Anita Burgh is the author of several bestselling novels, including *Distinctions of Class*, which was shortlisted for the Romantic Novel of the Year Award. *The Broken Gate* is her latest novel in Orion paperback, and in Orion hardback, *The Heart's Citadel*. She lives in Gloucestershire. Visit Anita Burgh at her website: www.anitaburgh.com.

THE BROKEN GATE

Anita Burgh

The Cresswell Inheritance
BOOK ONE

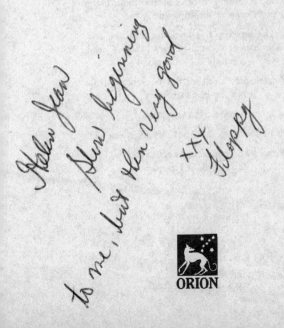

Helen Jean
Slow beginning
to me, but then very good
xx
Floppy

ORION

An Orion paperback

First published in Great Britain in 2004
by Orion
This paperback edition published in 2005
by Orion Books Ltd,
Orion House, 5 Upper St Martin's Lane,
London WC2H 9EA

1 3 5 7 9 10 8 6 4 2

A CIP catalogue record for this book is available
from the British Library.

ISBN 0 75286 542 0

Typeset by Deltatype Ltd, Birkenhead, Merseyside

Printed and bound in Great Britain by
Clays Ltd, St Ives plc

www.orionbooks.co.uk

For my grandson Ben Leith with love.

LOVE is a breach in the walls, a broken gate,
Where that comes in that shall not go again;
Love sells the proud heart's citadel to Fate.

Rupert Brooke 1887–1915.

Collected Poems 1916

Chapter One
January 1901

'How goes the enemy?'

The voice, rasping with effort, thick with phlegm, cut through the silence in the stuffy room, taking the assembled company by surprise. There was a swishing and rustling of silks, wafts of different perfumes, as the women leant forward. Two of the men immediately stood up. Another slouched in his chair, head flung back, mouth wide open, snoring.

At the bottom of the bed a small white-haired dog, lying with her head between her paws, was not sleeping. Not for one moment had she taken her eyes off her master. But now, at the sound of his voice, she lifted her head and her tail beat a tattoo on the covers.

'Five and twenty past six, Papa.'

'Mortie!' One of the women dug an elbow into the side of the sleeping man, who snorted loudly as he woke.

'What?' Looking confused, he leapt to his feet, swayed as if dizzy, then sat down with a bump.

'Morning or night?'

'Night-time, Papa.'

'What's he saying, Coral?' Mortie turned to the woman.

'Shush.' His wife made no effort to hide her irritation.

'Thank you, Hannah.' The sick man felt the air vaguely, as if searching for her hand. She took his and squeezed it gently, since he had no energy left to press hers.

'And Cariad?' At mention of her name, the dog's tail beat faster.

'She's on the bed – she hasn't left your side all day.'

The man appeared satisfied, for the lids closed over his rheumy eyes and a small smile played about his dry, cracked lips; no amount of cream alleviated their soreness. Hannah glanced down at his hand: the skin was white, the veins showed blue making his flesh look like marble, as if he was already dead.

The group around the bed sank back into their chairs.

'Perhaps I should go.' A large man, who had been sitting a little way from the immediate members of the family, stood up, his good-natured face creased with anxiety.

'It would be best to remain if Lady Cresswell told you to be here, Mr Greenacre,' Hannah said, and the estate manager, uncomfortable, sat down again.

At the foot of the bed, Melanie Topsham arched her back as if the long time she had been standing had made her stiff. Hannah smiled apologetically at her. There had been such a fuss about Melanie being in attendance but now they had all forgotten she was there.

'What did he mean? What enemy?' As she spoke Coral, Mortie's fashionably dressed wife, was smoothing the skirt of her ornate embroidered dress, rearranging the fabric, frowning at it. That done she checked her immaculately coiffed hair; the diamond and emerald butterfly pin fluttered, as if it were alive.

'He means the time, Coral,' Oliver Cresswell, her brother-in-law, whispered.

'Then why doesn't he say so? Why speak in riddles?'

'He didn't. Time's the enemy – his enemy. Can't you lower your voice? He's sleeping.' Oliver gestured to his father.

'"Stand still, you ever-moving spheres of heaven, that time may cease, and midnight never come . . ."'

'You know so many irrelevant things, Hannah.' Coral smiled as she spoke but there was no warmth in her eyes. Her rearranging of skirt and hair intensified.

'On the contrary, I'm always appalled at how little I know.' Hannah smiled back at her, which seemed to agitate Coral more: now she was tugging at her cuffs as if they, too, were misplaced – which they weren't.

'Lettice, stop sniffling,' Coral called, over her shoulder, to the girl who was curled up in an armchair; her white dress made her appear ghostly in the room's shadows. She was pressing a handkerchief to her face.

'Yes, Mama . . .' She could barely speak, and stuffed her handkerchief into her mouth to suppress her sobs.

'And don't slouch in that unladylike manner. Help with Felix and his toys.'

Lettice slid from the chair, knelt on the floor and, in a desultory manner, began to play with her little brother's wooden train set.

'Should Lettice be here? She's so distressed.' Hannah looked from her father to her niece. She was loath to let go of her father's hand, which, though he slept, clasped hers, to go and comfort the girl. She didn't want any of the others to take it, which was petty of her, and she was ashamed of the thought.

'It's her duty to be here. And what are you up to, Young Mortimer?' Coral asked her elder son, who was sitting at a table, his head in his hands.

'I'm reading, Mother,' he replied. He always spoke to her formally but Hannah suspected that he, too, was crying.

'You can't see over there. You'll damage your eyes – you'll go blind.'

'Not from reading he won't!' Young Mortimer's father laughed loudly, a shocking sound in this room of death.

'Really, Mortie, you can be so silly.' Coral sounded puzzled.

'Probably.' Mortie grinned good-naturedly.

'And what's that dog doing here? Get rid of it.'

'But Cariad's a great comfort to Father, Coral.' The

3

dog, as if she knew she was being talked about, slithered up the bed towards Hannah and nuzzled her hand.

'It's disgusting, put it out.'

'I think she should stay. Father asked for her.'

'Sentimental rubbish, Oliver, not what I would expect from you of all people. What do you say, Mortie, my darling?'

'Dog's no trouble. And if it's what Father wants . . .'

'You always take everyone else's side,' Coral said sulkily.

'Come on, old girl!'

'Please, everyone, can you not be quieter? He needs to sleep. He's so tired.' Hannah wished they would go away and leave her alone with him.

Two weeks ago her father had been full of life and she had been so excited by his visit: he had come alone and would be hers exclusively for once. The house was alive when his deep voice boomed along the corridors and his hearty laugh soared to the rafters. He was a handsome man with a fine physique. His hair was now as white as snow, but it was still thick and he wore it long, which gave him a leonine look. He'd never had a beard or even a moustache, despite the fashion, and she preferred him that way. But, best of all, his eyes were a clear, luminous grey and shone with his love of life.

But now he seemed to have shrunk to half his former size; his eyes were filmed and dull, his hair lank and lifeless. He no longer looked like the man she knew. Age, she realised, had caught up with him.

In London he had lived a soft life in the glittering circle that eddied around the Prince of Wales. He had eaten and drunk too much, had too many late nights for a man in his sixties, so he was far from fit when he had arrived just after Christmas. He'd also been suffering from a cold, which he had claimed was nothing.

She had tried to persuade him not to go hunting at New Year, fearing it would be too much for him, but he

4

had brushed away her objections, laughing at her fussing. He had taken a bad tumble and the inactivity when he was forced to rest had exacerbated his cold. The rapidity of his decline had taken her unawares. For three days she had watched as he slipped further from her, and a week ago the doctor had suggested she summon the rest of her family since, he said, they must prepare themselves for the worst.

Her hand was deadening but she did not remove it for fear of disturbing him. Her family had lived in this house for over two hundred years and it seemed right and proper that if her father were to die it should be here where he had been born. The thought made her shiver.

Hannah worried that she had been selfish to keep him here. Perhaps she should have taken him to London where they could have consulted the best doctors in the land. She feared their local doctor was not competent to treat him. She had been shocked when her stepmother Penelope had rejected the notion of asking for a second opinion on her father's condition.

'Hannah, my dear, how could you suggest such a thing? Think how offensive that would be to Dr Shelburn.' Hannah wanted to say that she thought her father's well-being was of more importance than the doctor's feelings, but she did not argue with her stepmother because she was afraid of her.

Everyone in the room settled back to wait. Hannah tried to remember when they had last been together like this, but it had been too long ago. Mortie and Coral preferred life in London, and her younger brother Oliver had been travelling the world restlessly for years now. As for Penelope, she made it no secret that she did not like Cresswell and came only when duty called.

How sad that it took death to bring everyone together.

'Vultures! That's what they all are,' her father had said, a few days ago. 'Flocking to the carrion.'

'Papa, don't talk in that way. I asked them to come to see you.'

'I didn't for one minute think they'd have come without being prodded.'

'Papa, they love you.'

'Love my money, more like. Putting in an appearance for fear I might change my will.'

'Papa, that's not so.'

'Hannah, my dear, I speak the truth. There's no need to try to protect me. I know what my family think of me.' He had beckoned her with his finger. 'But the secret is, I don't care. And, what's more, my will is made. I shall endeavour to haunt you all – I want to be present at the reading.' This idea had made him smile, then laugh until his frail body shook, he was gasping for breath, then coughing and spluttering. The sound had alerted his nurse who, her starched clothes crackling like the sails of a ship unfurling, entered the room and began officiously to tend her charge.

'What are we up to now?'

Hannah had seen her father's laughter turn to anger – he loathed his nurse. At least her appearance had stopped him laughing and, thus, coughing. 'Is it possible you might speak to me as an adult and not as a child?' he snapped.

'There, now, don't you get cross with Nursie. You won't get better that way—'

At that point her father had roared so loudly that Hannah had feared for him. How long ago had that been? Four days? Five? He'd still had spirit then – he could laugh, shout, be angry, react to the world around him. Now, in a matter of days, he was but a husk of himself, away in a place of his own, probably unaware that they were all with him. The nurse had said he was 'in the waiting-room of death'! Hannah had lost patience with her then.

Her father might think his sons didn't love him but she

6

knew better. Mortie, the elder of her two brothers, might be tactless and spoke too often before thinking, but he was not a bad man – 'Just stupid!' Oliver had said. Secretly Hannah thought he was right – she had so many uncharitable thoughts, these days. Mortie was noisy, and his jokes were terrible. He relished fine food and wine so he was corpulent – and indeed, such a glutton that he would never again be the slim man he once was. He was selfish, too, but in a childish innocent way, as if he was unaware he did wrong. He was usually forgiven for it.

Mortie loved his London club where he could play cards and talk at any time of day and night. She knew he felt safer in the city: he had once, in his cups, confided to her that to him the countryside was a fearful place. Hannah had no doubt that he loved his father, as he did his wife, children and siblings – in his way. She was sure he rarely thought about his own feelings, let alone anyone else's, and loved himself most of all. Somehow it made her love him more.

His marriage to Coral Picknall had been a mistake – for him and the rest of them. She was not an easy woman to like, convinced of her own superiority. She was no beauty either, for her nose was too large, her eyes too small and her lips too thin. Coral took a deep interest in fashion – in fact, as far as Hannah could make out, it was her only interest. She was always immaculately turned out, at great cost to Mortie.

In Coral's opinion she had done the family a great honour by marrying Mortie: his father was a mere baronet, while she was the daughter of a viscount. Over the years Hannah had acquired more knowledge of the Picknall family than she needed to know. And, unfortunately, Coral knew the pedigree of every other notable in the land: at the mention of a name, she would launch into a dissertation on their background while many an eye glazed over.

'Since, according to Coral, we're so low in the social

scale, why is she marrying him?' Oliver had pondered, the night before his brother's wedding.

'Perhaps she feared that time was passing and no one else would ask her.'

'Hannah! If I didn't know you better I'd have thought you were being catty!'

And she had been, for she could not warm to her prospective sister-in-law. But she had spoken the truth. Coral was twenty-seven when she and Mortie wed: devoid as she was of good looks, she also lacked the second asset necessary to making a good match – money.

While Hannah tried to remain polite and on good terms with her, Oliver was less restrained.

'Of course, the Picknalls were landed when the Cresswells were still painting themselves with woad,' Coral had said, rudely, only the other evening. What had goaded her, Hannah could not remember.

'So, you did us a great favour in marrying one of us,' Oliver had said, putting Hannah on her guard – he could be particularly sharp when he was bored. Hannah concentrated on her embroidery.

'Didn't I?' Coral laughed gaily as she fell into the trap. 'But it was my pleasure.' She fluttered her eyelashes at Oliver.

'But then, of course, everyone, even the grandest, has their price.'

'Oliver! Do you mean what I think you do?' She pouted.

'You must interpret it as you wish.'

'I'd rather have breeding than money any day!' Coral picked up her own embroidery.

'A family tree won't keep you warm in an attic.'

'Fortunately I shall never know.' Coral stabbed at the canvas.

'Quite. Mortie came along in the nick of time, didn't he?'

'I shall ignore such rudeness.'

8

Oliver stretched and yawned, all the time eyeing his sister-in-law. Oh dear, thought Hannah, and tried to concentrate on her work.

'Of course, you can't be sure, can you?'

'About what, Oliver?'

'That you'll always have money. What if Father changed his will? What if he didn't leave you two a penny?'

Coral uttered a shrill cry, which she adapted quickly into a laugh. 'Mortie, your brother's being horrible to me.'

'Don't tease her, Oliver.' Mortie looked up from his father's stamp album.

'Horrible Oliver says your father might change his will and leave you no money.'

'He wouldn't do that.' Mortie picked up his magnifying-glass with podgy fingers. Suddenly his head jerked up. 'Would he?'

'It wouldn't bother you, though, Coral, would it? After all, you didn't marry Mortie for his expectations, did you?'

'Mortie, stop him!'

'Oliver, leave her alone. Don't upset yourself, old girl, he's only teasing. I know you married me for love, didn't you?'

'But of course.' Coral fluttered across the room to plant a kiss on her husband's head.

'See!' Mortie didn't poke out his tongue, but from the schoolboy tone of his voice he might just as well have done so.

For all her faults, though, Coral had given them Young Mortimer, Lettice and little Felix. Hannah's niece and nephews were the love of her life. Given their parents' preference for London they had spent most of their childhood in Hannah's care – a responsibility she had taken on with pleasure, with the help of her old nurse Nanny Wishart.

Hannah stiffened with apprehension as the door opened and her stepmother, Penelope Cresswell, entered. She glided across to the bed – she walked as if she had wheels for feet and, try as she might, Hannah had never been able to emulate her. 'Any change?'

'He's sleeping.'

'A coma?'

'Sleeping,' said Hannah stalwartly. She could not bear to think that this was not a natural sleep from which her father would awaken and be just as he had always been.

Penelope, in her early fifties – Hannah had never been privy to her exact age – was still a handsome woman, even if the beauty of her youth had faded. But it was still possible to see how lovely she had once been. She was heavier now but since she was tall Hannah felt it mattered little because she carried herself with such grace. She had presence and a charm that could captivate a room full of people, but she also had a temper and spite that could empty it in a trice.

'I've ordered some food.' Penelope settled in the chair her son, Mortie, had relinquished to her. Hannah wondered how anyone could eat at a time like this. She knew she couldn't, but her stepmother had a healthy appetite and nothing curbed it – not even this. 'Hannah, my dear, Mrs Fuller says you ordered soup.'

'Soup?' Mortie seemed aghast at the very idea.

'I didn't think people would want to eat – Mother.' Hannah was unaware that she always halted before using that word to her stepmother.

'You should think of others, not just yourself, Hannah. You don't want to eat, but perhaps the rest of us do. Life goes on.' She bestowed a sweet smile on Hannah. She always did when others were about; when they were alone it was a different matter. 'I've ordered a cold collation.'

'You've ordered cats' meat!'

'Yes, Mortie. Since Hannah ordered only soup there's

no time for the cook to prepare a proper meal.' Again Penelope smiled. If snakes could smile that was how they would do it, Hannah thought. She'll soon be gone, she told herself, and then felt miserable: if she was to be rid of the woman who frightened her so, her father would have to die. *Or get better!* She sat up straight. How strange. It was as if a voice had spoken – she must have imagined it.

Once Hannah had wanted to love and be loved by her stepmother. But from the very beginning, with a child's awareness, she had known the woman would never love her. Her stepmother was not cruel or rude to her, but a dense barrier existed between them. When Penelope looked at Hannah, it was as though she looked through her. Hannah could never remember the woman touching her – if they passed in a corridor or a doorway, Penelope was apt to draw her skirts close to her as if to ensure that nothing of herself should touch her stepdaughter. Although she spoke naturally to her in company, when they were alone she ignored Hannah.

'She resents who you are, Hannah, my dear,' her grandmother had explained to her, when Hannah was still a child. 'You belong to your father's past, of which she was not part, and it's painful for her.' She could still smile at her grandmother's final remark on the subject. 'She is, of course, too stupid to behave in any other way.'

Soon after this conversation her grandmother had died and Hannah had never discussed the problem again. Nor was it solved – for what sort of woman would be jealous of a child? It wasn't Hannah's fault that her mother, Jane, had died. It wasn't her fault that her father spoke so often of her, and she could not be the only one who noticed how his voice softened when he mentioned her.

She had tried to imagine herself in Penelope's position but she knew she would love a motherless child, not hate it. She tried to understand, to be patient, to love. But at times, when the ostracism had particularly hurt her, a whisper of dislike entered her mind and, if her defences were down, mushroomed into a something that verged on hatred.

Years ago, just once, she had allowed herself to hate. The problem had arisen when she had fallen in love with Simeon, then the new curate. Over the years, she had lived at Cresswell mostly on her own, until Mortie's children were born. When Simeon had taken up his position, Hannah's loneliness had led to her infatuation with him. Added to that, she was nearly thirty, unmarried, and longed for children of her own. It was strange that she could see now so easily how and why things had happened, when at the time she had been unaware.

Although she had thought her father would be disappointed by her choice, she thought he would permit their union. But Penelope had made an unexpected visit to Cresswell and declared the match impossible. She had banned Simeon from the house.

Although it had taken Hannah time to admit it Penelope had been right, and eventually she felt grateful to her. Whenever she saw Simeon, who was now the vicar, she gave thanks for her timely escape. With his promotion he had become pompous, self-satisfied, with an intolerance of others' weakness that was almost wicked. What had hurt her, and still rankled, was that after permission for their marriage had been withheld, he had stayed in the parish. Shouldn't he have been so broken-hearted he had to leave?

'The praying mantis is here,' Oliver whispered, making her jump. 'Whitaker has just told me.' He glanced at the butler.

'I'd better see to him.' Gently she extricated her hand from her father's. Who had summoned him? How insensitive.

'Simeon, how kind of you to come. And Mrs Redman too.' She held out her hand in greeting. She did not know why she always felt embarrassed on meeting Laura

Redman – she had no yearning for her husband. 'But, really, there was no need for you to come so soon. My father's sleeping.'

'The note from your mother insisted that it was urgent.'

'I can't imagine why.'

'Where matters of the spirit are concerned, one cannot be too cautious . . . Perhaps we should wait here.' Simeon eyed the platters of food in the anteroom to her father's bedroom.

'I don't wish to offend you, Simeon, but my father will not want you here. He left strict instructions – no man of the cloth. And if he should hear you . . .'

'I shall be as quiet as the proverbial church mouse.' He smiled a lop-sided smile of self-congratulation at his joke – Hannah had lost count of how many times she had heard it.

'Simeon!' Oliver joined them, lighting a cigar. 'Such a long time since we last met.'

'To be true, and the loss is mine.' Hannah wished Simeon would not be so obsequious. 'So long away, Oliver, that you won't have met my wife.'

At these words Oliver glanced at Hannah. How typical of him to be concerned for her, she thought. She smiled to reassure him as Laura turned to be introduced.

Oliver held out his hand – and froze: his arm remained rigid in the air like that of a statue. At last, he gathered himself and shook Laura Redman's hand. Hannah noticed Laura was blushing but, then, her brother had that effect on women.

'Please help yourself to whatever you want. Come, Oliver, we should return.' She tugged at her brother's sleeve because he was still staring at the vicar's wife. She hoped he wasn't going to become besotted with her. That would never do. 'If you will excuse us.' They left the room and closed the door.

13

'Why were you staring at Mrs Redman so rudely?' Hannah paused by the bedroom door.

'She's very lovely.'

'Mrs Redman?' Her voice brimmed with surprise. 'Attractive, certainly, but lovely? No.'

'It was tactless of me, Hannah.'

'Don't be silly, I stopped feeling anything for Simeon years ago,' she said, and opened the door to her father's room.

The door and windows of the Cresswell Arms were shut against the storm that was brewing out at sea. The atmosphere was fetid with the pungent smell of cheap tobacco, the acrid vapour of the smoking oil lamps that swung from the heavy beams, the smoke that billowed from the inglenook each time the door was opened, and the sour stench of unwashed bodies. The cluster of men who huddled around the trestle table, on which stood casks of cider and ale, appeared unaware of it.

'He's not expected to last the night.' The boilerman, Sol Pepper, sucked on his clay pipe; the mouthpiece was dark brown from years of use. His fingernails were permanently black from the coke he stoked into the cavernous boilers that heated the many rooms of Cresswell Manor.

'Who told you that, then, Sol? Been invited into the big house all of a sudden?' the estate carpenter, Rob Robertson, asked. He was a large, burly man with a rumbling laugh that suited his bulk. When he laughed his whole body became involved: his arms waved, his legs jerked and even his black curls bobbed and swayed. The other men joined in, including Sol, whose mouth gaped to display the beginnings of white, mould-like cancer growths.

'You'm a stupid bugger, Rob,' Sol said. 'I met up with our young Dolly what's begun working in them kitchens.

It's no secret. There's no hope. That's what the doctor's told them.' He sucked noisily at the pipe.

'That Dr Shelburn knows naught! Told my old mum she'd never see Michaelmas and that was ten year ago now.' Fred Robertson, Rob's younger brother and one of the under-gardeners, took a mighty swig of his cider, the cause of the bright red complexion that belied the true state of his health.

'You'd have thought they'd have got a fancy doctor in from Barlton now, wouldn't you?'

'Or Exeter even, Sol,' Henry Beasley, the most junior under-gamekeeper, suggested.

'Perhaps it wouldn't be to their advantage if they did.'

'What's that mean, Rob?'

'Think on it. If he croaks, who benefits?'

'Mortie might be many things but he'd never want his father dead.'

'Are you sure, Sol? All that money, all that land and that sharp-tongued missus of his – you can't tell me *she* wouldn't want the old man dead 'cause I wouldn't believe you.'

'And what about the old trout?' Freddie asked.

'She's got a wandering eye already, and with her husband dead she could do whatever she wanted. My Molly says she likes a bit of rough – might be a chance for you, Henry,' Rob teased.

'That's if he could find what he was looking for in all that flesh!' Tubs Sylvester, the landlord, put in. He was well named since his stomach dominated his body. He often rested this protuberance on the table to take the weight off the rest of him. When he laughed, as now, it rippled.

'Hardly a cause for laughter, since the lord and master's son hates the country. What if he ups and sells us, lock, stock and sodding bucket? What then?'

The group turned as one to look at Bernard Topsham,

15

who, as usual, given his unpopularity, was sitting apart from the group.

'You're in a better position than us to know what's what, aren't you?' Rob grinned.

'You bastard! What you mean?' Bernard stood up and looked menacingly at the younger man, balling his hands. He was not tall but powerfully built. The men stood back, leaving Rob exposed to his wrath.

Rob put up his hand, warding off the man and his anger. 'No offence meant, Mr Topsham, but our Molly said Mrs Topsham had been called in to help with nursing the old bugger.'

'Yes, you're right.' Bernard swayed on his feet, and shook his head. He picked up his tankard, downed the remains of his ale in one, then staggered to the door. He yanked up the latch, pulled it open and paused briefly in the doorway. Then he launched himself abruptly into the night.

Sol crossed the room to slam the door. 'Thoughtless sod!'

'You were lucky there, Rob. He could've got nasty.'

'And who'd have won? Our Rob,' Freddie proclaimed proudly.

'Wouldn't have been worth it. And it's not right to hit a drunken man.' Rob held out his tankard for Tub to replenish and pushed a penny across the bar. No one was taken in: everyone knew that Rob would never fight, if he could avoid it – not out of cowardice but because he was a gentle soul.

'His poor missus will be in for a mighty lambasting tonight,' was Tub's considered opinion. 'Nice woman, too, and still pretty.'

'Our Molly says that Melanie Topsham thinks she's a cut above the rest of us,' Rob informed them.

'Your Molly would,' grunted Sol.

'And what does that mean?'

'Nothing. I think Melanie's the sort what likes to keep

herself to herself.' He turned his head. 'Not that your Molly would understand that,' he said in an aside. The rest of the company burst into laughter and even Rob joined in. 'Mind you, what Bernard said might be nearer the truth than we know. If the old codger snuffs it, what'll happen to us?'

'It couldn't be worse than it is now. The copse up at Longacre is sorely neglected, the cover gets thinner and thinner, and who'll be the first to complain when the partridge are poor?' Henry asked.

'Not Mr Mortie, to be sure. He couldn't shoot an elephant standing sideways on. I think he's scared of guns.'

'And I'm scared when he's got one in his hand, Sol,' Henry observed.

'There's no replanting as there should be,' Rob complained. 'A tree is felled or falls down and nothing replaces it – can't remember the last time we planted the saplings up. I asked that fool Greenacre, who said he had to wait for instructions. And that's not all. The pasture's overused. Too many sheep for it. Greenacre's fault again.'

'And have you seen the state of the watercress beds? Ruined!' his brother added. 'You'd have thought with the family fortune being founded on them they'd keep them going . . . Too rich for their own good.'

'Gawd, give me such a problem, Fred! It'll get worse with Mr Mortie, that's for sure.' Sol looked gloomily into his drink.

'Now, listen, it might get better. What if we *were* sold up? It couldn't be worse. A new owner might care for it and us much better, like.' Rob looked quite cheerful at the idea.

'The Cresswells sell up? Never. I don't see that happening.'

'But then, what have we been saying? Mr Mortie—'

Sol turned and spat – 'he hates it here, so it could happen.'

'It's a crying shame that Miss Hannah can't inherit. She cares.'

Henry spluttered into his beer. 'A woman? Inherit? Have you lost your mind?'

'It wouldn't bother me. We all know she loves the house and the land. And she's good to us, treats us as human.'

'Or half human, Sol!'

'I wonder what'll happen to her. The next Lady Cresswell won't want *her* around.'

'I doubt if she'd want to be – chalk and cheese those two.'

'Perhaps he won't die and we can all go on as before . . .'

'And pigs might fly!'

Hannah was once more beside her father. She was glad no one had taken her place – she didn't know how she would have reacted if she had found her sister-in-law or stepmother holding his hand.

Once again Oliver had taken up position behind her. Life was so unfair at times – or, rather, God was. Oliver should have been the first-born. He loved Cresswell, country life and country ways.

'Why are you leaving us?' Hannah had asked him, ten years ago, when he had suddenly announced, at only twenty-two, that he was going to America.

'Because I love this place too much. I've got to leave it one day so I might as well go now.'

It had been the first indication that Oliver was unhappy that the estate would never be his. Perhaps he knew what a poor custodian Mortie would be. Or perhaps anger drove him away, not grief or jealousy.

With no warning one of the dormer windows flew open, and a strong wind rushed in, blowing the heavy brocade curtains almost horizontal. Penelope Cresswell looked about her with annoyance, as if someone in the room was responsible for the racket.

'Perhaps Old Nick himself is trying to join the party,' Mortie joked.

No one laughed.

Oliver crossed to the window and, before shutting it, peered out into the night. 'There's a great storm brewing.'

'How strange,' said his mother. 'Your grandfather died on a stormy night. A Cresswell tradition, evidently.'

Hannah had to press her fist to her mouth to stop herself crying out at Penelope's insensitivity. She fought back tears – her father had often said, 'I can't abide a weeping woman!'

'How goes the enemy?' the hoarse voice repeated.

'Ten minutes after eight Papa, in the evening.'

'Thank you, Hannah.'

She pulled his covers straighter.

'Why does he have to keep repeating himself?' Mortie asked.

'He isn't aware that he is,' Oliver said sharply.

'It's wearying.'

'Undoubtedly far more so for him, Mother,' Oliver told her, with a cynical smile.

'And what do you find so amusing, Oliver?'

'There is nothing to amuse me here, Mother. On the contrary, I feel a great sadness.'

'You don't have to pretend with us. You are as impatient as I—'

'Don't presume to speak for me, Mortie. I wish Father no ill,' Oliver said quietly.

'Your profligacy has been a great trial to him,' Penelope said.

'What?' Oliver snapped. 'I am the least profligate member of this family. At least I spend only what I have earned. I don't live off my father's charity.'

'You're being impertinent.'

'In defending myself?'

'I wish . . .' Hannah's voice trailed off.

'Yes, Hannah?'

Hannah felt the familiar apprehension when she looked at Penelope. She took a deep breath. 'I wish everyone could leave their anger and antagonism at the sick-room door.' She sat back, her face set as if she was waiting for an onslaught to begin.

'Well said.' Oliver patted her shoulder. 'She's right. We should be united as a family and not fighting at a time like this. I apologise, Hannah.'

'You've changed, Oliver—' A rustle in the bed interrupted Mortie, and everyone focused on the patient.

At the foot, away from the lamps and in the shadow cast by the heavy bed curtains, Melanie Topsham leant forward too to gauge any change in the patient. Her face was composed, but Hannah had noticed that her eyes were sad.

'There really is no need for you to remain here, Mrs Topsham.' Penelope spoke, in her pleasant, melodious voice.

'I'd rather stay, Lady Cresswell, if it's all the same to you,' Melanie replied, as if to an equal, which took Hannah by surprise.

'You must be tired from standing with such devotion for so long. It was so good of you to come.' Penelope smiled at her – the smile that never reached her eyes.

'I am quite comfortable. It's not necessary—'

'But I think it is *most* necessary, Mrs Topsham. My husband needs his family – *only*.' She emphasised the last word so obviously that Hannah was embarrassed.

'I was invited, so presumably someone wants me here.'

Melanie looked at Penelope with no fear, Hannah thought admiringly.

The smile had left Penelope's face. 'You are insolent. I

would prefer it if you removed yourself. Now!' It was an order, and she would be obeyed without question.

'Then I shall wait outside.' Melanie moved with grace and dignity from the room.

'Who *did* invite her?' Coral asked, once the door had closed.

'Hannah, I presume.' Mortie stretched his large frame, threw his arms over his head and yawned noisily.

'What were you thinking about? A serving woman at your father's deathbed?' Coral sounded irritated.

'My father instructed me to.' Why the fuss about Mrs Topsham when Mr Greenacre sat stolidly in the shadows? Hannah wondered. She hadn't asked him to attend, and was puzzled as to who had.

'Your father? Why?' Penelope looked at her with surprise.

'He did not say and I did not ask – Mother.'

'How peculiar. When?'

'Last month.'

'Are you sure? Why? He wasn't ill then.'

'I know. But he said if I thought at any time in the future that he was unwell . . . if I thought . . .'

'The end was nigh?' Mortie suggested helpfully.

'. . . I was to ask her to come.'

'No doubt because she has nursing experience.' Penelope sighed.

'Then she can lay him out.' This insensitive notion came from Coral. Hannah longed to slap her.

'You should not be talking of such matters when . . .' Oliver indicated his sleeping father.

'He can't hear us.'

'How can you be sure, Mother?'

'The poor darling is drifting in and out of a coma.'

'What if, just then, he was *out*?' Oliver was not joking. He turned to the drinks tray he had had sent up and poured himself and his brother a large whisky.

'He can't last much longer, poor dear. The doctor told

me only this evening that we must not allow ourselves to hope.' Now Penelope was fussing with her clothes. 'He said he won't last the night.'

'We should ask another doctor to examine him.'

'I don't wish him to be unduly disturbed, Oliver.' She turned abruptly. 'Really, Hannah, if you're going to sniff in that unfortunate manner, I should prefer you did so outside.' She paused. 'It might upset your father and we don't want that, do we?' she continued, changing swiftly from sharpness to a kindly tone. She added a smile for good measure. 'My dear, you must try to control yourself for all our sakes. Fortunately we've been given time to prepare ourselves . . . . But you've always been rather emotional, haven't you?'

'Mother, he is her father.'

'And he's my husband, Oliver. Do you see me wallowing in self-indulgent tears?'

'An unlikely occurrence, Mother. Hannah loves him, that's the difference.'

'You can be insufferably rude, Oliver.'

'But always honest, Mother.'

Hannah wished they would stop arguing about her as if she were not there. She longed to speak up but couldn't find the words. There were times when she despised herself deeply.

'And you never asked Mr Greenacre if he'd like a drink, Oliver. Our apologies, Mr Greenacre.' Hannah noticed the smile Penelope gave the estate manager, as if they were friends. He was sitting on a chair that looked far too spindly to support his not inconsiderable weight. He had the healthy glow of one who worked in the open, and the air of someone who was not happy to be confined indoors in such circumstances.

'Nothing, thank you, Lady Cresswell. You're most kind.'

'I would appreciate it if you would get that child to bed, Coral. Really, it's too much.'

With an exaggerated sigh, Coral shooed Felix from the room.

'And you two. Go with your mother,' Penelope ordered. Neither needed any encouragement. Young Mortimer gave his grandmother a smart little bow, Lettice dropped a curtsy and they left.

'Mortie and Oliver, a change of linen would not come amiss. And you, Hannah, go and wash your face. When you have composed yourself you may return.'

'Yes – Mother.' Hannah moved swiftly to the door. In her haste, she slammed it.

Melanie Topsham might have left the sick room with dignity, but she was seething with anger. It was not the offensive manner in which Penelope Cresswell had spoken to her that had annoyed her – she had been involved with this family long enough to be relatively immune to their bad manners – but the way they talked of Sir Mortimer in his presence. It was unkind: they could not be sure he did not hear them. Or perhaps they didn't care if he did. Some here tonight were willing him to die, she was certain.

She was unsure whether to stay or to leave. Would it be impolite to sit? She rubbed the small of her back. She was tired and her spine ached from the hours she had stood at the end of Sir Mortimer's bed. If she sat in the shadows of the window-seat perhaps they would not notice her, perhaps even forget she had been there.

This morning's note from Hannah had been a surprise. She could not understand why the old man should want her, of all people, present at his death. But he was not dead yet, and that gave her hope. She tried to quell it – in her life she had found that hoping for good things was futile.

The bedroom door opened. Instinctively Melanie rose to her feet. Coral bustled out with her children but only

23

Lettice smiled at her. She was more like her aunt than her father, Melanie thought, as she returned the smile.

She sat down again. If they were going to ignore her she resolved to remain seated.

Then Mortie came out and crossed the room without acknowledging her, noisy as ever. Perhaps he had not noticed her. Should she speak to him? She bore him no ill will.

Then Coral Cresswell swooped back into the room, having deposited her children with the nanny. Such a sour expression she had, as if life had been unkind to her – and she with all her riches! On the other hand, Melanie thought, she had to suffer Mortie as a husband. Maybe she was being too hard on the woman. Coral stopped beside the table of food and a footman stepped forward to assist her, but she waved him away, rejecting all that was on offer.

'Mrs Topsham, you're still here?' The housekeeper had appeared at her side.

'Why, yes, Mrs Fuller, as you see.' Although she smiled politely enough, she stiffened. Mrs Fuller was a gossiping biddy, not to be trusted.

'A bite to eat?'

'No, thank you.'

'It might be a long night.'

'I'm not hungry.'

'Not like some as I could mention.'

Mortie had reappeared and was loading his plate with food as if he was afraid it was all about to disappear. Mrs Fuller leant towards her and Melanie was overwhelmed by the scent of peppermint mixed with mothballs. 'That Mr Mortie'll have a seizure one of these days, if he carries on as he is,' she whispered, pursing her lips.

Melanie said nothing, she knew that anything she said would emerge the next day bearing no resemblance to what she had uttered.

'Are you sure I can't get you a little something, Mrs Topsham?'

'It's most kind of you, Mrs Fuller, but not at the moment.'

'As you wish.' To her relief, the woman moved away.

Melanie stood up when Hannah came into the room. She liked and respected her.

'Dear Mrs Topsham, are you all right? Is there anything . . .'

'No, thank you. I want for nothing.' She noticed the dried tears on Hannah's face, the look of strain on her features. She would have liked to put her arms about her but, of course, that was out of the question.

'It was kind of you to come. I don't see nearly enough of you.'

'We're both busy, Miss Cresswell.'

'A most distressing occasion.'

'More so for you than for me, Miss Cresswell. I'm not sure what use I am to you, but if there is anything . . .'

'Just your being here is a comfort.' Hannah, clutching her handkerchief rather as a child hangs onto a comforter, hurried from the room.

Poor woman, Melanie thought. She deserves a better family than this.

One by one the family came into the room. Had Melanie been a betting woman she would have laid money on who would try to make her more comfortable and who would act as if she wasn't there. It was strange to be back. She had tried to make excuses not to come but the footman had been insistent. And everyone for miles around obeyed a summons from this family – it was how they all lived their lives. Even Hannah Cresswell, for all her kindness, would have been astonished if she hadn't come.

Mortimer Cresswell was aware of movement but hadn't the energy to open his eyes. There was no scent of lily-of-the-valley, which meant that Hannah was not there. He wanted her. He was aware of his wife – he could smell the musky perfume he had asked her not to wear because it irritated his nose. Now that he was in no position to object, it was typical of her to sprinkle it liberally about her person.

Poor Hannah. If he died she would be left to the mercy of his widow . . . Poor Hannah . . . He was drifting again, back to that comfortable blackness. A rustling noise and a more intense waft of his wife's scent attracted his wavering attention. Poor Hannah, what would her life be like? Penelope thought she'd deceived him, but he'd always known that she had only pretended to accept the child. Now . . . He could not die, he must not . . . But . . . Where was the energy he needed to live . . . ? It was so much easier to let go . . .

'At last . . .' Penelope's whisper pulled him back from the darkness. There were a few more words he could not catch. And then: 'My dear one.' There was a thump as if someone had stood up too rapidly and a chair had fallen.

'Lady Cresswell, this is not proper.' Mortimer heard the voice of his estate manager: although he, too, had whispered, it had been with a hoarse urgency.

'Of course it's not! Which makes it all the more enjoyable.'

Mortimer strained to lift his head. He concentrated on opening his eyes, but the lids were too heavy. He was conscious of a scuffling, the swishing of silk.

'No!' came an abrupt exclamation. 'Lady Cresswell, you are mistaken!' There had been anguish in that. Then more shuffling, more wafts of perfume.

'I've seen the way you look at me. There's no mistake!'

Mortimer felt his nostrils tickle – and sneezed.

'He's awake!'

'He can't be!' There was an almighty crash.

'Lady Cresswell! Are you hurt?'

Mortimer hoped she was – badly.

26

'I was just wondering, Lady . . .' Another voice. 'Oh, my dear Lady Cresswell, have you fallen?' Mortimer recognised the obsequious tone of the Reverend Simeon Redman. 'Laura, your assistance.'

'She caught her heel in the rug. I was just helping her,' Stanley Greenacre blustered.

'Let me assist you.'

'The carpet is frayed.' Penelope sounded annoyed – with herself, or with them? he wondered. 'I'm quite capable of standing, thank you very much. I do not need *two* men to haul me to my feet. Unhand me! And what are you grinning at?'

'I was not aware that I was.' Mortimer realised Penelope had attacked Laura Redman.

'Vicar, I asked you to wait outside.'

'So you did, Lady Cresswell, but Miss Cresswell was so distressed and the little children were sobbing as they passed me so I thought I might be needed.'

'Well, you're not. Not yet. Later . . .'

'Perhaps a prayer would give you solace in your hour of need, dear Lady Cresswell.'

Mortimer wanted to shout, 'Go! Clear out! Bugger off!' But the words would not form.

'How sensitive of you, Vicar, but can we not wait until my dear boys are here with their father? And shall we enjoy a collation first? One must feed the body as well as the soul, must we not, dear Vicar?'

How clever she was, Mortimer thought, the way she could suddenly turn on the charm. Sleep, that was what he needed . . .

Melanie looked up as Hannah returned, all trace of tears removed, just as Lady Cresswell, supported by the vicar and his wife, entered, with a red-faced, anxious-looking Stanley Greenacre bringing up the rear.

'Lady Cresswell, you look flustered.' Coral was immediately at her side.

'Mother!' Mortie spluttered, spraying crumbs across the room.

'She took a tumble,' the vicar explained.

'I did no such thing, Vicar! Whatever will you say next? The rug was worn. I tripped.'

'There's no worn rug in that room,' Hannah objected.

'My dear Hannah, if I say the rug is worn, it is worn.'

'Yes – Mother, of course – Mother.' Hannah blushed.

'Your father's alone. Go and care for him, there's a dear. I need a restorative. I think it best if you leave us, Mr Greenacre.' Her tone was cold, and his already flushed face was suffused with blood as though he were covered in claret. Mortie and his wife were fussing over Penelope. Melanie found herself wondering, if the old man died, whether they would be puttering over her as much as they were now. For who was she but the wife of an important man, and at his death, wouldn't her own importance be diminished? It would be interesting to see.

'And you! Why are you still skulking here?' Lady Creswell's angry stare was now focused on Melanie. She felt nervous – the woman was worse than the weather, constantly changing, she thought.

'I wasn't sure what to do or where to go, what was expected of me.'

'You're expected to know your place, which is not here with us at such an intimate time. Mrs Fuller, kindly show this woman to the servants' quarters in case she has forgotten the way.'

'But—'

'No buts, Mrs Topsham. You'll be summoned if needed, but I doubt you will be.' She turned her back on Melanie, who noticed how broad it was, how much sun it would block out if one should be standing behind her on a sunny day. Such thoughts were always a comfort: think of the ridiculous and people were never as imposing as they hoped they were.

She began to follow Gussie Fuller. As she passed

Oliver, he bent down and whispered, 'If he needs you, I'll come to get you.'

'Thank you, Mr Oliver.' She bobbed to him – which, to her satisfaction, she had avoided with his mother.

Why was he fighting sleep? Why not just let go? This sleep was like no other, it was of a depth he had never before experienced. No! he must not let go. He must fight. Death was waiting for him, not sleep. Mortimer listened as the vicar's voice, low and mournful, intoned a string of prayers for his departing soul, for his loving family – well, that was a joke. Who would miss him? Hannah, to be sure, and his dog . . .

His wife! If he'd had the energy he'd have laughed. She'd enjoy not having to lie to him, and spending his money with no restriction. At that he felt himself twitch. They'd made a mistake in marrying each other. He felt that he had kept his side of the bargain, but it had never seemed to cross Penelope's mind that she should keep hers.

He had been right about Oliver, though. Mortie was as greedy for his father's money as he was for food.

Mortimer was not hurt – it was what he'd expected from his wife and his heir. They couldn't wait for him to die, could barely control their longing to get at his money.

The prayers galvanised him to summon some energy. How dared this man presume to give him the last rites? Had Mortimer said that that was what he wanted? No, quite the contrary. Bugger this! he thought. He wouldn't give them the satisfaction of dying. Not yet!

'Jane,' he whispered, eyes tight shut.

'What did he say? I can't hear.' Penelope leant forward.

'I didn't hear either,' Hannah lied.

'Jane! Jane!' Summoning all of his scant power, Mortimer said the name as loudly as he could. What better way to annoy his living wife than to call out the name of the dead one?

'We shall be much more comfortable here,' Mrs Fuller announced, as she ushered Melanie through the door of her sitting room, which was behind the servants' hall. 'Some sherry?'

'No, thank you,' answered Melanie.

'After such rudeness from that insufferable woman you must need something.'

'No, really.'

'I thought you were most dignified.'

'Thank you.'

'Tea, then?' Mrs Fuller crossed to the mantelshelf, which was draped with deep-red fringed velvet. She yanked at the bell-pull to summon a maid. That done, she excused herself and left Melanie alone in the cluttered room.

It was many years since she had been here – long before Mrs Fuller had become housekeeper. She had been so nervous then as she waited for the woman in charge to come and interview her for the position as housemaid. It was her big chance, her mother had told her, her first step in the world, and if she behaved herself her future would be secure. Only she hadn't behaved, and her life had been ruined – or so everyone said. Melanie could never see it that way.

She sat upright on the velvet-covered sofa, which, while elegant, was overstuffed and uncomfortable. A desk stood beneath a glass-fronted bookcase, papers neatly arranged in the pigeon-holes – she wondered if it had a secret drawer, as these desks often did – and a large brass inkwell, decorated with dolphins and mermaids. That alone, if it was sold, would feed her family for a year, she was sure.

The walls were covered with dark-red flocked wall-paper and several paintings – surely they weren't Gussie

Fuller's. The room was cluttered with photographs in ornate frames, small boxes and odd ornaments. They must take a fair time to dust each day – but Mrs Fuller would order the maids to do it. Some people lived such indolent lives.

She stood up to study the photographs, interested to see what Mrs Fuller's family looked like. However, each frame contained a picture of a Cresswell or their dogs, cats, horses – she recognised them from long ago. Had the family become her life? It happened. Or was it simply that having no family of her own Mrs Fuller had borrowed them? How sad.

She picked up one of the photographs and studied Sir Mortimer's face. She liked him: he had always been polite to her and there was much for which her family owed him gratitude.

'I'm sorry, leaving you alone.' Mrs Fuller bustled back into the room. 'I can't rely on those girls to do anything right. Now, where was I?' She moved quickly about her room, the long chatelaine attached to her waist clanging noisily as she twirled about. She poked at the fire with a vigour that seemed at odds with her small-boned, birdlike figure. Then she was tidying papers, plumping cushions, patting her hair, a kaleidoscope of movement.

'You have a lovely room, Mrs Fuller. Some beautiful things.'

'Haven't I? Miss Hannah is most generous with *les objets* they no longer want.'

Melanie presumed she was supposed to be impressed by the French.

'Whitaker, Lavender and I have the pick of things,' she continued, pausing as a young maid arrived with a tray of tea. 'A whisper of whisky in yours?' She asked, once the girl had left them.

'Not for me, thank you.'

'You won't tell a soul if I imbibe?'

'Of course not.' Melanie wondered if the housekeeper

had left the room not, as she had said, to check the maids but to collect the bottle. Judging by her rosy colour, she'd had a nip before she returned. 'I've a long walk home,' she added, not wanting the woman to feel she was being censorious.

'They never think, do they? They order you to come, then never give a thought to how you'll get here or home again.'

'I'm not complaining. I like to walk and the storm's blown over.'

'Strange you were invited to join the family at such a time, wasn't it?'

'Very.'

'You've no idea why?'

'None.' She had, but had no intention of confiding. 'Of course, Sir Mortimer was close to my grandfather when he was a boy.' She felt she had to say something.

'I never knew that.'

'Yes, my grandfather Beasley was the gamekeeper, taught him to shoot, and about the birds and animals. My grandmother used to say Sir Mortimer spent more time in their cottage than in the big house. Just as Mr Oliver did with my father.'

'Your family's been on the estate for some time.'

'My father says longer than the Cresswells.'

'Hardly!' Mrs Fuller laughed in a ladylike manner.

'Why not? The fortunes of families can vary so much.'

'Of course, all this was long before my time.'

'Yes, I can barely remember my grandfather myself. Just the feel of him.'

'The *feel* of him? What a strange thing to be saying.' As she spoke Mrs Fuller poured a large amount of whisky into her tea.

'Not for me it isn't. I remember the texture of his jacket. The roughness of his hands. The smell of his baccy. His presence . . .' She felt sad: she had spoken of a time when she had been safe. When she hadn't known that people and events could harm her.

'You're a fey creature and no mistake.' Mrs Fuller laughed. Melanie smiled – she liked the description. 'And how's your family?'

Melanie was immediately on her guard. 'Very well, thank you.'

'Your husband?'

'Well.' More's the pity. And probably drunk by now.

'And that pretty little Xenia. She'll be finding herself a husband any day now. How old is she?'

'Nearly eighteen. I hope she bides her time before thinking of marriage.'

'But not if she finds the right man? You'd be pleased for her then?'

'*If*, I have always thought, is a very big word, Mrs Fuller.'

'Is she at home with you?'

'No, Mrs Fuller.' As you well know, she might have added but didn't. She took a sip of her tea.

'And that fine strapping lad of yours, Zeph – I can never remember his name.'

'Zephaniah is well.'

'They're high-falutin' names for . . .'

'For such as me? Was that what you were thinking? I understand. But when you have nothing else, the least you can do is give them beautiful names.'

'Quite.' Gussie Fuller didn't look convinced. 'Is he in employment?'

'He has a position in a solicitor's office in Barlton.'

'He has enjoyed such good fortune, your Xenia too.'

'Might I trouble you for more tea, Mrs Fuller?'

'I mean,' Mrs Fuller continued, as she poured the tea from a silver-plated teapot – everything in this room echoed the world upstairs – 'being so well educated. The likes of him. Most fortunate.'

'Wasn't it?' Melanie smiled sweetly.

33

'And being sent away to school. It must have been a grievous expense for you.'

'Not particularly. We didn't pay.'

'Really? Then who did?' Mrs Fuller leant forward.

'Don't you know, Mrs Fuller?'

'No, Mrs Topsham. I never liked to ask.'

'Sir Mortimer—'

'Sir Mortimer paid! Well I never!'

'I didn't say that, Mrs Fuller. I was about to say that Sir Mortimer realised my son was a clever boy and went out of his way to ensure that he was put forward for a scholarship to Blundell's School. I thought everyone knew that.'

'I see.' Mrs Fuller sank back in her chair with a look of disappointment, but then she sat up. 'But you were away from the estate for so long, how would Sir Mortimer have known?' she asked.

'Because my father told him.'

'And your Xenia too – she had a scholarship?'

'No, Xenia's a scatterbrain. Lovely but giddy, Mrs Fuller.'

'But I heard . . .'

'She went to school, yes.'

'Arranged by Sir Mortimer?' Gussie licked her lips.

'No, by his mother. Old Lady Cresswell was particularly fond of my grandmother – she was her maid for many a year. Now Xenia has a position with a family friend, a Mrs Featherstone in Exeter. The Cresswells have always looked after their retainers and their dependants.'

'Then times have changed. There's no doubting that.' Mrs Fuller pursed her lips. 'What do you think of them upstairs?'

'I have little contact with them. I hardly know them.' How sly she is, Melanie thought. 'Miss Hannah's always kind,' she added.

'Luckily for me it's Miss Hannah I normally deal with. Thankfully Lady Cresswell's rarely here.'

'So I gather,' Melanie said noncommittally.

Gussie Fuller leant forward in her seat, glancing at the door as if to check it was firmly shut. 'Lady Cresswell is a cross I'm finding harder and harder to bear. I, Mrs Topsham, am not used to such as she.'

'Is that so, Mrs Fuller?'

'I've heard many rumours of where *she* came from.' And she rolled her eyes towards the ceiling.

'Really?' This conversation might become dangerous, Melanie thought. 'Then I think you've been misinformed, Mrs Fuller. I've always understood her father was a banker of high standing.'

'Trade! Just as I said.' Mrs Fuller sniffed.

'Still, it's better than being in service, wouldn't you say?' Melanie stood up, buttoning her jacket. 'She's still Sir Mortimer's wife, Mrs Fuller. She deserves some respect.'

'Oh quite, Mrs Topsham. I didn't mean—' They were interrupted by a tap on the door. It was Hannah Cresswell.

'Ah, there you are, Mrs Topsham.' She was smiling. 'I thought I should tell you that my father is sleeping peacefully. The doctor has been and is very pleased with him. I feel he is quite astonished. He says that Father evidently had a crisis this evening, which is subsiding.'

'Such good news!' Gussie Fuller declared.

'I'm so pleased for you,' was Melanie's quieter response.

'I was thinking perhaps you would prefer to return home now, and I can send you a message in the morning if you are needed.'

'As you wish, Miss Cresswell.' Although it was the last thing Melanie wished.

'I shall call the coachman for you.'

'Bless you, no. The walk will do me good – I'm in need of fresh air.' Mrs Fuller looked offended. 'The sick room, you understand . . .' she added hurriedly.

35

The wind had dropped a little but there was still a stiff breeze, strong enough to make the blanket she wore, since she had no coat, swell out like a balloon. She sniffed appreciatively: she could smell the sea. There was no moon tonight but Melanie was not perturbed: she was used to the dark and the countryside. Many were the times she had walked late at night when her children slept – it was a good time for thinking.

What a strange night it had been, she thought, as she set out across the park, with everyone expecting Sir Mortimer's death, and then he had rallied. She wondered how that had come about for she, too, had thought the end was near. Had he heard someone say something that had made him cling to life? For Hannah's sake, she hoped it was not a false recovery: she had seen that before, the family thinking all was well only for the loved one to be dead a day later. She hoped against hope that the poor girl would not be subjected to another such night.

Poor girl! Melanie smiled. She must be at least six years older than I am. Yet there was a vulnerability about her that made Melanie want to protect her. And that was another funny thought – as if she, in her circumstances, could help such as Hannah Cresswell.

She pulled the blanket round her head, as her ears were tingling with the cold.

It had been interesting to see the house again. The short time she had been a maid there she had enjoyed being in such beautiful surroundings. Although she had worked hard it had been a pleasure to be trusted with some of the objects she had had to keep clean. And there had been such fun in the servants' hall, games, dances, flirtations – until she had spoilt it all with her stupid behaviour, her dreams.

She passed Flossie Marshall's cottage. She could see a candle flickering in an upstairs room and wondered if the new baby had come. She would call in the morning to see if help was needed. Poor Flossie: five children already and barely enough coming in to feed and clothe them adequately.

Next came the school house. There was a new teacher now, Miss Crick. She was young, pretty and enthusiastic but Melanie doubted that she could be as good as Miss Mason – she had been a fine teacher. If only I had been able to stay and learn more, she thought. Her parents had insisted she leave at the earliest opportunity to seek work. But there was no point in thinking what might have been – 'What's done is done,' her mother would have said, a pity she could not apply this philosophy to her own daughter.

The rows of thatched cottages stretched down the main road of the village. They looked pretty in summer or when they were under a blanket of snow, but they were not very comfortable to live in. The small windows made them permanently dark, and the damp pervaded every-thing, clothes and furniture, with a musty smell that never left her nose. After working at the big house and getting used to turning on a tap, Melanie longed for running water. She hated the communal pump, the gossiping women who congregated there, and the need to carry water in buckets no matter the weather. Still . . . they were lucky to have a house at all. Had it not been . . .

She doubted that the Cresswell family ever thought of what they had compared with others, how lucky they were. They took everything for granted – the lovely furniture, the curtains, pictures, wine, food, silver, the vases of flowers in the depths of winter. They no longer saw it, and she thought that was sad. So much had given her pleasure this evening: where did their pleasure come from? But while she had been there, taking it all in, another thought had crossed her mind: why should they have so much and she so little? It was not right. Most certainly it was unfair.

She pushed open the door that led into the scullery and

she smelt the unpleasant odour that all her scouring and cleaning never got rid of. She was as quiet as she could be, hoping he was abed.

'Is he dead?'

Her heart jumped as she heard his voice, slurred with the ale he had been drinking all evening.

'No, he's better.'

'More's the pity. What took you so long?'

'No one said I was to leave so I stayed.'

'And why were you invited?'

'I don't know. No one said.' She removed and folded the blanket.

'And you didn't ask? Was he going to leave you aught?'

'Bernard! What a thing to say!'

'Why not? Them buggers owe us.'

'I doubt they see it that way. Hasn't he done enough already?'

'Don't you bloody cheek me!'

She stood still, expecting a blow at any minute. 'I didn't mean to.'

'Up to your filthy ways, were you? Slut! Whore!'

She stood impassively as the blows rained down on her. She had known this would happen, hundreds of beatings had taught her that if she fought him he would beat her harder. Her cries of pain whipped him into a greater frenzy.

She did what she always did, separated her mind from her body. She concentrated on the words in her head repeating them silently over and over again.

'I long for you to be gone . . .'

'I long to be rid of you . . .'

'I long for you to die . . .'

'I will have my freedom!'

Chapter Two
January 1901

Oliver reined in his horse as they reached the summit of Childer's Hill. He had set out from the stables in darkness, wanting to reach the hill by dawn. He turned to the east where he saw, on the dark sky, a streak of yellow and pink light as if an artist had splashed colour on to a large black canvas. He waited patiently as the sun slowly emerged. It would be some time before it had the strength to melt the frost that covered the trees and grass in sparkling silver. He looked down from this vantage-point at his father's estate. Lights were evident, scattered like fireflies over the dark land. He could identify the home farm and, far to the west, the gamekeeper's cottage.

At the heart of the estate his father's mansion loomed eerily white, the many gables pointing to the sky. At dawn and dusk it reminded him of a beautiful woman appearing shyly from the gloom. He could just make out the battlements where, as a child, he'd played Cavaliers and Roundheads – he'd always insisted his brother was the latter. He wondered if his nephews played there too. There were many lights shining on the ground floor: the maids would be cleaning the rooms ready for the family to descend later. Then, on the upper floor, the glow of a candle moved rapidly past one window of the long gallery after another.

The horse took advantage of this halt to lower his head and tug at the frozen grass, his tack jingling.

'You won't get much joy from that, old boy.' Oliver's breath whirled like ectoplasm in the cold air. So often on his travels he had thought of and longed for this place. Now he remembered another morning ride, long ago, with his father beside him. Oliver had barely been able to keep up on his pony with his father's fine hunter. How old had he been? No more than seven or eight, he thought.

They had halted at this very spot, under the gnarled, ancient tree that crowned the hill, so bent from the ferocity of the wind it appeared to be curtsying.

'See that, boy.' His father had swept the air with his riding crop. 'As far as you can see, that's Cresswell land.'

Oliver had stood up in his stirrups, the better to see, and his heart swelled with pride that his father should possess all that, convinced, as he was then, that he must own the whole world!

Now Oliver lifted himself, holding this much larger horse firmly with his muscular legs. To the west he could see the dark purple smudge of Dartmoor – a place that had once filled him with fear. To the south were rolling hills on which were scattered the thousands of sheep his father owned. To the north was the sweep of Dunwell Wood, dark and dense. When he swivelled in the saddle to face east, he could just make out a sliver of the sea and one or two lights from Cresswell-by-the-Sea, too large to be called a village, too small to be a town, most of it owned by his father. Immediately below him was the picturesque hamlet of Cress where the estate workers lived, and the pensioners. Already he could make out figures in the gloom. There, right in the centre, placed as if by the calculations of a mathematician, lay the jewel: Cresswell Manor, with its church, park and pleasure gardens.

From this height it was as if he looked down on a vast tapestry that had not changed in the hundreds of years his family had owned this land. He stood, where countless of his ancestors had stood, to gaze with satisfaction as the dark of night was rolled slowly back.

He felt an overwhelming affection for the place. He had missed it so much: this land meant everything to him.

He glanced up at the branches of the trees, skeletally bare of their leaves, silhouetted against the sky. How many of his ancestors had made wishes here and what for?

He smiled as he remembered some of his own.

'You must walk three times round the trunk as you wish and you must never tell a living soul what you wished for,' Hannah had instructed him that first time.

'Why not?'

'Because if you do it won't come true.'

He'd walked round the tree three times, his eyes tightly closed, and he had wished for a pony. The next week he had been given Silver. His first ride had been to come back here and wish for a dog. He wasn't in the least surprised when his father had returned from the market in Barlton with a lurcher – Skimmer. A gun had followed, then a bow and arrows. The wishing tree was a magical place. When it appeared that Hannah would marry the curate he had hurried here and wished she wouldn't – and been tortured with guilt when the wedding did not take place and Hannah had looked so sad. His conscience had forced him to confess what he had done. At the time he had not understood why it made her laugh.

The tree had let him down when he had wished for his mother to spend more time at Cresswell – he smiled now to think that he'd once wished that! The tree had also failed when he asked it to make her love him – it was just as well that it had: as a man, he knew he neither liked her nor loved her. It had been a relief to acknowledge this, and the yearnings he had felt for her disappeared.

Despite the tree he still had to go away to school, and it did not make the bully die either.

He dismounted. He had been so happy when he believed in the tree. If only he could recapture that conviction. He looked about him to check that no one

41

was about. Then, solemnly, he walked round the huge trunk. 'Let me find love,' he intoned over and over, just as, long ago, Hannah had told him he must. *Love!* What a fool he'd been. To have found it and then lost it! 'Let me find love,' he said, one last time, and then, startling his horse, he laughed at his foolishness.

He climbed back into the saddle. He could just hear, on the still winter air, the clock over the stable gatehouse chiming the hour, and see the red brick wall surrounding the enormous kitchen garden. He'd asked old Robertson, the head gardener, why the walls were red when the great house was of granite.

Robertson had chewed his baccy, then with a mighty hawk he spat the tobacco, a good ten feet. How much he had admired the man's ability to do that.

'Them's warmer.'

'What? Red bricks?'

'Stands to reason. Have a feel.'

He had, and the walls were warm.

'Keeps them peaches on them there espaliers safe, see?'

The discovery that the source of the heat wasn't the bricks but a network of heated pipes that criss-crossed the wall had been another disillusionment. He still preferred the red-brick theory.

When he had been away on his travels, first in Africa and finally America, he could conjure up the warm, earthy summer scent of that garden. The distinctive smell of rich loam, of ripening fruit, of the flowers grown for the house. As a child it had been one of his favourite places. It was the Paradise in which he would like to find himself for eternity.

He frowned. Death would be the only way he'd end up here, stretched out in the family mausoleum. His pride that day as a boy had been short-lived: soon afterwards his world had tilted and was never the same again.

'And when I'm dead and gone, Oliver, all this will

belong to your brother and after him his son,' he had heard his father say, and wished he hadn't.

'And me?'

'Sadly, my boy, you must make your own way. Which I'm sure you will.'

'But that's not fair!'

'Life isn't, Oliver.'

'Why him? Why not me?' Even as a child he had never been afraid to speak his mind.

'It's called primogeniture – the eldest boy takes all. It's the way of the world.'

'But I love Cresswell. I love it more than Mortie does.'

'Perhaps you do, but it don't alter a jot. It'll still be his. Better get used to the idea.' His father wasn't speaking unkindly but firmly and quickly, as if he wanted the conversation over and done with. Oliver realised that he had planned the ride and the talk.

Even now, years later, Oliver could remember clearly how he had felt: it was as if he'd been hit in the stomach. Then he had felt a bleak surge of anger. He *had* to make his father change his mind. 'He'd sell it! He doesn't love it like me,' he argued forcefully.

'He can't.'

'What if he did?'

'He won't. He'll have his own son and then he'll be thinking in a more responsible way. And his son will have a son, and so it goes on.'

'And what if Mortie doesn't have a son?'

'Then it's yours.'

This should have been a comfort of sorts but it was not. Oliver had never been close to his elder brother but that day the anger with him had taken root. That Mortie was an easy going fellow did not ease his dislike of him. He began, at night, to plan how he could 'disappear' him. *Disappear*, was his word of choice to disguise what he really wanted – a plan, if not to kill him, to have Mortie's

43

life ended. He could smile now at the laboured twisting of his young mind to avoid the truth.

When Oliver was fourteen, Mortie, just into his majority, married Coral, and a year later, with a depressing inevitability, Young Mortimer was born, and the inheritance was secured with the arrival of Felix twelve years later. Oliver was now fourth in line and understood how princes felt.

School and university had changed him – saved him, even. There he had met other second sons. Some were eaten away with bitterness, others accepted their situation. He envied the latter, and refused to become like the former.

So far he had had a good life, and the anger had faded. He had little in common with his brother but he could now acknowledge that he loved him and always would. The sadness he felt today had been ignited by seeing again what he would never own. He had to control such feelings, he told himself. He was a rich man, and he had the satisfaction of knowing that he had made his own fortune. He had a pride in himself that Mortie would never enjoy.

But a new feeling was stirring in him, which he did not fully understand – discontent, restlessness. He would usually have thought it meant he was ready to travel again – but instead the idea filled him with horror. Had the knowledge that his father's time was limited, and that this place would soon belong to his brother, made him wonder if it were not time for him to put down his own roots? Or was it because he was lonely? Even when he was with others he often felt isolated and alone.

He wondered how Mortie felt about taking on Cresswell. To him it would be a trap, not a joy. He had never wanted it, and if he felt like that how long would it be before everything was ruined? Perhaps Oliver should offer to care for it for him. Was that a solution? But he would hate to ask his brother, as if he was going to him

44

cap in hand. He sighed as he took up the reins, and encouraged the horse towards the valley.

'Why, if it isn't Mr Oliver.'

'Beasley, how fortunate to bump into you.' The gamekeeper's face was redder than Oliver had remembered, a combination of the weather and the cider he drank copiously. Beasley had been the favoured companion of his childhood: he had opened Oliver's eyes to the signs that nature left for those who knew how to look, such as where the badgers lived and fieldmice hung on corn stalks. Beasley had taught him to use his nose to smell where the fox had been, and to detect when rain was imminent.

Oliver had loved his visits to Keeper's House over by Dunwell Wood; he felt more comfortable there than at home. There were always cakes and Mrs Beasley had made such a fuss of him. The sound of a snoring gun-dog, whiffling in front of a fire, the distinctive smell of its soaked pelt as it dried – to this day they meant security to him.

'I was sad to hear on your father.'

'It was a shock, to be sure. But the reports are more encouraging this morning. He had a reasonable night's sleep.'

'I didn't think we'd seen the last of him.'

'And how are you and Mrs Beasley?'

'We do fine, thank you, Mr Oliver. A touch of the rheumatism, but that's to be expected at our age.'

'I heard Henry had given up soldiering and was keeping now with you?'

'He should never have gone off like that – waste of time, if you ask me.'

'He must have learnt something?'

'Yes – to run!' Beasley said bitterly.

'Still, Mrs Beasley must be pleased to have him out of the danger of the Boers.' Oliver decided not to pursue this part of the conversation further. 'Will he be head keeper in time?'

'I'm not ready to leave it in anyone else's hands yet. And you sir, what are you up to?'

'Oh, a bit of this and that.'

'It's put a bit of weight on you, sir.'

Oliver laughed. 'You were never one for diplomacy, were you, Beasley?'

'No point in not saying what you see. You need to take care of that.'

'I'll see what I can do.' He grinned. 'I saw your Melanie last night up at the big house.'

'Did you an' all?' There was a pause as if Beasley was unsure what to say next. Oliver had heard rumours that they were estranged. 'Mrs Beasley and I would be most happy if you should feel like popping in for a cup of tea.'

'If she'll make her seed cake, I'd be honoured.' He began to move away.

'How was her?' Beasley asked abruptly.

'Melanie? I was concerned—'

'Naught to do with me.' Beasley turned suddenly and, head down, trudged away.

As Oliver moved off he glanced back over his shoulder at the sturdy figure of the gamekeeper. First he had not wanted to know about Melanie, then Melanie changed his mind . . . He must be all of sixty, Oliver thought, and yet fitter by far than he was. It was true that he had put on weight: the tightness of his hacking jacket proved that. He'd last worn it six years ago, the last time he had been here on a short visit, and this morning he'd had a job getting the buttons to meet. His breeches were the same. Town living was the cause. He should look for something to do. The thought he'd had earlier began to grow in his mind . . . a dynasty and an estate of his own to love.

He was passing the churchyard, which always made him shiver. The Cresswell mausoleum was in there and he was supposed to be buried there one day. He'd no desire for that to be his last resting-place – not beside Mortie and his wife.

A well-wrapped figure was hurrying towards the church. Simeon. Without thinking, Oliver turned his horse and trotted towards the imposing vicarage, which nestled beside the church. A maid was sweeping the steps. He dismounted quickly. 'Your mistress?'

The maid grabbed at her hessian overall and hurried into the house. He waited in the cold. He should go, he couldn't . . . But then why should he?

'Oliver? What are you doing here?' In a drab linen dress, Laura had appeared in the doorway.

'Looking up an old friend.' He smiled.

'Simeon is in church.'

'I know, I saw him.'

She blushed becomingly. 'You had better come in.' He followed her into the house and into the sitting room. 'Some tea? Coffee?'

'Nothing, thank you.'

She sank into a chair, indicating he should take the one opposite.

'You're about early?'

'I needed to think.'

'How is your father?'

'Better, thank you.'

'Such a relief for you all, the way he rallied last night.'

'Father is strong and . . . I had to see you, Laura.'

She stood up abruptly. 'Such a nice man, your father.'

'I do realise what a fool I was.'

She turned and stared at him. 'A little too late in the day, Oliver.'

'But why did you come here of all places?'

'Because this is where my husband works.'

'But you must have known you would eventually meet me.'

'I had no idea, I assure you. Had I known I would not be here. All I knew when I met Simeon was that he had a

47

living in the West Country – he wanted it to be a surprise.' She laughed at this, but it was not a happy sound. 'He never mentioned the Cresswells.'

'And if he had?'

'I would have told him.'

'And now?'

'I would prefer not to. But if it is necessary then I shall – of course.'

'I shall keep your secret.'

'Thank you.' She sat down again.

On the table in front of him he saw a picture book. 'You have children?'

'A son.'

He looked out of the window and a movement in the churchyard alerted him that Simeon was on his way back. 'Is he mine?'

'No, Oliver, he is not! How dare you even ask?'

'I had to know.'

'Well, now you do.' She was on her feet again, and this time her demeanour told him he was dismissed. He stood up.

'But Simeon?'

'I'm sorry?'

'Why marry someone like him?'

'I think it would be better if you left, Oliver.'

'You deserve better.'

'Simeon is a good man and has been nothing but loyal and supportive to me. There is nothing else to be said.'

They were interrupted by a clatter in the hall. The door opened.

'Mr Oliver, what a pleasant surprise. I saw the horse and wondered—'

'I came to thank you for your concern, and to let you know my father had a good night and is much better.'

'The power of prayer!' Simeon put his hands together piously. 'But you have had no refreshment. Laura, what are you thinking of?'

48

'Mrs Redman offered but I refused. I must be getting on, I have much to see to.'

'But of course, Mr Oliver. Call whenever you wish.'

'Thank you, Simeon.'

Simeon fussed him to the forecourt.

Once away from the vicarage he spurred on his horse – he needed to gallop, to rid himself of sad memories, wear off some excess flesh. His hair was tangling in the wind, which whipped smartly at his cheeks, making them glow, making them sting. He shouted out with exuberance at the joy of physical exertion. He'd missed this, he thought, when he pulled up the snorting, blowing horse. Trotting along Rotten Row, in Hyde Park, while chatting and gossiping with his cronies wasn't riding, not like this. He'd do some hunting while he was here.

As Hannah opened her eyes, savouring her sense of well-being, her dream lingered in her mind. She had seen three tall people, their backs to her. Then one had turned, a woman, and beckoned to her. She had had no face, but Hannah had been happy to follow her. Now she wondered where she would have gone.

She stared at the ceiling and waited for the familiar worries to rush in and knock aside her contentment. She knew they would come, was prepared for them. But nothing happened. Then she remembered. Last night when she had left her father, at the nurse's insistence, he had been sleeping calmly, his breathing regular, his colour better than it had been in weeks.

Had the vicar's prayers brought about the improvement – as Simeon had smugly claimed? She sank back on her pillows with a smile. She could afford to delay. He must still be well – if his condition had worsened in the night the nurse would have come to fetch her.

Simeon – smug. Such an unkindness on her part. And once she had thought of him as perfect. How perfidious of her!

49

When her alliance with Simeon had been forbidden Hannah had soon realised that she was not as unhappy as everyone thought she was. In fact she was content. It had been a fortuitous escape: what sort of vicar's wife would she have made when agnosticism had wormed its way into her mind? How could a vicar do his job if his soulmate was not of the same mind? She could imagine what the parishioners would have said.

She had never made the suitable marriage her father had hoped for. She had reasoned to herself that if she could mistake her feelings for Simeon, she would never know that she was truly in love. She had vowed not to marry a man she did not adore and now, at over forty, she had accepted she would never marry. Sometimes, to her annoyance, she still found herself hoping she might meet someone. And there were nights when she could not sleep for a longing to be held tenderly.

Sometimes she wondered how it would be when her father died. Would she be less at ease with herself? She loved him deeply and when he died . . . Just thinking of it made her stomach clench, her heart race, and tears prick her eyes. How would she survive without him?

The ornamental clock chimed on the mantelshelf. It carried on long past the seven she had expected and she sat up with a start. Ten o'clock? It must be broken! But light was peeping through a gap in the curtains! She had overslept. Why had she not been woken? And then she saw the tea tray . . .

She clutched her throat in fear. What if he was dead, and out of kindness she had been left to sleep? She swung her legs over the side of the bed, pulled on her peignoir as with agitated movements she searched with her feet for her silk slippers. She stood too quickly, the entire room spinning about her so that she had to hold on to the curtains of the bed to steady herself. At the ornate dressing-table, she glanced into the mirror – gilded, with two plump cherubs adorning the sides – that had belonged to her mother, yanked a brush through her thick long dark hair, pinched her cheeks and put a little salve on her lips. Then she took a deep breath and, heart pounding, raced along the corridor.

From the doorway of his room she saw her father sitting up in bed, supported by plumped pillows. 'Papa!' She clapped her hands with pleasure. 'You look so much better!' She felt dizzy, but this time with happiness.

'I've felt sounder than this, I must say, but it's an improvement on the last few days.' He was smiling at her, actually smiling! 'You look a little peaky, though.'

She shook her head, waved hands in the air. 'I don't ... I feel ... I don't know what ... Oh, Papa, you frightened me so!' To her horror, she began to cry and once started she could not stop. Her hands were fluttering even more now, as if, in some way, their movement could stop the tears. From time to time she twirled her handkerchief and gulped, 'Sorry,' then, 'So sorry,' and then, 'Sorry,' again.

'There, there.' Her father was trying ineffectually to pat her hand.

'Sorry,' she said.

'There, there.' It was as if their entire vocabularies had been reduced to these two simple words.

'I know how much you hate weeping women.'

'Only when the weeping's for ... effect or emotional blackmail. Those tears needed to ... be shed. You have ... touched me ... profoundly, dear child.' He sank back on the pillows, exhausted.

She saw that talking and trying to comfort her had been too much for him.

'I won't again. Please, try to rest.'

'There you are, Miss Cresswell.' The nurse had entered the room, holding a tray aloft. 'We wondered where you'd got to, didn't we, Sir Mortimer?' She said, in her irritating way.

'You did, I didn't.' Mortimer looked very cross. 'My daughter needed . . . sleep . . . So did I.'

'No more talking. You need to rest.'

'I'll bloody talk!' With enormous effort Mortimer pulled himself up in the bed. 'I ordered bacon and eggs . . . Disgusting gruel!' He pushed away the tray with its bowl of porridge, which the nurse had placed in front of him.

'It wouldn't be wise, Papa. You've barely eaten for a week.'

'Have a spoonful for Nurse. Show Nursie,' she spoke in her North country accent.

'Bugger it!' He pushed at the spoon, and porridge flew across the sheets.

'Now see what you've done! And I'd just put that nice clean linen on the bed for you.' The nurse tutted and fussed.

'Don't talk . . . as if . . . I . . . an imbecile. I pay . . . damn wages . . . Don't . . . forget it.' He banged on the bed with his fist.

'Papa, Nurse Burtonshaw's only trying to help you.'

'Noisy . . .'

'Why, Sir Mortimer, what a thing to say! I'm as quiet as a little mouse.'

'Your clothes aren't.' He beckoned to Hannah. 'Get rid of her – get me one that speaks English.' He spoke in a rush before the breathlessness caught up with him.

'Papa!' Hannah sighed at the petulance of the sick. 'I'm so sorry, Nurse. I'm sure my father doesn't mean it.'

'Yes, I do!' He frowned as he fiddled with the sheet.

'Don't you fret, Miss Cresswell. I've had worse than your father and that's the truth. Far worse.'

'Give me . . . time!'

His agitation was increasing and Hannah realised she had to get the woman out of the room. 'I'll help you, Nurse Burtonshaw. Let us get fresh linen.' She followed the woman from the room. 'I can't apologise enough,

52

Nurse. He's not himself. He's normally the most polite of men,' she said, once they were in the anteroom.

'The poorly can be trying, Miss Cresswell, as I said. Don't you bother yourself about it.'

'At least it's a sign he must be getting better. The really ill don't have the energy to complain, do they?'

Nurse Burtonshaw sucked in her lips so that she looked as if she had no teeth, and then exhaled noisily. 'I've seen this many a time, Miss Cresswell. I strongly recommend that you don't raise your hopes too high. Often the terminally ill rally just before the end. It's a false dawn, I fear.'

Hannah's hand flew to her mouth to stifle a cry. 'He seemed so much better. I can't believe . . .'

'Well, of course, you must think as you wish, but I was only speaking from experience. If you don't want to listen . . .'

Hannah felt an uncustomary spurt of anger. How dare this woman be so pessimistic? 'If your attitude is so dismal then he will relapse. He needs cheerful people about him.'

'And a lot of good that would do him.' The nurse swelled as if her indignation was inflating her.

'Far better than anything you seem to offer.'

'Well, really, Miss Cresswell! I'm only trying to protect you.'

'Then I wish you would not. I neither need nor want your protection.'

'He's going to die, you mark my words.'

At the look of satisfaction on the nurse's face as she made this pronouncement Hannah's anger surfaced. 'Nurse Burtonshaw, as you and my father are not the best of friends, perhaps it would be for the best if you left.'

'Well, I never! What next?'

'Next, Nurse Burtonshaw, you pack your bags. I shall, of course, make right your wages and arrange for a carriage to take you wherever you wish. Thank you, Nurse.' And before the woman could complain, Hannah swept out of the room. He *would* live, she would make sure of it.

Oliver was hungry from the exertion of his early-morning ride. 'Morning, Mortie,' he said, upon entering the dining room. His brother grunted. 'Morning, Whitaker.' He strode towards the sideboard, covered with silver chafing dishes. The pungent smell of methylated spirits from the small burners under them hung in the air, but he was so used to it that he didn't notice.

'Good morning, Mr Oliver. We've some particularly fine kippers arrived from Grimsby, sir.'

'Not today, Whitaker, thank you.' He began to pile eggs, kidneys, bacon and sausages on to his plate. 'No fried bread, Whitaker?'

'I'm sorry, sir. I'll send for more.' Whitaker, with an almost imperceptible wave, sent a footman on his way.

Oliver's attention focused on Mortie. 'You great hog! Give me some of that.' And he stabbed at one of the several slices on his brother's plate.

'Don't take my food!' Mortie stabbed at his hand with a butter knife.

'I've requested more from the kitchen, Mr Cresswell. The newspapers, Mr Oliver?' The butler pulled out his chair and flicked open his napkin.

'If you wouldn't mind, Whitaker, the *Sporting Life*. What's the news on Father, Mortie?'

'No idea. I slept like a log.' Mortie lowered his newspaper.

Whitaker gave a discreet cough. 'Excuse me, Mr Oliver, but your father had a good night's sleep and is greatly refreshed. He's even taken a little nourishment.'

Mortie ruffled *The Times* with evident irritation, and disappeared behind it.

'Thank God for that.' Oliver wondered if Mortie was

irritated because he was talking to him when he wanted to read his paper, or at the better news of his father.

'Your father has the constitution of a lion, Mr Oliver. I could never believe the end was nigh. However, there is a problem.' The butler coughed again, which indicated that he had something of a delicate nature to impart. 'It would seem, sir, that Miss Cresswell has dismissed the nurse.'

'Why?'

'I'm not aware of the reasons, but the woman is making rather a fuss below stairs and is somewhat incoherent. I have ascertained that she has not imbibed.'

'Well done, Whitaker.' Oliver had to suppress a smile – it was well known that Whitaker was not averse to a drop or two himself.

'Mrs Fuller does not know what to do with her.'

'If she's been dismissed I suggest we put her on a train to wherever she came from. More coffee, Whitaker, please.'

'What the hell has she done that for? Out of spite probably,' Mortie remarked.

'What a ridiculous thing to say,' Oliver remonstrated. 'Hannah hasn't got a spiteful bone in her body.'

'My wife interviewed the woman in London – she went out of her way to help. She said Hannah thought she was interfering. Now she's taken control, so Coral feels as if she is of no importance. Mother doesn't like it either.'

'Mother would never be satisfied with whatever Hannah did, as well you know.'

'Hannah acts without thinking. Stupid woman!'

'So you acknowledge she thinks! Which is more than you do!' He could never just have a conversation with his brother, always had to get in cheap jibes. 'And Hannah's far from stupid. If she has dismissed the nurse it will have been for a good reason. Thank you, Whitaker.' His replenished coffee was placed beside him.

'Who's going to tell Mother and Coral?'

'Why don't you, since you get on with them so well?'

Oliver began to study the racing form, then looked up as Hannah entered the room.

'How dare you dismiss the nurse?' Mortie was immediately on the attack. 'And if you're here, who's sitting with Father? He shouldn't be left alone.'

'Mrs Fuller has kindly taken my place while I have breakfast.' Hannah moved towards the sideboard and began to lift the lids of the dishes.

'So why have you dismissed the nurse? Did you consult with Mother?'

'No.' Hannah took some toast, and spooned marmalade on to the side of her plate. 'Tea, please, Whitaker.'

'You've no right to dismiss the woman.'

'Stop bullying her, Mortie,' Oliver snapped. 'What crime did she commit, Hannah?'

'She annoyed Father, who insisted she went.' Hannah took a seat at the table.

'Father? I don't believe you! He couldn't even speak last night.'

'He most certainly can this morning. I've sent for the doctor to examine him again. It's little short of a miracle.'

Mortie slumped back in his chair.

So I was right, thought Oliver. Mortie's disappointed that he's better.

'Are you sure?'

'Of course I am. However,' she looked sad suddenly and fumbled in her sleeve for a handkerchief, 'the nurse told me such rallies were quite common and often short-lived.'

'Perhaps she was taking her revenge – she probably wanted to upset you. Have you thought of that, Hannah?'

'I fear it might be the truth, Oliver. She is experienced.' Hannah sipped her tea, then pushed it and the plate of toast away.

'You must eat, Hannah, or you'll waste away. Then we'll have to start worrying about you.'

'I'm not hungry, Oliver, not with all this worry. What if she was right?'

Mortie threw his newspaper on to the table, leapt up and rushed from the room.

'You've cheered him up. He was quite upset at the thought that Father might recover.'

'That's a horrible thing to say, Oliver. Don't.'

'But it's the truth.'

'I can't believe such a thing of him. And in any case, why should he, of all people, be . . .' Her voice trailed away.

'Sister, dear, you have the most annoying habit of not finishing what you were about to say.'

'It was best not said.'

'It's still annoying.'

'Then I apologise.'

'I bet you were about to wonder why, when Father has been so generous to Mortie, he should want the old man dead.'

'As a matter of fact I wasn't.' But her blush indicated otherwise.

'No doubt Mother has poisoned his mind about Father. And he's not the brightest of candles. Then there's Coral and her endless demands – perhaps his allowance is insufficient for his needs.'

'I've often wondered why Father wasn't equally generous with you. He's a fair man.'

'But he was. He offered and I refused. I wanted to make my own way in the world – the proverbial second son.'

'And have you?'

'Yes.'

'Then I'm proud of you.'

'How fortunate I am to have you for a sister.' He took her hand and kissed the air above it. 'I've had an idea.'

'Yes?'

'If . . . I mean, I don't think he will, but if he did . . .'

'Papa?'

'Yes, if the worst happened,' he felt more relaxed now that he had found the right expression, 'it might be a good idea if you thought what you would do . . .'

'With Mortie inheriting Cresswell? I've thought that if Father . . .' She had to stop, she simply could not say *that* word. 'However,' she continued. 'On the one hand it would be hard to move out of the house. But on the other I don't think I'd want to stay. Yet I'd hate to live anywhere else.'

'I see.' He felt ridiculously disappointed.

'I have wondered if Mortie would let me have one of the cottages.'

'It would be hard for you after living here.'

'I don't know – one of the larger ones, of course, one that's fairly isolated, I couldn't live in the village with so many of the estate staff watching me. It might be nice not to have so much responsibility, only myself to consider.'

'But I'm sure Father will take care of you.' It occurred to him that financial matters were always wrapped up in euphemisms – why?

'That doesn't worry me. I have a legacy from my mother, hardly touched. But you were saying you'd had an idea.'

'Yes, I have. And if you think it impertinent or ridiculous, I'll understand. You see . . . I thought it might be a good idea if you came to live with me.'

Hannah looked surprised and touched. 'Me? How kind of you.'

'It's nothing of the sort. Pure selfishness, more like. You'd supervise the running of my home like a dream.'

'Me, in America? And when you took a wife?'

'You'd stay.'

'And if your wife didn't like me?'

'But she would.'

58

'How can you be sure? As far as I'm aware I've never been unkind to Coral but she doesn't like me.'

'Coral likes no one. But I wouldn't marry anyone who didn't love you as I do.'

'Dear Oliver. I don't know. It's an attractive idea but . . . I don't know if I would enjoy living in a foreign land. I love England so.'

'I didn't mean America. I meant here. Somewhere in Devon. It's time I put my own roots down.'

'Oliver, that makes me so happy. When Father's better we shall find you the perfect house. In fact, there is an estate for sale – but it's large and . . . Oh dear, I'm not sure how to put this without offending you.'

'How much have I to spend?' He grinned at the astonishment on her face when he told her how much he was worth.

'Such a fortune! I'm so proud of you. But the house I'm thinking of is quite close. The owner fell down a ravine on a mountain in Switzerland. And there was such bad gossip about him.'

'How much land?'

'I couldn't be sure, but probably about eleven thousand acres. The house is very grand.'

'And so am I!' He stood up and executed a courtly bow. 'So, what do you say?'

'If I have to leave here I will be honoured to join you. But I would insist on contributing my share of the expenses.' She hugged herself. 'I feel happier than I have in a long time, dear Oliver. Kind as it is, I hope it won't be necessary and that Father will live. Meanwhile,' she got to her feet, 'I've a nurse to find. Would you be going out riding again? If so, perhaps you could take a note to Mrs Topsham. She lives in Gardener's Cottage.'

'Is her husband the head gardener then?'

'No, he's employed to wind the clocks and mend things when they get broken. Not that he does either task well – Mrs Fuller is always complaining.'

'Why, if he is incompetent, is he retained?'

'I'm not sure. When they returned here about two years ago, Father insisted. It caused a lot of ill feeling at the time, though people seem to have forgotten now.'

'Do you know why he wanted her here?'

'No.'

'I've heard rumours,' Oliver admitted, 'but perhaps I shouldn't say.'

'Then don't,' she countered.

'You don't want to know?'

'Not particularly. In any case I'm certain you know nothing and are fishing for information I cannot provide. I'll write that note. I think we should make her a generous payment. She has little money – her husband drinks. Now, if you'll excuse me, I have to see the cook.'

'I thought that was the duty of the mistress of the house.'

Hannah gave him a look of amused resignation.

'Have you arranged matters?'

'Of course, Papa. Oliver will see Mrs Topsham – I've suggested she stays here until we find a substitute for Nurse Burtonshaw – and I've ordered some fish for your lunch.'

'I don't want fish! Steak and oyster pie.' She noted he was calmer, and he must be kept that way: he needed peace and quiet.

'That would be inadvisable, Papa. The doctor says you're to have a light diet – no meat, plenty of milk, eggs and fish.'

'Nursery food!'

'Food that will speed your recovery, Papa.' She smiled at him. 'However, he has agreed you may have a tankard of beer – but that's all.'

'The man is an . . . idiot, just . . . as his father before him.' He was agitated again.

'Let us see how you are tomorrow, Papa. The doctor is

only concerned for your recovery. Please, for me, listen to what he says.'

'Listen to whom, Hannah?' Penelope swept into the room, and Mortimer sighed audibly.

'We were discussing Papa's diet. I have suggested some fish.'

'Fish? Hannah, what are you thinking? Men need substantial food, and your father needs building up – steak, port, cheese, thick cream, even chocolate. Don't you worry, Mortimer, my dear, I am here and I shall see that you have whatever you want.'

'I really think that most ill advised – Mother.'

'Dearest Hannah, what can you possibly know of what a man needs?' Penelope flashed her a viperish smile. She began to plump a pillow, the first time Hannah had seen her do anything remotely domestic.

'Don't . . . want my pillows . . . rearranged! Fussing.'

'I'm making you more comfortable.'

'Then you're . . . failing . . . miserably.'

Penelope laughed gaily, a false sound. 'What a grumpy darling you are this morning,' she trilled.

'What fish . . . Hannah?' Mortimer looked slyly at his daughter.

'A nice sole, Papa, and I asked the cook to do a light champagne sauce to go with it.'

'Much good that will do him!' Penelope was now tidying her husband's bedside table.

'I look forward to it. Penelope, I feel . . . forty winks.' And he sank back on his pillows with a smile.

'How's a body to do what she's supposed to? Answer me that!' Eve Gilroy stormed into the kitchen, threw her receipt book across the room in the direction of Jose, the kitchenmaid, who ducked just in time. Still fuming, Mrs Gilroy slung a stool out of her way, skidded towards it, then kicked the book viciously so that it slid across the stone floor, cuttings and pages falling out, until it came to

61

rest under the pine dresser that stretched almost the length of one wall of the vast room. Then, her complexion ruby red with anger, the cook crossed to the dresser and poured herself a large glass of port, which she downed in one.

Jose Bealey, who had been standing rigid with apprehension, slumped with relief: if Mrs Gilroy had another glass of port she'd soon be over her tantrum. She continued to chop the scraped carrots into thin, perfectly matched sticks.

'Carrots is off! No need to waste more time on they.'

'Whatever you say, Mrs Gilroy.' Jose cleared the vegetables off the table. The cook was so angry that she hadn't even shouted at Jose for doing the vegetables at the kitchen table instead of in the scullery. But Jose had expected Mrs Gilroy to be closeted with Mrs Fuller for a good half-hour and had thought it safe to steal into the warm kitchen, away from the bone-numbing chill that lurked in the scullery.

'What's the racket about?' asked Dolly, the scullery-maid, looking up from the pots she was scouring.

'I didn't ask. I'd only have had my head bitten off, that's for sure. Mean old haybag.'

'Why are cooks always so bad-tempered?' Dolly picked up the hem of her apron to wipe her dripping nose.

'My mum says it's because of the heat. Or maybe it's the port fires her up. She drinks enough of it. She's certainly the nastiest pie-pusher it's been my misfortune to work for.' Jose covered the carrots with cold water. 'At least we'll have posh carrots for lunch. Dolly, you ought to talk to Mrs Gilroy about that cold of yours. You've had it for weeks.'

'Months more like. Can't afford to, that's the problem. If she gives me anything for it Mrs Fuller'll only stop it from my wages and then my dad will give me merry hell if I send him short.'

'Just so he can piss all your hard-earned wages away, I suppose.'

'Something like that.' Dolly carried the large black cast-iron saucepan across the scullery, the weight making the muscles bulge on her thin arms. She tried to lift it on to the drying rack but it was too heavy.

'Here, let me help you.' Jose gave her a hand. If her life was torment with Mrs Gilroy, Dolly's was far worse. 'When her goes all red like that I sometimes find myself wishing she'd drop down dead and put us all out of our misery.'

'I hope I'm around when it happens.'

'I wish you'd been here when Mrs Hodges was cook. She shouted but her was fair. Mrs Gilroy – anything gets her goat. Lucky for the cat I'd just let her out, otherwise she'd have gone flying too.' Jose began to peel the potatoes.

'I had to take some broth over to Flossie Marshall, what's about to pop – Miss Cresswell's instructions . . . I saw a lovely toff in the park,' Dolly said dreamily.

'Who was it?'

'I don't know. I hoped you would. He was tall and handsome, and on a horse he was, great big black thing.'

'Perhaps he was a ghost?'

Dolly shrieked. 'Don't say things like that, scaring me witless.'

'I couldn't do that, you'm no wits to lose.' Playfully she pushed her friend.

'Then when I got to the village I saw the clockman's wife.'

'Melanie?'

'Just walking along her was. I said good morning but she didn't answer. I think she was crying.'

'She wouldn't know how, hard as nails her is.'

'Someone told me you and her are related.'

'Her's a second cousin, twice removed on my father's side.'

'I don't understand that.'

'Neither do I!' Jose giggled. 'I don't have nothing to do with her. Me mam wouldn't like it. She says she's disgusting, a shame to women, having twins.'

'What's wrong with that?'

'It means her did *it* twice in one night and me mam thinks that's filthy.'

Dolly laughed. 'I thinks that's lucky for her!' she spluttered.

'So do I, but you don't know my mam! Her says as Melanie thinks she's a cut above everyone else, just 'cause her father's the head keeper – not as he speaks to her.'

'Why not?'

'Not sure, perhaps to do with the twins. And they went away to school, you know.'

'Honest? And her living in a cottage like that! Schools are expensive, especially them as you go away to.'

'You hear rumours. Perhaps he was her fancy man, been to see her.'

'Who?'

'The toff you saw.'

'Don't be silly, he's a gent.'

'Did he have a moustache?'

'No.'

'I don't think a man's a man when he ain't got a tash. Were his eyes blue?'

'I didn't get that close to see – more's the pity. He came back here later. I saw him ride his horse into the stables. I was carrying out the pig bins and he passed right by.'

'That's Mr Oliver Cresswell, been away from here travelling the world, he has. Molly said he was handsome. Said he was ever so polite too. We'd best beware in case he's got wandering hands.' At which she dived across the scullery, grabbed Dolly's waist and squeezed her hard. Her friend squealed with a mixture of fear and pleasure.

'What do you two think you're doing? Whatever next?

Jose, I'm surprised at you! What sort of example are you showing Dolly? And you, Dolly, there's pots by the cooker need doing.'

'But I've done them, Mrs Gilroy.'

'Not to my satisfaction you ain't.' She dived forward and, before Dolly could get out of her way, cuffed her hard around the ears. Dolly yelled.

'I've done the potatoes, Mrs Gilroy. Can I help Dolly? Her's not feeling too good.'

'No, you cannot. If you've done them tatties there's cabbage to be shredded, onions to be chopped. Help her? You've enough to do – and if you think you've the time I can find more. And where do you think *you*'ve been?'

'I beg your pardon?' Hilda, the pastrycook, asked indignantly. 'If you must know, I was writing letters. Not that it's any of your business.' Hilda was tying on her pristine white apron as she spoke. Jose admired her: although Mrs Gilroy was senior to her Hilda never put up with any nonsense from her. It always astounded Jose how thin Hilda was when, day in and day out, she made cakes and puddings all of which she sampled. Jose knew that if she did that she'd be as big as a barn. She and Dolly busied themselves on the far side of the room.

'Haven't I enough to do?' This was accompanied by a banging of more utensils.

'Eve, calm down – you've got yourself into a rare old state. What's happened?' Hilda asked.

'What's not happened! I spend all morning making my sauce, then it's not required. Change of menu! With an hour and a half to luncheon – that's what's the matter!'

'If we all help . . . Jose, come here. Now, let's be calm and organised, shall we, Eve?'

In response Eve Gilroy hurled a pot across the kitchen. It crashed against the wall, bounced on to the floor and missed the newly returned cat by an inch. It raced out, missing Hannah by a fraction.

If there was one thing that annoyed the cook more

than anything else it was a member of the family venturing into her domain. She swung round, eyes unfocused, spittle frothing at her mouth.

'What has happened?' Hannah looked concerned. 'You'll be doing yourself a mischief, *Mrs* Gilroy.' Hannah said out of courtesy to her position since she had no husband.

'How can I be expected to cook when I get different orders from different people? I deserve some respect, Miss Cresswell, that I do.'

'And we do respect you, Mrs Gilroy. You're the best cook we've ever had. Now, why don't you sit down? Hilda, some water for her.' Mrs Gilroy was now fanning herself with the oven cloth. Hannah held out the glass of water to her. 'I apologise for venturing here, Mrs Gilroy, but I gathered there had been a little bit of a problem.'

Her apology had calmed the cook but unfortunately the reference to problems reignited her anger. She rose from her chair and loomed over the table. 'I'd call it more than "a little bit of a problem", Miss Cresswell. I'm not a cook-general what has no standards.'

'Of course, you're not, Mrs Gilroy. Whoever suggested you were?'

'Did we or did we not decide on a little consommé, steamed sole with champagne sauce, and a small lemon jelly for your father's lunch?'

'We did. Has Lady Cresswell changed my instructions?'

'That she has. Summoned I was and out of time. How am I supposed to cook if I get sent for willy-nilly by all and sundry?'

'How irksome for you.'

'Now, with just over an hour to go, I'm to prepare a pie and a roast!'

Hannah tutted sympathetically.

'Well, truth be told, I were doing a roast anyway, but a

66

steak and oyster pie! It can't be done. Lady Cresswell seems to think I can perform miracles.'

Dolly stood with her mouth wide open with shock at the temerity of the cook to be speaking to her employer in such a manner.

'Mrs Gilroy, I don't want to upset you further but I should like you to continue with the menu I chose. Anything else would be too heavy for my father's digestion. So if it's not too late . . .'

Mrs Gilroy sat down. 'Will you be telling her ladyship?'

'But of course.' Hannah rose. 'There's always a lovely smell in your kitchen, Mrs Gilroy. It's always a pleasure to visit. I wish you'd let me come more often.' She paused at the door. 'Are you not well?' she said to Dolly.

'Me?' Dolly looked nervous.

'You seem to have a bad cold.'

'She's fine, Miss Cresswell. Her always sniffs like that.'

'She doesn't look well. I'll send down some medicine for her.' This announcement made Dolly blush to the roots of her hair, and the door closed behind Hannah.

'Put the kettle on, Dolly. You needn't think just because the mistress was kind you can slacken off.' Mrs Gilroy settled on her chair. 'Honestly, you two girls go at a snail's gallop. Get a move on.'

'Eve, you should be more careful. Her ladyship's the mistress of the house. You'd be wise to remember that.'

'Bah! Soon as the old boy coughs it she'll be back to London. I don't give a fig for her. Miss Cresswell will always look after us. If you ask me, Lady Cresswell was trying to get the menu changed just so the poor old man would have a seizure. And who'd have got the blame? Me!'

'You don't think so?' Hilda peered at her. 'Yes, you do! Well I never!'

'She's been sniffing around ever since she got here.'

'Who?' Hilda was leaning forward eagerly. The cook whispered in her ear. 'Never! He's married!'

'And when did that ever stop anyone? Here, you two, out!' Mrs Gilroy pointed at Dolly and Jose who, disappointed, shuffled out. 'If I was old Sir Mortimer I'd carry on living just to annoy her, that I would.'

On his way to the gamekeeper's cottage, Oliver stopped as promised at the cottage occupied by the Topsham family. 'Is your mother in, lad?' he called to a boy, who was chopping kindling in the small garden to the front of the house.

'It depends who wants to know.'

Oliver smiled at his cheekiness. 'Tell her Mr Cresswell's here to see her.'

'Sorry, sir.' His face had reddened.

'No need to apologise. A boy should take care of his mother.'

As he waited he glanced about him. Like most of the cottages in the village this one was in need of repair. The guttering was loose; the window-frames were rotting. He didn't understand: his father had always taken care of the tenants. Perhaps he should say something to Mortie. He didn't want to bother his father. Or he might speak to Greenacre – but the man seemed worse than useless as an estate manager.

Gardener's Cottage must have one of the best views in the estate, situated as it was at the end of the village, detached from the other houses. It was built into a slope that gave it an unimpeded view of the pleasure gardens at the house; the moors rose a long way behind.

'Mr Oliver!' Melanie Topsham appeared, hurriedly covering her head with a shawl. 'Your father?' She looked anxious.

'A marked improvement, Mrs Topsham. My sister was wondering if you would be so kind as to come to the house and assist her. The nurse has left and until a replacement can be found . . .' He gave her Hannah's note.

Melanie's expression reminded him of an animal unsure of its safety. 'Now?' She sounded anxious.

'At your convenience.' He had urged his horse closer to her. He could see a bruise on the side of her face, evidently the cause of her wariness.

'I'd have to get my husband's supper ready first.'

'Of course. Perhaps my sister could make arrangements for one of the other women to care for your family.' He smiled, fully aware of how disarming his smile could be. 'It would be helpful if you could stay at the house.' He saw he had startled her. 'That is, until we find another nurse. It would be much more convenient for my sister.' He spoke as one who expected no argument, but in fact he didn't like the bruise: he'd never had time for any man who felt it necessary to beat his dogs, horses and women. She would be safer, if only for a few days, with Hannah. Her husband would not dare to object.

'Thank you, Mr Oliver, but there is no need. I can make my own arrangements.'

'As you wish, Mrs Topsham. I'm just off to tea with your mother and father.' She did not react to this information so he saluted her with his riding crop and guided his horse back on to the main street of the village. He re-entered the park and cut across it towards Dunwell Wood and the Beasleys' home.

'It's so nice to see you back with us, Mr Oliver.' Hettie Beasley, her broad face wreathed in smiles, welcomed him. Her bulk was such that she took up the whole doorway, and her efforts to ensure that he entered her living room before she did led them to dodge and squeeze, flattening themselves against the walls. 'Why, Mr Oliver, such a figure of a man you are. There's no room for a little body like me.'

'My apologies,' Oliver said gallantly.

'Look who's here, Charlie. Our Mr Oliver, handsome as ever. Just as well I made one of my seed cakes, isn't it?'

'Mrs Beasley, what a treat!' Oliver entered into the game that he was not expected, that there was always a fine linen tablecloth on her table, that she and Charlie always drank tea out of the Crown Derby given her by Oliver's grandmother as a wedding present. That the crusts were always cut off the sandwiches, and that the jam was always decanted into a cut-glass bowl. It had always been like this. Before, he had taken it for granted; today he was touched by her efforts.

'Now, you sit there by the fire. I'll get an extra cup.' She buzzed out of the room.

He looked about the room contentedly. 'Everything's just the same.'

'Thank you, sir, for playing her game.'

'I find it charming.' He settled back in the well-worn but comfortable chair. 'You know, when I was a child I used to pray that you would adopt me and I could live here for ever and eat Mrs Beasley's seed cake every day of the week.' He laughed at the memory.

'It was our joy to have you here, Mr Oliver, that was for sure. You've been away too long.'

'Ten years . . . I've just seen your daughter.'

'Have you now?' Beasley began to fill his pipe with his pungent tobacco.

'She looked as if she'd fallen over.'

'Did her?'

'She was badly bruised.'

'Was her?'

'I was somewhat concerned. I don't wish to meddle but you don't think her husband is violent with her?'

'I don't think nothing, sir. And I'd appreciate you not mentioning Melanie in front of Mrs Beasley. As I say, sir, you've been away too long – there's a lot I need to talk to you about.' Beasley began the ritual of lighting his pipe slowly and methodically.

There was always the smell of milk and damp washing in Flossie Marshall's cottage, which was hardly surprising since the house was never without a baby in it. As soon as one was born another was on the way. She had been married six years and her sixth was about to arrive. Flossie's cottage contained little of any value, just a battered pine table with rickety legs, two wooden chairs, a rag rug on the floor, a small cupboard, a shabby armchair and several wooden boxes.

'Where's your mother?' Melanie asked the eldest, a serious-faced little girl, who was sitting in a corner on a box, feeding the last baby to be born.

'Scullery,' said Willow. They were all named after trees, and the others were Rowan, Ash, Maple and Aspen.

Melanie found Flossie scouring a pan. 'What will you call this one?'

'Melanie, what a nice surprise. Names, they'm getting harder. I hope it's a boy, I fancy Oak.'

'And a girl?'

'Cherry.'

'Nice, provided of course that the boy isn't puny.'

'Unlikely, given the size of his dad.' Flossie laughed loudly. Even when she wasn't pregnant she was a large girl – tall and broad-hipped with generous breasts. She had a wide, open face, which mirrored her temperament, and large, grey, trusting eyes. Melanie had few friends on the estate, but Flossie was one. The girl was what her own mother referred to as a 'tonic'. No matter how low she felt, Flossie, barely into her twenties, could raise Melanie's spirits. They were the poorest family in the village, and as such were ostracised by many – in large part, Melanie thought, due to Alf's work: he collected the night soil and mended the drains. She'd read about the Untouchables in India and had thought that the society she lived in was similar. She had befriended the family when they had arrived here, shortly after she had. Despite their struggle to survive, they were happy people who hardly ever complained.

'Here, let me do that.' Melanie took the pot from her. 'You should be resting.'

'What's that?' Again the happy laugh. 'I don't think it can be long now – I keep wanting to clean things. That's not at all like me.'

'I saw your light last night and wondered.'

'I'd hopes, but it came to nothing.'

Melanie dried the pan and put it on the shelf, which hung precariously on the wall. 'Where's Alf?'

'He's gone to clear the vicar's cesspit. The job came just in time – he'll need some money to go down the pub when the baby starts coming.'

'Flossie! He should be spending the money on you and the kiddies, not on boozing.'

'Get on with you. He has few enough pleasures in life.' They moved back into the living room. 'There's his baccy, his ale and, well, *me* I suppose.' She roared at her own joke.

'You're incorrigible!'

'If I knew what it meant, I'd know what to say.'

'"Wonderful" is what I should have said.'

'Oh, Melanie!' Flossie clutched at her ample bosom. 'That's the nicest thing anyone's ever said to me.' Her luminous eyes filled with tears.

'I didn't mean you to cry.' Melanie felt her own eyes prick. 'But you have so little and you're always happy. I envy you.'

'Envy me?' This seemed to take Flossie by surprise for she had to sit down on one of the chairs, but not until she had removed a stack of washing that lay jumbled and unfolded upon it.

'Let me.' Melanie began to fold the clothes, rough from over-washing and inadequate rinsing.

'You need a good man,' Flossie said, 'not that bastard you'm lumbered with.'

'I owe him – he took me in where many wouldn't have.' It was true, no matter how much she hated him.

'And you have to spend the rest of your life thanking him? I reckon you've paid him back a hundredfold.'

'Not really. I'm not a good wife to him.'

'Your house is always as clean as a new pin. He's always well fed, isn't he?'

'It's the least I can do. I hate him so much, you see, and I can't hide it, so the situation gets worse and worse.'

'If he didn't beat you you wouldn't hate him, so it's his fault. That's a huge bruise he's given you this time. I'd hit him back.'

'Then he'd kill me.'

'I'd run away.'

'I'd like to, but where would I go? And there's Timmy to consider. In any case,' she smiled slyly, 'you're bigger than me.'

This amused Flossie.

'Has Alf ever hit you?'

'Never. He couldn't hurt a fly, let alone me. But if he did I'd go and see my dad. He'd sort him out.' She clapped her hand over her mouth. 'I'm sorry, I forgot. You and your dad . . .'

'It doesn't matter. It doesn't hurt any more,' she lied. 'He and my mother lost more than me – they don't know their grandchildren.'

'It must be hard living in the same village.'

'It is, but when Bernard was offered his position here, we had to come. We weren't succeeding in Plymouth.'

'He don't seem to do much here neither,' Flossie said, in her no-nonsense manner.

'No, well . . .' Melanie had to look away. It was true: Bernard did less and less each week. It was her constant fear that Sir Mortimer would tire of his idleness and excuses and dismiss him. Then where would they go and what would they do?

'My Alf reckons Bernard knows something that the

family don't want the world to know. So if he don't want to do something he don't and naught's said.'

'What on earth gave him that idea?' Was that what people were saying?

'Well, there has to be a reason – he spends more time in the pub than working. Anyone with any sense would have given your husband notice months ago . . . unless?' At this Flossie put on an arch expression.

At this Melanie laughed, a delightful sound that wasn't often heard. 'You always say exactly what you're thinking.'

'I can't lie, though, can I? 'Twould be a sin, wouldn't it? Anyway, that's what Alf said. And we was wondering how you lived if him's not working. Everyone talks about it.'

'Then you tell them my husband works to bring in enough for us to live. He's not over-fond of graft.'

'What were you doing seeing my light last night? Out on one of your midnight walks, were you?'

'I was coming back from the big house. I'd been summoned to the old man's deathbed, but he hasn't died.'

'Well I never!' Flossie was impressed. 'Why was you invited?'

'To help Miss Cresswell with the nursing.'

'I thought they had a nurse,' Flossie said, sharp as a knife.

'So they did. But she's been dismissed.'

'She was there yesterday, my Alf saw her. Bossy old cow, he said.' She looked straight at Melanie.

'I can't tell you why I was there.' Melanie knew that unless she gave Flossie an honest answer she would continue to question her.

'Will you one day?'

'I promise I will.'

'What was it like?'

'I wouldn't trade places with one of them. Mortie and

74

his wife were carping – she's such a mean-looking woman. Lady Cresswell was making eyes at old Green-acre.'

'So it's true, then . . . And Mrs Greenacre's such a nice woman.'

'What can he be thinking of?'

'His nether regions.' Flossie's laugh rang out again and this time the children joined in. 'That Mr Oliver, what's he like?'

'Handsome and sad. There's no love lost between him and his brother. Well, at least, that's what I saw.'

'Sad, isn't it, when they have so much yet they don't get on? Family's for getting on and supporting, isn't it? Otherwise what's the point of them?'

'Exactly, Flossie. But not everyone's as lucky as you, are they?'

'Oh, Gawd! I've gone and done it again. Sorry.'

'It doesn't matter.'

'Can I ask? I mean it's none of my business and you can tell me to take my poky nose out but . . . why don't they talk to you?'

'Because I had to get married. They've never forgiven me for the shame.'

'Is that all? Good gracious me! If everybody on this estate felt like that then nobody would talk to anyone. Still, my mum always said your mother thought she was a cut above everybody else.'

It was Melanie's turn to laugh. 'That's what they say about me too.'

'Yes, but a lot of folks mistake shy for uppity, don't they?'

The clothes folded, Melanie looked about for some-where to sit. She chose a wooden box. 'I thought Miss Cresswell brought you a little sofa from the big house? I'm sure there was one here the last time I visited.'

'We sold it to the teacher. It was too grand for us. Plush velvet, if worn, but with the little ones it would have looked worse in a matter of days.' Flossie hauled herself to her feet and waddled towards the range. She lifted the lid off a saucepan and a rich aroma filled the room.

'That smells lovely,' Melanie said.

'Rabbit stew. Alf's favourite. I've made a huge one – then he'll have something to stick to his ribs in case Mother hasn't arrived.'

'You're such a good cook.'

'But you can make cakes and my sponge is like lead.'

'So your mother's coming to look after you?'

'I hope so. She likes having her hands on a baby, and I always feel safer if she's here.'

'Then I've an idea, but say if you or your mother don't want to . . .' Melanie explained that she needed someone to cook for Bernard and Timmy, and the Cresswells would reimburse her.

'Of course! Bless you, Melanie, for thinking of me.'

Back at her own cottage, Melanie tidied downstairs, made the bed and left a note for her husband – she'd rather do that than tell him in person. She said she had been *ordered* to go, which might calm him a little. And, in a way, it was true: how could she not go? She and Bernard were dependent on the Cresswells, so when the Cresswells said, 'Come,' they came. For generations, Melanie's family had been at their beck and call, and she had always accepted it. But these questions that had begun to plague her returned. Why?

Chapter Three
February 1901

Two weeks had passed since Mortimer's rally and change was in the air. The old Queen had died on the night that he hadn't. Although her death had been expected the whole nation was shocked. While some were excited by the thought of a new reign and the change it might bring, others felt bereft and afraid.

Mortimer was sad that the old era had passed, but Penelope fretted that they could not be with her husband's friend, the new King. Oliver felt challenges were afoot. It was doubtful Mortie was even aware of what had happened, although Coral had appeared in funereal black, claiming kinship through a cousin so many times removed that everyone's head began to whirl. Hannah was nervous at what the future might hold. Lettice cried and Young Mortimer went for a long, solitary walk. To the villagers it mattered not a jot who was on the throne: staying in work and earning enough to maintain their families was all that bothered them.

'Father's worrying me,' Hannah confided to Oliver, as they finished their breakfast one morning. 'He's no longer irascible. He agrees with everything.'

Oliver laughed. 'I'd have thought you'd be pleased about that?'

'I'd give anything for him to be difficult again. That would mean he was *really* getting better. As it is, he spends hours staring into space, saying nothing. It's as if he's no longer here.'

'What do Mother and Mortie think?'

'Before he left for London this morning, Mortie

commented on Papa's submissiveness. He said he thought he was becoming forgetful.'

'Not surprising when he's been so ill.'

'That's what I said. I haven't spoken to your mother. I don't want her to think I'm being critical of him.'

'Or you didn't want her to be made aware of something that perhaps she hadn't noticed.' He looked at her intently, but Hannah was rearranging the cutlery beside her plate. 'Certainly it's not like Father.' Hannah was now studying the prongs of a fork. 'What concerns you, Hannah? Do you think his mind has been damaged?'

Hannah dropped the fork. 'Don't say that!'

'Heavens, don't listen to me! Father's the first ill person I've been near. I've no idea what I'm talking about.' He laughed to lighten the atmosphere, but with little success. 'We need to talk to the doctor – you might be worrying unnecessarily.'

'But he's a simple country doctor, what will he know about such matters? I was wondering if we should get a specialist from Exeter or London, a man who understands such problems.'

'What problems, Hannah?'

'His sanity,' she whispered.

Oliver set down his cup. 'My dear, you should be careful in your choice of confidant. Your intentions might be misconstrued.'

'I don't understand.'

'Father is wealthy. They might think you're suggesting he's a senile old man unable to take care of his own affairs.'

'Why would anyone think I'd do that?'

'So that you acquire control of his money.' He spoke quietly, which made his words all the more ominous.

'Me?' Hannah clapped her hand over her mouth to prevent herself crying out. Then she removed it. 'How could anyone think that of me? I want only what is good for him.'

'Those who love you know that. But there are others, enemies . . . You must be aware that—' He stopped. How could he say that he meant his mother and sister-in-law?

'Oliver! if Father knew my worries he might think that of me too.'

'Exactly! So you must stop worrying. Give him time – his old enemy, now his friend.' He smiled. 'Think, Hannah. Father has had a brush with death and it must have frightened him – it certainly scared us. No doubt it has made him think differently. We must be patient.' He laid his hand on hers.

'How swiftly things change. Once Father was caring for us, now it's the other way round.'

'It's been a time of change for us all.'

'I'm so fortunate to have you here, Oliver. If I were alone . . .' She shuddered. 'I hope you intend to stay longer?'

'If you can bear with me.'

'Silly! It will be my pleasure . . .'

The door opened with a swish. 'Am I intruding on secrets?'

As always, Hannah stiffened at the sound of her stepmother's voice.

Penelope smiled falsely at her. 'Where are the servants?' She waved her arm and her riding habit, which was looped up to her wrist, flapped; Hannah thought she looked like a vast one-winged bat.

'We dismissed them,' Oliver explained.

'You usually breakfast in your room and we had no idea you would need them. Let me.' Hannah was already moving towards the sideboard. 'What would you fancy to eat – Mother?'

'You decide for me, Hannah dearest. I'm famished! I'll have you know I was up with the lark and have been out riding. So invigorating.' Her cheeks were coloured with a healthy bloom, and it was possible to see now, without the make-up she customarily wore, her once-famed beauty.

'You shouldn't venture out on your own in this weather, Mother. The roads are icy and snow is expected. You might have come to harm.'

'Nonsense! I've forgotten more about horses than you'll ever know, Oliver.'

What rubbish, thought Hannah. Oliver was an expert horseman, and for Penelope to ride was as rare as a heatwave in winter.

'It's dangerous, no matter how expert you think you are.' Oliver said this with a smile, and Penelope was unaware of the implied criticism.

'Such concern. How touching, dear son.' She patted his cheek. Perhaps they were getting on better, Hannah thought. It saddened her to see the distance between Oliver and his parents. Perhaps he had been away too long and they had expected their child to return, rather than this independent, confident man. 'There was no need for you to fear for me. Greenacre accompanied me so that I should come to no harm.' She laughed – as if at herself.

'Greenacre? At such an unsociable time?' Now Oliver was frowning.

'There were matters I wished to check with him.' She cracked open her napkin as Hannah approached. 'Good gracious, dear, so much food! I'm not a navvy!'

'I'm sorry, but you said . . .'

'Never mind. It's here now, and it was kind of you to fetch it for me.' She attacked the food with gusto. 'So, what was so secret that you needed to dismiss the servants?'

'No secrets. We were discussing Father and agreeing how well he was doing – how pleased we both were with his progress.'

Hannah looked at her brother with surprise. Did he

regard his mother as one of the enemies he had mentioned? Surely not.

Penelope leant forward as far as the rigid whalebones in her corset permitted. 'You think so? Then I am astonished.' She laid down her knife and fork deliberately. 'Are you both blind? Are you deaf? I am particularly surprised by you, Hannah. I thought you loved your father dearly.'

'I do.'

'Not enough to see that all is far from well with him.'

'What in particular?' Oliver asked.

'He can't remember what day of the week it is.'

'At the moment that is irrelevant to him.'

'He has no interest in anything,' she continued.

'Because he is concentrating on recovery.'

'He sits staring into space. He has become senile.'

'What makes you say that, Mother?' Oliver asked.

'Acquiescence was never your father's forte. From having opinions on everything he has an opinion on nothing. He has no notion whether his egg should be boiled, poached or fried.'

'Hardly cause for suggesting senility. Rather, he has no concern about how it is cooked. I often find it's easier to have food put in front of me than decide what to eat. You have just done exactly that.'

'Really, Oliver, are you suggesting that I am *senile*?'

'You used that criterion to suggest that Father is.'

'You're not taking this seriously. Your father is far from well. His mind wanders. I've been meaning for some time to discuss this with you both, but delicacy prevented me doing so – that, and the pain of it all. It is not easy for a woman to face these unpleasant facts about a man whose life she has shared for many years. It smacks of disloyalty. But someone has to speak up and that person is me.' From her riding habit she took out a delicate handkerchief and dabbed at her eyes. Hannah was sure she was not crying. Oliver watched, but made no move to comfort her. Then Hannah noticed that his hands were clenched, his knuckles white, and realised he was controlling himself. Why? Penelope was only saying what she herself had implied less than half an hour ago and he hadn't been angry with her.

'We have to act,' Penelope said, when it was apparent no one was going to comment on her weeping – or lack of it. 'On your rides, Oliver, have you not noticed the sad state of the land? Mr Greenacre has been most anxious about it. He wanted me to see for myself, and I was shocked.'

'There has been a measure of neglect.'

'I've done my best,' Hannah said defensively.

'I'm not accusing you, Hannah dear. We mean your father is no longer capable of running the estate.'

'So, what do you suggest, Mother?'

'I have been given the name of a doctor in Exeter, an expert on people's minds. He has a small, exclusive nursing-home there—'

'No!' Hannah exclaimed.

'It would only be until he is well again and has all his faculties. Do not take on so, Hannah.' This last sentence was tinged with irritation.

'Have you discussed this with Mortie?'

'He is in full agreement.'

'He would be.'

'And what does that mean, Oliver?'

'He would want the best for Father,' Oliver said, to Hannah's astonishment.

'I'm pleased you see sense.'

'And, of course, we should get Mr Battle from Barlton here to discuss his affairs and how they are to be managed. I presume you and Mortie have discussed the possibility of one of us having power of attorney?'

'Yes, I did. I can't tell you how wretched I feel. To think that dear Mortimer, with his acute brain, is unable to make decisions.'

'Why should that bother him when he has you to take all the right ones?' Oliver was drumming on the table with his fingers.

'Can he not stay here? Can we not care for him? Melanie Topsham and I have managed well these past weeks.'

'But what if he got worse, dear? What if he can't be treated here? In either case you'd be unable to forgive yourself. What if he took it into his head to go away? What if he should meet up with unscrupulous people who might influence him to our detriment? Melanie Topsham is such a one. I have never understood the necessity of having that woman care for him, and what her motives might be.'

'But he is fond of Mrs Topsham.'

'There! You see what I mean?' She looked arch. 'No, far better that he goes to the nursing home and *professionals* care for him. I don't want anyone saying I didn't do the best I could for my husband.'

'Why, Mother, are you so concerned that professional people should be brought in now? Hannah told me you didn't think it necessary when he was apparently dying.'

Fleetingly Penelope looked flummoxed, but recovered quickly. 'Because we had all been told there was no hope, and it would have been cruel to disturb him – as I explained at the time. Now, today there might be hope. This may be a reaction to his illness and he will recover – we must all pray for that – so other opinions are required.'

'Dr Shelburn's sensibilities don't worry you this time?'

'Really, Oliver, what a card you are! It was Dr Shelburn who recommended Dr Talbot from Exeter. He has an excellent establishment called the Cedars.'

'Should I ride over to Barlton to see the lawyer?'

'No need, Oliver, it's all arranged. They come tomorrow, medical and legal men together. So much more practical, don't you think? And this way no one can ever say anything detrimental about any of us or our actions.'

This was too much for Hannah. She pushed back her chair and rushed from the room, bumping into Whitaker on her way.

It was the custom for Whitaker, Mrs Fuller and Lavender Potts, Hannah's maid, to meet for sherry in Mrs Fuller's sitting room before they made their way to the senior servants' dining room for lunch. They only ate in the servants' hall on Sunday, at Easter and Christmas, when it was doubtful if they or the other members of staff particularly enjoyed the exercise. It gave them time to discuss any problems and to have a good gossip. When they took coffee, after the family had been served their luncheon, Mrs Gilroy joined them.

'A right to-do is boiling up aloft,' said Whitaker, whose father, a seafaring man, had instilled the odd nautical expression in his son. 'They're planning to put the old man away.'

Mrs Fuller nearly dropped the sherry decanter, but her instincts saved it. 'Never!'

The three huddled together in front of the fire. 'I heard them with my own ears – senile they called him.'

'They never did!' The housekeeper was incensed. 'What lies.'

'Acquiring power of attorney they were saying.' Whitaker looked pleased to be first with the news. 'And we all know what *that* means. He won't be allowed to make decisions, all transactions will be in *their* hands.'

'What did Miss Cresswell say to that?'

'Upset she was. Ran out crying. Cannoned straight into me. Not even aware I was there.'

'*That*'s why she's been so quiet and moody.' Lavender nodded.

'Listening at the door, were you?' Mrs Fuller asked.

'I simply overheard, Mrs Fuller. They made no effort

to lower their voices. Mr Oliver agreed with her ladyship's plans.'

'The snake! Away all those years, then comes home only when he thinks the poor old man's dying, and now wants to cheat him out of what's rightfully his. It's wicked.' Mrs Fuller was so upset that she had to pour herself more sherry. Then, aware of the accusing eyes upon her, she hastily topped up the others' glasses.

'They're coming tomorrow.'

'Who?'

'The lawyer – to get the papers signed, I presume – and a Dr Talbot from Exeter.'

'Talbot . . . I know that name.' Mrs Fuller frowned as she racked her brains.

'What can we do, Mr Whitaker?' Lavender was twisting her hankie.

'Very little, Miss Potts, against the might of the law and the doctors. I fear Sir Mortimer might have been scuppered,' he said despondently.

'They think he's gorn mad, Mr Whitaker.' Mrs Fuller shook her head in disbelief.

'I didn't hear anyone say those exact words,' Whitaker looked momentarily discomfited, 'but what else are we to infer?'

There was a tap at the door. 'Oh, really!' Mrs Fuller snapped. 'That'll be Dolly to tell us our repast awaits us.'

Mortimer felt that his strength was improving. As the weight returned, as his vigour built, he was purposely quiet and obedient, doing whatever the doctor or his wife suggested. He had chosen not to use one shred of his energy as he was intent on fuelling his anger.

'I like my glass there.' He pointed at a particular spot on the table by his chair, which was covered with books, spectacles, paper, pens. It looked like clutter but he knew where everything was.

'What a crosspatch you are this morning!' Penelope

laughed. 'There – is that the right place?' With an elaborate charade she put down his glass of beer.

'Thank you,' he said politely, yet filled with annoyance. He had difficulty controlling himself when she was near him. Her presence made him seethe with fury. They moved in a sophisticated circle where indiscretions were tolerated; and both had taken lovers over the years, but that was not the issue. There were rules, there were obligations, there was finesse. And Penelope had flouted them all.

How could she have contemplated committing an adulterous act not simply under his roof, but with himself in the room? And their children in the vicinity! Worst of all, it had been with an employee. Had she no shame? She had gone too far and he knew why – because she had thought it did not matter: that night she had expected to be his widow.

'You're always so short with me, so impatient,' she complained.

'I apologise.' His reply was calculated to puzzle her.

'I'm not used to nursing.'

'You are most kind.' Which only added to the conundrum.

'You must eat.' She held out a spoon to him. While others cajoled him into eating, Penelope ordered him – but then, he thought, she never *asked* for anything, always *demanded* it.

'What's that racket?' he asked suddenly.

'They're cutting trees up at Dunwell Wood. Don't you remember? You ordered Greenacre to see to it.'

'Did I?' He was sure he hadn't, even if he had intended to.

'Of course you did. Have you forgotten already?'

When she left the room Mortimer felt his body and mind slump with relief.

He laid his head back in the tall wing chair – he refused his bed during daytime: that, he felt, would expose his weakness. Something was afoot, but he could not put his finger on what it was. And there was no one with whom he could discuss his fears. Hannah, who had been such a tower of strength during the dark days, appeared to have gone to pieces now that he was so much better. How could he add to her problems by confiding in her? 'Really, Hannah, my dear, James and I can manage,' he had said to her, only this morning.

'But your linen?'

'It's organised, isn't it, James?' he'd asked his valet, who stood with bowl and ewer ready to help him wash.

'If you're sure?'

'We're positive. Now, you run along . . .'

When he had been seriously ill she had often been present when the nurse tended him. Now he was mortified that his daughter had witnessed his indignity. Then she had been controlled and capable, but now she seemed less able to compose herself, and cried at the least thing.

'I like my glass there,' he had told her.

'I'm sorry, Papa, I forgot.' In her agitation she had knocked it to the floor. During the flurry of maids being summoned to mop the carpet, Mortimer became aware that she was crying. 'You're tired, Hannah.'

'No, Papa, I'm sleeping well. I'm flustered, that's all.'

'But a spilt glass is hardly cause for tears, my dear.'

'I'm not crying.'

'I think you are. Why don't you get away for a few days? Have a rest, some sea air. Let us write to your godmother in Brighton and ask if you may go there for a few days.'

'No, really.'

'Then what about my sister in the South of France? Think of the sun, the warmth, away from this bitter winter.'

'I couldn't leave you . . . Not with . . .' She had rushed from the room in tears again.

Not with: what had she meant by that? Penelope. He'd have put money on it and he was a shrewd betting man.

'Well, I'll be off, Father, if that's all right by you?' Mortie had stood in front of him last week looking sheepish.

'Pressing engagement?'

'The Grangers have invited us – we couldn't make their last house party and Coral felt . . .'

'But of course you must go. Poor Coral must be bored here – such a social butterfly, your wife.'

'I wouldn't say that, Father. It's duty more than anything.'

'Of course, Mortie. When duty calls . . .'

'Exactly,' said Mortie, unaware of his father's irony.

'I trust you've been keeping an eye on things here while I've been laid up?'

'Well, not . . .' He frowned, obviously thinking hard. 'Greenacre appears to be pretty competent.'

'But no one takes care of one's affairs as well as one's own blood.' He had dodged the need to discuss Greenacre.

'Naturally, Father.'

If he wasn't so damned annoyed with his indolent son, Mortimer might have been amused by his discomfort during their conversation. He had long known the boy was idle, stupid and a glutton, but it had not bothered him unduly – until now. No doubt, he reasoned with himself, it was his brush with death that had made him realise what a disastrous heir he had.

He hoped that once Mortie had left for London he could forget about him, but instead he found himself fretting about what was to become of the Cresswells when his time came. This, more than anything, was eating away at his energy.

His grandchildren's daily visit pleased him. He hardly knew them, but that was unsurprising since he so rarely saw them. Young Mortimer was a sensitive, intelligent boy, a marked improvement on his father, so there was hope a long way in the future, and Lettice was the most lovely creature, even better-looking than her grandmother had been when he had first met and fallen in love with her. How he had loved her! And how could he have been so grossly duped? Felix was too young, though, and Mortimer found his chatter wearing.

'Good ride?' he asked Oliver, who was visiting before luncheon.

'Splendid. I went right to the top of Childer's Hill, down to Hunter's Copse then hacked over to Wheeler's Combe and back again.'

'Do you like Sergeant?'

'A fine horse.'

'He must be glad of the exercise.'

'He undoubtedly is.'

'See anything untoward?'

'One or two things. Nothing to worry about.'

'Could you see to them?'

'It would be my pleasure.'

'Staying long?'

'A while longer, if that's all right with you.'

'Stay as long as you want.'

Why couldn't he say to the boy, 'It's wonderful having you here.' Or even, 'It's a joy to see you, after all these years.' And what stopped him declaring, 'I love you!' There was a self-containment in Oliver that told Mortimer he was not needed – that Oliver did not need anyone. While this was commendable, it also saddened Mortimer for there was also an air of melancholy about Oliver as if he was disappointed in himself.

In this period of reflection Mortimer faced the fact that he had not been as good a father to his children as he had hoped. He had supplied them with the essentials and luxuries of life, but he had not imbued them with his own optimism and sense of self-worth. Mortimer was aware that he had faults, but he quite liked himself; he was not sure if his children liked themselves.

Friends he had had a-plenty – or so he had thought. He had been mistaken.

'Do you have friends, Mrs Topsham?'

'Friends, Sir Mortimer? I'm never sure what a friend is. I know people, and I am more disposed to some than others, but I doubt if they are *friends* in the manner to which you refer . . . though I like to think I have one.'

'And what do you think I mean?'

'People who would give you their last piece of bread. Who would show you loyalty and always be there in times of need.'

'Precisely, Mrs Topsham, and I don't think I have any.'

'But I'm sure you have.'

'Has anyone been to visit me? Enquired after me?'

'I wouldn't know.'

'They haven't.' He lapsed into a morose silence. He had thought himself such a popular fellow, with such a varied and wonderful social life. But where were those friends now? He had stretched his finances, large as they were, to the limit in entertaining the Prince, arranging house parties to amuse him – a difficult task when the man was so easily bored. He'd bought a steam yacht to take the man fishing in Norway. He'd had his shooting lodge in Scotland redecorated and furnished for him – he hadn't come, and Mortimer had sold the estate at a loss. He didn't like to work out how much the man had cost him. And all he had received from him was a brief note, not even a letter. 'He wasn't my friend at all.' Mortimer was unaware that he had spoken aloud.

'Some people feel they should not intrude when people are very ill,' Melanie suggested. 'Others are afraid of illness since it reminds them of their own mortality.'

'I fear you might be defending the indefensible.'

Of them all he preferred to be cared for by Melanie

Topsham. There was a calmness about her, an unobtrusiveness, which was what he needed at this time. She spoke only when spoken to, she had patience with him when he knew that he would sorely have tried a saint. Of course, it helped that she was a servant – except that she wasn't entirely. And yet, uneducated as she was, she was aware of it and dealt with the situation in a seemly way.

'We've failed you, haven't we?' he said suddenly.

'In what manner, Sir Mortimer?'

'We should have done more.'

'You've been very kind to us and we're grateful.'

'You should hate us.'

'Hatred corrodes the spirit.'

'Don't you ever think of what might have been?'

'It would be a waste of time to do so. What's done is done, and we cannot change the past.'

'You're very wise for your years.'

At this she laughed – a delightful sound, he thought. 'You flatter me, Sir Mortimer. I'm older than you remember me to be.'

'You remind me of my first wife.'

'I take that as a compliment, sir, since I've heard only good of her.'

In contrast to the present one, he thought. She'd have heard only bad of Penelope.

'They're having him put away.' Molly, the senior housemaid, rushed into the servants' hall where lunch was being laid.

'Who?' Jock, the footman, looked up from the *Sporting Life*.

'Sir Mortimer – who else? I overheard Lady C talking to her maid.' Maids and footman clustered around Molly. 'She said that once they'd got him into the nursing home they'd be going back to London – "and about time," she said.' There was an audible gasp at this information.

Jose couldn't get back to the kitchen fast enough. 'You'll never guess what's happened,' she gasped, interrupting Mrs Gilroy and Hilda.

'And what's happened to make you so rude as to interrupt a body?'

'Sir Mortimer, he's gone funny in the head. They're having him carted off.'

Mrs Gilroy had to feel behind her for her kitchen stool and plopped herself down on it and fanned herself with the oven cloth. 'What's he done? Who says?'

'Oh, the poor dear man,' said Hilda, who had sat down too.

'When?'

'Well, tonight, I suppose. No one said.'

'It's the first I've heard of it. What wickedness is afoot?' Mrs Gilroy stood up and took off her vast white apron. 'Jose, that pie needs another ten minutes, and keep an eye on the sprouts. I'll only be a minute.'

Mrs Gilroy bustled out of the kitchen, raced on her high-buttoned boots past the pantry, past the silver room, past the still room and tapped on Mr Whitaker's door. 'If you'd oblige me, Mr Whitaker, in Mrs Fuller's room?'

She continued along the corridor, aware of the stately plod of the butler close behind her.

'What a to-do!' she said, upon entering the room. 'If you've any of that sherry of yours, Mrs Fuller, I could do with a tipple.'

'You look done in, Mrs Gilroy. Sit you down.'

'I'm in such a state of shock I had to talk to someone. Thank you.' She took the glass of sherry and sipped deeply. 'It's Sir Mortimer. One of the maids overheard Lady Cresswell plotting to have him taken away tonight. He's gone weak in the head.'

'We know,' Mrs Fuller said.

'Oh!' Mrs Gilroy sat back looking deflated. 'But you didn't tell me.' She looked hurt.

'There just hasn't been time, Mrs Gilroy. We would

have told you when we all met up later,' Whitaker said. 'And it's set for tomorrow.'

'Then what do we do? Mr Oliver – he must be told straight away.'

'He's in league with his mother.'

'Oh, my Gawd! And Miss Hannah?'

'In despair. We were hoping to learn more from Lavender but she's with her now.'

'But Sir Mortimer isn't, is he – I mean, funny in the head, like?'

'Certainly he's forgetful, but aren't we all?'

'Speak for yourself, Mr Whitaker.' Mrs Fuller pouted, then giggled coquettishly.

'Where are they taking him? London?'

'Exeter. Some nursing home near Pennsylvania.'

'Not a Dr Talbot? Not the Cedars Clinic?'

'That was the name I heard mentioned.'

'But he's a charlatan.'

'Take a care, Mrs Gilroy, he's a professional man.'

'Don't any of you remember the scandal, way back in the seventies when poor Lady Alford was locked away by her husband who wanted to get his hands on her money? Wicked, he was.'

'That doctor would be too old, surely? It's thirty years ago – he must be dead by now.'

'Then it's his son.'

This appeared to placate them for they sank back into their chairs and sipped their sherry.

'But then—'

'What if—'

'You were about to say, Mrs Fuller?'

'After you, Mr Whitaker.'

'Ladies first, Mrs Fuller.'

She bowed her head graciously. 'What if he's a charlatan too?'

'How extraordinary! I was thinking along those lines myself.'

'Oh, the wickedness of it all. "*The heart is deceitful above all things, and desperately wicked.*" Jeremiah, chapter fifteen, verse ten,' intoned the cook. The other two raised their eyebrows. When Mrs Gilroy started quoting the scriptures, things were serious: it was the only time she did.

'They're taking him off.' The gust of wind from the open door made the smoke billow out into the bar.

'Who? Where, Rob?' Tubs looked up from the serious task of broaching a new barrel of beer.

'The old man. Sir Mortimer. Gone right orf his head, he has, ranting and raving something awful, he is.'

'Who told you that?'

'Our Molly came running over this evening. Said it was awful and that Miss Cresswell was taking on so that they feared for her an' all.'

'What brought this on then? I heard how he was doing so much better.'

'Tell you what, Tubs, this 'ere is like one of them up-and-down rides you get at the Barlton fair, and that's for sure,' Henry Beasley said.

'One day we're all set fair, the next we're all topsy-turvy,' Fred Robertson agreed.

'Straitjacket, you say?' Sol asked.

'Ay, frothing at the mouth he was, like a mad dog. 'Twas an awful thing to see, our Molly said.'

'Her saw him?'

At this Rob looked shifty. Then, apparently reaching a decision, he shook his leonine head. 'Aye, her did.' But there was sufficient doubt in his voice for the others to regard him dubiously.

'Bet her ladyship's behind this. Money-grabbing old witch. I've heard tales about her would make your hair stand on end,' Tubs said.

'Ask Bessie Greenacre what her thinks about her.' Sol took a gulp of his cider.

'Poor woman, what's her to do? "Here, Lady Cresswell, you stop messing about with my husband what's in your husband's employ . . ." Not a lot her can do, is there?'

'Have you seen him, Tubs? He's walking around with his tail between his legs. You'd have thought he'd look more like he'd had the cream,' Fred said.

'Perhaps it's her ladyship what's had that!' Tubs laughed, and the others joined in, slapping their thighs. It was a sign for their tankards to be recharged.

'Mind you, he's between wind and water, ain't he? How the hell can he tell her he don't fancy her? That he don't like 'em big?' Rob asked.

'I don't know. I can't see meself turning the offer down. I like a buxom wench and no mistake.' Sol rubbed his large hands together gleefully.

'Old Lady Cresswell never behaved like this, did her?'

'No, Rob, but she was a proper lady, not like this 'un.'

Everyone murmured in agreement.

'And what will Greenacre do if the old man finds out? He'll be getting his marching orders and no mistake.'

'Let's hope he do then, Tubs, 'cause the sooner he gets the push the better, if you asks me.'

'Still, he's probably safe enough, with the old man carted off to the asylum.'

'Straight up, that's the truth, and what a sadness it all is.' Sol looked gloomily into his empty tankard.

Lavender hurried silently along the upper corridor, holding the pale blue chiffon dinner dress she had just pressed. She sped past many doors, until she reached her mistress's room. 'Oh, Miss Cresswell. The things that are being said downstairs, it don't bear thinking about!'

'What sort of things?' Hannah was siting in front of her cherub-adorned looking-glass. She had not been enjoying her reflection: she looked wan and her pink-tinged eyes reminded her of a ferret's.

95

'The master. About the doctor coming and the lawyer, the taking over of his affairs. It doesn't seem right to me.'

'And from whom did you learn this?'

'One of the housemaids heard Lady Cresswell talking to her maid. She told the rest of us.'

'I see.' Anger, not an emotion with which Hannah was familiar but one to which she was becoming accustomed, began to goad her. 'Is everyone chatting about this?'

'I should think so by now.'

'It really is no one's business.'

'Yes, Miss Cresswell. But since it affected you I felt it was my duty to come and tell you.'

'Which was most kind of you, Lavender. But the staff are becoming alarmed about nothing. Lady Cresswell feels we should have a second opinion, and my brothers concur with this. There's nothing to upset yourself over.' Sometimes it was easy to lie and at others almost impossible. 'You may begin on my hair now.' She turned back to the mirror.

'But, Miss, that's not all.' Lavender picked up the silver-backed hairbrush, engraved with Hannah's crest, whose bristles she had washed that morning. She patted it on the palm of her hand to check that it was dry.

'What else?' Hannah's heart sank.

'This doctor, well, opinion is . . . that . . . well . . . that he's a charlatan.'

Slowly Hannah turned to her maid. 'That's a serious accusation to make of a doctor, Lavender – a respectable person.' The maid was blushing. 'You had better sit down. Who said this and why?'

'It was Mrs Gilroy remembered. It was a long time ago now, but I don't think you can be too careful . . .'

As soon as Lavender had finished imparting all she knew, Hannah was on her feet and rushing for the door, leaving the maid sitting with the hairbrush still in her hand. It was now Hannah's turn to rush along the corridor, her lace-trimmed peignoir flowing behind her,

her swansdown slippers not making a sound. She ran down the stairs as if her feet were not touching the treads. She pushed open a door in the main hall and entered the corridor where all the bachelor guest rooms were.

'Oliver,' she said urgently, as she tapped on the door. 'It's Hannah.'

The door opened. 'Well, this is an honour. Come in.' Hannah swept past him and into the room. 'I can only offer you whisky.' He grinned at her. 'No doubt you won't want that.'

'I've learnt something. How could you?'

'How could I what?'

'Take their side.'

'As far as I'm aware, I haven't taken anyone's side in anything. If you would excuse me, I must finish getting ready for dinner.'

It was only then that Hannah realised her brother was in his combinations with a pair of socks in his hand. 'I'm sorry,' she said, rather lamely. 'The doctor who is coming is a charlatan.'

'Is he, now? Who says?'

'It's common knowledge.'

'In what way?'

'He runs a home for people whose mental faculties are not all they should be. He has been known to agree to incarcerate people who are not impaired – for a consideration . . .' And she went on to explain the awful experiences of a certain Lady Alford.

'In the seventies, you say? Is it the same doctor?'

'I don't know.'

'I'm riding over to Barlton in the morning – there's an auction I want to attend.'

Hannah looked up at him. 'You've found a house?'

'Just curiosity,' he lied. 'Then I'll see what I can find out.'

'So you won't be here when *they* come.'

'I shall be back shortly after luncheon. Didn't Mother say they were coming in the afternoon?'

'What if you find out that all I tell you is true? What difference will it make? You're all in league together.'

'Hannah, what on earth do you mean?'

'This morning, at breakfast, you were agreeing with your mother. I couldn't believe my ears when I heard you.' Tears pricked her eyes and she closed them. How many more were there to shed?

'Hannah, listen to me, you silly goose.' She opened her eyes to see Oliver kneeling in front of her. 'I thought you would understand what I was doing. I didn't for one minute think you'd take me literally.' He took hold of her hand. 'I agree that Father is different, and a bit vague. But the rest? They incarcerate him over my dead body.'

'Really? You mean that? But why—'

'If I'm estranged from my mother – and I'm half-way there already – how are we to know what is happening? I'm lulling her into a false sense of security. With Mortie not here she has only me to turn to.'

'But he's coming. Tomorrow, on the morning train.'

'Is he now? So I'll meet him at the railway station. What could be better? Now, sister dear, you, too, must dress for dinner. Shoo!' As she passed him in the doorway he bent and kissed her cheek.

By the end of each day Mortimer was ready for bed. He'd never been one for taking his ease but now he regarded his canopied bed as a safe, comfortable refuge.

Melanie was hanging up his silk dressing-gown because James had gone to the kitchens to get him some milk.

'Damn, I forgot to tell James to thank Mrs Gilroy for my soufflé. It was perfect.'

'She makes a good one.' She was putting his velvet slippers by his bed ready for the morning.

'Have you been happy here?'

'Very much so, sir.' Melanie had indeed enjoyed it: after the sheer luxury of life here – even for a servant – the return to her cottage was a dismal prospect. As was the horror of life with her husband.

'You don't miss your family?'

'I manage to see my younger son most days.'

'And your husband?'

'He's managing well.'

'Is he able to cook?'

'No.' She laughed at the idea. 'One of the neighbours cooks and washes for him.'

'And the cleaning?'

'Another goes in and tidies the cottage for him.' What a kind man he was. No other employer would take such an interest. And it *had* all gone well. Flossie Marshall's baby had arrived but, like all her children, it was a fat, contented creature so Flossie, helped by her mother, had been able to do all she had promised she would. Bernard had not been unpleasant to her once, though, no doubt, her leaving money on the table every time she went there had something to do with it. She wondered if Bernard wasn't happier without her. Several times when Melanie had visited the house to check that all was well, she and Bernard had gone to bed. She did not enjoy these couplings, she never had, but if they kept him amenable it was a small price to pay. She had no desire for the arrangement to end: she wanted it to go on for ever.

'What would we have done without you, Mrs Topsham?'

'I'm sure you would have managed perfectly well. Miss Cresswell is a good daughter.'

'She's not good, Mrs Topsham, she's the best!'

'That's nice. Now, is there anything more I can do for you?'

'No, you run along – you must be tired.'

Melanie let herself out of the room, crossed the anteroom and opened the door of a much smaller room in which a single bed stood. This was where she slept in case she was needed. She could be summoned by a bell Sir Mortimer always kept to hand.

What an upsetting day it had been, especially for poor Hannah. Melanie's heart had gone out to her. And then all that gossip in the servants' hall. Was it true? Even if only half of it was, it was still an unpleasant tale. And her role in it? It wasn't just that if he was sent away she would lose her comfortable position here, it was the sheer injustice. Sir Mortimer was one of the sanest men she knew.

She heard the valet calling goodnight to him, heard the door to Sir Mortimer's bedroom shut. She stood up abruptly.

Sir Mortimer was sitting up in bed, his pince-nez on his nose, reading.

'Who's there?' He peered into the darkness.

'It's Melanie, Sir Mortimer. I wondered if I might have a word?'

Mortimer could not sleep. He tossed and rolled about the bed. He drank water and longed for whisky. He turned his pillow to the cooler side. He kicked the covers off because he was too hot. Then he was too cold and had to pull them back on. As usual, Cariad was on the bed until, disturbed by the constant upheaval, she slithered off and padded to her basket in the corner.

Earlier he had not been able to sleep for anger, and now there was fear – of the evil being planned against him, that he might not have the energy to fight them. This was how the elderly felt, he realised, when confusion set in. But he was not confused, he was fully aware – or was he? He had always prided himself on his logical mind, but tonight analytical thought appeared beyond him.

He sat up, and drank another glass of water. In the darkness he fumbled for the matches – and dropped them. 'Damn!' He hauled himself out of bed and felt with his bare toes for them.

Cariad raised her head, her nose in the air as if smelling out the cause of the outburst and then, deciding she need not be bothered, put her head back down and curled deeper into the covers. 'Damn!' Mortimer had dropped the matches again. 'How ridiculous of me,' he said aloud. He had had electricity installed downstairs but hadn't bothered with it in the upstairs rooms. He had always prided himself on being a modern-thinking man, yet here he was fumbling about in the dark, just as his ancestors had done. He heard the familiar hissing of the lamp as it ignited, and the light glowed warmly, an oasis in the large dark room.

He sat upright. He felt calmer now it was light. He'd set in motion the extension of the electric wiring first thing in the morning.

And that simple decision, he realised, had begun a logical train of thought. He had been panicking – something he wasn't used to. 'Not at all like me,' he said firmly. Cariad raised her head and wagged her tail.

'Cariad,' he called, and the small dog ran across the room, made two attempts to jump on to the high bed. He helped her up. 'Disturbed your beauty sleep, did I?' He stroked the dog's coat.

Melanie's information had shaken him. He shouldn't have been surprised by Penelope, but he had never thought she would go to these lengths. Incarceration. He shivered. What a nightmarish thought! Was Melanie right? Was the whole family, even Oliver, against him – except Hannah? Dear child.

Amid the clutter of books and papers on his bedside table he found the hand bell. He rang it. When no one came he had to ring it a second time. A flustered-looking Melanie appeared in the doorway. 'Sir? Are you ill?'

'A thousand apologies for waking you, Mrs Topsham,

but I need a few things. Some paper, a pencil and a very large whisky and soda.'

'Yes, sir. But . . . should you? The whisky, I mean.'

'I most certainly should, Mrs Topsham. I should probably have had several long before now. And if you could please wake my daughter.'

'Miss Cresswell?'

'I only have one daughter,' he smiled, 'as far as I know.'

'I'm sorry, sir.'

He waited impatiently, fidgeting about the bed so that he lost Cariad again. When he called her to come back she ignored him.

'Papa, what is it?' Hannah was tying the ribbon of her peignoir as she entered the room.

'I need to talk to you. And couldn't wait until the morning. Ha! Thank you.' He took the glass from the tray Melanie proffered.

'Papa, should you?'

'Why am I surrounded by nagging women?' He grinned at them both. 'I most definitely need this.' He took a satisfying swig of the drink. The two women watched him anxiously, as if they expected him to keel over immediately. 'Ha! That's much better.' He patted the bed so that Hannah sat down. 'Mrs Topsham has been telling me of gossip she had heard below stairs.'

'Was that wise?' Hannah looked sternly at Melanie.

'I felt it my duty, Miss Cresswell.' Melanie was in her nightdress, a shawl flung over her shoulders.

'You know what we speak of, Hannah?'

'I can guess, Papa. One can have no secrets in this house.'

'You are aware of what they're saying?'

'I am.'

'Who told you?'

Hannah looked intensely worried. 'Mother.' Her voice was barely audible.

'Would you have told me?'

'Papa, I don't know. I couldn't sleep for worrying about what I should do – what would be best for you.'

'Had you reached a decision?'

'I had. I was going to talk to you but I have been pre-empted.' She looked crossly at Melanie.

'You must not be angry with Mrs Topsham. She did what she thought was right.'

'She should have come to me.'

'I felt that there was only one person I could turn to and that was Sir Mortimer.'

'And very pleased I am that you did. What I need to know – since, as Mrs Topsham was the first to admit, what she had to tell me might have been mere tittle-tattle – is, who is involved in the plot to have me committed to a lunatic asylum?'

'Oh, Papa, it's not as bad as that. Mother thought you would be better off at a private nursing home. Papa, it's not an asylum.'

'You think so, Hannah? I don't. I'm sure it's been given an innocuous name so as not to alert people like me. Who is making these decisions for me?'

'Mother and Mortimer.'

'Not Oliver?'

'No, Papa. He's pretending to agree so that he can learn more of their intentions.'

'Ah!' Mortimer sank back on his pillows with a satisfied smile. 'That pleases me. It would have been difficult for you to stand up to them on your own, my dear. Mrs Topsham, would you be so kind as to go and awaken my son?'

As Melanie left the room Hannah took her customary seat beside her father and grasped his hand. 'I've been so upset, Papa. It's a relief that you know. But I feel dreadful – for in the very hour that Mother announced what she had done, I had already said to Oliver that I was worried about you and felt you had changed.' She coloured with embarrassment.

'I know I have. But I've had much to think about. And I'm tired, Hannah, I can't tell you how weary I feel. But . . .' he sat up straight '. . . I'm getting stronger. Now, tell me all you know . . .'

Five minutes later Oliver appeared in a padded silk, Paisley-patterned, dressing-gown. 'My son.' Mortimer held out a hand to him. 'A fine pickle I'm facing.'

'Father, don't be fearful. They can do nothing, I'm sure.'

'But what *could* they do to have me committed? That's what we need to know.'

'It's not a word I'm happy to use, Father.'

'It's just a word, dear son. I need to ask a favour of you.'

'Anything, Father.'

'First thing, I want you to ride to Barlton, fetch young Mr Battle.'

'I'm to pick up Mortie from the Exeter train with Dr Talbot.'

'Then ask Battle to ride here, post-haste, I need to see him before the others arrive. And, Hannah, as early as it is reasonable, would you please fetch the doctor from the village? And have James woken.'

'At this time in the morning? Papa, it wouldn't be fair.'

'I need him to organise my clothes.'

'Papa, there is plenty of time.'

'Now, Hannah. Kindly do not argue with me. It's important to me that none of you treat me as an invalid. Before you leave, Oliver, go to the office and bring me the ledgers. I need paper and pen. Then tell Greenacre to find a man who knows about the electric lighting.'

From having been silent and morose Mortimer was issuing orders willy-nilly. Hannah and Oliver looked at each other with amazement.

When he was finally alone again he still could not

sleep. But, oddly, he no longer felt tired. In fact, he was elated and full of energy.

'Husband it,' he said to himself.

Chapter Four
February 1901

At Henry Battle's villa, in the tree-lined avenue in Barlton, the door was opened a mere fraction. The maid was still in her nightclothes, holding a candle aloft. From her expression she was astonished to find a guest standing on the step at ten to six in the morning. He did not blame her.

'I'm not sure I can waken the master.' She answered his request belligerently, pulling her rather grubby robe tightly around her.

'And I'm certain you can. Now, run along and do as I ask. Tell Mr Battle that Mr Oliver Cresswell awaits him on a matter of some urgency.'

The maid thumped up the staircase, muttering audibly. Left alone in the hallway, Oliver looked about him. A shaft of light was coming from one doorway. He entered what was obviously the drawing room, where the gas mantles were lit. From the debris left on the floor a maid had been cleaning the grate. There was, as yet, no fire lit, but the house was warm. He touched the cast-iron radiator situated under a window; it was piping hot, unlike the tepid ones at Cresswell Manor.

The room was a good size, it was well furnished, and yet it did not feel overcrowded. From the outside the house had appeared intolerably small, but this room belied his first impression. Perhaps he should look for a pleasant modern house like this one – it would be less expensive to buy, let alone maintain, and it would be more convenient . . . He could even have one built to his own specifications.

He did not regard himself as pretentious but when he had thought of buying himself a home he had automatically decided on a mansion with land. When he had been on his travels, that had been his dream. It was what he had aspired to, worked and bargained for – even cheated for – in amassing his fortune. There was, of course, another reason: he wanted to prove he was as good as his brother – no, better than he was. The estate he was after now was larger than Cresswell. How foolish of him to saddle himself with such enormous responsibilities just to cock a snook at his brother.

'Mr Cresswell, what's amiss?' Henry Battle hurried into the room tying the belt of his dressing-gown, his face creased with anxiety. 'Is it your father? I sincerely hope he isn't . . .'

'Dead? Thankfully, no. He's much better, though not fully recovered. He has had double pneumonia,' Oliver said. 'I trust you'll forgive me for stealing in here but I was intrigued by your lovely house.'

'Thank you, Mr Cresswell, but compared with yours this is a poor shadow.'

'I'm not so sure. The simple life has many attractions.'

Henry Battle looked put out, and Oliver realised what a crass statement he had made. 'That must have sounded rude . . . I didn't mean – please accept—'

'No apology needed.' Henry held up his hand. 'I will regard your words as a compliment. So, Mr Cresswell, some refreshment?'

He pulled the bell and the maid reappeared, in uniform this time. He ordered tea and some cold meat, although Oliver insisted he wanted nothing: 'I shall be taking breakfast at the new hotel I've heard so much about.'

'The Victoria? Excellent food. It's already well patronised. A client of mine is the owner, and I'm sure she would like to hear your opinion of her establishment. However . . .'

'You must be wondering why I'm here at such an hour.

My father felt it imperative I see you as soon as possible and request you journey to Cresswell immediately.'

'But I'm going there this afternoon. Your mother summoned me.'

'And my father wishes you to go this morning.' He smiled, trusting that the man had sufficient wit to grasp the distinction between the two requests.

'Ha! I see.'

'I don't know if you have any indication as to what is going on?'

'I had heard your father was seriously ill, and I presumed it was something to do with his affairs,' he said, with commendable discretion.

'It most certainly is. And I'm sure you would be interested to know that we expect another visitor this afternoon – a Dr Talbot from Exeter.'

'Really? Of course, a doctor of the highest echelon. I shall change and drive out immediately.'

'I am obliged, Mr Battle.'

'It is my undoubted pleasure, Mr Cresswell.'

As Oliver left he met the maid with a tray of food and bowed in apology. His carriage was waiting for him in the bleak street, the driver huddled under a weatherproof, the horse bedraggled.

'The Victoria in Gold Street, Harold.'

The carriage clattered away. He would normally have chosen to travel in his father's new motor vehicle but he had chosen the carriage since he had thought that the noise of the combustion engine would wake his family at Cresswell Manor. Worse, it might have alerted his mother to what he was about.

The Victoria was everything people had said it was. The rambling old Prestwick mansion had been converted into a public hotel in so masterly a way that the guests felt they were being entertained in a nobleman's house. Clever, he thought, and wondered what potential there was for such in other cities.

It was just past seven when he took his place in the dining room and already the room was filling. There was a flurry of activity at the door and a man entered. He surveyed the room as if to ascertain that it was a suitable venue for him to grace – or perhaps he was ensuring that his presence had been noticed by everyone there. Oliver enjoyed observing people and guessing who and what they were. He recognised this man immediately. From his beautifully cut clothes and thick gold watch chain he was a successful man – and self-made: his outfit was a fraction too smart, too tailored, the cravat a shade too colourful. His expression showed him to be content with himself, and afraid of no one; he spent his money lavishly but wisely and expected immediate respect. From the fuss made of him, and the fawning by the head waiter, Oliver congratulated himself on being right. He hoped the man wasn't in town for the auction.

Oliver's breakfast was placed in front of him and he concentrated on the food and a copy of the *Barlton Gazette*, advertising the auction. He was soon deeply engrossed in an article on the history of the house and its contents.

'No! I shan't! It's so beastly early!' A young woman was standing by the man's table. She spoke in a melodious voice with a slight lisp, then laughed as she took her seat. She wore a large feathered hat so it was impossible to see the colour of her hair, but judging by her large brown eyes, the arched dark eyebrows, she must be a brunette. Oliver preferred fair women, preferably with grey eyes. He'd never known why. But despite this he acknowledged she was beautiful, and he was not alone – many in the now crowded dining room were watching her with interest.

Despite her youth she was poised and sure of herself. The man was watching her with adoration in his eyes – poor fool, thought Oliver. How could he believe that such a creature was with him for any reason other than his money? He must be twice her age. But from the rope of pearls on her delectable bosom, and the diamond brooch she wore, he had paid her well. She could not be a lady, he noted, since she was wearing diamonds before luncheon.

Women! He missed them. It had not troubled him when he was at home, but now that he was watching this fine specimen, a longing stirred in him that he could have done without.

Hannah rode her bicycle across the park towards the doctor's house on the edge of the village. She could have asked one of the grooms to deliver the message but she had decided that discretion was necessary. She could have saddled a horse – before her father's illness it had been a rare day that she didn't ride – but she enjoyed pedalling along . . . and she knew it annoyed her stepmother. Both Penelope and Coral thought it unladylike and that the tweed bloomers she had purchased were coarse and unseemly. Hannah wished she could wear trousers all the time.

Also the ride gave her time to think: a bicycle warranted less concentration than a horse. At around six that morning, after a mostly sleepless night, she had reached a conclusion. She now felt she had been caught up in the reaction of Lavender and Melanie, and too much affected by the gossip that swirled about the house. She could understand Oliver and her father's concern about the lawyer and the doctor coming, but was that because their male pride had been hurt? Were they offended that Penelope, a woman, should take into her hands affairs they thought the exclusive domain of men? She could not believe that even Penelope would be so wicked as to scheme to have her husband removed. Was it not more likely that she was showing wifely concern? Since she did not like her stepmother she felt she should give the woman the benefit of the doubt. And if, as she had initially thought – or, rather, had been led to think – there was a conspiracy, it would mean Mortie was involved and she refused to believe that. Mortie was far too good-natured and lazy to be involved in a plot. She had to pedal harder as she climbed the slight rise by Cobbler's Spinney. In any case, what would be the point?

Their father had been distant with them, but what father wasn't? Spending time with and showing interest in children was for women. And although her father had rarely been at Cresswell Manor, his presence always was. He was unfailingly generous to all his children and grandchildren. She herself had a plentiful allowance, and from the way he and Coral lived so did Mortie. She was sure, too, from the quality of Penelope's clothes and jewellery, that her stepmother never went without.

Her father's many long absences had been sad for Hannah, but the estate ticked over without him. Well, perhaps there were parts that needed attention – Dunwell Wood had been looking untidy, but if the trees weren't being felled Hannah was sure her father had had good reason to leave them. And then she had heard the familiar sound of axes and known that work was being done. There, she thought.

She arrived at Ferndean only slightly out of breath. The large villa was owned by her father and rented by the doctor – she hoped he was in and not visiting the sick.

'Miss Cresswell.' The maid who opened the door bobbed in greeting. She looked vaguely familiar and Hannah wondered if she had once worked at the manor.

'If I might see the doctor . . .' Yes, she was sure now she should know the girl – if not her name. It had been so much easier in her grandmother's day when all the maids were called Jane.

'Miss Cresswell, this is a pleasure, so early.'

'I felt like some fresh air and it's a pleasant morning, if cold. Cycling can be so exhilarating. But, Doctor, if I might have a word?' She glanced at the maid who still hovered, evidently awaiting orders.

He showed her into his sitting room, where she sat on an overstuffed armchair and marvelled that such a small room could hold so many objects. It was fortunate that crinolines and large bustles were no longer fashionable or it would have been impossible to move across it.

'I gather you recommended a Dr Talbot to Lady Cresswell for my father,' Hannah said, without preamble, for she knew how dedicated and busy the doctor was.

'Not I, Miss Cresswell.' He was frowning. 'Are you sure?'

'I must have misunderstood.' All her previous reasoning was slipping away.

'Certainly, about a week ago Lady Cresswell enquired about doctors for nervous disorders and I told her that Dr Talbot had a good reputation in these parts.' Hannah reeled. 'But I had no idea she intended Sir Mortimer to see him. I had the impression it was for a female friend of hers – ladies' nerves being so much more fragile.' He smiled but Hannah did not respond as her worries came screeching into her head pushing logic roughly to one side. 'Why would your father need to consult someone like Dr Talbot?'

'My stepmother is concerned about him.' Her voice emerged as a squeak.

'That is natural. Any wife would be. But he is recovering well, far better than I had anticipated.'

'I had got it into my head that you would be seeing him this afternoon.'

'I shall, of course, be attending your father, as I do every day, but no specific time has been arranged.'

'I see.' Her heart sank further. 'Father would be most grateful if you would pay him a visit. He is somewhat agitated by . . .' She trailed off. The nightmare was back. 'Before luncheon,' she added. 'That is imperative.'

'I shall be there.'

'Thank you, Doctor.' She was on her feet.

'Take care on that dangerous velocipede of yours.'

'It's safer than a horse, Doctor.'

As she pedalled back towards the manor she was filled once again with worry and puzzlement. The doctor had said little, but she was sure he had been covering shock at her news. She felt sick now with apprehension and her nerves were as taut as violin strings.

Thank heavens Oliver was still here. How wrong she had been to doubt him. He was obviously far wiser than she had given him credit for. He was the last person to be swayed by gossip, and would not panic in an emergency. She had heard him leave long before dawn for Barlton, which she had thought unnecessary. But it hadn't been.

It was at times like this that she longed for her own mother to advise her . . . 'Thinking that way won't help!' she said aloud, her breath swirling in white vapour on the freezing air.

She wondered how Oliver would get on this morning. He hadn't said anything but she was sure he was attending the sale of the house and estate she had told him about. And she knew from the *Barlton Gazette* that the auction was today. She hoped so: it was a fine house and so close. Yet it was mysterious that he hadn't discussed it with her or taken her to see it. Perhaps he liked to make his own decisions with no influence from anyone else, but that was unfair of him if he wanted her to live there with him. Surely she could expect to have some say?

She was always thinking of herself. That made her pedal faster. Maybe he had given up the idea, regretted that he had mentioned it to her and was too embarrassed to tell her.

How well did she know Oliver? They had been apart for so long and both of them had changed. There was a hardness about him now that she was sure hadn't been there in the past. An air of loneliness too. He needed a wife, and she prayed that if he found one she'd be pleasanter than Coral.

She waved at Rob Robinson as she sped past the sawmill, and wondered if Coral would be arriving too. She should discuss with Mrs Fuller the arrangements if everyone who was coming wished to stay the night. If they did, she should invite others to dinner. Was it too late? Would they be insulted? No, she could explain. She would ask the doctor and his wife. Simeon too, perhaps.

As always, she found that it was best for her to keep her mind busy: if she was making arrangements, her worries disappeared.

The house loomed into view, and she thought how little help to anyone she was at the moment, least of all to her father. As she went through the arch to the stableyard she resolved to stop being so weak and useless. She must make herself a true support.

She had decided something else during the long night. If her stepmother was going to be spending more time at the manor then Hannah had to control her fear of the woman. Penelope had never harmed her, just been distant. And what could she do to Hannah in the future to hurt or damage her? Nothing.

She tooted her bicycle's horn as she rode into the stableyard, and Ferdie came out to meet her as she put her feet on the ground. She dismounted and he took charge of her machine.

The banqueting room of the King William Hotel was crammed. Oliver made his way to the front where he had booked himself a seat. He looked about him at the throng and wondered who would bid against him.

He had told no one what he was about. He wasn't sure why. Perhaps because he didn't want Hannah to be disappointed if he failed. And if no one knew he had bid for it, no one need know if he did fail. Every time Oliver thought he had conquered his pride something happened and it wormed its way back into him.

He thought he detected four other potential bidders and that the rest were rubbernecks – a handy expression he'd learnt in America. He had tried to find out from the auctioneers what the competition was but they had been evasive. When he had tried to buy the estate privately they had refused his offer, saying the vendor wished to go to auction. It had been a frustrating few weeks.

He shouldn't have set his heart on it, he knew that only too well. If you wanted something too badly two things were likely to happen: the price always miraculously increased, or you didn't get whatever it was anyway. A bit like women. He smiled to himself.

There was a rustle of silk, a breath of expensive perfume – Worth, he thought. Someone whispered, 'Excuse me?' in a low, musical voice, and accompanied the words with a sweet, apologetic smile and a fluttering of long eyelashes. The lovely woman from the hotel breakfast room insinuated her way past him, her boa brushing him. She was a professional coquette if ever he'd seen one. She took a seat on the opposite side of the aisle, closely followed by her companion. He was swathed in a sable coat that brushed the floor, the top of his cane was gold, and he, too, smelt of expensive cologne, sandalwood; his hair glinted with pomade. His olive complexion was pockmarked and his cheek bore a scar – from duelling? A *parvenu*, Oliver thought, but what a handsome figure he cut, with an air of mystery which would be irresistible to many women.

The auctioneer climbed on to the rostrum, a short, rotund man with an expression of deep satisfaction with himself. There was a loud shuffling as people took their seats, and those already seated sat up straight. Others carried on talking. The auctioneer brought down his gavel with an almighty bang, obviously a man who expected to be obeyed. The muttering ceased, but there was further rustling as people settled themselves into more comfortable positions, not easy when they were crammed together so closely. There was much coughing and clearing of throats.

'Ladies and gentlemen.' Another bang of the gavel. 'It's my pleasure and honour to offer to you, on the instructions of the Honourable Edward Prestwick . . .' The auctioneer made a dramatic gesture with his hand and everyone turned. A young man, looking deeply embarrassed, was on his feet at the back of the hall and acknowledged them. He looked too young to own such a property, and Oliver wondered why he had decided to sell it.

He looked remarkably cheerful about it, not in the least sorrowful as Oliver would have been.

'I shall open with the bidding for lot one, the house, pleasure gardens and parkland of Courtney Lacey, amounting to five hundred acres. Are we ready gentlemen?'

The bidding was fierce and fast. The auctioneer, more used to the speed of a cattle market, was difficult to understand: he spoke quickly in a thick Devon accent. Soon there were just two bidders left – Oliver and the scar-faced stranger. Oliver's pulse rate increased. Each time Oliver bid, the stranger smiled, paused until Oliver was sure that victory was his. Then as the auctioneer raised his gavel, as one and all in the room held their breath, with an almost lazy gesture the man raised his hand and upped the bid. A sneezing fit held up the proceedings for a precious minute in which Oliver recovered himself: he was aware that he was offering too much, that he had long passed his top limit and they still hadn't bid for the farmland, village and cottages. The auctioneer looked at him, and he shook his head. 'Going, going, gone!' The saver banged on the podium. 'To Mr von Ehrlich!'

Oliver felt sick with disappointment, but acknowledged his adversary's good fortune with a gracious wave. He stood up, and made his way to the back of the hall, stepped into the public bar and ordered himself a large whisky. For the best, he told himself, as he downed it in one and ordered another. It wasn't meant to be.

'Who got it?' a man at the bar asked another.

'Some foreigner – van Earlick or some such outlandish name. He's been here about a week, snooping around. Nice enough fellow – a bit on the swanky side and too rich for his own good. He must have lost his senses – all that money for a house, it don't make no sense, does it? No land as yet, and what's he going to have to pay for that?'

'Not much. The auctioneer should have left the house till last.'

'Madness! But it was the foreigner's bad luck that another idiot was there this morning.'

Oliver hid behind his copy of the *Barlton Gazette*, embarrassed by his narrow escape.

Mrs Gilroy was singing. This was such a rare occurrence that the maids were soon suppressing giggles and rushing off to tell others. Eventually everyone serving in the house had heard the rather fine contralto voice.

'That's one of my favourite hymns, Mrs Gilroy, and beautifully sung, if you don't mind my saying so?' They never used each other's Christian names when their juniors were present.

'Thank you, Mrs Fuller. You can't beat a good hymn.' She took a deep breath and 'The Church's One Foundation' ascended to the raftered ceiling.

Mrs Fuller went back towards her sitting room, passing the butler on the way. 'That makes a pleasant change.' Whitaker nodded towards the soaring sound. 'She's a lovely voice, don't you think, Mrs Fuller?'

'Very nice,' the housekeeper answered, a tad wasp-ishly, not liking his appreciation of her rival.

'And to what do we owe the pleasure?'

'She gets bored, Mr Whitaker. There hasn't been enough to do in the last few weeks.'

'Aren't the staff and family enough for her?'

'Well, we have such plain menus, don't we?'

'I'd hardly say that was so, Mrs Fuller.'

'It depends, I suppose, on what you're used to.' As soon as she had said this, Mrs Fuller wished she could take back the words. 'I am, of course, only repeating what Mrs Gilroy herself says, that it doesn't allow her to use her skills.'

'But she has the family to cook for.'

'But with Sir Mortimer ill, Miss Hannah not fancying much, Mr Mortie and his family away, and Lady C shut in her room, she finds it upsetting. But this evening they're entertaining and she's a large dinner to prepare so she's as happy as a lark.'

'I have to say, Mrs Fuller, that I never thought, from my time here, to see such people entertained for dinner – a lawyer and a doctor! Lunch is more suitable for such as they, or maybe a light fork supper. But dinner!' Whitaker's face wore a dolorous expression.

'Times are changing, Mr Whitaker. We should change with them.'

'You might, Mrs Fuller, but I prefer the old ways. Do you realise they'll be using the front door?' He blanched.

James and Lavender were sitting opposite each other at the large table in the centre of the servants' hall. Lavender was pleating the dark red moquette cover that was spread over it after meals. 'It will be strange without you here, James.' She looked downcast. 'Does it depend on what happens to Sir Mortimer?'

'It's not just that. I'm ready for a change.'

'But where would you go?'

'I'd be given good references, and I've made good contacts working for Sir M. I could go anywhere. Haven't you noticed there's more jobs than people to fill them, these days? Anyway, I don't want to be a servant for the rest of my life.'

'What else would you do? This is all we know.'

'There are the hotels now.'

'Lady Cresswell says you should only stay in one abroad.'

'But she's wrong. Hotels are becoming respectable. And there's America.'

'America!' she repeated, in a hushed tone.

'I was talking to Mr Oliver about it the other day. You can do anything you want there, he said. The sky's the limit, provided you're not a shirker. He said there was a shortage of good valets, and employers with money to burn. I could earn double what I do here.'

'You mentioned it to *Mr Oliver*? Are you mad?'

'No! Keep your wig on. I said I was enquiring about America for a friend of mine who was thinking about emigrating.'

'And you think he believed that? He's not stupid. He'd have known it was you.'

'But what if he did? We have to look to our own future. If the old man dies, what'll become of us then?'

'I'm sure Mr Oliver would take you on. He's got no man of his own yet.'

'But I've just told you I might not stay a servant. I don't want to end up like old Whitaker. There's got to be more to life than emptying an old man's slops.'

'I don't know what's got into you, James Thistle! Time was when you were content. I am. You can't be happy if you don't accept your lot in life.'

'And what's your future to be, then?'

'I'll stay with Miss Hannah. If her father was taken away, or if he died, she'd need me.'

'But what if she was left with no money? What if she

had to move out of here? She doesn't get on with her sister-in-law.'

'That's true.'

'So where would she go? What sort of establishment would she have? Perhaps she couldn't afford someone as skilled as you and make do with a young village girl.'

Lavender felt faint. She moved uncomfortably on the hard Windsor chair. 'It won't happen,' she said, with a confidence she was far from feeling.

'Let me tell you, I've heard odd things.' He beckoned to her to lean across the table. 'The old man isn't as rich as everyone thinks, you know.'

'Isn't he?'

'No. There was the Newmarket fiasco, and then he invested heavily in gold prospecting in America, only he wasn't one of the lucky ones. And there was a pile of bad investments.'

'What was the Newmarket fiasco?'

'Fellow sold the master a string of horses on the recommendation of the Prince – as he was then. Fit for the knacker's yard, they were. Funny business, racing. You need to know what you're about.'

'But Sir Mortimer knows a lot about horses.'

'Racehorses are different. It's not like buying a hunter or a coach-horse. Least, that's what I learnt – only he didn't.'

'But if the King suggested it?'

'Exactly! He couldn't ignore advice from His Royal Nibs. Duped, he was. And you know what I think? The old P of W saw his other mate heading for Queer Street and thought, who, of my rich friends, can help him out? Poor old Sir Mortimer happened along at the wrong time. And the bankrupt was more important to the Prince than our Sir M. He considered him rich enough that it didn't matter if he lost some, but if his other friend lost everything he'd be banned from Society.'

'That all sounds a bit far-fetched.'

'You don't move in those circles. It's cat-and-dog all the time, everyone fighting to be in with the Prince. It'll be worse now he's King.'

'Poor Sir Mortimer.'

'He shouldn't try to curry favour.'

'That's not a very nice thing to say, James.'

'But it's the truth. Upshot is, I reckon he was using the money he would have left Miss Hannah.'

Lavender sat back in her chair with a look of horror. 'Oh, the poor sweet lady. Still, she's got money from her mother's estate.'

'Enough for the sort of house she's used to? I don't think so.'

'But there's all this.' She waved her arm, not to indicate the servants' hall but all that lay outside.

'Not much use if he's up to his ears in debt.'

'I can't believe it!'

'You'd better. And now you see why we have to think of ourselves.'

Oliver enjoyed stations, and the crowded platform at Barlton was no exception. He liked the noise, the shouting, the hurly-burly of passengers about to depart. He relished the jostling for position to see the trains' arrival. The atmosphere was full of excitement, expectation – and the sadness of those steeling themselves to say goodbye.

On the platform Oliver always felt as if he had stepped into another world, that he had become isolated from his normal life and problems. Today, to his surprise, he felt an overwhelming urge to get on the next train, no matter where it went. He'd be free again, as he had been for years. In returning he had become involved with the lives of others – the last thing he wanted. Isolation suited him better. He didn't want to be entangled in the dramas of his family. It would be so easy to escape. He looked towards the booking hall. He took a step in that direction . . .

But it had been good to be back. For three weeks he had felt a well-being that had been absent for some time. There had been moments when he'd felt that he belonged.

It would not be fair to leave Hannah and his father to deal with the rest of the family. His father, while recovering his spirit, was still weak physically, and Hannah had been through so much in the past weeks: if he left she might go to pieces. He had to acknowledge that a few weeks ago he would only have considered himself.

There was something else. He fidgeted with his collar, uncomfortable with his thoughts. Laura Redman: married or not, he had to see her again.

The station staff were galvanised into action. Porters began pushing their trolleys through the crowds, bells were ringing. Oliver heard the clunk of the signal at the end of the platform, saw the red light glowing. The arrival of the station-master, resplendent in his top hat; moving pompously about his domain, bowing at some, looking disdainfully at others, was the final indication that the arrival of the train from Exeter was imminent.

Oliver looked up the track and saw the great iron engine approaching, whistling shrilly, steam billowing on either side as if it carried clouds, which had fallen from the sky. People pressed forward as if oblivious to the danger of standing too close. Oliver took a step back: ever since he'd seen a man fall under a train in Chicago, he'd always avoided the rush of the engine along the platform.

He waited – not for him the dash up and down the platform as others did, looking for their friends and loved ones. He'd see them soon enough. He hoped vehemently that they had missed the train.

The crowds opened up and, for a second, a woman stood out from the throng. Oliver smiled. It was almost as if he had antennae to tell him that an attractive woman was in the vicinity. This one was tall, unfashionably slim, and dressed in the height of fashion. Porters, smelling the scent of money, were soon clustered about her, to the annoyance of other passengers. She pointed imperiously with her umbrella at an ever-growing pile of cases being unloaded from the train. Oliver was taken by the darkness of her hair, the luminosity of her skin, the black eyes that, even at this distance, he could see were large and luminous. She was not beautiful in the accepted sense, but striking. Nor was she young, in her early forties, he assessed, but still lovely. It was then that she saw him, and Oliver experienced the discomfort of having an attractive woman regard him with no interest. Then the crowds closed again and she had vanished.

'Oliver! Good of you to come and meet us.' Mortie was bearing down on him, a cigar in his mouth, swathed in a large overcoat with an astrakhan collar. His top hat was set at a rakish angle. Oliver despised his brother, but how he loved him.

They shook hands in greeting. 'This, Oliver, is Talbot.'

A much smaller man, with faded brown hair touched with grey, and a pleasant expression stepped forward. 'My pleasure, Mr Cresswell.' His handshake was firm. This meant nothing to Oliver, who had learnt that often the firmest handshakes were those of con-men.

'I thought luncheon in the new hotel – the Victoria, I'm most impressed with it,' Oliver said.

'I told the doctor we should be getting over to Cresswell straight away.'

'I trust you're not in a rush, Doctor. I came by carriage but I arranged for the motor vehicle to come for us at two.'

'Can't be helped, then.' Mortie shrugged. 'And I could eat a horse.'

'It will give us a chance to talk, Mr Cresswell, in comfort.'

'Precisely, Dr Talbot.' Oliver led the way out of the station and to the hackney carriage he had arranged. If Talbot was a charlatan he was a pleasant one.

A little later, they were settled at a table in the hotel dining room. Faced with a long, complex menu, Mortie took an inordinate amount of time to decide on mulliga-tawny soup, turbot, and game pie, only to call the waiter back and change the turbot to sole, and the pie to boiled mutton with caper sauce.

'Have you decided for sure, Mortie?'

'I think so, except that the roast looks appealing.' His greedy little eyes had alighted on the meat trolley as the waiter, with a flourish, took off the dome to reveal a huge sirloin.

'You can't have everything, Mortie, old chap. And *we* shall die of starvation if you don't make up your mind soon.'

'The doctor is well on the way to doing so – soup and fish? It wouldn't keep a woman alive!'

'I prefer not to eat meat. And I am unaccustomed to the large luncheons that seem to be in vogue. I think better on a light diet.'

'I *never* think, so it's all right if I eat.' Mortie chuckled.

'Wine. Do you wish to choose, Mortie?' Oliver asked.

'My pleasure.'

At least it would keep him occupied and less likely to change his mind over his food again, thought Oliver. 'Your expertise is in disorders of the human mind, I gather,' he said to the doctor.

'It is, sir. Though, of course, I am qualified in all aspects of medicine.'

'I had presumed so. And how does one learn about the mind?'

'I studied in Austria. They are doing much pioneering work there. It has been most interesting . . .' While the doctor was explaining his knowledge and theories, Oliver noticed his rival, von Ehrlich, arrive in the dining room.

He now had two women with him, the young one and the fascinating woman he had seen on the platform that morning. Lucky devil! Oliver knew which one he would favour. As if he had become aware that someone was watching him, von Ehrlich looked in his direction and acknowledged him with an elegant bow.

Oliver stood as the man approached.

'Mr Cresswell, I gather.' Von Ehrlich bowed again.

'Mr von Ehrlich.' Oliver bowed in his turn.

'I trust you're not too disappointed?'

'The richer man won.' Oliver smiled. 'I apologise for pushing the price so high.'

Von Ehrlich shrugged as if the money was of no great consequence. 'The land came cheap.' From his pocket he took a slim gold case, which he flipped open. 'My card, Mr Cresswell. I hope we shall have the honour of your acquaintance?'

'Undoubtedly, Mr von Ehrlich.'

The man swung round and returned to his table.

'You might have introduced us.' Mortie complained.

'I hardly had time, did I?'

'Odd-looking cove. Foreign, isn't he?'

'Evidently.' Oliver smiled – Mortie could be guaranteed to state the obvious.

'What did he get that you wanted?'

'Nothing of consequence – a property. You were saying, Dr Talbot?'

The doctor began again, explaining what was evidently of great importance to him . . . but Oliver found the presence of the lovely woman too distracting.

'Oliver, are you listening?'

'Sorry, Mortie, I was engrossed in what the doctor has to say.'

The doctor smiled and Oliver had the unpleasant feeling that he knew he hadn't heard a word.

'Would you believe the doctor wants sober-water poured in his wine?'

'If that's what he wants.'

'I owe it to you all, especially your father. I gather from your mother that you are all concerned about the state of his mind.'

'Some of us more than others,' Oliver replied.

'You've noticed changes in him?'

'He's a bit vague, has trouble with his memory, but he's been very ill. He seems normal to me.'

'Which, of course, invites the question, what do you mean by *normal*, Mr Cresswell?'

'I would say my father's normal behaviour would be what is normal for him.'

'Rubbish, Oliver. He's gone off his noddle.'

'I gather you don't agree with your brother?'

'I don't,' Mortie averred. 'Doctor, you should understand that Oliver runs away from matters he does not like. He's like an ostrich – aren't you?' In reply Oliver merely smiled. 'My father, Dr Talbot, rambles incoherently. He hides things.'

'How would you know? You haven't been at home for weeks,' Oliver reminded him.

The doctor held his hand up to stop him. 'What sort of things does he hide?' he asked.

'Toast. Even a fried egg – put it under a cushion. Can you imagine the mess?'

'Did he give a reason for doing so?'

'He did, Doctor. He said my family were starving him to death.' Mortie was puffed up with indignation.

'Hannah never told me this,' Oliver said.

'Didn't she? Well, Mother jolly well will. You ask her. And he went berserk, began to break furniture because he thought people were stealing his money.'

'Who told you this?'

'Mother, of course. I can't remember the last time Hannah bothered to write to me . . .' He paused to load his fork with as much as he could get onto it, then pushed it into his mouth.

126

Oliver looked at his brother in disbelief. Mortie had just told the doctor a series of bare-faced lies. So this was how his mother intended to persuade the man that her husband was incapable. He was glad he felt about her the way he did: if he had loved her he would just have suffered painful disillusionment. With the doctor present he did not know the best way to approach this: if he made a fuss he might appear to be protesting too much and thereby give credence to what Mortie was saying. 'Talbot, he's withdrawn, he doesn't talk to us. He can't make decisions. It worries our mother,' he said eventually, deciding that honesty might be the best defence.

'I expect she is. It can be a trying time for everyone. And there are the feelings of guilt to contend with,' the doctor replied.

'What guilt?' Mortie looked up from filling his mouth.

'Having to decide what is best for your father.'

'Oh, that!' Mortie returned to his food.

Chapter Five
February 1901

After his doctor's visit, Mortimer felt calmer and more confident. At his insistence, in front of the lawyer, Shelburn had reassured him that he was not concerned about his mental state. Since he had left, Mortimer and Henry Battle had been closeted in the library for most of the morning. The long oak table had disappeared under a sea of paper and ledgers. Although it looked chaotic the purposeful manner in which Mortimer picked out documents and books implied that he was in control of everything.

'Did you note all that down?' Henry turned to the young man sitting at a smaller table, notebook and pencil to hand; he had been making copious notes.

'Yes, Mr Battle.'

'Then read that back to us.'

'Before you do, tug the bell pull for me, there's a good chap.'

The youth read out the long list of fields and their acreage, woods, copses and estimates of trees standing, farms and rents, cottages and expenses. All of these items were listed alphabetically.

'Well done, young man. I'm sorry I don't know your name,' Mortimer said, as the boy finished, his voice husky from the effort.

'Topsham, sir.'

'Is it now?' But Mortimer said no more. A footman appeared in answer to his summons. 'Ensure this young man is fed and given something to drink, then bring us coffee.'

The two older men watched the gangly boy walk awkwardly to the door, as if he was aware that they watched him.

'An impressive young man,' Mortimer said, once the door had closed.

'He's the best assistant I've ever had and he's not eighteen until next month. He's hard-working and very ambitious.'

'Then you had better look to your laurels, Mr Battle, or he'll be taking your clients from you once he has his articles.'

'He has some time to go for that, Sir Mortimer.' Henry laughed. 'At least, I hope so.' He began to pile his papers. 'I don't wish to be presumptuous, Sir Mortimer . . .'

'When people say that they invariably are.' Mortimer smiled, and Henry looked abashed. 'If you wish to give me the benefit of your opinion I shall be happy to listen. I don't need to act on it, do I?'

'No, sir, but I don't wish to offend you.'

'Mr Battle, I dealt with your father for many years. He never offended me, and I doubt that you will.'

'Very well. In the . . .' He coughed. 'Although I have the details to prepare your new will, I wonder if it would not be better if we wrote a temporary document today, Sir Mortimer, while I'm here . . . Without wishing to sound over-dramatic . . . But, well . . .' He looked distinctly uncomfortable. 'I will then work on the final missive in my office – it is a complicated matter and will take time.'

'In the circumstances. Was that what you wanted to say?'

'It is difficult—.'

'I understand. You know what I appreciate most about you, Mr Battle? It is the manner in which you understood immediately the situation I find myself in. No questions, no doubts, no recriminations. You have just got on with the job in hand. I like people as decisive as you.'

'Thank you, sir.'

They paused when the footman returned with a coffee-pot, cream-jug, sugar bowl, cakes and biscuits. 'We can manage, Jock.' Mortimer dismissed the servant, then poured the coffee. 'It's a strange thing, Mr Battle. I've been so tired until today. Now I feel galvanised, as though I have a new lease on life.'

'Better you should feel that way than . . .'

'Demoralised? Yes, you're right, Mr Battle. You must often find yourself knowing the secrets of your clients but never sure how much of your mind you can speak. Do you see much of this sort of drama?'

'Well, we're not yet certain—'

'Come, Mr Battle, neither of us is that naïve surely?'

'It's a sad situation. For some time I have thought it was preferable to be comfortably off rather than wealthy. I have noticed that the rich man's health is of great interest to many people.' At this Mortimer laughed loudly. 'I have also observed that members of a family often think they know better how a person should spend their money than they do themselves.'

'Any other pearls of wisdom?'

'The deathbeds of the rich are invariably more crowded than those of the poor.'

At this Mortimer roared with laughter and slapped his thigh.

Melanie was taking advantage of Sir Mortimer being out of his room to clean it. She had asked Mrs Fuller for her permission, which had been granted. The housekeeper had even told a maid to assist her. Molly was now rolling up the rugs to take them downstairs for a good beating in the open air. Melanie had been washing the ornaments in a large bowl of soapy water.

'Big improvement in the old man, isn't there?'

'Sir Mortimer, you mean,' Melanie said, on her guard and her dignity. She was fully aware of what the others on the estate thought of her and she was not going to make any slips that might be misreported. 'Very.'

'You could have knocked me down with a feather when I saw him up and dressed all smart, like.'

'He looks well.' She was admiring a fine piece of Dresden as she patted it dry with muslin.

'We heard he was going to be put away in the asylum.'

'I can't imagine where you got such an idea from. He's made a remarkable recovery.' She spoke briskly, aware that the girl was fishing for information.

'Odd, though, isn't it, the lawyer turning up at that time this morning? You should have heard Mr Whitaker. He said no one of quality called before eleven.'

'I doubt Sir Mortimer regards his solicitor as being of the quality.'

She did not see the face Molly pulled at her behind her back, or that she stuck her nose into the air for good measure before she picked up the rugs.

'Let me help you.' Melanie took one end of the roll. It was heavy and difficult for the two women to carry. On the landing they banged into a chest. Molly's cap had fallen over her eyes and she knocked a picture askew. Melanie caught an ornament as it was about to tumble to the floor. They manhandled the rugs down the back stairs and out into the yard, then hauled them on to a washing line. Molly rolled up her sleeves, took up the bamboo beater and belaboured them.

As Melanie went back into the house, and was passing the kitchen she heard a voice she recognised. She stopped dead in her tracks. It couldn't be! She peered round the door. 'Zeph!' she exclaimed.

Mr Battle's assistant was quickly on his feet and rushing across the stone floor towards her. Everyone else in the kitchen was consumed with curiosity as they hugged each other.

'Let me look at you,' Melanie held him away from her, her face brimming with love. 'What are you doing here?' She looped her arm through his and led him out of the kitchen.

'Well I never. And he didn't even say thank you for my seed cake.' Mrs Gilroy looked put out.

'Who is he?'

'Her son, Zephaniah.' Mrs Fuller preened at being the one with the information.

'What a God-forsaken name.'

'What can you expect from someone who thinks themselves a cut above?' sniffed Mrs Gilroy.

Hannah could not settle to anything. The novel that had gripped her yesterday was dull today. She mended a small tear in a dress, but her stitching was so poor that it would all need unpicking. She was all fingers and thumbs at the piano and the music was discordant. She tidied her glove drawer, then began on her handkerchief sachet but quickly tired of that too.

Although she knew it would annoy her she sought out Mrs Gilroy in her kitchen. She compounded the cook's annoyance when she queried if all was well for the dinner this evening and insisted on inspecting the fish. Mrs Gilroy's umbrage was evident.

Inadvertently she upset Mrs Fuller too. She had no idea why the housekeeper should appear put out – she always checked the rooms when guests were expected and might stay overnight. Suddenly she realised that perhaps the staff were worried about her father too. She found that touching – but if they were concerned everything must be worse than she had imagined. When she went into the library to see him, her father was engrossed with the lawyer and his ledgers. He looked at her vaguely as if her interruption was about to make him lose track of his calculation. She left them to it and went back upstairs. On the main landing she met Penelope. Her stepmother was berating a maid who stood wanly with dustpan and brush in her hand and a carpet sweeper beside her. 'If you did your work when you were supposed to I would not have come across you with all this equipment.' She pointed at the offending objects.

'Yes, my lady. I'm sorry,' Molly answered looking steadfastly at the floor.

'You know the rules. No housekeeping accoutrements to be visible.'

Despite her better judgement, Hannah felt she had to speak out. Molly was a good worker and the last thing Hannah wanted was for Penelope to dismiss her. 'Excuse me – Mother. Molly has had extra work this morning, helping to clean Father's room.'

Molly looked at her with gratitude.

'What's that got to do with me finding her coming out of my room?'

'I'm all behind this morning, my lady, and that's the truth.'

'I wasn't speaking to you! So, what is your explanation, Hannah?'

'No doubt Molly was unable to get into your room earlier.'

'You mean I have to plan my sleep for the maids' convenience?'

'No.' Her heart was thudding. At this upsetting time, the last thing she needed was a confrontation with Penelope. She took a deep breath. 'As I said, Molly had extra duties and it's hard for the maids when people don't keep to a routine.'

'I would like to point out to you, Hannah, that I am the mistress of this house, something you appear to forget regularly.'

'I'm sorry – Mother.'

'Why can't she do my room when I'm at luncheon?'

Hannah's sigh was audible. 'Because she has other duties at that time – Mother.'

'This house is run like a bordello.'

A giggle escaped Molly.

Penelope glared at her. 'Are you happy here?'

'Sometimes,' Molly said stalwartly. Hannah admired her honesty.

'Then I suggest you watch your tongue, young woman, or you will not be here much longer.'

'Yes, my lady. Sorry, my lady.' Molly bobbed. Penelope turned on her heel and stalked along the corridor to her room.

'I'm sorry, Miss Cresswell. I was tipped off she'd gone downstairs and I thought I'd time to nip in and do her room. We're at sixes and sevens today.'

'I understand, Molly. I suggest you spend the next couple of days behind the scenes. Tell Mrs Fuller I said so.'

'Thank you, Miss.'

As she passed her stepmother's room Penelope called, 'Hannah, a moment.'

She felt sick with tension as she entered the room. Her stepmother was at her dressing-table.

'Please do *not* argue with me in front of the staff, Hannah. It leads to insubordination. And it shows how little respect you have for me.'

'But I didn't mean—'

'You prance about this house as if it were your own, and I hasten to remind you that it isn't.'

'I apologise. I didn't mean to offend you. I was just trying to explain the situation.'

'You may go now.' She returned to the looking-glass.

'I should like to say – Mother,' Hannah had paused at the door, 'I have never regarded this house as belonging to anyone but my father.'

At Penelope's look of malice, Hannah wished she hadn't said that. But it was the truth. However, in the circumstances, antagonising her stepmother was not a sensible thing to do.

Dismissed like one of the servants, Hannah walked along the corridor. She despised herself – was it only this morning she had resolved not to be so afraid?

She stopped at her father's room. 'Let's go for a walk, Cariad,' she said to the little dog, who looked as bored as she was. Cariad's tail whacked the floor.

When they got downstairs it was raining. In the flower room Hannah found an old riding mackintosh. It was a man's and swamped her, but no one would see her so what did it matter? It must belong to her father for it smelt of his cologne – sometimes when he was away she would go to his dressing room and pour some onto her handkerchief. It made him seem closer.

As Cariad scuttled about in the undergrowth and Hannah stood waiting for her, she put her hands into the pockets. In one she felt the lace edge of a handkerchief. She pulled it out. She looked at it, idly noting the monogram, an ornate L. She began to put it back but a waft of perfume issued from it. She pulled it out again. What was her father doing with a woman's handkerchief in his pocket?

'Come on, Cariad,' she called to the little dog, who had evidently been rolling in the mud. 'Just look at you! Round to the back and the pump!' She had to call Ferdie several times before he appeared out of the stables, curry-comb in hand, and gave him instructions to bathe the dog immediately.

In the house she walked along the stone-flagged corridor, passing the kitchens, from which the most wonderful smells were issuing, and the pantries. All was bustle, the servants running hither and thither. They were smiling, she noticed: the atmosphere in the house had changed. And it wasn't just the servants, she decided, it was almost as if the house itself was happy to be having guests, if only the lawyer and the doctor, but it was an indicator that life might be returning to normal. Or was it? She shuddered as she remembered what was happening. Don't think about it, she told herself.

If her father . . . She corrected herself. *When* her father was better, they should entertain more. She was becoming too reclusive. She might suggest to him that they had a large house party, but would people come so far from London? Her stepmother was always complaining that Cresswell was too far from *civilisation*. Maybe when he left, as surely he would eventually, Hannah should go with him. She had always regarded herself as content at Cresswell but she was no longer sure: the happenings of past weeks had made her question everything when before she had been happy to accept what people said.

She entered the pressing room. James was working on one of her father's suits. 'I hoped I'd find you here, James.' She pretended not to see the cigarette glowing in an ashtray, and inspected one of her skirts, as if checking the mud had been brushed out satisfactorily. 'This mackintosh of my father's, could you see to it? Cariad jumped up at me – look at the mess she made.' She showed him the pawmarks.

'Leave it with me, Miss Cresswell, I'll see to it. Nice walk?'

'Very pleasant, thank you.'

'Not exactly the weather for it, if you don't mind me saying.' He was staring at her bedraggled hair, and Hannah patted it self-consciously – it was plastered to her head. What a fright she must look. 'Rain has never bothered me. When one lives in Devon, one gets used to it.' She smiled. 'A minute.' She delved into the pocket of the coat. She didn't want a servant to find the handkerchief.

She was crossing the hall when she saw Melanie in conversation with a young man who was standing with a hand on the library door knob.

'Miss Cresswell.' Melanie bobbed to her. 'Might I introduce my son, Zephaniah?'

'How do you do? How nice to meet you.' She held out her hand to the tall youth. He had Melanie's fine grey eyes, her height and her good looks.

Melanie and Zeph watched her mount the stairs. 'What's she like to work for?'

'I don't work for her, just her father. She's nicer than the others. Still arrogant, mind you, but I don't think she's aware she is! How long do you think you'll be here?'

'We'll finish with Sir Mortimer this afternoon.'

'What are you doing?'

'I shouldn't be discussing it. It's confidential.'

'Then I'm sorry I asked, but who would I tell?'

Zephaniah looked from left to right, then leant forward to his mother. 'Rewriting his will,' he whispered.

'Really?' Melanie felt her heart jump.

'I'm not doing that. I mean, I'm not privy to what's in it. Mr Battle is. I'm just collating figures for them.'

'Good heavens, Zeph, I'd never have asked if I'd thought it was so important. And I'd never expect you to break such a confidence. I don't want to know a thing.' And she didn't. She was appalled. If Sir Mortimer was changing his will she was responsible. After all, by telling him of the gossip she'd heard, she had set this sorry business in motion.

'I'd hoped you'd be staying the night.' She wanted to get off the subject of wills.

'We are. I overheard Sir Mortimer telling Mr Battle he was expected to dine. He looked very pleased. I think Mr Battle likes hobnobbing with the gentry.' He grinned.

'I'll get a message to Flossie Marshall to cook you some supper.'

'Will you be there? I don't want to go home . . .' His voice trailed off. Melanie knew he'd been about to finish 'if it's just Father there', but he was too loyal for that. She knew he feared his father, and sometimes she saw on his face an expression that bordered on hatred.

'You'd like to stay here?'

'It must sound ungrateful but, well, yes, I would.'

She patted his arm. 'I understand. It's nice to have a little luxury, even if it's only for an evening. I've enjoyed my stay here. I quite dread leaving.'

'This is what you deserve.'

'Me? What a dear son you are.'

'I'd best get back.' He nodded towards the library door.

'Forgive me, I've kept you. I hope to see you later.'

Penelope Cresswell had been lurking in the vicinity of the hall for the past hour. Whitaker regarded her with his normal superior expression. Had she any idea of his thoughts she would have dismissed him in a trice.

At the spluttering and clunking sound of an approaching motor vehicle, Whitaker stepped towards the door, took a large umbrella from the elephant-leg stand, and clicked his fingers at the footman, who skidded ahead to open the door. Whitaker was about to step out on to the porch, when he was pushed aside unceremoniously as Penelope moved out and took up her position on the steps. Whitaker opened the umbrella and held it over her head. They were joined by Hannah.

Whitaker disapproved of many things but at the top of the list was this noisome vehicle. They had to 'move with the times', Mrs Fuller had told him, and if these were the times he had to move into he was unsure that he wanted to.

'How kind of you to come, Dr Talbot!' Penelope gushed, as the doctor bowed over her hand. 'I trust you had a good journey.'

'An extremely swift one,' he said, with a touch of irony.

'I would like a word in private, Doctor.' She beamed at

him, eyelashes fluttering. 'There are confidential matters I would prefer . . . I wish to protect my dear boys, you understand?'

'I think I do, Lady Cresswell.' He looked questioningly at her.

Penelope was puzzled. Then she had the grace to look a little flustered. 'This is my daughter, Miss Cresswell.'

Hannah was astonished. Penelope was always at pains to let strangers know that Hannah was not her daughter. She looked up shyly into a face with such kind brown eyes and such a dignified mien that she was quite taken aback, and couldn't think what to say.

'How do you do, Miss Cresswell?' He held out his hand.

Hannah blushed as she took it, though she couldn't think why.

'You need not have bothered to come down, my dear,' Penelope said.

'I heard the car – Mother. I wanted to meet the doctor too.'

'He has enough to contend with.'

'On the contrary, I should like to speak to all the members of your family . . .' he paused '. . . Individually.'

Hannah could have hugged him, especially when she saw irritation flash across Penelope's face.

At the sound of a galloping horse everyone looked towards the drive. A soaked Dr Shelburn reined in his mount and jumped to the ground.

'Dr Shelburn! What on earth are you doing here?'

'I've come to see my patient again, Lady Cresswell.'

'There's no need for that. We've called in Dr Talbot.' Penelope turned her back on him.

'On the contrary, Lady Cresswell, it would be most valuable if I could speak with Sir Mortimer's physician.'

Penelope regained her composure and led the way into the house, across the hall and towards the carved oak staircase, black with age.

'Papa is still in the library – Mother.'

'But he should be in his room. He will tire himself out. Oh, the silly man, he gets so confused when he's tired, Doctor.'

'I expect he does, Lady Cresswell.'

'But I want him to be at his best for you.'

'I'm sure you do, Lady Cresswell.'

The library door opened and, immaculately dressed, his eyes alight with intelligent interest, Sir Mortimer strode into the hall. 'Dr Talbot, I presume. How very kind of you to come all this way to chat to me.'

Penelope gaped – Hannah thought she looked like a gasping fish.

It was an afternoon of huddled groups, of people meeting behind closed doors, of much whispering and looking over shoulders. Suspicion stalked the corridors and all were agog downstairs.

'Heard anything?' Mrs Gilroy looked up from larding the beef fillet.

'It's how I imagine the corridors of power are when a great debate is in full force,' Whitaker replied, and put down the tray of leftover cakes he had brought from the drawing room.

'Who's Lord Salisbury up there, then?'

'Need you ask?' Whitaker laughed.

'Lady C, no doubt.'

Whitaker suddenly sat down.

'You look done in, Mr Whitaker. Cup of tea?'

'That is most kind of you, Mrs Gilroy.' He put his head into his hands.

'You all right?' Mrs Gilroy asked. 'Whisky needed here, I think, Hilda.' The pastrycook fetched the bottle from the pine dresser that dominated one wall of the kitchen and added a slug to the tea that the cook had already poured.

'I've worked for this family for over thirty years, Eve,

and I thought I knew them. It's distressing to find that I don't,' Whitaker muttered.

'It must be.' Mrs Gilroy felt quite faint at his use of her Christian name. He was never normally so informal. 'Poor Edward,' she dared to say. 'It reminds me of my sister. I thought I knew her, and then our mother died and I haven't seen hide nor hair of her since – of course, her taking Mother's rings without a by-your-leave might have had something to do with it.'

'It's Mr Mortie has shocked me most. I've always felt well disposed towards him, even if he hasn't given us much cause to admire him. But I heard him, with my own ears, lying to that head doctor from Exeter. Lies, all lies!'

'What did he say?' Even Hilda, who had been beating meringue, stopped to listen.

'That Sir Mortimer claims he can understand what his dog is saying.'

'My great-aunt does that. Lots of people say they know what their dogs want. That's no proof.' Hilda was indignant.

'He said his father was raving one evening and throwing his food on the floor. Well, I never saw it.'

'Did he say he *saw* it, or did he say he'd been *told* it?'

'What are you implying, Mrs Gilroy?' Whitaker had returned to his normal formality.

'Mr Mortie's hardly the sharpest knife in the box, is he? He has many faults but I never saw him as a liar. Since it's not in his nature to lie then perhaps he's of the belief that others don't. So if a certain somebody had told him that had happened, he would believe her – or him, as the case might be,' she added hurriedly.

'And if he'd been throwing food about, who would know it? We would, of course, since the maids would have been sent to clear up the mess,' Hilda added.

'Of course! You're right, Mrs Gilroy. I had allowed distress to impinge on my logic.' Whitaker cheered up, picked up his teacup and drank with relish. He sat up straight, almost as if he was on parade. 'And, Mrs Gilroy, I trust you will forgive me my presumptuous lapse of a moment ago.'

'Get on with you. How long have we known each other? I've been here two years, so it's about time we were all a bit more friendly. The times, as Gussie keeps saying, are changing!'

'Eve's right,' said Hilda. 'There's enough formality upstairs.'

'I deem it an honour, then.'

'Ah . . .' The two women sighed in unison.

'In my opinion, that calls for another cuppa – *Edward*.' Mrs Gilroy scurried about. 'And we might as well finish up these fancies that Hilda made and they couldn't eat. Jose!' she yelled. 'Plates and forks!'

'Very kind, I'm sure. But, then, there's been the oddest thing. That doctor – you know you said he was a charlatan? Well, you were right, Eve. He's asking them all what their dreams are.'

'He what?'

'I couldn't help but overhear Miss Hannah. It seems she dreams of people with no faces.'

'How peculiar. Me, I dream in colour. Why only the other night – Put them there, Jose.' The kitchenmaid was taking as long as she could to lay the plates and forks. 'Get a move on, girl. We're having a private conversation – *if* you don't mind!'

'Sorry, Mrs Gilroy.' Jose scuttled back to the scullery.

'As you were saying, Edward?'

'I heard him asking Miss Hannah and then Mr Oliver what they'd been dreaming. Of course, as I said, *she* told him, but Mr Oliver said what the hell – pardon my language – was the point of him telling his dreams? He got quite huffed. The doctor said that he could understand them from their dreams.'

'I've never heard such poppycock in my life! Foreign is he?'

'No, English.'

'How very strange.'

Jose, who had been listening at the door, moved away when the older servants related their dreams to each other.

'Find anything out?' Dolly was sitting in the corner her feet up on a stool.

'I think they've all gone doolally. Talking about dreams, they are.'

'Other people's dreams are always dull.'

'You should have heard Mrs Gilroy's! She said she was in a forest full of snakes and Mr Whitaker rode up on Sergeant, dressed in hunting pink, to rescue her!' She shrieked with laughter.

'That wasn't a dream, that's her hoping!' It was Dolly's turn to screech with laughter.

'Poor soul. She's left it a bit late in the day, hasn't she?'

'Any chance of a cuppa?' The outer door had opened and Ferdie stood on the step, shivering with cold, holding a bedraggled dog in his arms.

'Poor you! Come in, but you can't bring a dog in here. Mrs Gilroy would kill me.' Dolly had stood up and was straightening her skirt.

'Of course you can, Ferdie. That's Sir Mortimer's dog, Dolly. Cariad can go anywhere her wants.'

Ferdie put the dog down and she made a beeline for the kitchen. Jose had been right: they all heard the butler and the cook cooing over her and evidently feeding her titbits.

'You're soaked!' Dolly stated the obvious. She picked up a towel and gave it to him.

'I had to bath that bloody dog, and me in the middle of grooming too.'

'Who asked?'

'That Miss Cresswell.'

'She's nicer than the others but none of them ever

think, do they? We're just there at their beck and call.' Jose tutted sympathetically.

'Still, they pays our wages. And her did arrange that cough medicine for me – not that it's done much good,' Dolly said.

'Don't be so level-headed, Dolly!' Jose laughed. 'It does us good to have a moan.'

'Any chance of a cuppa?' Ferdie asked again.

'Sorry, Ferdie, I'll get you one.' Dolly looked pointedly at Jose and rolled her eyes. Jose took the hint. She picked up a basket the laundrymaid had dropped off, and tiptoed across the kitchen towards the below-stairs laundry store. As she passed the footman's pantry she heard a whistle. 'Jose, come here.' Jock whispered.

She looked to left and right. 'Just a minute, then.'

Jock took the basket from her, put his arms about her, pinned her against the table and kissed her while his hands groped under her skirt.

The door was ajar. They heard footsteps and sprang apart. As Whitaker passed he pulled it shut and didn't register them.

'Christ!' Jock's legs buckled.

'We must be mad!'

'Meet me tonight in the stables.'

'I'll try,' Jose said, weak with excitement.

'Might Hannah and I speak to you privately, Dr Shelburn?' Oliver had been waiting in the hall for the doctor's return. He had gone to collect his wife and change for dinner. 'That is, if you would excuse us, Mrs Shelburn?' He bestowed on her a smile of such charm that Maisie Shelburn's cheeks burned with pleasure.

'Of course. It's been an anxious day for you,' she managed to say.

'If you would be patient for just a few minutes, Mr Cresswell? The vicar and I have been summoned to your father by the lawyer – something to do with documents, I gather.'

'We shall be in my sister's sitting room. Whitaker,' he summoned the hovering butler, 'show Mrs Shelburn into the drawing room, and when the doctor is ready, bring him to my sister.'

He made his way to Hannah's sitting room and tapped on the door. It was opened so quickly she must have been standing waiting. 'Oh! Where's Dr Shelburn?' Oliver explained. 'But what would Father want Simeon and the doctor for?'

'I think—' But Oliver got no further for Jock appeared, weighed down with a tray of decanters. Hannah checked that nothing was missing. 'You needn't have bothered with that.' He was amused: when guests were expected, Hannah usually ordered far too much of everything, food and drink.

'I want him to feel comfortable.'

'He'll be blind drunk if you're not careful. But since it's here . . .' Oliver poured himself a large whisky and soda.

'If I might have a small sherry?'

'But you don't drink.'

'I do sometimes – when I feel the need.'

The third knock heralded the doctor.

'Come in, Doctor.' Hannah held open the door.

'I shall get straight to the point,' he said, and much to Oliver's amusement waved away her offer of a drink. 'You need have no fear. Dr Talbot regards your father as perfectly normal.'

'Thank God.' Hannah sank into a chair, unaware that she was fanning herself with her handkerchief, something she would never normally do.

'How did he reach his conclusions so quickly?' Oliver enquired.

'You don't become as expert as Dr Talbot without being a good observer of people,' the doctor told him.

'Did he speak to everyone in the end?'

'I don't think I betray any confidences if I tell you he was greatly impressed with you both, how honest you were with him, that you had been genuinely concerned for your father, but not, I hasten to add, to the extent of thinking he was not in control of his faculties. I assured him you had already spoken with me on the subject. I said, and he agreed, that your concern was natural, and that you accepted readily my explanation that it was necessary for your father to adjust to the fact that he is ageing, that he had been near death.'

'Yes,' said Oliver, certain Dr Shelburn had not had such a discussion – there hadn't been time – but if it made him happy to appear of such importance, Oliver was content to say nothing.

'And my brother Mortie?' Hannah asked. 'He was so adamant . . . I don't understand him at all. He's such a good-natured man, you know.'

Suddenly the doctor looked trapped, as if he did not want to say any more.

'We need to know, Doctor. We shall keep your counsel.'

'I should not be telling you this, Miss Cresswell, but . . .' He paused, evidently weighing the ethics of his position. 'It has to be said that your brother's account matched your mother's word for word, and Dr Talbot concluded that he had not witnessed anything untoward and was simply repeating what he had been told. Eventually, he admitted this. Mrs Topsham gave a glowing report of your father, as did his valet. Which, of course . . .'

'Was that necessary? Discussing my father with the servants?' Hannah's face showed her dislike of this.

'It was very necessary, Miss Cresswell.'

'Why?'

'They know your father well and could be regarded . . .' the doctor gave a discreet cough. '. . . as impartial. Dr Talbot takes his role most seriously.'

'Of course.' Hannah did not look convinced. 'So Papa can stay here?' she asked, happy to change the subject.

'Undoubtedly. I have recommended he goes to bed – he exerted himself far too much today. He still needs to guard himself and take care of his health. We are not out of the woods yet, Miss Cresswell, and the next few weeks will be crucial to his well-being. I trust you will continue to care for him.'

'It's my pleasure to do so, Doctor.'

He stood up. 'Perhaps I should say that, as yet, no one else is privy to this information.'

Left alone, brother and sister looked at each other. 'I could cry,' said Hannah.

'And a lot of good that would do.' Oliver patted her hand.

'Don't worry, I won't.' She smiled up at him.

'You like Dr Talbot, don't you?'

'He seems a very nice man.' She knew she was blushing.

'I didn't mean in *that* way.' Oliver grinned at her.

'I don't know what you're talking about.'

'I think you do.'

'Dr Shelburn was avoiding discussing your mother, wasn't he?' Hannah changed the subject, feeling flustered, embarrassed and confused in turn.

'The fact that he did damns her, doesn't it?'

'But why did she say such things? That's what I don't understand. She's not an evil person.'

'I'd agree. Opinionated and difficult, but not wicked – or so I thought. But perhaps she is, and we didn't see it. It's obvious that our parents don't like each other very much.'

'Oliver!' Hannah was shocked as she always was when her brother said what she had been thinking and felt she shouldn't.

'Dear Hannah, we must be honest with each other if

we're to understand anything. There's no use in pretending that things are as we would like them to be rather than as they are. I begin to think Mother was disappointed when he didn't die.'

'*Oliver!*'

'Just listen. Over the weeks, Mother had become used to the idea – no doubt she had even begun to plan her life as a widow. Neither of us is trapped in such a marriage so we don't know how we would feel.'

'I wouldn't wish anyone dead.'

'I didn't say Mother did so *intentionally*. Perhaps she's not aware of what she was thinking.'

'I can't even think of living without him.'

'But you love him and she doesn't – that's the difference. Don't you see the importance of facing the truth to understand? Having him committed was her way of being free of him.'

'If you can reach such conclusions, so can Papa. What will he do?'

'Not a pleasant position to be in, is it? Quite frightening for anyone, but especially for someone who is weak from illness. Perhaps that was why he summoned his lawyer.'

'His will?'

'It had crossed my mind when I learnt that Mr Battle had asked the doctor and Simeon to attend him.'

'How awful this all is. I always thought we were reasonably happy.'

'It's how families are, my dear, innocent sister. It quite puts me against marriage.'

Hannah shook her head as if to rid herself of such unpleasantness. If he was thinking in this way had he changed his plans too? She wondered if she should mention the handkerchief she had found in her father's coat, but decided against it, although she was not sure why. 'I haven't had time to ask. How did the auction go?'

'I was not fortunate.'

'Was it Courtney Lacey?'

'The same. It was probably for the best, as Nanny Wishart would say.'

'It wasn't meant to be, as she would also say. But I'm sorry. Who bought it?'

'A foreign family. He looks like a pirate, duelling scar and all.'

'Good gracious, in Devon! How exciting.' She picked up her evening bag and gloves. 'I met Mrs Topsham's son today. A lanky boy, with a fine face.'

'I've been thinking about her. Do you think Father has a care for her?'

'I hope I misunderstood your meaning. He cares for all those on the estate.'

'I meant if he liked her – as a woman.'

'What a dreadful thing to say! How could you even think such a thing?'

'Perhaps there is something in their past that makes him care about her.'

Bag and gloves tumbled to the floor. 'That's a disgusting suggestion. I don't think you should say such things to me.' But the perfumed and initialled handkerchief flashed into her mind again. She could almost smell its perfume. How much did she know about her father?

'I apologise. It was disrespectful of me.'

She could not look at him, she was so embarrassed. 'Please, Hannah, don't be angry with me. My curiosity got the better of me. And you must admit it is a mystery. Melanie was her parents' pride and joy when she was young – I remember from the days when I spent so much time with Beasley – and now they don't speak to her and with that in mind, why did she come back here, of all places, when it must make everything more difficult for her?'

'It was all most unfortunate.' Hannah was studying her hands intently.

'How long has she been back?' Oliver ventured.

'A couple of years. You must have forgotten, but about eighteen years ago she ran away and married someone her parents didn't approve of – at least, that's what I've always been told and it's what I believe.' She frowned, and looked at her brother with an anguished expression. 'I don't think I shall ever be able to forget what you've just said about Melanie and Papa.'

'So why didn't the Topshams stay away? And why did Father insist on her caring for him?'

'Do we have to continue this discussion?'

'Yes, Hannah. I need to know so that in future I'm forewarned of anything that people might say against him.'

'Very well. Papa was in Plymouth on business. The Topshams were living there and were in dire straits. Her husband couldn't find work – people say he's a drunkard and I fear that's probably true. Father chanced across her in the street and she recognised him. He felt sorry for her – you know how he feels responsible for the estate workers and their families.'

'The husband appears to do little work now. Why?'

'I think you should ask Papa about these matters, not me.'

'I see. She is, of course, an attractive woman . . .'

Hannah stood up. 'Father is a kind man. Often when people do good things wicked people can only see bad.' With that she collected her bag and gloves again and swept from the room. Once outside, she turned back. 'Perhaps you would be better off slandering our father to Mortie – he knows more of the world than I do.'

'I already have. He knows nothing.'

But Hannah did not hear: she had slammed the door noisily – for her.

Despite her conversation with Oliver, Hannah was determined that nothing was going to spoil the evening. Her father was well, sane, and not about to be taken from her. And she was not alone: the others were sparkling, too, as if a great weight had been lifted from them.

Mortie – who, as the day had progressed, had become more and more depressed – was in fine form now, laughing and joking with the lawyer, whom he seemed to know well.

'Has the doctor told him too?' Hannah whispered to Oliver.

'I don't think so.'

'But he's so happy.'

'Fuelled by whisky.'

'Oliver, you always think the worst of him. It's understandable that he's a little merry. It's been a horrible day. I think he's feeling remorse for the things he said about Papa.'

'He should have thought before he said anything.'

'It would never have crossed his mind that your mother could possibly be lying.'

'You always say *your* mother. Never *our*.'

'Well, she isn't mine, is she?'

'You sound as if that's a relief to you.'

'How silly of you. It's not. I'm just being pedantic.' But she was blushing.

'I don't blame you.'

'I think Mortie's attitude is really rather endearing.' She was desperate for Oliver to change the subject.

'Stupid, is how I would describe it.'

Even the arrival of Penelope did nothing to change the mood. In fact, Penelope was in exuberant form, charming the men, being considerate to the doctor's wife, kind to the servants, ablaze with diamonds and rustling in heliotrope silk.

'You see her now, Oliver, she's happy too with the news of Father. How could we have thought for one minute that she did not have his best interests at heart?'

'Or she has not yet been told of the doctor's conclusion,' was Oliver's response, as Whitaker appeared and announced that dinner was served. Hannah was more than content that Dr Talbot was to escort her into the dining room and that she was to sit beside him. The prospect made her feel quite giddy.

Only one thing marred the evening for her: Oliver made far too much fuss of Laura Redman, who appeared embarrassed by his attentions. And as she moved away from him Hannah noticed her perfume which reminded her of something but she couldn't remember what.

'Dearest Mortimer, it is late and you should not be troubling yourself with your family.' Penelope led the way into the bedroom, her colour a little higher than usual from the amount of claret she had drunk. Mortimer was sitting up in bed, propped up with a dozen goosedown pillows. Instead of the usual subdued lighting lamps were placed all around the room so there were no dark areas.

'On the contrary, I wish to see you all. There are matters to discuss.'

'Would the morning be better?'

'No, Penelope, it would not. I have things to say, and until they are said I shall not have a good night's sleep.'

The others looked at each other. What did this mean?

'You must have every oil lamp in the house here!'

'I want to be able to see you all. Now, if you would kindly be seated.' He indicated the semicircle of chairs that Melanie had arranged for him. He waited patiently while they took their seats. 'Are we settled?' Mortimer looked at them all with a benign expression. 'Then we shall begin.' On his lap he had a notepad. 'I trust that you are all happy with Dr Talbot's conclusions about me.'

'Papa, how could you ask?' Hannah half rose from her chair.

'We have not been told, even though I asked,' Penelope said sweetly. 'I was told you wanted to tell us yourself.'

'Yes, I do. I am happy to report that the doctor considers me well. I am not senile. I am perfectly sane.'

'Top hole.' Mortie grinned.

'It was what I expected,' Oliver said quietly.

'My dear one. Such a relief to us all, but especially for me.' Penelope spoke in a tight little voice, with a fixed smile. She waved her handkerchief agitatedly. The perfume it released was not, Hannah noticed, the one that annoyed her father so and made him sneeze.

'I was, you will realise, somewhat taken aback that you thought it was necessary for me to see him.'

'It was a family decision,' Penelope said hurriedly.

'Was it now?' Mortimer looked long and hard at his wife and she had the grace to lower her eyes. Mortie suddenly found that his collar was far too tight for him. 'At first I was angry, but then I realised it was a good thing. It made me stop and think. It made me see I needed to do things, take decisions that I should have taken long ago. The first resolution I have made is to give up my previous life. I intend to spend most of my time from now on at Cresswell.'

This caused mixed reactions. Hannah clasped her hands with pleasure. Oliver grinned and nodded. Mortie seemed uninterested, and Penelope looked horrified but said nothing.

'I had intended to see you one by one, but then I decided this would not be a good idea. There is too much tittle-tattle in this family and what I said might have been misreported.' At this there was a great deal of movement as if everyone's seat had become uncomfortable. Mortimer looked at them in turn, as if gauging their reaction. 'I have decided to see you together so that you can all hear what I have to say to each of you, and then there can be no wrongful interpretation. Hannah.' He faced her. She felt nervous, as if she had done something wrong.

'You have been a good daughter to me – the best a man could hope for.'

'Oh, Papa.' She looked down in confusion.

'But I realised I had not made adequate provision for you should I have died. As you are all aware, when that day comes this property passes to Mortie. Coral, of course, will be mistress here, Hannah. Unfortunately she is not the easiest of women and there is a risk that she might make your life difficult—'

'I say!' Mortie blustered. 'I don't like this. She's my wife, after all.'

'And it is commendable that you rise to her defence. However, I am certain that other members of this family would be in agreement with me.'

'She can be opinionated,' Penelope said.

'I doubt if you could, or would want to, stay here, Hannah. So I propose, in the absence of a dower house, that we build one. It shall be your home until you no longer need one – if you should leave to marry or when it is your turn to join me up above.' He smiled.

'Or down below!' Mortie guffawed.

'Where are you planning to build the house, Father?'

'I thought over by Dunwell Wood, Oliver. It would be protected by the trees on the north side and would face south with good views.'

'Papa, I don't know what to say,' Hannah murmured. 'It's so kind of you. I had, of course, wondered what I would do when . . .' She was unable to say the words as if voicing them might make it happen.

'How would she be able to run it, Father?' Oliver asked.

'It's good you should be concerned about your sister's affairs.'

'I was just going to say that too,' Mortie said sulkily.

'I shall, of course, make you a sufficient allowance for your household expenses, Hannah. The maintenance of the fabric of the house will be the estate's responsibility.'

'She has her legacy from her mother,' Penelope said waspishly.

'Money that I would rather was not touched. She is my daughter, Penelope, something you have always been at pains to forget.'

'Mortimer!' she exclaimed but no one took any notice of her.

'Oliver,' her husband went on.

'Sir.'

'I wish I knew you better. I regret the years you have been away and that when you were younger I did not spend more time with you.'

'I feel the same, Father.'

'When you left I felt that you were petulant and angry with the cards you had been dealt. That you were resentful that your brother was to inherit and not you. But, I think it has been the making of you, my son.' At this Mortie slumped in his chair. 'You obviously need no financial assistance from me.' Mortie brightened. 'I'm proud of you.' Mortie slumped further. 'But I would ask a favour of you.'

'If I can be of assistance.' He would never admit it to anyone but Oliver's throat constricted and his eyes pricked.

'Might I ask if you intend to stay in the vicinity?'

'I think so. My roots are here and I have tired of travelling. I tried to buy Courtney Lacey, but failed in the bidding.'

'So Battle told me, which has emboldened me to suggest the following. You would be doing me a great favour if you took over the running of the estate.'

'But it's my estate!'

'Not yet, Mortie.'

Oliver sat still for a moment, all eyes upon him. 'Father, I would enjoy helping you – for the time being. But I could not commit myself to a long period, not in the circumstances.' He looked pointedly at his brother.

'It's the answer I would have expected from you.'

'We had planned, Oliver and I – when we thought the worst – to live together. Perhaps Oliver would like to join me?' Hannah said.

'A sensible suggestion, Hannah, but you misunderstood me. I rather hoped you would stay here with me, running this house as you do. The dower house would be for when I am dead and buried.'

'Oh, Papa, there's no question – you're right, I did misunderstand. I thought if you were going to be living here permanently . . .' Her voice trailed away as she took a surreptitious glance at her stepmother. How could she stay here if Penelope was going to be here too? It would be impossible – her father didn't understand.

'Mortie.'

'Father.' Mortie managed to sit up straight and fiddled with his collar. Penelope leant over and patted his knee reassuringly.

'We have listened to what Oliver has said. What he didn't say was, "What is the point of me taking over this estate if one day it will be Mortie's?"' He looked at Oliver, who nodded. 'You don't get on – I've been aware of that for years. But I think, Mortie, you would be well advised to persuade your brother to remain here. You know nothing of the estate. You have even less interest in it. You will bleed it dry, and you need someone to prevent you doing so. I am not concerned for you but for Young Mortimer. I wish this place to be well husbanded so that he will have a worthwhile inheritance.'

'I'd make sure it was.'

'I don't think you would. You are too idle and uninterested.'

'Father!'

'That is unforgivable, Mortimer. How could you speak to our son in this manner?'

'I have to speak the truth for Young Mortimer's sake.

It is my obligation to ensure that the estate is not neglected.'

'Such hypocrisy, Mortimer! The place is falling about our ears as you speak.'

'An exaggeration, Penelope. But, yes, there is neglect, which is why I've asked Oliver to help me. I intend to put right that dereliction of my duty. There is something else, Mortie. I must warn you that I am not as rich as I was. When I die you will have to cut your cloth accordingly. I suggest you start to learn to control your wife.'

Mortie jumped to his feet.

Hannah felt herself blushing for him. This was awful, she thought.

'I don't know what you mean,' he said.

'Yes, you do, Mortie. Coral is only interested in money. She is a bully. She controls you. If you don't reverse this trend you will have a miserable life. And, unless you control her spending, a poverty-stricken one. I have to warn you now that the allowance I give you will be decreased by ten per cent in the next fiscal year.'

'You can't do this, Mortimer.' Penelope was now on her feet.

'Yes, I can. I can do whatever I want. Which leads me to you.' His look was so ominous that Penelope sat down again.

'You want us to leave, Father?' Oliver asked.

'No. As I explained, I want everyone to know what is said. I would prefer to have this talk with my wife in private but too much is twisted in this family for me to take such a risk. If this is embarrassing for her, she has only herself to blame. You have behaved in a deceitful manner, Penelope, and I will not accept it. You have broken all the rules. I will not go into detail but you know to what I allude.' Penelope looked at him defiantly. 'You compounded it by trying to have me committed to an asylum.'

'I did not!'

'Don't make matters worse by lying. I have the documents here that detail our separation.'

'*Our what?*' Penelope was on her feet again.

'Father!'

'Papa!' Mortie and Hannah spoke in unison like a Greek chorus. Only Oliver remained silent.

'I do not wish us to remain together.'

'How dare you do this? How dare you humiliate me in front of our children? How dare you contemplate making me look foolish in Society? How dare you?' Her voice rose until she was screeching.

'I don't expect you to leave tonight, but I would like you to be gone by noon tomorrow.'

'No!' she screamed, then fell in a swoon on the floor.

Mortie and Hannah were quickly at her side.

'Have you some smelling salts?'

'She has not fainted, Hannah. She is pretending, she often does. Get up, Penelope, or I will cut your allowance by a hundred pounds.' There was silence from the floor. 'Two hundred.' No response. 'Five hundred.'

There was a moan from the heliotrope bundle on the floor. 'Where am I?' Penelope said weakly.

'Discussing our future. Please don't pretend to faint again.'

Mortie helped his mother to her feet. She looked so flustered and tearful that Hannah fetched her a glass of water. 'Thank you, Hannah dearest.'

'Instead of being hysterical, just stop and think, Penelope. You are getting what you wanted – a life without me. We shall both be happier.'

'But how will I manage?'

'I intend to be generous. I shall purchase you an alternative residence in London.'

She seemed mollified by this, and settled back with a thoughtful expression to mull it over.

'But, of course, your expenditure will not be as high as it is now, since you will not be moving in Society.'

'No? How cruel!' The crescendo of noise began again. If it had not been impolite Hannah would have put her hands over her ears.

'I must object, Father,' Mortie put in.

'You can object all you want, Mortie, but it's none of your business. I would have preferred not to humiliate your mother in this manner, but it is her fault that I felt it necessary.'

'Mortie!' Penelope wailed.

'Don't fear, Mother, you have me.' He helped her to her feet and she leant heavily against him. 'Father, I can never forgive you for this. I shall never set foot in this house again as long as you live.'

'That is your privilege, Mortie.'

'My darling boy.' Penelope held his hand tightly. 'Mortimer, I think you have become a monster. I shall consult a lawyer over this.'

'I think you should.'

'How am I supposed to survive with no *entrée* into society? I will never go to Court again – I will lose my friends!' The tears were genuine now.

'I am sure you will find other society to amuse you – if not so illustrious. Perhaps in Italy or France.'

Penelope let out a little squeak and, to her horror, Hannah saw her father was enjoying himself. What had her stepmother done to warrant such anger?

'I never wish to see you again!' Penelope flung at him.

'I understand.'

'Come, Mortie.' She swished from the room, Mortie behind her.

At the door he turned. 'Father, I meant what I said.'

'I'm sure you did, Mortie.'

Oliver and Hannah were poleaxed by the suddenness of their father's decision. Both were unable to understand fully what had happened.

'I'm sorry, but I felt that, any other way, she would

confide in you both, twist my words and poison your minds.'

'I see that, Father,' Oliver said, but Hannah remained silent, unsure of what she felt.

Eventually she said, 'But you lose Mortie, Papa. How can you even contemplate that?'

'His stout defence of his mother was a good thing so there's hope for the boy yet. And don't fear, Hannah, he'll be back. Coral will make him come.'

Hannah looked at her father in astonishment. He understood everything about all of them and she hadn't known it.

Chapter Six
August 1901

Stanislas von Ehrlich stood on the sweeping lawn of his latest acquisition with contentment on his face. He had dreamt of this moment for many years, secretly cherishing his plan, confiding it to no one. In the dark days, which had been many, it had kept him going, given him the impetus to fight and claw his way back. Despite the vicissitudes of his life, the moments of failure, he had never denied this vision, never once relinquished the certainty that it would become reality – eventually.

And here he was!

He wished he could prolong this moment, the exquisite sense of achievement he felt. He looked about him, memorising the colour of the leaves on the trees, the flowers, the position of the sun, the strength of the breeze, all to aid his memory when the initial euphoria died away, as he knew it would.

There were many he wished were here to witness his triumph: some, like his father, for revenge; his wife, for sentimental reasons; and others, for the pleasure of seeing their fury, their jealousy, that he had succeeded and they hadn't. The thought pleased him.

He looked at the line of windows on the southern side of the house. The wall was so long that they marched, identical in height and width, like glistening soldiers in the sunshine. So many rooms to own! He had not bothered to count them but his aim was to sleep in every bedroom – ideally with a different woman in each. That thought made him laugh, a deep, joyous sound that was taken by the wind and tossed towards the house. He saw a maid peer, astonished, from one of the windows.

He began to walk across the knot gardens, past the fountain, towards the maze, then turned to look at the house from a different angle. Without doubt, it was an amazing achievement: he had come here from a small semi-detached villa in the northern suburbs of London in the space of eighteen years.

He wished with all his soul that May was with him. His wife had never lost her faith in him when many had. A simple soul, she'd been always afraid she would let him down. 'They're buying my expertise and cunning, not my wife,' he had reassured her, not knowing in saying this he was making matters worse.

His shopkeeper father felt so strongly that May was not good enough for him that he had banned her from his house. Of course, Stanislas never went there either. The deathbed reconciliation had been, as far as he was concerned, a farce put on for the sake of his mother. It was as well his father had died: had he recovered he would have made Stanislas's life hell.

He had had to prove to the world that he was right in his choice of wife. He showered her with jewellery, dresses, hats and furs so that eventually she had had everything a grand lady would expect. They moved from one house to another, each larger and grander than the one before. But at each stage she became quieter, more distant from him. Not that he noticed: he was too engrossed in the pursuit of wealth – until the day she killed herself.

Grief and guilt nearly destroyed him. For a time he had forgotten his dream but then it had been the one thing that had galvanised him into more work, planning and scheming. He knew that it was because of May that he was here.

On the day of her death he had resolved never to fall in love again: the pain of loss was too much to bear. And he hadn't. He had had many women, his money saw to that, but he never gave them anything of his soul.

He began to walk back towards his fine new home. There was much of which May would not have approved. Success had changed him and he was harder than the man she had known and loved. He was ruthless, which she would not have liked. He was arrogant – she would have abhorred that.

And then there was their daughter, Esmeralda. May would have disapproved of the way Stanislas spoilt her, but he loved to be able to indulge her. His own mother said he was ruining her, but how could anyone be ruined by love? It was in his nature to give and in Esmeralda's to receive. They made a perfect couple.

'Sir! Sir!' His secretary was running towards him, waving papers.

'What now, Joynston?' There was almost a hint of weariness in his voice.

'I'm sorry to bother you, sir, especially today, but I've a communication from Bean and Walters in relation to the shipment of pig iron. They send fulsome apologies but it is delayed.'

'Then cancel it.' Stanislas put his hands behind his back, bowed his head and walked on. Joynston had not been with him long enough to know that this posture indicated he was not only angry but thinking hard.

'Cancel it, sir? At this late date?'

'Yes.'

'But how can we?'

'There was no cover for delay in the contract we signed.'

'But—'

'There are no *buts* in business, Joynston.'

'But the consignment?'

'There will always be others. And they will have learnt a lesson. They will not let me down again – when and if I give them a second chance.' He stopped dead so abruptly that the young man inadvertently overtook him. 'What do you think of my new house, Joynston?'

'It's very fine, sir.'

'Suitable for me?'

'No doubt about it.'

'Are the arrangements made for the ladies?'

'I gather so, sir.'

'I saw banks of white flowers growing down that way.' He pointed towards the kitchen gardens. 'I've no idea what they're called but I'd like large bunches picked and put in Miss Esmeralda's rooms to welcome her.'

'It will be my pleasure, sir.'

'I meant for the gardener to pick them, not you.'

'But of course, sir.' And he was hurrying away along the gravel path, coat flying, papers waving, a bit like the rabbit in that book he'd once read to his daughter. In fact, if he was honest, it was the *only* book he'd read to her. He watched as the figure disappeared into the house. Poor Richard Joynston. He was from a good family, but with no money, no prospects, just a willingness to please – and in love with Esmeralda. Not a hope in hell for him there. He doubted if she knew the secretary existed, and if she did, he'd never permit it. At the first spark of interest from her Joynston would be out of a job and moved a million miles away.

Stanislas had plans for Esmeralda. He had made sure she had been brought up correctly: he was no gentleman but she'd had the best education in how to be a lady that his wealth could buy. He lavished money on her so that she always looked a picture – her dress bills alone would support dozens of families for years. She moved, spoke, ate, drank, relaxed in a different way from any other woman in his family. No doubt she harboured dreams of marrying for love, but he would ensure that she married for standing and wealth.

The sound of a cavalcade of motors puttering up the long drive alerted him. He began to walk back to the main entrance. He did not hurry – they were still some distance away. He could imagine them peering out of the windows, breathless with excitement, wanting to be the first to get a glimpse of their new home. And what a view it was. They would chug round the steep bend – Clutter's it was called, he must find out why – then past fifty yards of giant rhododendron bushes, which formed a tunnel, and the house would emerge, through the stand of beeches, across the park, in all her beauty. Just like a lovely woman drawing back her veil. The house was more substantial and important to him than any woman, apart from Esmeralda – the ruler of his heart. He smiled at his sentimentality – this was all he ever allowed himself.

The cars ground to a halt. The chauffeur had no time to open the door before his daughter erupted from her vehicle, a tumbling mass of laughter, followed with more stately elegance by her companion.

Esmeralda engulfed him with kisses and hugs. 'I thought we'd never get here. It's been *such* a long journey. I'm quite fatigued.'

'Half an hour at least!' He laughed as, from the second car, the chauffeur helped his mother alight.

'It's the most wonderful house I've ever seen, just as you promised.'

Esmeralda was jumping from one foot to the other, so like a little girl. He hoped she would stay that way for ever. 'Don't I always keep my promises?'

'It's so big, Papa. Enormous. Grand. Exquisite!' Her wonderful dark eyes grew wider and larger at every exclamation.

'A suitable abode for my princess.' He swooped on her, lifted her off the ground and swung her in the air until she squealed with glee. 'So, what do you think, Mother?' he asked the small, plainly dressed woman standing silently on the forecourt.

'I think you might have overstretched yourself, Stan.'

'Dearest Mother. Trust you to rain on my fireworks.'
But he had expected no less from her. 'And Miss Beatty?'

'A very fine residence, Mr von Ehrlich. And I trust you
will all be most happy and content here.'

'Thank you. I hope we shall be here for ever more, and
that you will be with us.'

'We shall see,' said Agnes Beatty, as enigmatic as
always.

'So, ladies, shall we enter?' He held his arm wide, like a
guide at an historical monument in Rome, to shepherd
the women under the portico, through the large oak door
and into the front hall of Courtney Lacey.

'What are the flags, Papa?' Esmeralda pointed at the
tattered banners, high in the hammer-beam roof.

'Old battle honours.'

'But you never fought in a battle, Papa.'

'No, but neither did the man I bought them from.'

'And the paintings? Look at that creature. I swear he
has a cast in his eye.'

'Men of standing, no doubt.'

'Are they the ancestors of the man who sold you the
house?'

'No, he took his with him. I've no idea who these
people are but sooner or later everyone will think they're
ours.' He laughed. 'Shall we take tea in a little while in
the drawing room?' And he led the way up the wide oak
staircase. 'I can just see you floating down these stairs in
a ballgown, my darling.'

'When, Papa? Oh, yes, a ball! For me. How wonderful.
As soon as possible. Please!'

'But we don't know anyone to invite,' he said.

'We shall, Papa. We must meet people immediately.
Miss Beatty, do you know anyone in this vicinity?'

'A few.'

'Then you must invite them to tea. I insist.'

'That would not be correct. We should call on them
first and leave our cards.'

'But why? It could take *for ever*!'

'It is so that they can decide if they wish to receive you.'

'But they know you.'

'Of course, but they don't know you. I have told you, Esmeralda, you must learn to listen.'

'Yes, Miss Beatty.'

It never failed to amaze Stanislas that Agnes Beatty could control Esmeralda in a way he could not, even if he had wanted to. But that was what the woman was here for. Like his secretary, Agnes was from an impeccable family but as poor as a church mouse. What was the point of breeding if you couldn't afford anything? he thought. 'Do you like this room, Mother?' He indicated the upstairs drawing room, long casement windows on one side, dressed in heavy, slubbed silk curtains.

'It's not very cosy, is it?'

'Look at the ceiling, Mother.'

The plasterwork above them was intricately carved. It was pristine white and looked as if it were made of sugar by an expert confectioner, good enough to eat.

'A dust trap.' His mother sniffed.

'Since you won't be dusting it, there isn't a problem, is there?' He smiled at her. There were times when he would have liked to hit her.

The huge fireplace, in which, despite the time of year, a fire roared, was of white marble with a coat of arms carved in the front. When Stanislas was ennobled, as he was determined one day to be, he'd have a new one built.

'It's cold in here.'

'Mother, it isn't.'

'I hope those chandeliers won't fall on us. Crush you to death, they would.'

The crystal chandeliers, weighing several hundred-weight, were ablaze with light. The generator that had come with the house had been inadequate and he had replaced it with an enormous one, which, to his satisfaction, would take a small fortune to keep going.

'So, Mother?'

'It's very nice. I don't understand why you bought second-hand furniture when you could have had everything new from that nice Mr Gillow.' Winifred looked dismissively at the antiques, some of which her son had purchased with the house and others for which his agents had scoured the land.

'I like old things – that's why I love you so much!'

'None of your sauce!' She pushed him playfully.

Stanislas had reserved one of the towers for his own use because it was away from his mother, Agnes's superior gaze and Esmeralda's chatter. He had a suite of rooms there and he'd had a telescope installed on the highest level. It amused him to spend time surveying his land from this high vantage: it lay before him like a colourful tapestry. 'All mine,' he would say, as a satisfied smile played about his mouth.

He refocused the powerful telescope on a cloud of dust moving along the drive. 'Visitors!'

A slim and agile man, although he was in his middle years, he sped down the stairs, overtook the footman and wrenched open the mighty front door, surprising an astonished-looking coachman, whose hand was raised to bang the door knocker.

'Sir. Lord and Lady Prestwick.' He held out a card, the corner of which was neatly folded.

Stanislas did not bother to read it. He bounded down the steps two at a time, raced over the gravel and opened the carriage door, much to the consternation of the occupants.

'Lord and Lady Prestwick, what an honour! I'm so proud you favour me with your presence. Come in!' In one fluid motion Stanislas was lowering the carriage steps with the expertise of a coachman and making expansive gestures towards his open door.

'Well . . . Yes . . . Cards . . .' Theo Prestwick harrumphed.

'Stanislas von Ehrlich.' He shook the hands of the elderly man and his buxom wife – they had matching warts on their cheeks, he noticed, and matched in ugliness. Stanislas normally avoided unattractive people, unless business, or titles, was involved. 'Come,' he said.

'How very kind . . .' Dulcie Prestwick glanced uncertainly at her husband.

Theo levered his not inconsiderable bulk from the carriage, which swayed alarmingly. 'This is most decent of you, von Ehrlich. Come, my dear.' He held out his hand to his wife and the carriage continued to rock on its springs as he helped her down. Once she had alighted the oscillating body of the coach ground slowly to a halt.

Stanislas fussed back and forth as he led the way, unaware that his behaviour recalled that of a major-domo in a public restaurant.

'Since this was your family residence, there is no need to explain any of the house to you, my lord. You must regret its sale.'

'Not in the least. Best thing that could have happened. Never could stand the place. My late brother-in-law owned it. Left it to my son, you see.' He explained.

'You may show me since I have never been here before, Mr von Ehrlich,' Lady Prestwick told him.

'Never?'

'We are newly returned from our honeymoon.' She blushed.

'I hope you'll be happy here—' Theo began, but did not finish: a young woman was skimming down the stairs so fast her feet seemed barely to touch the treads.

'Visitors! How exciting! Hello . . . How do you do?' she said breathlessly, as she skidded to a halt in front of them.

'Esmeralda! Manners!' Stanislas attempted to sound cross but failed: he was laughing with delight as his daughter jumped up and down with glee. 'But I forget my own manners. Some refreshments.' Stanislas clicked his fingers at a footman standing by.

'It is most kind of you, von Ehrlich, but we are on our way to an appointment and we must not be late.'

'Have you far to go?' Stanislas looked bleak.

'To Cresswell Manor, to dine.'

'Our neighbours! But if you are held up you can telephone to tell them you are delayed. I gather they have an instrument too.' He brightened measurably at this idea.

'But we shall not be, so there will be no need,' Theo said firmly, though he smiled to offset the tension in his voice.

'A glass of Madeira? Sherry?' Again he clicked his fingers – an unfortunate gesture. 'You see, you would be our first guests.'

'In that case, we will stay just for five minutes. But there's no need for refreshments.' Leading the way, Stanislas was unaware of Theo's resigned expression as they climbed the stairs. 'Have you met the Cresswells?' he asked, once they were settled in the drawing room.

'Not yet, unfortunately. We have been here but a short time. No doubt we shall.'

When Agnes Beatty entered the room Theo Prestwick lumbered to his feet. She smiled in their direction and took a seat as far away as possible from the assembled company. She looked puzzled when no introductions were forthcoming.

'It was Cresswell's wretched son who bid against me and pushed the price of this estate through the roof.' Stanislas grinned.

'But much to my son's pleasure!' Theo rejoined.

Stanislas jumped to his feet and shook his hand with enthusiasm. 'I like a man who speaks the truth.' And he laughed, showing perfect white teeth. 'They say Sir Mortimer's a friend of the King. Is that so?'

'I gather he is. But rather him than me – an expensive hobby, the friendship of kings.'

'How wise you are, Lord Prestwick. Such friendships are not for me either,' Stanislas lied.

'Tell me, Lord Prestwick, is it true all the horror stories we have heard about the previous owner of this house? Young women being incarcerated and auctioned like furniture?' Esmeralda laughed gaily. There was an audible intake of breath from everyone else and Dulcie Prestwick grabbed her large tapestry bag as if it were a life-raft.

'Esmeralda!' Miss Beatty hissed.

'Where did you hear such rubbish?' Stanislas demanded.

'Everyone says it, Papa. I'm sure Lord Prestwick won't mind silly little me asking.' She giggled, a little nervously.

'If you will forgive us, Mr von Ehrlich, Miss von Ehrlich, madam,' he bowed in Miss Beatty's direction, 'we must leave. Come, my dear.'

Stanislas accompanied them to the hall, apologising for the tactlessness of youth and assuring them he had no idea what his daughter meant. Theo Prestwick reassured him that it did not matter – which they both knew was a lie.

Stanislas waved them on their way. As soon as the carriage had disappeared, he strode back into the house slamming the oak door. He thundered up the stairs and stormed into the drawing room. 'You stupid girl! How could you humiliate me so?'

'I didn't think.'

'You *never* think.'

'Oh, Papa, don't be so grumpy.'

He raised a fist.

'Mr von Ehrlich, have a care.' Agnes Beatty stepped forward.

He swung round to face her. '*Have a care* – you tell me? You are failing in your duties, madam!'

'Papa, please!' Esmeralda grabbed his sleeve. Agnes stood her ground, not a smidgen of fear in her eyes. 'I'm *so* sorry. I shall write tonight and beg forgiveness.'

'As well you might.' Stanislas turned on his heel, horrified by how close he had come to hitting his daughter.

'What are they like? Do tell.' Hannah was agog, and once their guests had settled she couldn't wait to hear their opinion of the new neighbours.

Dulcie and Theo looked at each other, as if hoping to sense what the other might be about to say. 'Well . . .' they said in unison.

'You first, my dear.'

'I couldn't possibly,' Dulcie demurred.

What a sweet couple they were, thought Hannah. She was glad that Theo Prestwick, whom she had known all her life, should be so patently happy. 'Ah, here's everyone else.' Hannah had been proud of how much better her father looked until she saw the shock on Theo's face. He had not seen his old friend since before his illness.

'Mortimer!'

'Theo!'

Once greetings and introductions to Dulcie had been made they all took their seats. Whitaker and Jock served tea.

'May I offer my congratulations on your marriage? Both Hannah and I were so sad to miss the wedding.'

'But your health is more important than that, Mortimer. Did you enjoy the South of France?'

'It was pleasant, but it's good to be home. Two months was too long to be away.'

'And Penelope, she is well?' Theo asked.

'Well . . .' Mortimer began, but fortunately there was an agitated flurry, as Coral and Mortie, newly returned

172

just as his father had predicted, swooped on the guests, prevented him saying more.

'A thousand apologies not to have been here to welcome you. I trust Hannah took care of you?' Coral wore her usual fixed social smile. 'We were just saying hello to the children. We've only just arrived from Cowes and the Royal Yacht.'

Hannah was embarrassed by Coral's boast.

'You look well, Mortie. Heavens, it must be a good fifteen years since I last saw you. When I left Courtney. Must be. Good Lor'! Time—'

'Don't mention time to Papa, sir. It's his enemy.' Mortie found this very funny and looked hurt when no one else did.

'It's the enemy of us all, Mortie.'

Mortie nodded sagely, even though he was unsure what was meant.

'Oliver, it's good to see you. I feared you would never return from your travels.'

'The lure of home became too great, sir.'

'Your father must be pleased to hear such sentiments. I was sorry you failed in your endeavours to purchase Courtney, dear boy.'

'It wasn't meant to be, sir. No doubt I shall find another.'

'So, you really intend to stay, Oliver?'

'Yes, Father.'

'Then I am more than content.' There was, Hannah was sure, a hint of tears in his eyes.

'I'm glad Oliver didn't succeed. It would have been so dull to have him as our neighbour rather than interesting strangers, don't you think?' Coral said brightly.

'I was asking our guests about our new neighbours, Papa. Are they pleasant?' asked Hannah.

'Are they suitable?' asked Coral.

Dulcie and Theo again looked at each other. 'It's

difficult to say, Hannah. They are not exactly . . . well . . . like us. Not quite sure how to put it.'

'Foreign, is he, with a name like that?'

'He sounds English, Mortimer. He has no accent.'

'Perhaps he calls himself that to make himself appear more interesting,' Oliver suggested.

'I can't see why he should feel the need to do so, Mr Oliver. He's very intriguing and has a strong presence. Wouldn't you agree, Theo?' Dulcie asked.

'I would, my dear. There's a charm about him, a spontaneity I rather liked.'

'I did feel that he might be trying too hard to impress – which is not a nice thing for me to say . . . I understood and felt sorry for him. Oh dear.' Dulcie looked anxious.

'But we asked your opinion, Lady Prestwick.'

'You did, Miss Cresswell, but I need not have given it.' Hannah was struck by how her plain face was lit by the sweetness of her smile.

'You said you understood him. Do enlighten us.' Coral's sharp voice made Dulcie stiffen visibly.

'What I mean . . .' She paused as if marshalling her thoughts, then sat up straight and continued. 'Our society is so rigid on who is acceptable and who isn't. No doubt Mr von Ehrlich knows full well that many won't accept him because he is in trade.'

'Trade! Whatever next?' Coral fanned herself, and Mortie laughed. Fortunately no one appeared to notice Hannah's discomfort that the very thing she had been thinking had now been said.

'I should point out that I, too, am *in trade*, Mrs Cresswell.'

'But it's different for you, Lady Prestwick. You have your husband's standing.'

'Ah, yes, but that is his, not mine, and there are some who will be happy to remember that.'

Dulcie looked at Coral with steel in her eyes and Hannah saw she would have to revise her first impression of the woman. She had strength that Hannah had not noticed at first.

'I'm sure I don't know about such weighty matters,' Mortimer put in. 'The one thing that concerns me is, do you make my friend Theo happy?'

'Happy, my dear Mortimer? I feel I have died and gone to heaven!'

'Oh, Theo!' Dulcie was overcome by the compliment.

'I thought your hotel amazingly comfortable and efficient, Lady Prestwick. In fact, so good that I would like to discuss with you various ideas I've had about hotels in general,' Oliver said.

'Thank you, Mr Oliver. One can never be sure with a new venture how it will be received. It will be my pleasure to discuss it with you.'

'We should all go there for luncheon or to dine.'

'In a restaurant, Sir Mortimer? I've never eaten in a public place.'

'Then it's time you did, Coral. We must move with the times. And all this talk of trade, who is and isn't acceptable, is pointless. Money has to come from somewhere.' He gazed at her sternly, but Hannah doubted she understood how rude she was being.

'We're trade. Cress-growers, that's us.' Mortie imparted this information helpfully, while his wife scowled at him.

'Really? How interesting.'

'Yes, Lady Prestwick. We have always owned the same cress beds, and it's where our name comes from. I can show you if you wish.' Mortie appeared quite animated.

'Lady Prestwick doesn't want to see boring old cress beds, Mortie,' Coral reproved him.

'Oh, but I do, Mrs Cresswell. Such matters are an endless source of fascination for me.'

'They are in a sorry state, I fear,' Oliver said.

'And does this Ehrlich man have other family?'

'His daughter is a lovely creature, Mrs Cresswell, but a little too forward for her own good,' Theo pronounced.

'Do you agree, Lady Prestwick?'

'She's a beautiful young woman but in perpetual motion, which might prove trying with time. And I'm not sure about the lisp – why do young girls play these games.' She chuckled, which, for Hannah, removed any hint of spite from her comments.

'Stunning dark eyes as well as the lisp?' Oliver asked.

'Yes.'

'His daughter!'

'Oliver! Do I note a hint of interest?' Coral teased him.

'I confess I'd jumped to the wrong conclusions. And was there another woman, dark too, foreign-looking?'

'There you have it, Oliver. Von Ehrlich didn't introduce her and we felt quite embarrassed for the poor woman, just sitting there unacknowledged, like a governess. But my wife and I decided she couldn't be that. She had too much style and was expensively dressed,' Theo told her. 'We cannot be sure, but we wondered if she was a companion.'

'Not his wife?'

'La, Oliver, yet more interest!' Coral laughed.

'I presume he would have introduced his wife. But, then, who knows with these coves?' Theo slapped his thigh and sent a side table flying. Objects skimmed this way and that, and in the mêlée of apologies and reassurances no one noticed that the gong to dress for dinner had sounded.

Below stairs there was a buzz of activity. This small party had come in the nick of time. With only Oliver in residence it had been many weeks since the last, and everyone had had too little to do.

'Idle hands, Mrs Fuller, idle hands,' the butler was heard to say, so many times that everyone's patience was stretched to the limit. Mrs Gilroy had suffered most – she had thrown several tantrums.

'What's the point of my life?' After one port too many, the cook had been found, several times, slumped over her kitchen table bewailing her fate.

'Now, now, Eve, don't take on so. The family being away has a great advantage. It gives us all time for a nice tidy!' Mrs Fuller had said cheerfully each time, in an effort to chivvy her along.

'If you say that once more I'll – I'll – boil your flaming head!' Whenever she shouted this, Mrs Gilroy banged on the table so that the flour sifter, the pepper pot and the salt box jiggled. Mrs Fuller might have pointed out that she wasn't the only one repeating herself. She decided to have a word with Mr Whitaker.

'Edward, this can't continue. Eve is likely to have a seizure if she carries on like this. And the drinking! It's all too much.'

'There, Mrs Fuller,' Whitaker had said – he still found it uncomfortable to use the Christian names the women preferred. 'It won't be long now and they'll all be back.' And the housekeeper had noticed a glazed look in the butler's eyes, and that his colour was unnaturally high. He had evidently been at the Madeira. There was only one thing for her to do: she turned to the sherry.

There was a sigh of relief when the telegram had arrived to say Sir Mortimer and Hannah were returning from the South of France where they had been staying with his sister, who was married to a Frenchman. But peace had been short-lived below stairs: Lavender, who had accompanied her mistress, had regaled them all with the superiority of French cuisine.

'Who wants to eat food that's been mucked about?' Mrs Gilroy stood with her arms akimbo.

'But, Eve, you've no idea—'

'I've *every* idea. Food is what I know about. Meat what's orf, smeared with sauces to disguise the taste, that's what you've been consuming, Lavender. Slugs and snails and puppy dogs' tails, that's what Frenchmen are made of!'

'Oh, Eve, you are a card!'

'Then you won't be wanting any of my cooking, then? Won't be good enough now you've turned into a Frenchie.'

'Of course it will. There's no cooking as good as yours.' Hurriedly Lavender made amends.

A week after Sir Mortimer's return the dinner for the Prestwicks had been arranged. The maids rushed about with piles of linen, buckets of coals, ewers of water, closely followed by Mrs Fuller, who checked all their activities with gimlet eyes.

'What's the new Lady Prestwick like, Edward?' she asked, as they passed in the corridor, going in opposite directions, he with a tantalus to be filled, she with a bunch of flowers to be arranged.

'Trade, Mrs Fuller.'

'Never!'

'It's all those changes you keep going on about. She isn't the part, doesn't even look it. Tragic, in my opinion . . .'

The menu for the dinner was pinned to the kitchen noticeboard. Dolly, who could read and was proud of it, had studied it with great interest. 'So much food for so few people, it's disgusting,' she said to Jose later, as they prepared the last of the vegetables. The gardener had moaned when Mrs Gilroy decided that carrots, peas, broad beans and cauliflower were not enough and sent him to pick some runner beans. Dolly was slicing them into the finest slivers. She'd already let the knife slip twice and had had to bandage a finger, which stuck up awkwardly.

'Gluttons, all of them,' said Jose.

'And why do they need soup, then the entrées, then a second course?'

'I said, they're gluttons.'

'And why, if they'm having lamb, do they need chicken too?'

'Don't forget the fish, all the puddings and the dessert.'

'And why do them end with cress? Cress is for sandwiches.'

'Not here it isn't. They eat it right at the end to cleanse the palate so the port tastes good with the nuts and the cheese.'

'How do the women stay so thin, then? If I ate like that I'd be as big as a tram in a week.'

'They play with it, pretend to eat it – shocking waste it is. I don't know why Mrs Gilroy doesn't throw it at them. You watch – half the plates come back with the food still on them. Them as eats then goes and tickles their throats with feathers.'

'Like the Romans? To make themselves sick?'

'You do know a lot of pointless things, Dolly. What use is that in a kitchen?'

'Not a lot, but I hope to do something with it one day. And when I'm a mother, I'll be more interesting for my children. All my mum talks about is making jam, washing, and how hard done by she is – I don't want to be like that.'

'My mother says books are dangerous and they don't do you no good.'

'There are days when it's a good thing to get carried away, especially when old Gilroy's throwing one of her huffs. I can escape in my reading.'

'If she finds you with your nose in a book she'll box your ears with it.'

'No, she won't – Miss Hannah gives me books to read. She wouldn't dare.'

'How's that?'

'One day she saw me on the back steps reading the

newspaper before I lined the bins with it and she asked me if I liked to read and I said yes, and she said she'd send down some books for me and she did. What's more, she said I could keep them if I wanted. So there.'

'What's Ferdie think of it, then?'

'He gets fed up. Says I'm turning into a bookworm. But, oh, Jose, when I gets me nose in I can go anywhere, be anyone. Leave all this behind.' And she indicated the bleak scullery, which even in summer was still cold and damp.

'How are you and Ferdie doing?'

'All right.'

'You done it yet?'

'Done what?' Dolly looked innocent, while knowing full well what Jose meant.

'You know, let him get in your knickers.'

Dolly shrieked. 'No, I have not, and if I had, do you think I'd be stupid enough to tell you?'

'What you waiting for? I have.' Jose looked dreamy.

Dolly laid down her vegetable knife. 'Jose, you silly girl. What did you do that for?'

'If you don't know then there's no point in explaining, is there?' She giggled. 'It just sort of happened. One night – you know how it is, and we started . . . and Jock . . . Well, I couldn't stop him and, truth be told, I didn't want to. And wham bang! We'd done it.'

'Jose!' Dolly was wide-eyed with horror. 'He won't respect you.'

'I don't bloody care, not when he can make me feel like he does!' She laughed.

'You're mad!'

'No, I'm not. Jock says he's going to marry me.'

'And you believe him? Why would he bother when he can get it without?'

'That's an awful thing to say.'

'It's the truth, though. And even if he did marry you,

how would you survive? They don't allow married couples here.'

'Other places take couples.'

'And what sort of establishments do you think they are? Low class, I'll be bound – nothing like this. You'd be going down not up.'

'Well, it's none of your business, is it?'

'I thought we were friends.'

'What's that got to do with it?'

'You look out for your friends, least you do in my book.' There were tears in Dolly's eyes.

'Oh, Dolly, I'm sorry. Don't be cross with me. I love him, that's the simple truth, and I wanted you to know.' And she tumbled into Dolly's arms just as a red-faced Mrs Gilroy appeared.

'Game chips!' she screamed at her kitchenmaid.

In the drawing room Coral had automatically taken charge, pouring the camomile tea herself. Hannah tried not to look disgruntled. Coral *was* Mortie's wife and all this *would* be hers one day, she reasoned, but her resentment was growing. Coral was older by three years but this was Hannah's domain.

'Are you sure you wouldn't like a small glass of champagne, *Lady* Prestwick?'

'I am more than content with this delicious tea, Mrs Cresswell. Such lovely carnations. Are they Malmaison?'

'They are,' Hannah said. 'No matter where I am, when I smell Malmaison I think of home. My aunt in France said the same.'

'Isn't memory wonderful? When I smell lilies I am transported to my hotel.'

'Oliver is so impressed by your hotel. It's a big compliment for he's stayed in the very best around the world,' Hannah told her.

'It has been an exciting venture.'

'But aren't you afraid, *Lady* Prestwick? You can't

know who your guests are. I could never stay in the same building as strangers. Such a dangerous business to be involved in. If it failed, are you not afraid of . . .' Coral's voice trailed off.

'Losing everything?' Dulcie smiled her disarming smile. 'No, I'm not concerned.'

'I expect your involvement was thrust upon you at the sad demise of your late husband. Just a few months ago, wasn't it?'

'He had barely started on his plans. The decisions were all mine.'

'How extraordinary. And I learnt that you own the large shop in Barlton – always surprisingly well stocked.'

'Randall's Emporium. Yes, that's correct.'

'A woman of substance!'

'I am.' Dulcie looked amused.

'Was the shop your husband's?'

'No.'

'How extraordinary!'

'It might appear to be extraordinary to you, Mrs Cresswell, but I've been out of step with my sex all my life. I am never what people expect. And, incidentally, my husband died over a year ago. I don't know why but people seem to think it was only yesterday and that I wed my present husband in too much haste.' She turned to Hannah, who was blushing for Coral. 'You were going to show me the plans of your new house, Miss Cresswell?'

'Are you sure you want to see them?'

'I wouldn't if I were you, *Lady* Prestwick. They're tedious and dear Hannah becomes so in the showing.'

Hannah loathed the way Coral had the ability to say *Lady*, as if she was laughing while keeping a straight face. It made her want to protect Dulcie Prestwick.

'Architecture is of great interest to me,' Dulcie told Coral.

'Your Graceteign is such a beautiful property. As a

child I often went there for tea with my grandmother. I remember the most wonderful garden . . .' As she spoke, Hannah was laying out the plans for the new dower house on a card table.

'It is a jungle now but we intend to restore it.'

'And the giant bronze stag?'

'Still guarding us.'

Coral rose to her feet, barely suppressing a yawn. 'If you'll excuse me, I must go to my little ones.'

Hannah stifled a grin. Coral didn't bother with her children from one month to the next, but with guests she found it necessary to pretend that she did.

'I do hope Coral did not offend you with her questioning. She tends to speak without thinking.'

'How kind of you, but I think she knows exactly what she's saying.' Again that smile removed all reproach.

'She has a tendency to see problems before they emerge.'

'Have you not noticed that those who have too little to do have a much greater tendency to pessimism? I'm sure she meant well.'

'It's just that she . . .' Hannah began, then changed her mind. She did not know Dulcie well enough to confide in her. Nor should she be disloyal: Coral was her sister-in-law, even if she didn't like her.

'It will be easier for you when you have your own house,' Dulcie said. Hannah looked at her with surprise. It was as if she had read her thoughts. 'I'm sorry, I shouldn't have said that.'

'No, I don't mind. It's true. I'm mistress here for most of the year and then it's taken away from me. I have to admit I do resent it somewhat.' She laughed to cover her embarrassment at her confession. 'But although I am excited by the new house I dread the day I move. It will mean that my dear papa is no more.'

'Won't your stepmother move there with you?'

Hannah looked at the older woman, weighing her up.

'She won't be with me since she and my father have separated,' she said, in a rush.

There was an almost imperceptible pause. 'I did wonder . . . Before dinner . . .' And Hannah understood that this innocent-seeming woman had manoeuvred the conversation, and found she did not mind. 'I do think it's brave of them. It is so tragic if people who do not care for each other are forced by society to continue to live together. So much unhappiness could be avoided.' There was an expression on Dulcie's face that made Hannah wonder if she was speaking from an experience in her past. 'I have heard it said that the death of a dear one is preferable to the scandal of a divorce, but I cannot agree with that.'

'They won't divorce, I'm sure of that.' The very idea made Hannah feel cold – the shame it would bring, the scandal. 'But everything would be easier if everyone thought like you. Poor Papa has lost many friends.'

'Then they weren't true friends.'

'He is no longer welcome at Court.'

'Which, no doubt, saves him a lot of expenditure.' They giggled. 'There is so much that is wrong in our society, don't you think?'

'In what way?' As far as Hannah was aware there was little wrong with her way of life, apart from her relationships with Penelope and Coral.

'There should be a fairer distribution of wealth. It is not right that we have so much when many have so little.'

'Of course,' Hannah agreed, but was not sure why. It wasn't a matter to which she had given thought. The Cresswells looked after their tenants: was more expected of them?

'I am sure you noticed your sister-in-law's reaction to the fact that I own my businesses. Now, why should that be?'

'It is unusual.'

'Exactly. But why should it be so?' Dulcie had flushed

with excitement as she warmed to her theme. 'For years I lived a normal life for a woman of my station, until circumstances forced me into business. And although it is wrong to boast, I have to say that I am very good at it. What saddens me – no, annoys me – is all the years when I could have been doing exactly that and was deprived of my vocation.'

'But you did many other good things. I've heard of your home for orphans and the library for the poor. So commendable.'

'My point is that I wasn't allowed a choice. As you weren't. We simply accepted that we women should not do such things, as if our brains were incapable of considering serious matters.'

'Certainly when my brothers went away to university I envied them and wished I could go.'

'And I suspect you wish that you had had the same schooling as they.'

'I do. I find it so confining merely to have had a governess – even though mine was sweet to me. There are many things I would like to have learnt. I'd like to be able to contribute something.'

'Exactly!' Dulcie clapped her small, pretty hands. 'The next generation must be allowed to fly free, be given opportunities. How I wish I was younger – I would be so involved in changing things. Perhaps . . . I have some interesting pamphlets if you would like to read them?'

'I would. What are they about?'

'Many things. Inheritance for one. Why shouldn't women have the same inheritance rights as men?'

'In what way?'

'Why should primogeniture not apply to women? Then this, since you are your father's firstborn, would all be yours and you wouldn't need to move into the lovely house you are having built.'

'I had never given thought to such a radical idea.'

But they could not pursue this topic any further for the

door opened: they were joined by the gentlemen and a happier-looking Coral.

Hannah, though tired, could not sleep. Her mind was whirling with so many ideas, most of them new to her. She was thinking about Dulcie Prestwick, how interesting and unusual she was. She had never met anyone like her in her life. She wondered if she was unique or if there were many women like her. She was physically unattractive, yet her manner and spirit surmounted this. She seemed straightforward but was far from that – Hannah had marvelled at her sharpness. She observed so much and reached logical conclusions quickly. In fact, Hannah thought, she had a mind like a man's. She smiled in the darkness: she doubted Dulcie would regard that as a compliment.

And she would be right. All her life Hannah had thought men superior to her in intelligence and ability. But where had such an idea come from? Nanny, of course, had worshipped her brothers, and Hannah had been brought up to regard marriage as her destiny, that it was best for her, a woman. That she had not found a husband labelled her a failure to many people. Her father's separation from his wife would lessen her chances of marrying, for what respectable man would wish to be involved with a family tainted by such scandal? It was strange how little that seemed to matter now.

The way her thoughts were developing was interesting. She turned over and closed her eyes, but sleep was still elusive. Dulcie had appeared such a docile little woman yet she was quite revolutionary. She had silenced the table when she had launched into a passionate defence of the emancipation of women. When Mortie had snorted with derision and pointed out that women would not understand enough of politics to be given the vote, Dulcie's pitying look had made everyone else laugh.

There was no doubt left in those present as to who, of the two, had the greater intelligence.

All these new ideas had touched a nerve in Hannah. Once the things had been said, they seemed so obvious. She wondered why she couldn't have thought them for herself. She was in a more favourable position than most women. She was unmarried and thus had no husband or children to consider. Compared with most, she was free – she could do as she liked. She was even more fortunate than many since she had money of her own. In the unlikely event that her father disowned her, she had the wherewithal to survive. Thanks to her mother, she needed no man to support her. She had never considered this before. She was already an independent woman and had not realised it. What she did with her inheritance was up to her.

She was not discontented – far from it. She was happy most of the time. She had a good life and had come to terms long ago with her childlessness. But this evening's conversation had shown her that the irritating feeling she sometimes had of dissatisfaction, and which she had never understood, might be because she needed to do something else. She must look beyond running someone else's house and caring for someone else's children! Good heavens! She had never thought like this. Perhaps a degree of selfishness might be a good thing after all.

But she had no skills, no talents, no training. Certainly she could never run a business because she had no head for figures – balancing the household accounts was always a nightmare for her. She painted moderately well, but could never teach the subject or sell her work. She hadn't the patience to write a novel, as her aunt was attempting to do. She couldn't cook. She knew how to run a large house and deal with servants, but her father would never agree to her running a stranger's house or, God forbid, a hotel! Of course, there were always good works – perhaps she could help Dulcie there. But was that what she really needed? What else was there? She knew about gardening.

At that she sat bolt upright in bed. That was something she knew a lot about. Over the years she had been tutored and guided by the gardeners, and had planned and planted the Cresswell Manor gardens, which everyone admired. She slumped back on the pillows. But how could she make a career out of it? Everyone she knew had lovely gardens, so no one would need her advice. Unless ... Hadn't Dulcie Prestwick said her garden was a jungle? She could approach her and suggest it. Of course she would do it for nothing – talking about a fee would be too embarrassing. She resolved to speak to Dulcie before the Prestwicks left in the morning.

She got up and padded into her sitting room. On her desk was the household ledger, which she should have completed yesterday. She sighed as she opened it. It wasn't just that she hated doing sums, it was the state of the shopkeepers' receipts – fish scales invariably clung to the fishmonger's and blood smeared the butcher's . . .

'Very satisfactory.' Whitaker sorted one key from the large bunch he carried, unlocked a small metal cash box and put into it the money the staff had received from the Prestwicks. It would be his task later to share it among them, according to the rules he had devised. Only staff who had had personal contact with the guests were eligible, except Mrs Gilroy, who was regarded as a special case. The largest share went to the senior members. It never crossed his mind that this might be unfair: there were many who received nothing and it was a constant source of disgruntlement with them.

'How satisfactory?' asked Mrs Fuller.

'Most.' He slammed the lid of the box, locked it and placed it in the silver vault, which led off his office. His secrecy about the tips led to a degree of suspicion: Lavender, Mrs Fuller and Mrs Gilroy often wondered if he wasn't pilfering some for himself – not that they had ever confided in each other.

'His lordship couldn't have afforded a gratuity of that magnitude a few months ago – right up Queer Street he was.' He sat down at his desk. 'Take a seat, Mrs Fuller.'

'Thank you, *Edward*.' She made a fuss of sitting, hoping he would notice her. He didn't. 'He's done well for himself, hasn't he?'

'As has she – marrying into the nobility and looking as she does.'

'He's no oil painting.' Mrs Fuller felt quite offended for her ladyship.

'No one would have married her if she hadn't as much as she has, that's for sure,' Whitaker remarked.

'They seem happy together.'

'Anyone could be happy if they have enough funds.'

'Really, Edward, I'm surprised at your cynicism.'

'I speak as I find.'

'Of course, had it not been for her age, the speed with which they married might have had tongues wagging even more.' She looked arch.

'A year only.' The butler pursed his lips. 'Unseemly.'

'I heard she didn't even go into half mourning but straight from black into her bridal gown.'

'It makes you wonder what's happening to our world, Mrs Fuller. Mind you, I don't see what age has to do with it.'

'I meant that a year is a long time at their stage in life.'

'In my opinion there are no exceptions.'

'Still, we don't know all the facts, do we?'

'But someone of breeding would have respected the niceties.'

'Hasn't his lordship breeding enough, then? After all, what's sauce for the goose . . .' She wagged a finger at him.

'Now, how may I help you, Mrs Fuller?' he barked.

'It's an unfortunate matter.' She looked suitably

demure. 'It's about Jock. I think you might have to speak to him. He's up to no good.'

'Jock is a fine footman. He has a great future ahead of him.' The butler was immediately on the defensive.

'Not if he indulges in hanky-panky with one of my girls, he won't.'

In slow motion Whitaker removed his spectacles and cleaned the lenses. 'I don't believe it,' he said at length. If it was possible to sit to attention that was what he was doing now. 'If there's anything going on – and you would have to prove it to me – then it's because your girl has been bothering him.'

'*Bothering him!* You don't seem to understand me, Mr Whitaker. He has been chasing her.'

'Who?'

'The kitchenmaid.'

'I don't believe it. Jock has far too much class to consort with a *kitchenmaid*! It can't be true – he'd be risking his career.'

'He started as a hall-boy so there's little difference between them, except age. And Jose is a good girl, who could go far too, if she's not led astray by such as he.'

'She can't be that good if she's got her claws into my boy.'

Mrs Fuller got to her feet. 'Very well. There appears to be no point in pursuing this conversation, *Mr Whitaker*. If you won't speak to him then I shall have to go to Miss Hannah and tell her.'

'You can't speak of such matters to a lady.'

'You give me no alternative.' She swung round to leave.

Whitaker got to his feet. 'Very well, Mrs Fuller. I'll have a word with him, if you think it necessary. But the solution would seem to be to dismiss the girl. It'll be—'

'Please, don't say it, Mr Whitaker, you've said enough.'

As she swept along the lower corridor, her chatelaine

clanking, she was muttering, unaware of the maids who were giggling at the state she was in.

'I shall never understand that man!' she said, as she stormed into the kitchen. 'How dare he?'

'How dare who?' Mrs Gilroy looked up from the steak and kidney pie she was decorating with pastry leaves.

'Edward. He's blaming it all on our Jose.'

'And quite right too. Forward little minx.'

'We don't know that, Eve.'

'We can guess, though, can't we? She's got a bold eye on her.'

'I expected better from you, Eve.'

'She knew the rules. She broke them. She'll have to go.'

At this, a great wailing noise came from the corner of the kitchen. 'I didn't see her there,' said Mrs Fuller, looking at the huddled figure of Jose, who was making sandwiches.

'You needn't expect any sympathy from us, young woman. You should have kept yourself proper instead of behaving like a tart,' Mrs Gilroy yelled across at her.

'But I didn't. We did nothing.'

Dolly had just entered the kitchen and looked at Jose with amazement.

'Honest, Mrs Fuller. I haven't done nothing wrong. I can't be sent away. My mum'll kill me.'

'You should have thought of that! You knew what Lady Cresswell expected from her staff,' Mrs Gilroy snapped.

'Her ladyship can get up to all sorts, then, but no one else can?' Jose was defiant.

'How dare you be so forward-speaking of your mistress?'

'Well, she isn't my mistress no more, is she?' Jose said belligerently.

'What do you think, Hilda?' Mrs Fuller asked.

'I don't think an accusation is sufficient for someone to lose their position. This is gossip.'

'Gossip? I saw them with my own eyes – spooning, they were.' Mrs Gilroy slammed her rolling-pin on to her pastry board with a crack.

'A kiss doesn't prove anything,' said Mrs Fuller.

'With a footman? Disgusting!'

'It weren't disgusting. It were lovely. There were nothing wrong in it. We love each other – we want to be together for ever.'

'Depraved, you are,' Mrs Gilroy told her.

Jose whipped off her apron and flung it on to the table. 'And what about you? I've seen you making sheep's eyes at Mr Whitaker. You're just going for me because you can't get what you want.'

'You lying bitch! You speak to me like that again and I'll slap you good and proper!'

'You lay one finger on me and I'll have the law on you.'

'Jose!' Dolly said, in a barely audible whisper.

'And I'll tell you what's more! You and Mrs Fuller here, you're both wasting your time, it's Lavender he likes. So there!'

'Mrs Fuller, what do you intend to do about her?'

'Go to your room this instant, Jose.'

'I'll go when I'm good and ready.'

'Jose!' Dolly tugged at her sleeve, but Jose was past hearing.

'You're a bad-tempered old witch. No one likes you, with your shouting and swearing. And you're a rotten cook!'

'That's too much!' Mrs Gilroy shouted, picked up the pie she had been trimming and threw it at Jose, who ducked. It hit the wall.

'You're dismissed, young woman,' Mrs Gilroy shouted.

'No, I ain't. I'm walking!'

'Well, did you ever!' the housekeeper exclaimed.

'In all my years, I never heard the like of it.'

'She's such a pleasant girl too,' Hilda said, in a voice tinged with regret.

'For her sake, I hope she isn't up the duff.'

'But she said she hadn't done anything wrong.'

'And you believed her? Oh, Hilda, I sometimes think if the devil walked in you'd say, "What a nice man," and give him one of your pastries. Dolly!' Mrs Gilroy shrieked.

A frightened-looking Dolly came back into the kitchen from the scullery. 'Clear that mess up. I'll have you know, it was our lunch. It'll have to be leftovers now. And, Dolly, you're the new kitchenmaid.'

'Me?'

'Don't be idiotic, child. Who else?'

'But poor Jose, it might all blow over. She might come back.'

The cook put her hands on her hips. 'You listen to me, my girl. Nothing's going to blow over. She'll be gone by evening and let that be a warning to you. And don't cry. If there's one thing I can't stand it's a crying kitchen-maid.'

Jock sat on the bench outside Mr Whitaker's pantry, his palms damp with sweat, his stomach churning. He'd have had to be deaf not to hear the shemozzle which had come out of the kitchen half an hour ago.

'Jock.' The butler, immaculate as ever in his morning uniform of black jacket and pinstriped trousers, appeared at the door. 'Come.'

Jock stood in front of the desk. 'You know why you're here?'

'Yes, sir, but I—'

Mr Whitaker held up his hand to stop him. 'I never listen to gossip. I asked you to come here to answer one question. Did you have carnal knowledge of Jose Beasley?'

'No, sir.'

'Which is exactly what I thought. You cannot be too careful, Jock. Keep any conversation to business matters with these young women. You're a good-looking fellow and, from my experience, I have observed these maids have feverish imaginations. You have a good career ahead of you. Don't risk it.'

'No, sir.'

'That will be all.'

'Thank you, sir.'

Outside the butler's pantry Jock leant against the wall for a second, then whistled his relief at his narrow escape. He strutted back to the footmen's room. There, he put on the green felt overall he wore for cleaning the silver and took up where he had left off. A little later he glanced up to see Jose at the door, her face tear-stained. 'Yes?'

'I've been given the push – or, rather, I gave myself the push before Mrs Gilroy could.'

'Was that wise?'

'What do you mean?'

'What about your character letter? No one will take you on without one.'

'I'll find something. I'll buy a newspaper. We'll get positions somewhere.'

'We? But I've got a place here.'

'You won't want to stay after the way I've been treated, will you?'

'I'm not losing out because you couldn't keep your knickers on.' He picked up his yellow buffing cloth.

'Jock! You're not saying these things.'

'You knew if we were caught you'd be dismissed.'

'And what about you?'

'I was lucky. Whitaker believed me, and your lot didn't believe you, did they? But even if he hadn't it's doubtful he'd have dismissed me. I'd have said you led me on with your wicked ways.' He laughed. He could see that Jose was bewildered.

'But I love you,' she said.

'And I don't love you.'

'But you said!'

'I said a lot of things. It didn't mean I meant them.'

Her hand moved so quickly that he didn't see her pick up the knife and fling it. It was only when it was about to pin his hand to the table that he moved. He was lucky: the knife only nicked him but blood spurted everywhere.

'Bitch!' he shouted.

'Bastard!' she countered.

Chapter Seven
August 1901

Of all the days of the week Melanie loathed Monday more than any other. As her mother and grand-mother had always done, so did she – the washing. Having collected a bucket of water from the communal pump in the village she now hauled it on to the brick copper, which was so large it took up a third of the space in the room – she hated it. To get the water hot enough she had to have it lit by six in the morning. It was not the easiest fire to light and keep in. To ensure the draw she had to have the door open to the yard, no matter the weather, which added to the discomfort.

She stood on a small rattan stool to remove the wooden lid and was enfolded in a cloud of steam. With a wooden stave, she swirled the clothes about in the soapy water. She hated the smell of boiling clothes, she hated the steam making her hair lank and dull, she hated everything about Monday.

'Still, they says as it's good for the complexion,' Flossie Marshall had told her encouragingly this morning, when she had dropped off her own washing. She hadn't a copper, and Melanie, taking pity on her, had offered to put some of Flossie's bits in with hers. Flossie's pile was much larger than she had anticipated and she was regretting her impulsive gesture – God knew when she would be finished.

If anything, Bernard loathed Mondays even more than she did. He complained about the upheaval, the smell of damp washing, the fact that his dinner would be cold meat and baked potatoes. If it was raining, his moaning reached a crescendo: he disliked having clothes and linen draped everywhere to dry. He would usually round off his grumbling by telling her what a mess she looked. It was, she had decided, the only day he even noticed her.

Of all the things Melanie could complain about it was that for the rest of her life she knew what she would be doing and when. On Tuesdays she'd be ironing everything she'd washed on the Mondays – if anything, it was more tiring than the washing, standing for so long in one place and lifting the heavy irons from the range. She stabbed at the grey water as if it was its fault she had so much to do. They'd have chops, two veg and a steamed pudding for Tuesday's midday dinner.

Wednesdays she'd be doing the bedrooms, cleaning and scrubbing every surface in the fond hope that she'd get rid of the damp smell which permeated everything. They'd have stew and treacle tart.

Thursdays she would be in the garden trying to coax more vegetables to grow. She resented the garden: if Bernard had worked hard she wouldn't have minded caring for it, but as he did as little as possible, she felt it should be his responsibility, not hers. They would have boiled ham and jam tarts.

On Fridays for ever more she would take whatever vegetables and eggs she could spare to the market in Cress. They would have fish – whatever was cheapest in the market – then bread and jam. If she had done well with her sales she might buy some fruit, but invariably she hadn't enough money.

On Saturdays she would be cleaning and scrubbing the downstairs room, the small porch, the front doorstep, the kitchen and the scullery, in case anyone called the next day – not that anyone ever did, but like her mother and grandmother that was what Saturdays were for. They would eat eggs and streaky bacon, then suet pudding with jam.

Sundays she did nothing – according to her husband. A

day of rest, he called it, while she cooked the big meal of the week: the roast and a tart. She would do the sewing and make any repairs, then sort the washing for Monday. Round and round. She went from one week to the next, like an animal in a cage, and would until she was an old woman – if she lived that long.

She swore when she saw she had let the fire get too low, and added more kindling. And yet she shouldn't feel sorry for herself: they were luckier than most – they had plentiful food on the table. She had to be careful, but they could manage on Bernard's wage despite his drinking. Her time in Plymouth had shown her what real poverty was like. She could never go back to that, and the constant fear that she would not have enough to feed the children. She had learnt how tenuous their hold on life was when there was not sufficient to eat and thus fight illness, which was a constant threat.

She had not wanted to return to Cresswell and face her parents' intractable attitude to her, but she'd had no choice. Here they were safe: no one starved on the estate, while those who were old and pensioned had a roof over their heads until the end. Even the poorest, like Flossie, were given food from the kitchens of the big house.

Despite her husband, she had considered herself fortunate until she had helped to nurse Sir Mortimer. Before that, her life had been as it was now, and she had accepted it. Since her stay in the house her discontent had grown. She was turning into a miserable, moaning woman, which was not what she wanted to be. It was as if a window had opened and she had seen what life could be like, which made her lot seem worse.

'You've got your health, that's what matters,' Flossie, with a wise old head on young shoulders, had said, when Melanie had confided in her. Melanie thought only that good health would simply prolong her misery.

'Of course, if you were happier with Bernard you'd be happier in yourself, wouldn't you?'

'Would I?'

'Oh, yes. I wouldn't swap my Alf and my life with him for all the silks and satins in the world.'

It wasn't the silks and satins Melanie wanted, or to be part of the Cresswell family – too many of them hated and plotted against each other. What was it she didn't have now that was causing this dissatisfaction? 'It's not their possessions I want. It's the orderliness of their lives, the cleanliness. They live in a world of light and sparkle.'

'Achieved by others working their arses off.' Flossie chortled.

'That's true.'

'You'd feel guilty having others wait on you.'

'Maybe, but I think it's a guilt I could learn to control. They have time, Flossie. Time to get up, wash and dress, time to sit and read, time to do whatever they want and not what's expected.'

'Except they're probably expected to do other things.'

'Such as?'

'Visit the sick, play Lady Bountiful, go to church, write letters . . .' She pulled a face. 'I'd hate to have to write letters.'

'It isn't fair, though, is it, that they should have so much compared with others?'

'Fair? What's fair in this world? Nah, it don't bother me. While they've got what they've got, at least my Alf can make a living.'

'But think how much he does and how much he gets for it. While they sit on their thousands of pounds.'

'But they aren't going to give me their money, are they? And if they shared it out with everyone, with all the people what live in this here country, we'd probably end up with two pence. They're welcome to it, as long as my Alf gets his wage.'

Of course, what Flossie had said was true, Melanie thought, as she carried another basket of washing out to the line – at least the sun was shining and there was a good drying breeze. But being true didn't make it right. What she'd have liked to know was why her family and the Cresswells, living here side by side since time began, had not had equal good fortune. 'Brains,' she said aloud. 'Or cunning.'

If it wasn't for Timmy ... She stood up straight, looking out over the view across the Cresswell land, regarded as one of the finest in the kingdom. If it wasn't for Timmy she'd go. She'd pack a bag, slip away in the night and never look back.

But she couldn't go, there was her younger son. Just thinking of running away was dangerous: today she could not imagine resenting Timmy but—

'Mum!' He was running across the back garden to her. 'Mum, Miss Crick wants to see you.'

'Why? What have you done?'

'Nothing.' He sounded affronted, then grinned.

'Do you know why?'

'She just said to ask you to see her. She said as when you're good and ready, but she's there now.'

Melanie looked down at her damp apron and patted her bedraggled hair. 'Now?'

'Please.' She looked at her son's anxious expression. She did not want anyone to see her looking like this but perhaps she'd better go. If she didn't she'd only fret to know what it might be about – as Timmy was already. In the house she changed into her best dress and brushed her hair. She had unruly curls she had never been able to control. 'You stay here. I won't be long.'

Miss Crick was at her desk in the schoolroom, checking the writing on the slates. 'Mrs Topsham, I'm glad you could come.'

'I'm sorry I look a bit of a mess. Washing, you understand. But I thought I'd best come straight away, then I need not worry.'

'There's nothing to worry about, quite the contrary. Timmy's a bright boy, Mrs Topsham.' Melanie smiled with pride. 'He has an enquiring mind and is eager to learn.'

'He's always been the same. If he gets his head into a book you can forget talking to him until it's finished.'

'He has a good chance of being awarded a scholarship to the grammar school in Barlton.'

'You think so?' Melanie's heart lifted.

'I'd be surprised if he wasn't.'

'Then he should be given the chance. There's just . . .'

'The cost?' Miss Crick smiled at her. 'His tuition would be free – it's an excellent school. The main expense would be his uniform, pen and pencils. And, of course, his travelling costs to Barlton each day. I have ascertained that there is a train from Cress that would get him there in the morning and home in the evening. It would be a great chance for him.'

'I would have to discuss this with my husband.'

As she walked home Melanie's mind was in turmoil. How was it to be managed? One of her greatest dreams was that Timmy should have an education that matched his brother Zephaniah's – the unfairness of their situation haunted her. How could she find the money? What would Bernard say? It would be up to her to find the wherewithal, but provided his drinking money remained the same she did not think he would object. He wasn't cruel to the child, just not demonstrative. It was unlikely he would care one way or the other. She resolved not to tell Timmy until she had discussed it with him – just in case.

Back at the house she began to tidy up. She had time to get straight: loathing Mondays as he did, Bernard would spend longer than usual in the Cresswell Arms.

Later, when his supper was on the table, she realised with relief that tonight he wasn't very drunk.

'Bernard, I've some wonderful news,' she said, once Timmy was safely in bed.

'What's that?' He paused momentarily in shovelling food into his mouth.

Melanie explained. 'I'm so proud of him.'

'Why? He hasn't even done the test.'

'But you know what I mean. Our son, thought to be that clever.'

'He might fail.'

'Miss Crick says he stands a good chance.'

'He's not to take it.'

'Why?' Her heart pounded with anger.

'Because I says not.'

'You have to have a reason.'

'I don't have to explain myself to you.'

'Is it the cost of the uniform?'

'We can't afford it.'

'I've thought of that. I can speak to Mrs Fuller at the big house – they're taking on more women from the village for cleaning. Some say they're economising, others that they can't get the servants. I know she likes—'

He brought his fist down on the table with a thud. 'That's typical of you. Run to the bloody Cresswells. He isn't going and that's that.' He stood up, pushing his chair back.

'But this is his chance. Bernard, please—'

'And who gave me a chance? Answer me that.'

She had stood up, but now she sat down, the truth dawning. 'You're jealous! You're jealous of your own son! I can hardly believe it. You don't want him to get on in the world because you're a failure.' Her voice was raised as she stood up and leant across the table. Her head jerked back when he hit her.

'That's right, hit me. It's all you know to do.' Another blow landed, making her ears ring. 'How can you punish him? What's he done to you?' The punches rained down on her. She was not silent, not tonight: she was screaming at him, not feeling any pain as he lambasted her.

'He's going! He's going to have that chance!'

'Over my dead body.'

'What bliss that would be!'

She had gone too far: he pushed her, banging her head against the wall until she slumped to the floor. Then he began to kick her. 'No! Don't!' she cried out, aware that her son had rushed into the room and was trying to restrain his father. She tried to stand but found she couldn't. The pain was the worst she had ever experienced, too much for her, and she fainted dead away.

Every morning, whatever the weather, Oliver rode over the estate. During the months he had been there he had found much that he was not happy about. Everything looked as beautiful and lush as it had for centuries, but when he inspected it closely he found many small things that showed serious neglect. He had organised a list of work to be done – it was going to cost a lot of money. He had put aside his own plans for the time being.

'Father, Greenacre is incompetent,' he'd said, just before his father left for France.

'He does for me.'

'He should be replaced.'

'I have no wish for that.'

Oliver had tried to explain the position, but he soon grasped that he was wasting his breath. His father did not want to listen.

It was a puzzle to Oliver that he should keep on someone who was incapable of doing the work. The man was out of his depth: whenever Oliver spoke to him about estate matters, he looked like a frightened rabbit. What complicated things for Oliver was that he was a pleasant fellow and, despite everything, he liked him.

'Greenacre, the gate at the end of the lower drive, near Dunwell Wood, is still broken. I pointed it out to you months ago. Why has it not been mended?' Compared with some of the problems, this was a minor matter, but it was a prime example of the inefficiency he was uncovering.

'I'll have it seen to, sir.'

Talking to the man was difficult: he never looked straight at Oliver but always at a point over his shoulder. This had led Oliver to wonder if he had been embezzling funds, yet that was hard to believe since he was a decent man. All the same he had checked out the ledgers, which he had discovered were in a sorry mess and would take weeks to sort out. A cursory glance made him think the man had not been stealing, merely disorganised.

He had a theory that he had rejected at first, but once his father had returned from his convalescence in France in fine fettle and still rejected any criticism of Greenacre, Oliver wondered if he was right. There had been several signs that his mother and Greenacre had been up to no good, snide remarks and snippets of gossip. Was his father keeping him on because it was the final insult to his wife? Banish her and keep the other culprit? If so, it was devious of him – and irksome for Oliver, who had given his word that he would help.

'The breach in the wall on the Barlton Road side that I mentioned weeks ago is still there. If it isn't attended to it will crumble further. Why has it not been repaired, Greenacre?'

Then there were the neglected woods, hedges, weeds, the lake, the thatch that needed replacing on too many of the cottages, the drainage in the village to attend to to prevent an outbreak of illness. He doubted if the cress beds would ever recover. Oliver added items to his list every day.

After complaints from the head gardener, the estate carpenter and the blacksmith, Oliver lost his temper. For five minutes he vented his frustration on Greenacre. The answer he received was not what he had expected: 'If bills are not paid on time I can't get the materials to do the things you request, sir.'

'What on earth are you talking about, man?'

'Suppliers are reluctant to let us have materials, sir. There's nothing I can do about it.'

There was such irritation in his voice that Oliver thought the estate manager was finally showing a little spirit. 'You hardly need suppliers to mend a broken gate!' was his reply.

He was standing by that gate now. It was at the end of one of the minor drives into the estate. Oliver could not remember ever having seen it closed before, but now it would be impossible to shut it even if they wanted to. It had once been a fine example of wrought-iron work but one of the hinges had broken and it hung at a drunken angle. It needed painting too, and there were signs of rust. Soon a new gate would be required, which would be far more expensive.

Afraid that it was dangerous and might fall on an animal, Oliver had hauled over a large piece of a tree trunk to lean against it; now if it went it would fall on to the hedge, not the drive.

'Taxes,' had been his father's monosyllabic reply when, upon his return from France, Oliver had queried the lack of investment in the land.

'I'm sorry?'

'Death duties.'

'But you're no longer dying.'

'My time is undoubtedly limited.'

'I wish you wouldn't say such things, Father.'

'I'm a realist, aware of how ill I've been. I'm resigned to the knowledge that it is doubtful I shall regain my health completely. I won't make old bones. I'm trying to limit the damage when I do die.' He refilled his glass with port. 'Ever since the eighties and the agricultural depression things have been hard – the income from the land has halved since then.'

'All the more reason to maintain it to a high degree.'

'You think so? If the land is improved, its value increases and, with it, the taxes due on death.'

'But if you neglect it too far the amount of money required to restore it might exceed the tax.'

'At eight per cent I very much doubt it.' Mortimer poured more port and Oliver hoped it was not harmful to him.

'Does Mortie know about this?'

'No. Do you think he'd be interested?'

'Maybe not, but I should think Young Mortimer might have something to say about it eventually.'

'Not for a long time, though, and who is to say that by then estates like this will not be just a memory?'

'I doubt it.'

'Do you? I don't. I foresee the end of the order of things as we know it. Ramsay MacDonald and his cohorts will see the end of our sort.'

Oliver laughed. 'Your illness has evidently made you a pessimist.'

'Then we're back to the realism I was talking about. Shall we join dear Hannah?'

His father was out of touch with values. Oliver thought it unlikely that Cresswell would attract high taxes, but then he remembered the sum for which Courtney Lacey had sold. Perhaps his father was right after all.

There was a further worry. This neglect was not a new phenomenon: it had been going on for some time. Oliver wondered if his father was as solvent as he had been led to believe. But he could never mention *that* to him.

He looked at the gate again. At this rate he was going to have to organise its repair himself. Perhaps if he offered to take over the complete running of the estate for his father there would be no need for a manager, and his father would have no excuse to keep him.

Greenacre had been curious about his concern for the gate when there was so much else to be attended to. But he couldn't know its importance to Oliver: it was here that he'd met Laura Redman, by chance, walking on a rare warm day in February.

At the sight of her his pulse had raced in a way he'd never thought it would again. He had dismounted, they had chatted politely, and he had walked back with her to the vicarage. She hadn't wanted him to accompany her.

'Why not? We do nothing wrong.'

'I'm a married woman, Oliver.'

'I don't need to be reminded.' Though he tried to smile it emerged a sorry and twisted thing.

'It's not seemly.'

'We shall walk in the centre of the drive.'

'People might gossip.'

'They never stop! We can't let our lives be ruled by busybodies.'

At the vicarage she'd turned to say goodbye.

'I'm very thirsty,' he'd said, wheedling.

'Then I suggest you ride home post-haste.'

'Just a tiny one . . .'

'I have no alcohol.'

'But I like tea.'

She had shaken her head at him in a tolerant way and allowed him in. It was all so innocent, or seemed to be; had she known what he was thinking as he'd watched her pour the tea, greet her child, she'd have had him thrown out. Even more so if she'd known he'd pocketed a handkerchief of hers – a childish thing to do.

They had what he referred to as a chance second meeting and then a third – on his part little was left to chance. Daily he'd lurked here at the same time in the hope that she would come. He had wondered after the third time if she, too, could not rely on chance so took her walk at the same time and to the same place so that he might find her. Such a thought made that pulse of his race even faster. Then he had ventured to suggest they meet here. And they had. Over the last few months it had become a regular rendezvous.

They talked, it was all they did – he was disappointed, but proud that he had managed to control himself. And he had time, he was not going anywhere, he told himself. All this had happened while his father and his sister were away and he was glad: he would not have liked Hannah to discover what he was about. But, then, what was that? He was looking for Laura's friendship, that was all. He'd missed it after they had parted. He laughed – he knew he lied to himself.

He had decided he would stop these meetings once his family had returned. But they had been back a couple of weeks now and here he was, impatiently looking at his watch. She was late and Laura was rarely that. And he knew as well as he knew that tonight was a full moon that he could not go on like this, that he did not want to.

'Oliver, I'm sorry.' She appeared, pink of cheek, her hat crooked, as if she had been running.

'I'd wait for ever for you.'

'Oliver!' she said warningly.

'I was merely being gallant.'

'I'm glad it was no more.'

They set off on the walk they always took, out of the broken gate, down the road, then turning off into a narrow lane that, with summer, had become a tunnel of foliage, a dark, cool, secret place. They had to walk in single file, Laura first, Oliver admiring the sway of her hips, the proud angle of her head. His horse's reins were over his arm, Sergeant bringing up the rear.

'Why were you late?' Oliver asked, when they reached their destination, a small clearing in Dunwell Wood, the river Cress bubbling through it.

'What's that noise?' She looked alarmed.

'The workmen building Hannah's house, that's all.' He was spreading a rug he had brought with him on the ground.

'Why did you bring that?' she asked, suspicious.

'Because I'm tired of sitting on damp grass.' He laughed and saw she relaxed. There was no need to tether Sergeant: he would contentedly crop the grass until they were ready to go.

'I was late because Simeon was delayed in getting back for luncheon,' she said, as she lowered herself on to the plaid rug.

'Do you tell him you meet me?'

'No.'

'Why not?' He sat down beside her.

'He might misunderstand.'

'What is there to be misunderstood?'

'I keep reminding you—'

'*I'm a married woman*,' he said for her. 'I know,' he said, with irony. 'Do you remember when we—'

Laura put up a gloved finger and pressed it to his lips. 'Memories can be dangerous, Oliver.'

'I treasure mine.'

'As do I.' But she looked fixedly at the river as she spoke.

'Laura . . .'

'Don't.'

'You always knew what I was thinking.'

She turned to face him. 'No, I didn't. I didn't know when you were going to leave without warning.'

He concentrated on the river. It was inevitable this conversation would take place one day. He had not looked forward to it.

'I was afraid,' he said eventually.

'You? Afraid? Of what?'

'Responsibilities – finances – what it would mean to marry and support you. I didn't have the money, Laura. That was the only reason I went as I did.'

'Why didn't you tell me?'

'Had I known I was going to succeed I would have. But how could I know what was going to happen? I could

209

never have allowed myself to be responsible for you, of all people, living in poverty.' What he said was true but also the reverse. He had run away because he couldn't afford to marry her, and also because he didn't want to – he had been too young to settle. That was the truth.

'And how do you think I live now?'

'Simeon seems to do well.'

'There are other sorts of poverty than financial, Oliver. I would have waited for you, come what may.'

'I didn't know that.'

'Because you didn't ask.' Tears trickled from Laura's fine blue eyes and slid down her cheek. She made no move to wipe them.

'Laura, my darling.' He took hold of her hand. 'I don't think I can continue seeing you like this.'

'I know, it's hard.'

'I want to kiss you, make love to you, as we used to. Remember those long hot sunny afternoons in London when all we wanted was to devour each other?'

She made a soft, sibilant sound.

'We have no choice,' Oliver said. 'We cannot continue meeting like this.'

'You're right. We cannot. Or we can—' And, before he knew it, Laura had taken his face in her hands. 'I love you, Oliver. I want to be yours again.' And she pressed her lips to his.

Hannah was excited but tense too. She was cycling to inspect her new house which was being built, infuriatingly slowly, close to Dunwell Wood, one of her favourite places on the estate. What if, when it was finished, she didn't like it? she thought, as she bounced over the rutted lane. What on earth would she say to her father? She had not been over since her return so that when she rounded the bend in the track she nearly fell off her bicycle at the progress that had been made. It was beginning to look like the picture the architect had shown her.

'I never thought to see so much of it built!' she exclaimed to John Snape, the young architect from Barlton whom her father had commissioned. 'We've been lucky with the weather.' He stood awkwardly, as if unsure whether he should take command of the bicycle or not. 'Would you care to see inside, Miss Cresswell? It is possible now to see how it will look.'

Hannah propped her bicycle against a tree, solving his dilemma. 'I shall be thrilled to. And I've one or two ideas that I am hoping will not be too late to incorporate.'

'I'll see what I can do,' he said, with the resigned tone of one who had heard this before. 'This will be the drawing room.'

'It's much bigger than I thought it would be.'

'That's most satisfactory, Miss Cresswell. Most of my clients at this stage say how small it is.'

'I am devastated that the walls are finished. I'd hoped for french windows there. But, obviously, it's too late.'

'I think we could manage that.' He looked ruefully at the newly plastered walls.

'Really! How thrilling. Because, you see, I would like a long terrace built, with steps over there, down into the garden.' Mr Snape was making rapid notes. When she had first met him she had thought him alarmingly young, but she had been reassured by his confidence and the photographs he had shown her of other houses he had designed. 'You must think me rather silly not to have thought of this before.'

'Not at all, Miss Cresswell. Many people have a clearer idea of what they want when they see the building taking shape.'

'There's something else. On the plans, I presume these are to be the servants' rooms in the attic. I'd rather there were fewer of them and that those remaining were larger.

And here . . .' she stabbed at the plan with a gloved finger '. . . there'd be room for a bathroom.'

'Are you sure, Miss Cresswell? For the servants?'

'Yes, Mr Snape, I am. Good staff are becoming harder to find and keep. The young girls much prefer to work in the towns, in factories – I can't imagine why. If we make them as comfortable as possible they may stay longer.'

'As you wish, Miss Cresswell.'

'There's another matter. I feel the bedrooms might be on the small side. I think I'd be better off with seven, rather than the ten you planned.'

'As you wish, Miss Cresswell.'

'Did you bring the catalogues for the fire surrounds? I do hope they're of wood – I think that would be more fitting.' It took her but a minute or two to select those she liked. 'Now, I have something I want you to see.' She delved into the wicker basket on her bicycle and took out a folder of cuttings and booklets. 'You see, I want it simple but elegant. No darkness. No clutter. Lots of light wood and . . . Here they are. I thought these wallpapers would be perfect.'

'Ha, William Morris, the very thing!'

'You think so? Good. And here . . .' She was searching again in her folder. 'This furniture. I would like it ordered when the time is right. Modern, uncluttered, you see.'

'But I'd presumed—'

'That I would furnish it with antiques? No, Mr Snape, I want everything brand new.'

'Your choice will suit my design to perfection.'

'Another thing – I really won't ask for anything more! I need a study or studio close to my suite.'

'I suggest the turret room, with perhaps a balcony for enjoying the sun from the southern aspect – it was not on the plans but can be incorporated.'

'That would be splendid. It's for my work, you see.' There, she had said it! *Work!*

'Might I ask what that is?'

'I design gardens.' She didn't yet, but it sounded better than to say she *wanted* to. And it wasn't a complete lie, since she had done so much planning at Cresswell Manor. 'I've a commission from Lady Prestwick who wishes me to help her with the restoration of her garden at Graceteign.' Exaggeration was easy! But it was a beginning and Mr Snape need not know that.

'That is most interesting, Miss Cresswell. Perhaps we can be of use to each other. I have a thriving business in building new villas – not on this scale, you understand – but very respectable. And often people are not sure what to do with their gardens. But, as my wife points out to me, I can only identify a rose with confidence . . .'

She had been a little disappointed at mention of his wife – so much for her thoughts the other night about a husband. She smiled at her inconsistency.

As she pedalled home she was humming with joy. That had been the most satisfactory meeting of her life. The house would be perfect – it was almost a shame she would not be moving in immediately. Abruptly she stopped herself thinking like that: she could only move when . . . She slowed down . . . Unless . . . though nothing had been said, she could not believe that Penelope had been banished for ever. Whatever she'd done, Hannah's father was punishing her by giving her a fright. If she returned, Hannah was determined not to be under the same roof . . . But, then – she was pedalling harder again – Penelope had been gone for six months so he must have meant it. Think of something else, she told herself.

The conversation with Mr Snape had made her head whirl with ideas. Seeing the area that would be her garden had made her eager to start planning it too. As soon as she reached home she intended to get started with her pencil and paints.

It was then that she saw Oliver emerge from the lane

beside the broken gate on the beech drive, leading their father's horse. She was about to call his name when she saw that someone was with him. It was Laura Redman. How convenient! She had meant to call on her later this afternoon to discuss the progress of the schoolmistress. Her mouth was already open when she saw Oliver bend down and kiss Laura full on the mouth. The handkerchief! The handkerchief! The monogrammed. So it was Laura!

Hannah's bicycle wobbled so violently that she skidded across the path and ended up in the ditch, her feet over her head, water soaking into her clothes. She felt so foolish and hoped they hadn't heard her fall. She wanted no one to see her like this but, more, she didn't want to see them, having witnessed that kiss.

She picked herself up, and tested her limbs gingerly. Nothing was broken. However, her bicycle had not fared so well: one of the spokes had broken. She brushed her clothes, trying to remove the mud and twigs and set off on foot up the long drive. Of Oliver and his companion there was no sign.

'Oh, Miss Cresswell, what happened to you?' Harold, the coachman, approached her.

'I had a silly tumble, Harold.'

'You'd be safer on a horse, Miss.'

'Perhaps you're right. But my poor bicycle is broken.'

'Ferdie!' he yelled. 'See to Miss Cresswell's bicycle. Miss.' He touched his cap as Hannah made her way to the back door of the house. A few moments later as she crossed the hall she noted a strange umbrella. They had visitors. She ran up the stairs to tidy herself, just in case . . . Was it Dr Talbot? She could not stop herself hoping it was. He had said he would call, and she had written to him from the South of France, reporting on her father's progress and telling him when they were due to return. But, disappointingly, she had had no reply. It would be nice to see him again. There was a calmness about him that she had found comforting. More importantly, he was not married.

'Oh, lor' Miss Cresswell! What on earth has happened?'

'A ditch and I became far too well acquainted.' She removed her coat, Lavender fussing about her. 'I hope you can clean this for me.'

The maid looked at the tweed jacket and bloomers with a professional eye. 'They should brush up. I'd better let them dry, though. I trust you don't want them in a hurry.'

'No, my bicycle has to be mended. Who's visiting?'

'I don't know, Miss. The footman came for you but he didn't say, and I didn't ask. He said your father wanted you but I said you were out on a bicycle ride. Apparently your father requests you join him. I gather there was quite a fuss.'

'The cream blouse with the high collar, my dark blue velvet skirt and the matching boots.' As she looked at her reflection she wondered who it might be. There had been no cards left and people didn't just turn up – at least, the people she knew didn't.

Lavender did her hair for her and helped her with the tiny buttons on the sleeves of her blouse – ten of them. She sprayed a little perfume on a clean handkerchief and made for the stairs. She hoped Oliver would not be there – he was the last person she wanted to see just now. She was too shocked and annoyed with him to be civil. She needed time to think about what she had seen, decide how best to deal with the appalling situation.

When she entered the drawing room Hannah felt as if all the air in the room had been sucked out and left her breathless. She stood immobile, like a statue, in the doorway.

'Miss Cresswell?' Whitaker was looking at her with concern.

'Hannah, are you unwell?' her father asked.

'Forgive me.' She laughed nervously. 'You must think me so rude. It was the shock, you see – but you've just broken my dream.' She looked at the three strangers standing in the room: her dream people had faces now.

'Then you must make a wish immediately,' the older woman suggested, in a low voice of great beauty, and she smiled at Hannah, such a lovely smile that she was transfixed by it.

'I shall.' There was only one wish for Hannah to make: that her father would continue to improve.

'Our neighbours, Hannah. Let me introduce you.' Coral, newly arrived on a visit, fussed forward, oozing charm.

'What a pretty dog,' she said to Esmeralda, who was holding a small Pekinese – evidently the reason why Cariad was skulking under a side table, her beady black eyes watching intently every move that was made.

'He's called Mr Woo. Isn't he the sweetest creature you ever saw?'

'I said to Miss von Ehrlich that it was just as well we only had Cariad and not a great aggressive dog, or Mr Woo might have been eaten as a snack,' Coral said, but Hannah was fully aware, even if Esmeralda wasn't, that the girl was being reprimanded for bringing him.

'Papa said I should not bring him but he cries when I leave him.'

'As all creatures would, to be sure.' Mortimer smiled indulgently.

'Oh, Sir Mortimer.' Esmeralda fanned herself.

'Shall you enjoy country life, Miss von Ehrlich? It can be rather dull and tedious. There are few dances or parties – I'm so afraid you will be bored and leave us *toute suite*.' Coral's false charm and cold eyes led Hannah to think she found their visitor too attractive by half.

'Then we shall just have to have our own, shan't we, Papa?'

'If you say so, my dear.'

'And I do hope you will all come. Then I shall *never* be at risk of *ennui*.'

'From your name are we to surmise you are not English, Mr von Ehrlich?' Coral enquired.

'I am English, Mrs Cresswell, but my father was German. We came here over forty years ago.'

'Escaping from a pogrom, were they?'

Hannah could not look at anyone: she was too embarrassed by the implication in the question.

'Not as far as I am aware, Mrs Cresswell,' Stanislas said good-naturedly. 'No doubt all families come from somewhere.'

'I am descended from a knight who came here with William the Conqueror,' Coral said, with pride.

'So, you prove my point, Mrs Cresswell.' Hannah would have liked to whoop with joy at Coral's being put in her place. He really was *most* charismatic.

'If it is not impertinent, Miss Cresswell, do please tell us your dream. Oh, do please!' Esmeralda asked prettily.

'It's very strange, I dreamt I met you.'

'How creepy. It makes me go all shuddery.' Esmeralda shivered.

'But you had no faces.'

Esmeralda let out a little squeal of fear.

'A doctor who had studied in Vienna with another doctor called Freud said it was because I was fearful of something,' Hannah went on.

'You don't think you were being warned against us?' Stanislas asked, with an amused expression.

'No, please don't . . .' Then Hannah laughed. 'I think you're teasing me, Mr von Ehrlich.'

'Perhaps I am.' And he looked at her so intently that she felt quite light-headed.

'I find that fascinating,' Agnes Beatty said, in that wonderful voice – One would never tire of it, thought Hannah.

'Have you second sight, Miss Cresswell?'

When Stanislas smiled, his face was transformed: although Hannah had, at first, thought him ugly she could see now that he was curiously handsome. 'Not that I know of. It's never happened to me before.' Hannah was used to being flustered, she spent her life being so, but this was different: she was perturbed because these people made her feel as if she was the only person in the room who mattered to them. It rocked her composure.

'My grandmother is fey. She reads tea leaves and the tarot cards,' Esmeralda offered.

'Really?' Hannah was startled by this revelation: it was not the sort of thing one should impart to strangers, she thought.

'I tell her she's a witch. She'd have been burnt at the stake years ago.' Stanislas laughed.

'Do you consult her for yourself, von Ehrlich?'

'For business you mean, Sir Mortimer? No. If one relied on such matters to succeed one would not be successful for long.' He proceeded to hold forth on investments, standing on the hearth rug, his feet wide apart, swaying back and forth as if he was holding court in his own house. Such confidence, thought Hannah.

'Are you settling at Courtney Lacey?' Hannah asked, when Stanislas had finished and an uncertain silence had descended.

'Very well, thank you, Miss Cresswell. It's a lovely house. But no ghosts, much to Mother's disappointment.'

'I got lost in the maze. I was shrieking with fear. I thought I might be trapped for ever and die of starvation.' Esmeralda laughed gaily.

'And what happened?'

'Father sent the gardener to rescue me.'

'And I expect you would much rather it had been a knight on a coal black stallion.'

'Why, Sir Mortimer, how clever of you to read my mind.' She patted his arm and smiled at him as if she was flirting with him. To Hannah's astonishment, her father was flirting back.

'I should be most interested if you know anything of the history of the house you could impart to me, Miss Cresswell.'

Agnes Beatty had joined Hannah. She wondered what her relationship was to the others. She was too well dressed to be a companion or governess, but Hannah did not think she was a relation either. 'I'm afraid I know little about it. Of course I know Lord Prestwick the original owner but I never met his brother-in-law, the last owner, who had purchased it from him. He did not mix much in society – not, Miss Beatty, that there is much socialising hereabouts.'

'No doubt Mr von Ehrlich will change that. He likes to entertain and is happiest when he can watch his guests enjoying themselves.'

'How very commendable.'

'And what are your interests, Miss Cresswell, if I might be so bold?'

'I fear not as many as there should be. I like to read, and I play the piano, but not well. I should like to be able to paint, but try as I might . . .' There was her nervous laugh again. She hated to be asked this question: she felt she had so few attributes that people would tire of her quickly.

'I've never understood why, just because one is female, it is presumed that one is automatically skilled in the arts. No one thinks less of men because they cannot paint, play or sew.'

The very idea of men sewing made Hannah laugh, but happily this time.

'And you?'

'I cannot do anything.'

'I find that hard to believe, Miss Beatty. You look as if you would be accomplished in many things.'

'What a joy to hear you say that. Perhaps no one will discover how unskilled I am. I hear you like to bicycle?'

'I do.'

'It is, without doubt, the most wonderful way to exercise. Perhaps we could venture out together one day?'

'I should like that very much.' Hannah looked at her with renewed interest. Agnes had sought her out and she had never had a friend. Perhaps this woman would become one. The thought prompted a smile, but it disappeared when Oliver walked in.

'What are they like, Mr Whitaker?'

'*Parvenu*, Mrs Fuller. A Johnny-come-lately if ever I saw one.'

'What makes you say that?'

Dolly was carrying in the senior servants' tea tray. She was delaying as much as she could, wanting to hear. She wondered what '*parvenu*' meant – she'd look it up when she had a minute for there was a dictionary with Mrs Gilroy's receipt books.

'Look at the time they left.'

'I was surprised when they ordered tea for three more. Never heard the like.'

'Exactly, Mrs Gilroy. Fifteen minutes on a first call, the rules say, and they should be abided by. It's what oils the wheels of society.'

'What does?'

'Etiquette, Mrs Gilroy. It is what made the Empire great.'

'If you say so, *Edward*.' She was still infusing his name with meaning, but he was still refusing to react.

'The young woman's face was painted.'

'No!'

'Flashy dressing, Mrs Gilroy.' He sucked his lips in with disapproval. 'Too much jewellery for the time of day.'

'Really? Got good jewellery, have they?'

'Large, Mrs Gilroy. On the large side.' His voice brimmed with disdain. 'And the young woman brought her dog!'

'Her dog! What sort of person visits with their dog? In someone else's drawing room! Well I never!' The cook bristled with indignation. 'Haven't you finished with that tray yet, Dolly? You're all fingers and thumbs. Get a move on. I miss my Jose, it has to be said.'

'Really, Eve? I thought you said she was a slut.'

'She was a good little worker, Gussie. Not like some as I could mention.' She fixed a steely eye on Dolly.

'Does anyone know where she's gone?' Mrs Fuller asked.

'Back to her mother's, I presume, I never asked. Try one of these dainties Hilda made, Gussie.'

Dolly left the senior servants and went back to the kitchen to have her own tea. She could have taken it in the servants' hall but she didn't feel like the noise and banter today. And she hated to be in the same room as Jock, who carried on as if nothing had happened and he was not responsible for getting poor Jose the push. It was so unfair when the two of them had been involved and only Jose was punished. She had no time for the other maids, who blamed Jose as well. They argued that she had known the rules so had only herself to blame. Dolly believed she was the only person in the world who saw the injustice.

She was missing Jose far more than she had thought she would. How could they dismiss a girl and not make sure she was safe, with somewhere to go? She could be anywhere. The white-slave traffickers might have got hold of her and she could be in a harem by now – well, perhaps not quite: she'd only been gone two weeks and it would take longer than that to get to a sheikh's house, she decided. She wondered what it would be like to be the plaything of a rich man. Not that she had any plans or the opportunity, she told herself. Everyone went on as if it were the end of the world to be seduced away. But was sin so bad? What was the point in being good in this world. Kept women had goosedown beds, gilt beds, great wooden ones and Dolly had a mattress on a pantry floor and an old stained bolster long given up by people senior to her. Mistresses had silks and satins while she had this dour uniform and one dress for church on Sunday. Hell and damnation awaited them, they said. But what if there wasn't a hell – as there might not be a heaven? What then would be the point of being good all your life?

She was fed up with being told that people were better than her. Who said and who decided, that's what she wanted to know. Why being senior, titled or rich gave others the right to be downright rude and unfair was a mystery.

She had thought she wanted to be a ladies' maid, but now she wondered if she really did. She was even beginning to wonder if she wanted to stay here. It had been all right when Jose was here and she'd had someone to talk to. But now there was no one. She had hoped that Ferdie was going to be a friend but all he wanted to talk about was horses, which was of no interest to her. The end had come when, one day, she had given him an illicit cup of tea and he had tried to get into her knickers. She'd thrown him out, dirty guttersnipe.

And if Jose did go wrong, whose fault would it be? If she had no money and the only way to survive was to sell herself, then whose fault was that? The Cresswells! She poured tea into the tin mug she invariably used. What annoyed her most was that the likes of the Cresswells could allow a girl to be dismissed without a character reference yet hand out money to the Waifs and Strays Home in Barlton. There was no rhyme or reason for it.

She hauled the large dictionary on to the table. '*Parvenu*'. Here it was. 'A person of humble origin who has gained wealth or position and risen in society . . .' Well, what was wrong with that? What snobs the others were. And with what reason? They were only servants. In the Cresswells' eyes they were nothing, and yet because they worked here the housekeeper, the butler and the cook thought they were something. How silly.

'When I'm a man, when he hits you, I shall hit him back.' Timmy's face was strained. 'I'll stop him.'

'And a great son you are to me.' Melanie leant forward to kiss him and had to hide a wince of pain. He had said *when* not *if*. He thought it inevitable, as she did. 'It's kind of you, but I don't want you to hit anyone – ever. It's wrong and only bad people do so.'

'But Dad hits you.'

'And when he does it he is wrong to do so.'

'But Miss Crick says we're to honour our father and mother. It says so in the Bible. How can he be wrong?' He was frowning, his confusion evident.

'He just is.'

'But you told me once to respect him.'

'Maybe he deserved your respect then. He doesn't now.' Oh dear, she thought, what a muddle it all was. 'You see, Timmy, it's difficult for me to explain to you. Your father doesn't like me—'

'But he must. You're lovely.'

'Dear Timmy. It's true, though. There's something about *me* that makes him cross and then he lashes out . . . And . . .' Her voice trailed off, how did she explain the inexplicable to a child. She would have liked to say that his father was a useless, idle bully, that he was so stupid he had to use his fists since his tongue always let him down. But she couldn't. He was Timmy's father. She couldn't teach him to hate, that would be even worse.

As she moved about her kitchen she did so gingerly. The pain in her chest was not lessening and she was certain she had broken a couple of ribs. She had strapped herself up with a binder, which helped a little but not enough.

'You've got to scarper, Melanie. He's going to kill you, that's what. Just look at the state of you.' Concerned she hadn't seen her friend for nearly a week, Flossie had popped in to find out what was wrong. They were sitting at the kitchen table, and for the past half-hour Flossie had been advising Melanie.

'Trouble is that giving advice and seeing what should be done is always easier when it isn't your own problem.' Flossie was cradling her mug with both hands, blowing every so often on the steaming tea.

'Everything you've said is true, and you're right that I should go. I've thought of all these things. But how?'

'He's getting worse, isn't he?'

'He drinks more so he's more violent. The more I try to please him, the worse I make it.'

'Poor you.' Flossie patted her hand.

'And if I did run away, what about Timmy?'

'Take him with you, of course.'

'But he loves his father, and Bernard's never cruel to him. They love each other. How could I deprive the boy?'

'I think you're daft.'

'You're probably right.'

'But if you're killed he'd lose both of you. You'd be dead and his father would be strung up, so Timmy would be worse off.' As always Flossie spoke her mind.

'There's truth in that. But where would I go? I've no money.' She smiled at her well-meaning friend.

'There's only one thing you can do. You've got to go and see your mother. Tell her everything and how afraid you are. Bury the hatchet. She won't turn you away.'

'You don't know my mother,' Melanie said, with a cheerless laugh.

'Mine says yours is a lovely lady, kind and thoughtful.'

'Then your mother doesn't know her either.'

'But she says she's well thought of hereabouts.'

'Oh, yes, she is. Everyone thinks she's wonderful – and

she is, kind and thoughtful to everyone. Except me. She'd throw me out.'

'It's worth a try. She might help you, and you won't know unless you ask.' She sniffed at her baby's bottom and pulled a face. 'Time to be getting along.'

Melanie stood on the back doorstep of her parents' cottage. With the palm of one hand she gently pressed her side to ease the pain. She had been sick with nerves before she set out, which had made her chest worse. As she stood waiting for her knock to be answered she felt the waves of nausea building again. She took deep, hungry gasps of air to stem it.

'Mother.' The door had opened.

'What are you doing here?'

'I need help, Mother.'

'Don't we all? What's makes you special?'

'Please. This is not easy for me. I need . . .'

At this point Rob Robertson, his axe over his shoulder, came into view. 'You'd best come in,' Melanie's mother said. 'Don't want that nosy creature seeing you here – it'll be all over the estate before you can say Jack Robertson.' She didn't smile, and Melanie doubted if she knew she had made a joke: her mother did not make them, let alone understand them.

Nothing had changed in the eighteen years since she had last set foot in this cottage: the same chairs, the familiar pair of pictures of hunting dogs on the wall, the same highly polished brass ornaments and fairings on the mantelpiece, the same smell, the same kettle on the range . . . Everything was just as it had been when she was a child, the same but different.

'I'm making a pie,' her mother said unnecessarily, since all the ingredients were on the kitchen table. She returned to rubbing the lard into the flour. From her jerky movements, Melanie wondered if she was nervous too.

'You always made the best pies,' she said, sniffing appreciatively at the meat simmering on the range.

'No point in trying to butter me up, Miss.'

'I wasn't. It's the truth.'

'I presume you're here for something. You wouldn't come otherwise.'

'I'm not asking you to take me back.'

'Just as well. It would be a waste of breath.' She had picked up a knife and, with a vicious swipe, sliced more lard into the mixture.

'I need some money.'

The floury hands were suddenly still. Her mother stared at her. If it was true that women became their mothers with age, Melanie never wanted to be like her, so bitter-looking, so angry.

'I should think everyone needs money. I know I do.'

'This is an emergency and I'd pay you back.'

'I don't see you for eighteen years and then you come and demand money. Who do you think you are?'

'Your daughter,' she said quietly.

'Don't remind me!' her mother replied, with bitterness.

'It was you sent me away. It was your choice not to see me. I've been back two years and have you sought me out? No. Did you answer the letters I wrote you? No. You've avoided me. Why, you don't even know Timmy.'

'I don't like letter-writing. You never called, only the once. What was I supposed to do? Crawl after you? Not me! You've another think coming.'

'And when I did come that once, what reception did I get? Don't you remember? You turfed me out. I was too afraid to try again.' Melanie could not imagine treating her own children in this cold manner. But arguing wasn't helping her or Timmy. 'But now, Mother, I'm begging you, please help me.' She hated having to plead, but she had no choice.

There was a clatter at the back door, the sound of boots being removed, a coat being hung up. Melanie's heart jumped into her mouth. Was it her father? She was afraid of his wrath but she hoped it was him: of the two he was more likely to be sympathetic than her mother.

'Melanie, is it you? Here?'

She smiled up at her brother. 'Yes, I'm not a dream.'

'Pity you aren't.'

'Mother!' Henry objected.

'You keep your nose out of this.' Their mother pointed her kitchen knife at him.

Henry looked abashed and Melanie felt sorry for him. He'd tried to get away from their mother once but had returned with his tail between his legs. She had seen him several times since he had got back from the army, but he was always looking over his shoulder when he spoke to her, afraid their mother would find him. Eventually he had stopped seeking her out. He could not stand up to their mother. No one could.

'You all right, Melanie? You don't look it.'

'I'm fine, Henry, honest. And before you ask, I walked into the scullery door.' She touched the bruises on her face and smiled to make him think they were nothing.

'A likely story.' Her mother sniffed.

'Anything I can do?' Henry asked. 'Was it Bernard? If it was I'll see to him.'

Don't interfere. And you help her, Henry, I wash my hands of you too and I mean it.' She pointed her knife at him threateningly. 'Go and get washed up. I want to talk in private.'

Henry looked as if he was about to argue.

'Do as she says, Henry. For me!' Melanie looked at him pleadingly. Reluctantly he crossed the room.

'And no listening at doors,' their mother shouted after him. 'Right. Explain yourself, now you're here.' At least she had laid down the knife. 'You can't demand money and not give reasons.'

'I need to get away from here, and with no money I can't.'

'At least that would be a blessing.'

Melanie chose to ignore the jibe. 'I need help to set myself up near Barlton. Timmy's up for a scholarship at Barlton Grammar.' Perhaps that would persuade her.

'Educating another out of his class, are you? It'll end in tears.'

'He's very clever. Miss Crick says so. He should have the chance.'

'Am I to conclude you're planning to leave your husband?'

'I have to. He doesn't want him to go to the school.'

'He's the one who should decide.'

'It's not just that. I dare not stay . . .' Again she touched her bruise in the faint hope that her mother would understand.

'You shock me more than I can say. He's been good to you. Not many would have taken you on and that's a fact.'

'If I stay he'll kill me. He beats me and the beatings are becoming more severe.'

'A woman is hit because she needs it.'

Melanie looked at her boots so that her mother would not see the fury in her eyes.

'What did you do?'

'Nothing. He drinks. That's why.'

'You married him for better or worse. You've made your bed, now lie on it.'

'You don't understand, Mother.'

'Yes, I do. You've been a great disappointment to your father and me. If you go now you'll be an even greater one. And how can you contemplate leaving your child?'

'As I told you, I was planning to take him with me.'

'You can't do that. He belongs to your husband. He has already indicated he doesn't want him to attend that school.'

'But Timmy loves me.'

'Love! That's all you were any good at talking about.

228

You go. I've a good mind to give you something just to send you on your way, but you don't take that child with you!'

'I can't leave him.'

'Then you'll have to manage some other way. I won't be part of such wickedness! Of course, you could always go on the game – you'd be good at that!'

Melanie pushed back her chair and stood up. 'I don't have to tolerate this.'

'What did you expect?'

Melanie's hand was on the latch.

'All you've ever done is bring shame to this family.'

At the door Melanie turned. 'Did your mother speak like this to you? Did she cast you out?'

'Of course she didn't, she had no cause – I didn't let her down.'

'Didn't you? Really? Wasn't she ashamed that yours was a shotgun marriage? Wasn't she humiliated that I was born seven months after your wonderful wedding that you were always telling us about.'

'You never were!'

'Don't lie. I've checked the church records. You just hope everyone's forgotten. Well, I haven't.'

'You were premature, everyone knew that.'

'At eight pounds? For God's sake, Mother, don't add blatant hypocrisy to all your other sins.' Melanie swept out, oblivious to the pain in her chest. She slammed the door behind her.

She had gone only twenty yards when she heard footsteps pounding along behind her. 'Melanie! That was wonderful!' Henry's eyes shone with admiration.

'There was nothing wonderful about it. It was very sad.' She had to blink back the tears that were blinding her. She turned to walk away, but Henry grabbed her sleeve.

'Is it true? Do you really think he'll kill you?'

'Of course it isn't,' she lied. 'I just said that to try to get some money out of her.'

'I don't believe you. I've heard the gossip about him and you. I should have done something before.'

'Henry, don't be silly. If you believed only half the gossip you hear in this place you'd still be wrong. Honest, I'm fine. I just don't like him any more and I want to get away for Timmy's sake more than my own.'

'You didn't walk into a door, did you?' he persisted, and pulled her closer to look at her bruise. In doing so he jarred her chest. She blanched with pain and yelped. 'It's worse, isn't it? He's hurt you somewhere else.'

'I fell down the stairs and hurt a rib. That's all.'

'All?' Henry bellowed. The rooks in the trees panicked into the air. 'I'm going to see to him.'

'No.' It was her turn to grab his sleeve. 'Don't. If you do anything I shall never speak to you again. I mean it.'

'But I can't let him do this to you—'

'Henry, listen to me. Do nothing. If you try to help me you'll make matters worse for me, don't you understand?'

Though it was summer, the fire in the Cresswell Arms still billowed acrid smoke into the bar and the customers, as always, were oblivious to it. The only concession to the change in temperature was that most of the men congregated a little later, making the best of the long evenings to work in their gardens.

'Went to have a look at that deng great house they'm building up by Dunwell. What's one old spinster need all those rooms for?' Rob complained.

'As if the big house baint big enough to house all the buggers,' said Sol, savouring his first pint of the evening.

'Mind you, would you like to live with that sourpuss Coral when the old sod dies?' Freddie Robertson asked his brother.

'Is her as bad as everyone makes out?' asked Tubs,

who was not employed by the Cresswells so knew them less well.

'Worse,' Rob nodded approval at his own conclusion.

'What were you doing up there, Rob?' Sol asked.

'Cupboards. You'm never seen so many. That's the trouble with owning too much. You'm have to have somewhere to put it all. There's cupboards for china, for sheets, for boots. And that don't count the kitchen and that there scullery. And one room, I don't lie, all cupboards, nothing else.'

'What for?'

'Clothes.'

'Is it just you going to build them?'

'No, Tubs. I told her, I said, "Miss Cresswell it ain't possible. No body could make all these here cupboards in the time you say." I told her I had my other duties and if I fell behind then her father would have my guts for garters. I said I needed an assistant – no, I *demanded* one.'

'You?' Sol smirked.

'Well, sort of.' Rob shuffled his feet.

'And what did she say?'

'"Do your best, Robertson," that's what she said. And how the hell am I supposed to be doing that?'

There was a general mutter of agreement while tankards were replenished.

'And the garden,' Freddie added. 'That's going to cost a packet. The plans – you've never seen aught like it. A water garden, a rose garden, herbaceous borders – I hate them. Hard work, that's what they are. And today she announced she's going to start an arboretum.'

'What's that?' asked Sol.

'A collection of trees, that's what that is.'

'Trees? Bugger me, haven't they got enough of they?'

'Like you, Rob, I pointed out I couldn't be doing it all meself. That we're short-staffed as it is with the main gardens. "I'm sure you'll manage, Robertson." That's what she said to me. Butter wouldn't melt in her mouth.'

'And will you get extra wages for the extra work?' Sol asked.

'Will we hell! It's not right. Bloody slave labour, that's what it is.' Freddie was steaming now.

'We should all down tools until it's sorted. That's what we should do.' Rob nodded, evidently satisfied with this idea.

'Oh, yes, and get thrown out of our houses? Lot of good that would do us, Rob.'

'But if you all did it, what could they do?' Tubs suggested.

'Wouldn't make no difference.'

'Another pint, Tubs, if you don't mind? But you know what annoys me more than anything is all that money going on that there deng dower house and not a penny spent on our cottages. My thatch is in a sorry state. I've patched it best as I can but it needs ripping out and starting again.'

'Then there's the damp.'

'Unhealthy, damp is.'

'But what I don't understand is in his father's day we had less money but we had more, if you know what I mean. Old man Cresswell always looked after us. Bad-tempered old bastard he was but the cottages were in good repair. He was a fair man. This bugger, he charms your arse off and don't spend no money on anything he's not involved with.' This was one of the longest speeches anyone had heard Sol make, and it was met with an astonished silence.

'Cutting off his nose, though, ain't he?' Tubs broke the spell. 'The whole village will collapse at this rate and it'll cost him ten times what patching up would do.'

'It isn't patching up we need, it's good maintenance, like in the old days,' said Freddie.

'That new cove over at Courtney Lacey, he might be a

foreigner but he's looking after his staff well. All the cottages are being renovated, water laid on,' Rob informed them.

'Water!' they chorused.

'That's what I said. The thatcher's been working non-stop ever since he bought the place. He's got so many maids no one's overworked.'

'Everyone says he's a Johnny-come-lately and don't know how to behave.'

'I tell you what, if that's so I'd rather work for new money than this skinflint lot.'

'Maybe things are changing,' said Tubs. 'I had Mr Oliver here the other day. He's got plans.'

'What sort?'

'This place. He's got good ideas. We're going to have the bedrooms done up, a bathroom put in—'

'A bathroom? What on earth for?'

'Guests, that's what for. He reckons that where we are, right by the sea, if we were smartened up we could put up holidaymakers. New bar we're getting too. It'll be too grand for the likes of you.' Tubs laughed.

'And if they do this place up how long do you think you'll last? They'll shove you out and have someone smarter in. I'd put a florin on that, I would.'

'Nah, Rob, they wouldn't get rid of me. There's been a Sylvester here since time began.'

'And do you know what I heard the other day? My Molly'd been talking to the old man's valet and he said—'

At this point the door opened and Bernard Topsham stumbled in to his normal frosty welcome. It was evident to all that he was already drunk for he stood in the middle of the bar swaying ominously. The stench of beer on him made even this hard-drinking group back away. 'Get a move on, Tubs. You could bloody die of thirst waiting for you to move your fat arse.'

The assembled company glanced at each other. Despite

his nickname, Tubs did not like rude comments about his size – only he could joke about it.

'Mind your manners, Topsham, or you won't be getting nuffing.'

Bernard slapped a penny on the counter. 'Who says?'

'I do.' The two men squared up to each other.

Bernard looked at the barrels, licked his lips, and muttered something the others didn't catch. 'What was that?' Tubs demanded.

'A pint, *please*, and a rum.'

That was the nearest Tubs would get to an apology. To the disappointment of the others he poured the pint. Bernard picked up his tankard and stumbled to the seat by the inglenook, mumbling to himself. Rob made a circular movement with his finger at his temple.

'You! Watch it!' Bernard roared at him. The tension in the air increased.

'Sorry, Mr Topsham.' Rob grinned nervously.

'Bloody hell, he's pickled!' Sol whispered.

'I won't give him no more. Strikes me he's spoiling for a fight and I don't intend to give him the pleasure,' Tubs said.

'Oh, go on, Tubs. A good fisticuffs would suit us fine.' Rob laughed.

'So that you could run – as you always do?'

'That's not fair.'

At this point the door burst open and a wild-eyed, dishevelled Henry Beasley rushed into the room. 'You bastard!' He made straight for the fire and his brother-in-law.

'Watch it, Henry, he's sozzled.'

Henry did not even hear Tubs. 'You come out and fight me. Instead of whipping my sister, you can try and whip me.' The young man stood menacing and strong, glowering at Bernard.

'Watch it, whippersnapper.'

'Don't you—' Henry dragged the older man to his feet.

The effort made him lose his footing momentarily and Bernard, as drunk as he was, took advantage and hit the boy in the face. Henry swayed, regained his position and thumped Bernard's ear. Then he smashed his nose.

'Outside, both of you!' Tubs roared, coming round from his side of the bar. 'If you'm going to kill each other you bloody well do it out in the yard.'

'Mind your own sodding business.' Blood dripping from his nose, Bernard turned on Tubs.

'It *is* my sodding business because it's my bar! Now—' He put out his hand to restrain Bernard, who hit him hard on the head. Tubs stood, looking dazed. He shook his head, as if trying to clear it. Then, his stomach undulating as he staggered towards his adversary, he let out a great bellow and hurled himself at him. Bernard stepped nimbly to one side and Tubs banged into the fireplace just as Henry kicked Bernard in the stomach with his heavy boot. Bernard doubled up in agony as a cheer rose from the onlookers. Tubs pushed himself away from the side of the fire and took a step towards the others. He stopped abruptly, his expression suddenly showing puzzlement, surprise and finally fear. He clutched at his chest, let out an animal groan and, like a great tree, fell to the floor.

Rob, Freddie and Sol looked at each other and then, as one, raced to the aid of the landlord.

'Tubs!'

'Tubs, answer me.'

'Come on, Tubs, you silly old bugger!'

'He's dead.'

'He can't be.'

'He bloody well is.'

'You killed him, you bastard!' Sol was on his feet ready to take on Bernard. But Bernard was on the floor of the bar, and beside him lay a red-stained poker. They stood, mesmerised, as a trickle appeared from his head, then a stream and finally a torrent of blood. It streaked across the wooden boards in a ruby red, shining river of inevitable death.

Of Henry there was no sign.

Chapter Eight
September 1901

Melanie was aware that crying was not going to help her today or improve her lot in the future. But understanding was one thing: stopping the tears was another. Fortunately Timmy had asked if he might sleep in the secret den in the woods he had built with his friend Sammy Pepper, the boilerman's son, so he did not know she was upset.

She knew she had to make decisions quickly. She knew that if she delayed, her will to leave would weaken. She would ask Hannah Cresswell for a letter of introduction that would, hopefully, give her a good character. Then she would go to Barlton and find work. She could perhaps find employment in an inn, if not a private home . . . How easy, how rosy, it sounded. But if she did . . . She fumbled for her handkerchief. If she left Timmy with his father he would never go to the grammar school.

From her pocket she took the letter that Miss Crick had given her that morning. Timmy had won the scholarship. It was up to her to find the money to send him.

Suddenly she brightened. If she mentioned his success to Hannah, perhaps the family would help as they had in the past. Or was it too much to expect? Would they think her presumptuous? Despondency returned. But what if she asked them to tell Bernard it was his duty to give the boy this chance? He would have to listen to them – even he would not dare disobey.

But the thought of leaving her son, of not seeing him . . . Bernard, she was sure, would ban her. The tears flowed again. She chose to ignore a thumping on her door. She wanted no one to see her like this. The battering continued. She put her hands over her ears in a futile attempt to shut out the noise.

'Melanie? Are you there?' She was aware that the door had opened. 'Melanie?'

'I can't see you at the moment, Flossie. Please go away.' She tried to control her voice so that her friend would not know the state she was in.

'I'm sorry but . . .' Flossie ignored her and entered the room. 'Oh, my love . . . I'm so sorry . . . I had to come . . . Something awful has happened.'

'Timmy?' Melanie stood up immediately, clutching her throat with fear.

'Bernard.'

She sat down again. Her sense of relief made her feel so weak that her legs could no longer support her.

'I think you should come.'

'Where?'

'The pub.'

'What for?'

'Melanie, just come. Alf says he's hurt. You should be there—'

'I don't care if he is.'

'He might be dead. Alf wasn't sure.'

'Dead?'

Flossie had picked up Melanie's shawl and was shaking it out, holding it up, coaxing her.

When they opened the front door Melanie could see the villagers standing on their steps, looking at her cottage, all with curious expressions on their faces. At sight of her tear-stained face there was a murmur of sympathy, which was new to her. She pulled her shawl over her head, so that its folds covered her face. She and Flossie, her latest baby clutched on her hip, scurried down the track, the others following in a crocodile, and turned on to the road that led to Cress-by-the-Sea, and the inn.

The bar was full of people. The crowd parted, just like the Red Sea, Melanie thought, as she moved forward.

Two men were lying on the floor. She saw Tubs first, then Bernard.

'So much blood,' she said, in a strange little voice which she was surprised was hers.

'Should you sit down, Melanie?'

She heard a chair scraping on the stone floor. 'No, thank you, Rob.' How kind everyone was being, how strange that was. They never normally were, not to her.

'I'll stand.' She needed to. When he woke up he'd leap at her. She had to be in a position to run.

There was another flurry at the door as the doctor arrived. He knelt down, took his stethoscope out of his large black bag and placed it on Tubs's chest. The buzz of speculation increased, and he looked irritated.

'Shut up, everyone! The doctor can't hear,' Freddie Robertson shouted.

There was a general shushing noise since those at the back had not heard. It was as if the room held its breath. When the doctor took the stethoscope out of his ear there was a general and noisy exhaling. He shook his head. Everyone groaned, Tubs had been a popular man.

There was a stir at the door as the local constable, Humphrey Grimshaw, appeared. The doctor and the policeman nodded at each other, then the doctor concentrated on Bernard.

Melanie was aware that she, too, had stopped breathing. Please don't let him hurt me, she was saying to herself over and over.

'I'm sorry, Mrs Topsham, there's nothing I can do. Your husband has passed on.'

Melanie gasped and her hands flew to her mouth. There was a sigh of sympathy from the villagers. They were not to know that Melanie was suppressing a cry of relief.

'Who witnessed this?' Constable Grimshaw had his notebook in hand, pencil poised.

Rob, Freddie and Sol had their hands up, but looked shifty. 'Anyone else?'

'No,' Sol said loudly. The other two looked at him in surprise.

'No,' they said in unison, quickly recovering themselves.

'All those who witnessed nothing will kindly leave.'

No one moved.

'Out!' the constable shouted.

Disgruntled, the villagers did as they were told, only to regroup in the yard.

'Now, if you could tell me what happened, one at a time?'

The three men looked at each other. 'You go first, Sol,' said Rob, and Freddie nodded, looking scared.

'They had an argument.'

'What about?'

There was a long pause as Sol thought what to say. 'He was drunk. Tubs ordered him out.'

'And?'

'Bernard wouldn't go.'

'And?'

'So Tubs came out from behind the bar.'

'Yes?'

'Bernard called Tubs fat.'

'Fat?'

'Yes, Tubs don't . . . didn't . . . like to be called that. He got angry.'

'You agree with this?' Constable Grimshaw asked Rob and Freddie. They nodded enthusiastically.

'Tubs whopped him one. Bernard hit him back.' Sol lapsed into silence.

'Then? Come on, man!'

'I'm not sure . . . I didn't see . . .'

'One of you must have seen?'

'I did.' Rob stepped forward. 'Tubs whammed into the wall there.' He pointed to the side of the fireplace. 'Winded him, it did, so he picked up that poker . . .' he pointed to where it still lay beside Bernard '. . . and . . .' He lifted his arm high miming its arc through the air.

'Bit short to do that and hit him there, wasn't he? Bernard was tall.'

'He was like a madman. He could have taken on an army.' Freddie put in his pennyworth.

'Is this possible, Doctor?'

'I should say that's exactly what happened.' The policeman, concentrating on the doctor, did not see the look of relief that passed between the three men.

'Mrs Topsham, would you like us to make the arrangements?'

'That would be most kind Constable.'

'Will you stay with her, Flossie?'

'I will, Humphrey.'

'I really don't need anyone,' Melanie murmured.

'It's for the best, Mrs Topsham.'

Flossie put an arm round Melanie as they made their way back to Melanie's cottage. All the way people were standing at the edge of the road and fell silent as she approached. Men doffed their caps. How ridiculous, she thought.

Once in the safety of her home, she ripped off the shawl, oblivious to the pain in her chest, and began to laugh, and the laugh rose higher and higher.

'Melanie, stop! People will hear you.'

'I don't care if they do,' she spluttered.

'Well, I do. Stop it!' Flossie ordered her sharply.

'But I'm so happy!' And the shrill laughing began again. Flossie moved quickly across the room and slapped her hard. 'Now stop it!'

Melanie stroked her cheek where the slap had landed.

'I'm sorry, Flossie. I can't grieve, I'm *pleased* he's dead. I've dreamt of this day.'

'If you take my advice, you mustn't do or even think anything you might be ashamed of in the future. A man is dead. There's nothing funny about that, nor is it a cause for joy. It's no matter he was a bastard.'

Flossie's words were like cold water sluicing over her and Melanie slumped at the table, crying.

'That's better.' Flossie put the kettle on.

But Melanie was not weeping with grief, but from a mixture of relief and fear. How on earth would she manage now?

The room was dark, the curtains pulled against the summer sun. The only light was from two candles which, since they were the cheapest, sent spirals of acrid smoke into the room. Melanie sat alone, the storm of tears over. She was exhausted, with the strangest feeling of emptiness.

Last night the men had brought Bernard home. Rob had knocked up two simple coffins, and Flossie had lined Bernard's with some old curtains Hannah had given her. They were a pretty rose-covered chintz, and made Bernard look softer, kinder. Sad that he could only look so in death.

She had been here all night. No matter what she thought of him she could not leave him alone. It would have been wrong. But she wished she was anywhere but there.

Who was watching over Tubs? she wondered. She hoped he was not alone. He was a widower and she'd no idea if he'd had family. Someone would be with him, she told herself. Her main concern was Timmy. Last night when she had pulled herself together, she had gone to Dunwell Wood to look for him. She had walked through the pretty wood in the summer twilight, calling his name. She had no idea where his den was. Every so often she would stop and listen, hoping to hear him and Sammy talking. But she heard nothing.

'Timmy! Are you hiding from me?' The wood was small and it did not take her long to walk through it and back to the middle again. 'Timmy, please, I need to talk to you.'

There was a rustle in the undergrowth. 'Timmy?' She had to smile as his dirty face appeared over a rise.

'Mum? What are you doing here?'

'I came to find you, I've something sad to tell you. Let's sit down here.' She indicated a place beneath a tree. 'Are you all right? Have you been crying?' She saw now that the dirty face was tear-streaked.

'I fell over.' He wiped his nose with the back of his hand.

'Don't do that,' she told him instinctively. 'Doesn't matter,' she added. 'Where's Sammy?'

'In the den.'

'Timmy, your father's had an accident. I'm sorry but—'

'I know. He's dead.' A large tear trickled down his cheek, making a white path through the dirt.

'How do you know?'

'Someone told me.'

'Who?'

'I don't want him dead.' He was crying now in earnest. She took him into her arms. 'Timmy, you can't stay here now.'

'I know.'

She stood up and held out her hand. 'Come on. Let's find Sammy and go home.'

'You can't! You can't go in there.' He looked frightened.

'Why not?'

'You're too big. I'll get him.' Before she could say anything he had run back into the trees. A minute later he returned with Sammy, a nice boy, but today he couldn't look at her, which she thought strange.

'I don't want to go home. I want to go to Sammy's.'

'We shall have to ask Sammy's mother if you can.' She led the two boys out of the wood and back to the village.

Mrs Pepper had showered her with hugs, kisses and assurances that she was there if Melanie needed her. Timmy, she had said, could stay as long as he liked.

As she walked back to her own cottage, aware of the shy stares, the friendly smiles, the handshakes of condolence, she wondered why there should be such a change. No one had liked Bernard, and her mother had ensured that no one liked or wanted to know her, save her good friend Flossie. Why was everyone acting in this way? Perhaps it was death they respected, its inevitability, not her husband.

All the time she had watched over Bernard in his coffin she had feared he was merely sleeping. She wished she could leave him but it was her duty to watch through the night. If only Timmy was here she could use that as an excuse not to sit by the coffin.

All that night and today she had tried to feel sorrow as Flossie thought she should, but she couldn't. In the clear light of day she was still relieved. She had stopped laughing – that was from shock, she was sure. She felt ashamed of herself now, and it was yet another example of how wise young Flossie was.

'Think of the happy times,' she told herself. She sat frowning, but no pleasant memories came to her. In the early days, before he had been violent, he had been kinder, more considerate, but she hadn't been happy. She never wanted to marry him in the first place.

She had been too young, too afraid, and there had been her parents' constant nagging and insistence that she must. She should have stood up to them. It hadn't been fair on him or herself, and certainly not on the children. She moved her body: she was stiff and aching. If they had not married and Bernard had found another woman, he might have been happier – might never have become the man he did. Everything might have been different, and he would not be lying there dead.

And her legacy from him? Memories of misery. He'd had nothing else to leave her. She paused. Except Timmy – and 'Freedom,' she said.

If they were to survive she must pursue her plans in earnest. At least Timmy would have the education he deserved.

'Who's that?' she called. There was no reply. She went to the door. 'Hello?' No answer. She pushed open the scullery door. There, at the back door and swinging round to face her, was Timmy. He had a loaf of bread in one hand and, in the other, the leg of lamb she had cooked last night, but which had not been eaten. 'Timmy, what are you doing?'

'I needed some food for the den.'

'Aren't you at Mrs Pepper's?'

'Yes.'

'Then what do you need food for?'

'Fun.'

'I don't understand.'

'We thought we'd have our tea at the den and then go back to Sammy's. Mrs Pepper says as it's all right.'

'You be careful.'

'I will.'

She let him go. A whole leg of lamb. At least grief wasn't interfering with his appetite. She settled back in the chair and resumed her vigil.

'Mum, where are you?' She heard a voice call from the door.

'Zeph! Thank God you've come.' As her elder son put his arms about her she felt safe for the first time in months.

'It really is impossible!' Coral flounced into the room and

slammed the book she had been carrying on to the console table.

'What has happened?' Hannah did not look up. She was sitting close to the window in the morning room painting an impression of Dulcie's knot garden.

'Your father says Mortie is to attend this man's funeral. Mortie hates funerals! Your father will be insisting he drinks cider at the inn next.'

'Father is right. It's our duty.'

'You might see it as an obligation, Hannah, but I don't. We don't live here.'

'No, but you will one day,' Oliver interrupted. He had entered behind her.

Hannah's paintbrush hovered for a minute. Then she cleaned it and began to pack away her paints. She would return to her own rooms – she was avoiding being alone with Oliver.

'I still don't see the necessity. They loathe us behind our backs.'

Hannah looked at her with astonishment. 'I don't think that's so, Coral.'

'I think she may be right, Hannah.'

Hannah looked at Oliver with the chill in her eyes that had been there since she had seen him with Laura Redman. 'How do you know that? You've only recently returned here – you're like a stranger to them.' She dried the brush, aware she had probably hurt his feelings. 'Melanie Topsham has been very kind to this family so we should be represented. But please, Coral, don't feel you and Mortie have to do anything you don't wish to do. I have decided I shall go in any case and can represent you.' She snapped her paintbox shut.

'Women at a funeral? Whatever next? Only lower class women attend.'

'I wish to change the tradition – especially if Mortie won't go. What has he decided, or is he obeying your orders?'

246

'He talks of duty. But I don't think Mortie would recognise duty if it bit him.'

'That's hardly fair, Coral.' But Oliver was smiling.

'You know my husband, Oliver. If your father said jump through a hoop he would.'

'He's a good son,' Hannah said quietly.

Coral moved towards the window. 'It will be a gruesome experience. Now Young Mortimer says he wishes to attend.'

'How touching.'

'He's too young.'

'To attend or to show respect?'

'Hannah, there are times when you are so proper and perfect I would like to scream! He is not going and that is that. I will listen to no arguments.' With that she swished from the room. Hannah began to follow her.

'Don't go, Hannah. I want to talk to you.'

She had almost reached the door but politeness made her pause. 'Yes?' She made her voice distant.

'You're avoiding me.'

'I don't think so.' But she could not look at him.

'And you speak to me only when you must. If I enter a room you find an excuse to leave it.'

'I'm sorry if you should think so.'

'What is it? How have I offended you so?'

Hannah stood clutching her painting equipment. 'I'd rather not discuss it.'

'Is that fair? You and I were always so close. I find this coldness very hurtful.'

'What did you expect?'

'Since I don't know what I have done, how can I expect to understand?' He spoke gently. 'Is it something to do with Laura?'

This took Hannah by surprise and she did not know where to look, what to say.

'It is, isn't it? Come, sister, sit here and talk to me, please.'

Reluctantly she sat on the chair he had pushed towards her.

'I should explain,' Oliver went on.

'There is nothing you can say.' She wished she was anywhere but there. 'Some things are unforgivable. I'm sorry, Oliver.' She rose.

'How do you know?'

'I saw you kissing her, down by the broken gate. Oliver, how could you? A married woman!'

'Do you think I'm proud of myself? If you do, you don't know me. I'm ashamed.'

'Then why be with her?'

'I cannot be without her. I love her.'

'I don't believe you. If you did, you wouldn't put her in such a dangerous position. She risks all for you – husband, marriage, child, reputation. I'm appalled.'

'Hannah, don't judge us too harshly. She is unhappy with Simeon.'

'She took her vows. Many women find themselves in miserable marriages but they don't do as she has. Look at Melanie – married to a brute, but did she run away, was she unfaithful?'

'Laura has not committed adultery, with me or anyone.'

'She kissed you.'

'That is not the same. It was just a kiss.'

'She thinks in an adulterous way, no doubt.' It was incredible to her that she should be having this conversation, using words she hated, that horrified her. 'I never thought I would say it but perhaps it would have been better if you had not come home.'

'Hannah!'

'I'm sorry, Oliver, but I have to say what I've been thinking now I have started. All I can think is poor Simeon, poor Laura and wicked you.'

'We're not hurting Simeon.'

'You take his wife from him!'

'I don't. He never had her – she never loved him.'

'Then why did she marry him?'

'She was lonely and unhappy, grieving for a lost love. She met Simeon and he asked her to marry him. Miserable as she was, she accepted. Sadly she has lived to regret it.'

'Then she is selfish.'

'She would agree with you. Don't be hard on her, Hannah, she's a good woman.'

'Good? And she the vicar's wife!'

'You have never loved so you cannot understand.'

'That's cruel, Oliver.'

'But it's true. To love someone, to lose them and then to find them again, it is beyond comprehension that she could turn her back on the chance of a little happiness.'

'Happiness! That's all you talk about. Those who search only to be happy are invariably the most selfish.'

'When *you* fall in love with someone, I will accept your criticism of us. You seem to think I'm self-obsessed and don't think, but I'm riddled with guilt and fear for the woman I have loved for many years.'

'It's you? Her lost love?' Hannah asked. Tears were forming in her brother's eyes.

'It's all my fault, you see. She's the sister of a friend of mine from Cambridge – that was where we met. We should have married. But I felt I was too young . . .'

'As you were.'

'And I distanced myself.'

'So that's why you went away?'

'I was foolish. I should have explained myself to her. I should have told her I would seek my fortune and return to claim her. Instead, coward that I was, I left her with no explanation, no letter, no communication.'

'That was too cruel of you.'

'I know. I don't need to be told.'

'Poor Oliver, poor Laura.' She held her arms out to

249

him. 'I'm so sorry for you both, even if I can never approve.'

'I knew you'd understand.'

'I understand your love, your sadness, but you know it must end. You cannot continue.'

Oliver looked closely at her. 'Dear Hannah, don't make me stop seeing her. We do nothing wrong. We walk and we talk, and when we say goodbye we kiss each other farewell. That is all.' He was lying, but he thought it was probably the best thing to do.

Melanie was surprised at the number of people who had come to pay their respects. Because she had disliked Bernard, it had never crossed her mind that others might have liked him.

'Don't be silly, Melanie. They're coming because of you. No one on the estate cared for him,' Flossie assured her.

'Me? But I've always felt no one approved of me.'

'You'd be surprised. There's plenty of gossip about you, of course, and I've heard as some think you're a bit stuck up . . .' At this Melanie had to smile – it was so typical of Flossie. '. . . but most people felt sorry for you. They were afraid of him, though, and thought it best to keep away.'

'I wish I'd known.'

'Well, you know now. I've made you some rabbit stew.'

'It's kind of you but I find I don't want to eat. Mrs Pepper brought me some too, so Zeph and Timmy have plenty – it won't go to waste.'

'Rabbit?'

Melanie grinned. 'Yes.'

'I'll take mine back, then.'

'Please do.' Melanie sighed. 'Isn't it strange how everyone brings me food when it's the last thing I want?'

'It's because they want to help and don't know what else to do. Have you seen your brother?'

'Henry? No. I thought he might call in but no doubt my mother's told him he can't. Why do you ask?'

'Just curious, that's all. He rushed out of the pub just as my Alf was arriving and no one's seen hide nor hair of him since.'

'Do you need to see him?'

'No, nothing like that . . .' Flossie's voice trailed off and she looked uncomfortable. Melanie looked at her curiously but they were interrupted by yet another knock on the front door – the door that was never used unless Death visited.

'Miss Cresswell!' She was surprised to find Hannah on the doorstep, and yet she supposed it was what she would have expected of her.

'We are all so sorry for you in your loss.'

'Thank you, Miss. Would you like to come in?'

Hannah hesitated. 'Just to pay my respects.'

Melanie showed her into the front room. 'He looks so peaceful, Mrs Topsham.'

'Doesn't he?' For the one and only time since she'd known him, she thought.

She waited as Hannah bowed her head to say a little prayer. Melanie wished she could, but was unable to find it in herself to do so. 'Would you care for a cup of tea?'

'How kind – if it's no trouble.'

'The kettle has been on permanently ever since the accident.'

'Flossie, how nice to see you. How are the children?'

'Well, thank you, Miss Cresswell.'

'That's good.' Hannah put the basket she had been carrying on the table. 'Such a pleasant cottage this one, isn't it?'

'Yes, Miss,' said Melanie, thinking, If you don't have to live in it. Whenever Hannah visited the village there was an awkwardness about her, Melanie thought, and

251

wondered suddenly if it was because she felt shy and did not know what to say.

'I thought you might enjoy these.' From the basket she took Kilner jars of food. 'Mrs Gilroy tells me that is beef and that is chicken and that is . . . I can't remember.'

'Hope it's not rabbit. She's got a lot of that.' Flossie nodded towards the dresser where two further bowls of food stood, and giggled. 'I don't wish to be rude, Miss, but perhaps it would be better if you gave it to some of the old cottagers.'

'I think we offer food since we don't know how else to help you. Mrs Topsham, if there's anything you need, you will let us know, won't you?'

'I will, Miss Cresswell.'

'Show her, go on!' Flossie urged.

'I can't.' Melanie glared at Flossie as she spoke.

'What is it?'

'Nothing, Miss Cresswell.'

'If you won't tell her, I will. She's had notice to vacate this cottage, Miss. And him not even in his grave.'

'That's not possible.'

'Show her,' Flossie persisted.

'I should like to see, Mrs Topsham.'

From behind the dog ornament on the dresser Melanie removed the letter that had arrived yesterday. She handed it to Hannah, who frowned as she read it. It was signed by Mr Greenacre. She looked up at Melanie. 'What can I say? All I can do is apologise. Rest assured, Mrs Topsham, this is an unfortunate error. I know my father never ordered it.' She was placing the gingham cloth back into her basket. She was evidently flustered and was pink with embarrassment. 'If you'd excuse me? I fear I've no time after all for the tea.' She was half-way to the door.

As Melanie opened it and Hannah stepped out Hettie Beasley walked past.

'Mrs Beasley, I'm just going. You will want to see your daughter in private.' Hannah held open the gate so that

Hettie had no choice but to enter, a rigid smile on her face.

'I'll be in touch, Mrs Topsham.' Hannah waved the letter.

They watched her mount her bicycle and pedal off.

'You can go now, Mother. The coast's clear.'

'Now I'm here I'll pay my respects to Bernard.'

Melanie held open the door for her, then stood back and let her go in alone. She scurried into the kitchen. 'It's my mother!' she whispered to Flossie.

'I'm going.'

'Please stay!'

'No, thank you. Afternoon, Mrs Beasley. You're looking well.' This was rather a pointless thing to say for the older woman had entered the room, her face ashen, her handkerchief pressed to her eyes.

'I'll see you out, Flossie.'

'Don't bother. I know the way.' The door slammed as Flossie made her escape.

'He looks peaceful.' Hettie blew her nose. 'You've disguised his wound very well.'

'I didn't do it. Mrs Pepper and Mrs Robertson laid him out for me. I couldn't. Tea?'

'Well, now I'm here . . .'

Melanie hadn't expected her to stay – she was sure her mother was only there because Hannah had seen her.

'You needn't stay if you don't want to.'

'No, I was on my way here. There are matters to discuss.'

'Yes?' Melanie placed the refreshed teapot on the table, then collected a cup and saucer from the dresser.

'Will you be staying?'

'I don't know.'

'It would be better all round if you left as soon as possible.'

'Is that what Father thinks too?'

'Of course.' She blew on her tea and puckered her lips

to sip it, which exaggerated the considerable moustache on her upper lip.

'I shall decide later.' She wasn't about to tell her mother of the eviction: she didn't want to see her gloat. 'There's no hurry,' she lied. 'After all, I've lived on this estate for the past two years and we've managed to avoid each other.'

'I didn't mean that. I'm worried about the gossip.'

'What gossip?'

'Don't tell me you haven't heard. It's about Henry. Have you seen him?'

'No. Why?'

'They say he killed your husband.'

'Henry? Don't be silly! Our Henry wouldn't do that.'

'I can't sleep I'm so worried.' To Melanie's astonishment, her mother began to cry.

'Mother!' She sat rigid, unsure what was expected of her. She watched as her mother's shoulders heaved. She felt nothing, which was odd when she remembered the hours she had spent crying for her lost family. 'Calm down, Mother, and tell me what you've heard.'

After much patting of eyes and gulping of air, Hettie pulled herself together. 'There's talk that he hit Bernard and ran away.'

'Who said this?'

'Several people.'

'But the men who were there say it was Tubs.'

'I know.'

'Then that's what happened.'

'But if it's not true and if this gets to the police he'll be arrested and hanged. My life will end.'

'What's happened?' Zephaniah, who had been out for a walk, stood in the doorway, his tall frame silhouetted against the sunlight.

'Zeph, this is your grandmother Beasley. She's upset.'

Zephaniah's face froze. 'I'm glad.' He turned on his heel and stalked back into the garden.

*

As dawn broke Melanie slipped silently out of her house. She pulled her shawl around her against the early-morning chill. She had chosen to set out at this time so that no one saw her. A mist hovered over the valley, heralding a glorious day, the dew heavy on the grass. Such beauty, she thought, for such ugliness to have taken place amidst it.

When Zephaniah had come home last night, several hours after he had left in a rage, he had calmed down.

'There's no need to be angry for me, Zeph. I'm used to the way my parents feel about me.'

'But I love you, and I cannot be in the same room as her.'

'You don't have to be – I doubt she'll be back. I'm sure she only came today to maintain her good standing in the community. Even she wouldn't dare to slight the dead. But I wish you could meet your grandfather. He's a kind, sweet man.'

'He still ignores you.'

'Because of my mother.'

'Why can't he contact you himself? Why do what *she* wants and not what he wants?'

'My mother's a formidable woman. He stopped dis-agreeing with her years ago. He just wants peace. I understand that.'

'I don't think that's excuse enough. I have no wish ever to meet him.' He had gone to bed still angry and she didn't want him to be. She didn't want her problems to mar his youth.

As she moved through the park, she kept to the edge, even though it meant she had to walk further, but she didn't want anyone to see her from the manor: the maids would be about by now.

Should she have confided in Zeph, she wondered. She was weary with this extra burden. But it would not be fair to add to Zeph's worries – he was so young, so inexperienced. No, she'd been right last night when she'd resolved not to tell him, especially given his position in a solicitor's office.

It amazed her still that one act of stupidity on her part, so many years ago, had brought such unhappiness to others – just like the ripples from a stone thrown into a pond. Had she not been so weak her parents would still love her – though she felt her father did anyway. Her children would not be so bitter – it was obvious Zeph was, and he told her that Xenia was too. And Bernard would still be alive.

Henry! She stumbled on a tree root, distracted by the thought of him. He had been so angry and upset the last time they met that he might have gone in search of her husband and fought with him. She couldn't believe he'd intended to kill him. Not the Henry she knew. But if he had he was in serious danger. As her mother had said, he could be hanged. Her stomach knotted. All of it was her fault.

She had reached Dunwell Wood and could hear her father's retrievers barking. No doubt they had heard her and soon her father would be out and about. The trees closed around her. She had watched Timmy the other day and followed the route he had taken, ducking down to get through the undergrowth, having to pull her skirt free of brambles, several times getting caught by the hair. Now she could smell woodsmoke. It was difficult to be quiet since the branches snapped and swished as she moved along.

She felt like a cork in a bottle as she emerged into a clearing, her son's den, made from branches and twigs to one side, a smouldering bonfire in the middle.

It would be difficult to know who was the more surprised, Melanie or her brother.

'Henry!'

'Oh, hell!'

'What have you done?' she stumbled as she rushed towards him, afraid he might run away.

'I didn't mean to hurt him, Melanie, that's the honest truth.' He was backing away from her. 'He flew at me. I couldn't – I didn't mean to hurt him.' He was shaking. She saw a livid bruise on his cheek and touched it gently. 'I thought he was going to kill me.' There was such fear in his eyes.

'I know, I know . . .' She remembered how Bernard could look when he was angry. It could have put the fear of God into the strongest man. 'Henry, listen to me.' She took his arm. 'No one knows.'

'Others were there.'

'They're saying that Tubs killed him. You'll be all right.' She tried to inject confidence into her voice. 'You can't hide here. It'll make people think you've done something. You must go home.'

'I can't.'

'You can and you will. Listen, I've spoken to Mother.'

'You spoke to her?'

'Yes, she called on me.' Even in these circumstances she could not help but smile at his astonishment. 'I reassured her it wasn't you. You have to face the gossip – you can't stop it. But if you don't go home they'll know it was you.'

'Melanie!' He looked close to tears.

'I know, I know.' She tried to keep exasperation out of her voice. 'It's hard.'

'I'm sorry.'

'No need to apologise to me, you've done me a favour.' There she had said it. It was what she thought, and Henry, she supposed, was the one person she could be honest with. 'I think you should attend the funeral with me. It would look odd if you didn't. Then you should leave here. Find work as far away as possible.'

'Leave here? Go where?'

'I don't know, do I?' She regretted her irritation. 'Father will help you.'

'What do I say to them?'

She looked down at the ground and noticed a line of ants transporting crumbs, like giant boulders on their frail bodies, across the grass. That was how she felt, like an ant with a great burden. 'I suggest you say you arrived, saw the fight and ran away because you were scared. No, that doesn't sound right.' She frowned. 'It might be better to say you saw it and were afraid you might join in so you decided it was better if you left. But when you heard he'd been killed you thought you might be accused and panicked. Yes, I think that sounds more likely, don't you?'

'I don't know what to think.'

'If you don't pull yourself together you might be arrested, sent to trial and hanged.' She spoke sharply. She had to. He would damn himself if he didn't control his terror. 'Come on, put that fire out. Let's get you to Mother's.' She helped him cover it with earth and bundle up his few possessions – mostly, she noticed, with wry amusement, belonging to her and brought here by Timmy. She brushed her forehead with the back of her hand. She felt so tired and wished herself a million miles away.

'Henry! Thank God you're back. Where have you been? Are you hungry? Quickly, come in.' This was said as Hettie looked about her as if expecting the whole village to descend on her cottage and take her son away. She began to close the door, having ignored Melanie, who turned to leave.

'Melanie.'

'Dad!' She looked back to see her father standing in the cottage doorway.

'Girl, I don't know what to say—'

'Neither do I.'

'Melanie, love.'

She said nothing, simply slipped into his arms. She felt

the roughness of his tweed jacket, smelt his tobacco, and wanted to stay safe like that for ever.

'This nonsense has gone on long enough. Come in.' He stroked her hair.

'I'd better not.' She wiped away a tear.

'I'd rather you did. This family is in trouble and it should be together.' She followed him but could not help thinking that when she had been in trouble no one had said this to her. But that was the past and, for Timmy's sake, maybe she should be forgiving even if she knew she would never forget.

'Did you kill him?' Hettie was asking Henry as they entered the kitchen.

Henry looked trapped. He glanced across at Melanie, who was willing him to find some courage.

'No. I saw him – on the floor.'

'Then why did you run?' Hettie looked at him sharply.

'He panicked,' said Melanie, because Henry was incapable of speech.

'I wasn't asking you.' Hettie looked at her daughter with the customary coldness.

'I panicked,' Henry repeated miserably.

'Dad, I've been talking to Henry and I've suggested perhaps it might be a good idea if he moved away.'

'Moved away? Now what mischief are you planning?' Hettie glared at her. 'Not content with ruining your own life, you wish to destroy your brother's too. You're evil!'

'Hettie, watch your tongue.'

'It's the truth. She was born wicked.'

'Hettie, enough!' he shouted. 'What do you want to say, Melanie?'

'It might be better for *him*.'

'You're jealous – you want him out of the way.'

'I'm protecting him, Mother, from the gossip.'

'He says he didn't do it. What's he got to be afraid of?'

'Even when he's innocent there will always be people

who think he isn't. There will always be tittle-tattle. And I don't think he's strong enough to weather it.'

'Not hard, like you, you mean.' Hettie stood with her beefy arms folded.

'As you wish, Mother.'

'I think she's right, Hettie, and I can find him a position.'

'I don't want him to go.'

'And I, Hettie, am telling you that he *is* going. And no—' he held up his hand, 'there'll be no more argument. It's decided.'

It would have been impossible to say who, in the kitchen, was the most surprised by this statement – including Melanie's father.

'Xenia! You're early!' She was trying to divest herself of her shawl so that she could kiss her daughter. 'What a beauty you've become.'

'Mother, I'm so happy to see you. A friend of Mrs Featherstone brought me in his motor-car.'

'A motor-car?'

'Yes, it was most exhilarating.'

'How beautifully you speak!'

'Thank you, Mother.'

Melanie stood back and looked at the lovely young woman, more like a stranger than her daughter. Why should this be? She did not feel like this with Zephaniah. She gave up the attempt to kiss her.

'Who was the kind gentleman?'

'Mr von Ehrlich. He has just moved here – he's very rich. Where's Zeph?' She pulled her skirts closer to her in a fastidious manner as if she didn't want anything in the cottage to touch her.

'He was here. Tea, some lunch?'

'I couldn't eat a thing. I suppose I should say I'm sorry, Mother, for your loss.'

'Perhaps so, but it's not necessary.'

'What time is the funeral?'

'At two. I think I hear your brother. I'm sure you'll have much to talk about.'

Soon she heard them chattering and was glad that Zeph had returned. She saw so little of Xenia, who lived in a different world now: Mrs Featherstone was a wealthy woman with a beautiful house. But she still felt close to Zephaniah, and she didn't see him often either.

An hour later Melanie, in her best dress, opened the door to Rob Robertson and the pall-bearers. Nothing was said. Rob took a large screwdriver from an inside pocket and held it aloft. The closing of a coffin was a dreadful sound, she thought, no matter who was in it. She heard the bang of the lid, the twisting of the screws, and shuddered.

Rob entered the room. 'A word, Melanie. Private, like.' He looked pointedly at her children.

'Would you mind waiting in the garden?' she said to them.

They waited until Xenia, who had taken the longest, had left the room.

'It's about Henry.'

Melanie's stomach clenched.

'I thought I should say as you've nothing to fear. You know . . .' Big Rob looked awkward.

'Thank you, Rob. And the others?'

'Mum's the word. Perhaps I shouldn't say this of the dead, like, but we all hated him.'

'I understand, Rob. You're not alone, and we're grateful to you all. I'm touched.'

'Well, that said,' Rob looked bashful, 'are you ready? I can hear the bell.'

'Of course.' She hadn't noticed it tolling and wondered how long it had been going on.

The coffin had been placed on a farm cart that someone had decorated with flowers and leaves. It was pulled by

Sol's aged cob. Melanie walked behind holding Timmy's hand. She had tried to hold Xenia's but her daughter had avoided her. Zephaniah was behind her. How beautiful they were, and how proud she was of her three children.

When they reached the church it was already packed. Melanie knew that this was not an indication of Bernard's popularity: it was the custom for the whole estate to attend every funeral.

She was aware of rustling and whispering as she reached the front pew to find her parents and her brother already ensconced there. She smiled at her father and ignored her mother as she took her place. She was touched and surprised to see Hannah in the Cresswell family pew. Women such as she never attended funerals, and certainly not one of theirs. Even Young Mortie and Lettice, looking pale and pretty in black, had honoured her. It was at times like this that Melanie saw how protected and safe she was. But not for much longer.

As the sound of the first hymn died away Simeon Redman climbed into the pulpit. She did not recognise the man whose virtues he extolled. Either the vicar had known a different Bernard, or had not known him at all. She was gratified to hear the occasional snort from the congregation.

At the end, as Rob and the others took up the coffin again, she did not know what to do. Should she go first or would the family? Hannah Cresswell and her father stopped in the aisle. Sir Mortimer indicated that she should go first, and with her family, she followed Bernard out, knowing the Cresswells were behind her, feeling it was wrong. She blinked as they moved from the darkness of the church into the hot, sunlit day.

She remembered little of the interment in the cemetery where her ancestors lay and where, it had been planned, she too would be buried one day. Not now, she thought. She'd never want to lie in the same soil as Bernard. And she was tired of being a hypocrite: she wanted to go home.

'Mrs Topsham, you know you have all our sympathy.'

'Thank you, Sir Mortimer.'

'I would be most grateful if, at your convenience, you would call at the house.'

'Of course, sir. Tomorrow?'

'Before luncheon.' He lifted his hat and was gone. He left a worried Melanie, who was sure that he wanted to tell her she must vacate the cottage.

Chapter Nine
September 1901

'It seems so wrong to be going out to enjoy ourselves after a funeral.' The coach swayed as it turned out of the drive. Hannah disliked this brougham: its motion always made her feel sick. She wished she was with her brothers and Young Mortimer, who were riding behind them.

'I don't see why, Hannah. It's not as if the man was anything to us.' Coral was fussing as usual with her clothes. Hannah wondered why she couldn't get dressed and forget what she was wearing. 'Vanity,' was Nanny Wishart's opinion.

'We're involved in the lives of anyone employed on our estate,' Mortimer said.

'Really, Sir Mortimer?' Coral queried, and coloured.

'Hannah, you should do nothing this evening but enjoy yourself.'

'I shall endeavour to do so, Papa.' Looking out of the window she saw two young people walking along the road. 'Lettice, look, it's Melanie Topsham's children.' As they drew level they both waved.

'Twins, aren't they? I find twins somewhat vulgar.'

'Oh, Coral, you can be so funny.' Hannah was laughing.

'I don't see why. I didn't mean to be.'

'I know – that makes it funnier.'

'Hannah!' Her father frowned but there was a twinkle in his eye.

'They have such outlandish names. I mean, for someone of her class it is somewhat presumptuous, don't you think?'

'Why? I think they're rather lovely.'

'You've become so egalitarian, Hannah. It's most amusing.'

'I don't see why she can't call her children whatever she wants. I like the name Zephaniah – she told me it means "Jehovah has concealed".'

'Concealed what?' Coral laughed gaily. 'Really, Hannah, you do know some curious things.'

'I like Xenia as a name. It sounds like music,' Lettice added shyly.

Hannah was glad that Coral had given in to the girl's entreaties to be allowed to come too this evening: she went out so little and it was time she mingled more with society. Both children had been so excited when their invitations had arrived. It might have been different if she had found out that Lettice had slipped into the funeral. 'I like Mrs Topsham,' had been her explanation, and Hannah had thought that was enough. They had decided to keep it from her mother.

'You're right, Lettice. The children are so beautiful they deserve exotic names.'

'It's hardly surprising they are. Melanie is a good-looking woman.'

'Do you think so, Sir Mortimer?' Coral sounded surprised.

'You evidently don't, Coral.'

'She has a certain pleasantness of face, but her features are a little coarse for my preference.'

'I think she's lovely,' Hannah said.

'And Young Mortimer agrees. He told me he thought Xenia was pretty,' Lettice informed them.

'I can hardly believe he said that. Lettice, you make it up. He has far too much taste to do so,' Coral snapped.

'I wonder what Melanie will do now.' Hannah thought it safer to change the subject. 'I've been thinking I might talk to Mrs Fuller to see if we can't find her a position in the house.'

'Is that wise, Hannah? Do we want her in the house if her brother killed her husband? It might run in the family!' Coral gave an exaggerated shiver.

'Since he didn't, I don't see any problem.' Hannah tensed with fury.

'Nor is there. I don't wish any member of my family to repeat this scurrilous gossip, Coral.' Mortimer spoke so fiercely that Coral blushed deeply, and an uneasy silence descended.

'Blue suits you, Hannah.' Coral attempted to retrieve the situation.

'Thank you.'

Five minutes later they had entered the drive of Courtney Lacey. Although it was not yet dark the huge mansion was ablaze with light. Coral perked up dramatically as the carriage crunched to a halt, the door opened wide and Stanislas von Ehrlich bounded down the steps in welcome.

There was an exciting flurry as grooms appeared to take the men's horses. Stanislas was noisy in his effusive greetings and then, in a squealing, whirling mass of pink and lilac silk chiffon, Esmeralda erupted down the steps, her jewelled slippers sparkling as she ran.

'I've been beside myself with anticipation,' she trilled.

'I live in hope that one day my darling daughter will behave like a lady.' Stanislas was smiling, besotted.

'On the contrary, Mr von Erhlich, I think that's the most marvellous welcome I've ever received.' Mortimer bowed over the girl's hand and she giggled prettily.

'And, Miss Cresswell, you look so pretty,' Esmeralda cried.

Unlike her normal self, Hannah felt drawn to kiss the girl's cheek, which made Stanislas smile even more indulgently.

'And, Mrs Cresswell, welcome.'

'Miss von Erhlich.'

'Lettice! We shall be great friends, I know it.' Esmeralda gave the astonished girl a hug. 'And three gentlemen Cresswells. What luxury!' Esmeralda clapped her hands with childish pleasure, but Hannah could not help noticing that she was looking at Oliver.

Stanislas and Esmeralda led the party into the house. 'You will wish to refresh yourselves. Daddy, you look after the gentlemen.' She took Hannah by one hand, Lettice by the other, and raced up the stairs at a fine pace.

'Dear Miss Ehrlich, you're too fast for me,' Hannah protested, as she felt her arm about to be yanked out of its socket.

'I'm sorry, Miss Cresswell – it's just that I'm so excited to have you all here.' With a flourish she opened a linenfold door. 'I wanted you to see my room. Don't you think it's the loveliest one you've ever seen?'

'It's charming.' Hannah looked about her. She had not lied: in a chaotic, pink and white, frilled and ruched way the room was pretty. 'It's like . . .' she paused '. . . It's like walking into a wonderful dream, a cloud.'

'I think it's the most beautiful room ever.' Lettice gazed around it and Hannah could see she wanted one just like it.

'Do you like this?' Esmeralda flung herself on to the bed, which was shaped like a vast swan. Curtains of the finest muslin, embroidered with tiny pink roses, billowed above it.

'It's wonderful.' Lettice bounced on to the white silk cover too.

'And you, Mrs Cresswell?'

'Quite unusual, isn't it?' Coral sneered.

'It is, isn't it?'

'If we might . . .' Coral glanced about her.

'Of course. I'm sorry, I got quite carried away. My Bridget will assist you. I'll wait for you in my sitting room.' She looked shy now, aware of her blunder as she left them with the young maid who had appeared.

'*Quelle horreur! Cette chambre est grotesque!*'

'I like it,' Hannah answered, in English, aware how rude it was to speak in a foreign language in front of someone who did not understand it.

'Really, Hannah, you can be so obtuse when you wish. No, not like that,' Coral snapped at Bridget, who had removed Coral's hat and was straightening her complicated hairstyle. 'It might be suitable *pour un enfant*. Five years ago Lettice would think this beautiful *mais, pas maintenant*.'

'I like it *now*,' Lettice said stalwartly.

'Don't be ridiculous. Of course you don't!'

'I don't think Esmeralda's a woman. She's still a child – which, in my opinion, is part of her charm. Long may she stay so. No, thank you, Bridget, I can manage my own hair.' Hannah smiled at the maid.

'Such lovely perfumes!' Coral was opening and sniffing at bottle after bottle, dabbing several on her wrists. She was behaving as if she had none of her own, Hannah thought.

'That's me ready. Lettice?'

'I'm nervous.'

'There's no need to be. Thank you, Bridget, for your help.'

'*C'est mon plaisir, Madame, et aussi obligatoire pour moi*,' Bridget said rapidly, on a low note.

'What did she say?' asked Coral, as they passed into Esmeralda's boudoir.

'I didn't catch it.' That would teach her, Hannah thought.

The room they entered was another extravagant confection. There, they were welcomed exuberantly by Mr Woo.

'You all look even more beautiful,' was Esmeralda's greeting.

'Who is to be here?' asked Coral.

'The Prestwicks, father and son. *The Honourable* Edward has just married the most ravishing woman and I'm green with envy for he is the most charming of men. But Phoebe is so sweet and I forgive her for marrying him, and she is my new best friend.'

'Not the girl . . .' For once Coral took notice of Hannah's warning glare and stopped mid-sentence. All of the county had been abuzz with gossip at the future Lord Prestwick marrying a simple country girl earlier in the year.

'Then there are the Drummonds from near Chudleigh – more Father's age. The Portleys from South Beer – she's *so* pretty and rides a horse with such panache. The Fidgets – isn't that the most funny name you ever heard?' She laughed. 'And the . . .' She carried on listing the local grandees. It crossed Hannah's mind, given the illustriousness of some of the names, that perhaps some had accepted the invitation out of curiosity, not neighbourliness. Hannah knew most of them, which she always found such a disappointment; she hoped to meet new people and always that there might be a nice gentleman who would notice her. 'All in all I think we're thirty, so we can dance afterwards – I insisted Papa arranged an orchestra. Such fun!'

'And Miss Beatty?'

'I don't know where she is.' Esmeralda leant forward. 'She's in a bit of a sulk,' she whispered.

'Why?' Coral's ears had pricked at the hint of gossip.

'I can't remember.'

Hannah felt disappointed that Agnes Beatty might be absent.

'There, Edward. A nice cup of tea and some of my fruit cake. Funerals take it out of one, don't they?'

'Normally so, Mrs Gilroy.'

'"Surely he hath borne our griefs, and carried our sorrows," Isaiah, fifty-three verse two."'

'On the contrary, there was a remarkable absence of mourning, most unseemly – *in my opinion*.'

'But, Edward, had there been would you not have regarded that as unseemly too?'

'An unrestrained exhibition most certainly. But a small showing of sorrow would not have gone amiss – *in my opinion*.' Whenever he said that his chest swelled and he looked quite fierce. No one dared to disagree with him.

'So, everyone was there?'

'The whole village.'

'Henry Beasley?'

'Supporting his sister.'

'Despite the rumours?'

'I never listen to gossip, Mrs Fuller.'

The housekeeper coloured at the implied criticism.

'Difficult not to hear it, Edward,' Mrs Gilroy said, 'when that is what everyone is saying. I never believed it of the boy for one minute, but unfortunately that sort of mud tends to stick. He'll have to move away – *in my opinion*.' She grinned broadly but the joke seemed lost on him.

'I don't like to criticise the family, as you know, but I was shocked to see Miss Hannah and Lettice there. Women at a funeral? Well!'

'I wish I'd known they were going, then I'd have gone too. Wouldn't you, Eve?'

'That I would have. A good funeral makes you feel glad to be alive, sets you up for the day.'

'Young Mortimer was looking at Xenia Topsham in a most unfortunate manner,' the butler continued.

'No!'

'Really?'

'Young Mortimer!' Mrs Gilroy, Lavender and Mrs Fuller spoke like a chorus.

'Most unfortunate.' Whitaker looked even fiercer.

'But everyone says she's very lovely.'

'And very forward, Mrs Fuller. Another slice of fruit cake, if you would be so kind, Mrs Gilroy.'

'I'd thought to approach Miss Hannah and suggest I find her work here. She's a good seamstress,' the housekeeper said.

'The family won't like that. There's a little too much closeness to Sir Mortimer, if you ask me. That Nurse Burtonshaw said as much before she left.'

'Really, Mrs Gilroy! Listening to tittle-tattle again!' Their gossip was interrupted by a tap on the door.

'I'm sorry to interrupt, Mr Whitaker, but I thought as I should come and find you straight away.'

'What is it, Jock?'

'One of the silver matchbox covers is missing.'

'Missing? What are you talking about? How many are there?'

'Eleven, Mr Whitaker.'

'Eleven!' Whitaker twirled on the spot. 'No one is to leave. All staff are to be confined to their rooms. We search forthwith.'

'But what about the ones who have free time?'

'Cancelled, Jock. We shall seek the culprit from attic to cellar,' the butler declaimed.

'It'll turn up, Edward.'

'Mrs Gilroy, I have never lost one item of silver on any watch of mine. And there is not to be a first time!' And he fussed out of Mrs Fuller's sitting room.

'Just as well the family are dining away tonight, otherwise there'd be complications.' Lavender stood up. 'I must get going. With Miss Hannah out, I want to sort her gloves and underwear.'

'Will he search their drawers?'

'Don't be silly, Eve. What would be the point of that?'

'Fairness, that's what. Maybe one of them's taken it. And if he's searching he needn't think he's looking through my smalls drawer.' Mrs Gilroy straightened her pristine white overall.

Gold plates, gold goblets, gold cutlery and the largest vase in the centre of the table full to tumbling with flowers and fruit – some of which Hannah had never seen before – threatened to overwhelm them. Ivy trailed the length of the table, rose petals scattered among it. The candelabra – gold, of course – were so numerous that there was barely room for anything else on the table. Even the glistening glasses were rimmed with gold. While Hannah appreciated a well-set table, this was too opulent, too fussy, for her. The vegetation in the middle of the table made it impossible to see anyone sitting opposite, which she regretted since Agnes Beatty, who had come down to join them after all, had been placed there.

Then Agnes's face appeared round the side of the vase. She had parted some of the greenery with a fork, and smiled in a conspiratorial way – as if Hannah thought, she had read her thoughts.

A string quartet was playing behind a screen, as if they had been banished. Rather than performing classical music, as one would have expected, they were playing modern tunes. Stanislas was evidently enjoying it since he was drumming on the table in time to the rhythm with his fork.

'You like my music, Miss Cresswell?'

'It's very jolly, Mr von Ehrlich.'

'Can't stand the sort of music one is supposed to like.'

'You've my agreement on that, von Ehrlich,' Mortie boomed, relaxed and happy that he had apparently met someone after his own heart.

Hannah wondered who had done the place settings: she saw that Esmeralda was seated beside Oliver and that the two were deep in conversation, as if no one else was present. Oh dear, she thought. She was not sure that an interest between those two was a good thing. From the occasional frown he gave in their direction, Esmeralda's father was obviously of the same mind.

'Such lovely weather we're having,' she said to the man sitting at her right. His place card said he was Charles Trentworth and he was not from these parts – she had never seen him before.

'How mightily original of you, Miss . . .' He picked up her place card between fastidious finger and thumb and peered at it myopically. 'Miss Cresswell,' he concluded, in a voice so full of boredom that she blushed.

'I never know what else to say to strangers on such occasions.'

'How wearisome for you . . . And everyone else, come to that.'

At this sneer she went an even deeper crimson.

'I have not noticed any scintillating conversation from your lips either, Mr Trentworth. On the contrary, I cannot recall anything of note you have ever said, or anything of any charm,' Agnes interrupted. Startled, Hannah saw that Agnes had again lifted the trailing leaves and ferns to defend her. She felt like rushing round the table and kissing her.

'Had I done so it would have been wasted on you, wouldn't it, Miss Beatty?' he replied. 'I always cut my cloth for the person, so to speak.'

'Are you always so insufferably rude?' Hannah found the courage to say. Then she turned her back pointedly and concentrated on the Mr Hepworth on her other side. 'Are you from these parts, Mr Hepworth?'

'Sadly no. Such wondrous scenery.'

'It is, isn't it?'

'And such lovely ladies to entertain we mere men.'

Hannah found herself stared at, in the most intense way imaginable, by the darkest brown eyes. She was blushing yet again, but for an entirely different reason as her heart pitter-patted away with excitement. 'You look like Lord Byron.' She could not imagine what had made her say such a thing.

'If only I could write poetry like him . . . for you.' The last two words were spoken in a voice that dipped so low she wondered if she had imagined them.

As the meal progressed she was in a daze of excitement. She was not used to such attention – it made her mind whirl. And she could not think of anything else to say to him either, and was glad when he turned to Dulcie Prestwick on his other side. But her thoughts were racing. Was he the one? Had she found him at last?

'I think my granddaughter is taken with your brother, Miss Cresswell.' Stanislas's mother leant across the table from her place at the head, which was unfortunate since her dress fell forward displaying an expanse of old flesh.

'They seem to be getting on well, Mrs von Ehrlich.' Hannah delicately patted her lips with her napkin.

'Bit old for her, don't you think?'

Hannah spluttered into the linen. 'Perhaps a shade but I'm no expert on such matters.'

'Stan's hoping for a title for her.'

'Stan?' Hannah looked puzzled.

'He likes to call himself Stanislas, but he'll always be Stan to me. Does your brother have a title?'

'No, he's a younger son.'

'Then he's wasting his time. And you're drunk!'

'I beg your pardon?' Hannah began, and then, to her relief, saw that the old woman was glaring at the butler.

'Perhaps a little, Madam,' the butler answered, with amazing dignity.

'Then instead of guzzling it yourself, serve a bit more at this end of the table!' And Mrs von Ehrlich waved her glass. Hannah did not know where to look – she'd never seen such behaviour before – but, to her surprise, as the embarrassment faded she found it funny.

Finally the ladies withdrew.

'Miss Cresswell, your brother is a delight. Such an

interesting man.' Esmeralda had sought her out immediately.

'He is, isn't he? He has done many things, and been to so many places. Lucky for him.'

'Don't you travel?'

'Very little, though I went to the South of France this year.'

'I simply adore Cannes. Papa insists we go each winter. He says it's the only time to be there – when the King is there. Gracious, I think I've just been very rude . . .' She giggled.

'No, it was not rude. I gather it *is* so. But my father needed to convalesce, you see, so we didn't go at his usual time.'

'Do you think it would be safe for me to love your brother?'

'I really couldn't say.' Hannah felt flustered by the question. 'I don't know what you mean by "safe".'

'Does he have another interest? Is there a rival to little me?'

'No,' she lied. But she consoled herself it was not really a lie for he had promised her that they were just friends. 'No, there is no one else, as far as I am aware,' she added, for insurance.

'You make me *soooooooooooo* happy. I will confide in you – I already love him,' she whispered.

'But you hardly know him.'

'Where love is concerned, acquaintance is sufficient.'

'Esmeralda, this painting, would you explain it to me?' Coral called her away.

'It's by a Mr Turner, I believe.'

'Is it finished?' Coral queried.

Hannah was not sure how she felt about the confession she had just heard. Of all the young women in the world she felt that Esmeralda was probably the least likely for Oliver to fall in love with. She was too young, too flighty, too false – that was not kind. What had made her think it?

'I'm sorry I interrupted your dining companion.'

'Miss Beatty, I shall always be grateful to you. I'm not good at such functions. I find empty chit-chat beyond me.'

'You were simply being polite. Charles Trentworth should be called Charles Worthless. He is a disagreeable young man with far too high an opinion of himself.'

'Is he rich?'

'Rather poor, I gather.'

'It's usually the rich who think they can be rude with impunity.'

'And he's not a very good judge of who is wealthy.'

'And the other man, Mr Hepworth?' She felt her heart race at her mention of his name.

'A lecher and a fraud.'

'Good gracious me.' She was deeply disappointed.

'I know I should not be so dogmatic, especially when he is not here to defend himself. But I warn you, he looks for money – he has none of his own.'

'Does Mr Ehrlich know only impecunious men?' She managed to smile.

Agnes laughed, a delightful low, bubbling sound, which was infectious and Hannah joined in.

'What's the joke?' Esmeralda was back.

'We talk of the dreaded Hepworth.'

'Oh, I felt so sorry for you, Miss Cresswell, when I saw you placed beside him. He is odious. He fancies he looks like Lord Byron. Tell me, did he say he wished he could write poetry for you?'

Hannah was concerned that her regret must show on her face. 'As a matter of fact, he did.'

'Ha! What fun! That means Papa owes Miss Beatty and me fifty pounds!'

'It was very wrong of us, but we wagered he would. I just wish it had not been to you.'

Hannah felt Miss Beatty place a hand gently on hers. 'It was nothing. I'm glad you won.' She smiled crookedly.

'I so hoped you would come this evening. I heard about the funeral and was afraid you might not,' said Agnes Beatty.

'I did wonder if we should, but dear Lettice would have been so sad had we not. And well . . . Our attendance was purely duty, Miss Beatty. No one liked the man.'

'So difficult, isn't it? One loathes to be hypocritical and yet when society expects, what else can one do?'

'Are you well? Only Esmeralda said . . .' And then she wondered how to continue: she could hardly tell Miss Beatty that the girl had said she was sulking.

'We had a little huff before you arrived. I threatened not to dine with you all. But when I heard you were here I changed my mind.'

Hannah felt awkward again, but was not sure why.

'Miss Cresswell, my garden.' Dulcie Prestwick had joined them. Hannah would normally have been happy to have her company, but tonight, oddly, she wished she could have spent more time alone with Agnes Beatty.

The sun poured through the long casement windows as Lavender pulled back the heavy curtains. 'Good morning, Miss Cresswell,' she said, and put down the tray of tea.

'The sun is bright. What time is it?'

'Nine thirty, Miss. There's something . . .'

'I overslept!'

'No, Miss. I took it upon myself, since you were so late last night, to let you sleep. Miss . . .'

'That was very kind of you, Lavender. But late night or not, I've still much to do today. What time did I retire?'

'About two o'clock.'

'Dear me. How rude of us to stay so late! What will the von Ehrlichs think of us? My writing case, Lavender.'

'You had a nice time, then, Miss?' Lavender asked, as she fetched the finely inlaid box.

'We danced until I thought I should fall over. Mr von Ehrlich is a particularly fine dancer. Then we played games and danced some more. It was so jolly that time just flew by. Only the Lord Lieutenant and his wife left early, and that was hardly surprising since they're nearly eighty. You should have seen Lettice, she had such fun . . . Oh, it was lovely.' She sank back on her pillows recalling the evening.

'And the food?'

'Sublime.'

'I'd best not tell Mrs Gilroy, then.' Lavender laughed.

'But Mr von Ehrlich employs a French chef.'

'I'd best not tell her that either. Mrs Gilroy's none too keen on anything French.'

'Then just tell her it was not as good as hers. Imagine, though, I ate a mango! I never have before.'

'I don't think I ever heard of such a thing.'

'Still,' she opened the sloping box, picked up her pen and inspected the nib, 'I must write my letter. I'll wear the rose linen today. I'll ring when I'm ready.'

'There's just one thing, Miss.'

'Yes?' Hannah looked up. 'What is it?'

'Mr Whitaker would like to talk to you.'

'What about?'

'I couldn't rightly say.' Lavender looked trapped.

'I think you do know.'

'He said I wasn't to discuss anything with you.'

'Whitaker said that?'

'Well, yes.'

'Then I'm ordering you to tell me.'

'Something went missing last night. He's very upset.'

'He thinks it was stolen?'

'Yes, Miss.'

'What was it?'

'A matchbox cover.'

'Hardly the Crown Jewels!' Hannah laughed.

'It was silver, and Mr Whitaker said it was not the value, it was the principle.'

'Of course. And did he instigate a search?'

'Yes. We went through all the servants' rooms but we didn't find anything.'

'We?'

'Mr Whitaker, Mrs Fuller, Mrs Gilroy and myself. I didn't like doing it one little bit, Miss.'

'I'm sure you didn't. Tell Mr Whitaker that I will see him at ten thirty. The minute I've written this letter, get Ferdie to ride over to Courtney Lacey for me. That will be all.'

How horrible, she thought, once her maid had left. It was loathsome when something like this happened. The repercussions would continue for a long time; she knew that from the last time it had happened. Then a couple of pounds had been stolen – not an insignificant sum for the footman, whose money it had been. But there had been such an upheaval, and the suspicion had continued for weeks with whispers and innuendo, a perfectly awful time for everyone. The culprit was never found. Perhaps it was the same person. She'd discuss the possibility with Whitaker.

'This is most unfortunate, Whitaker.'

'It is, Miss Cresswell. I thought to come to you rather than your father.'

'That was considerate of you. I don't want him bothered by this.'

'I wasn't sure what to do with Mrs Cresswell being in residence.'

'Of course.' It must be difficult for the staff – Hannah herself was often unsure if she was in charge. 'I think my sister-in-law would see this as my concern.' Coral was the last person Hannah wanted to know about this, for the time being. She would only offend everyone. 'And you found nothing?'

'We did not.'

'Did you talk to the outside servants?'

'I didn't think it was necessary, Miss Cresswell.'

'But what if our thief had an accomplice, someone who doesn't work in the house, and gave it to them?'

'Most remiss of me. I should have thought.'

'I would like you to note who is particularly close to anyone working outside. And perhaps we should have an inventory of the contents of the silver room, Whitaker.'

'I'm sure that's not necessary. I keep a meticulous eye on it.'

'Evidently not meticulous enough,' she said sharply. 'Who searched the searchers?'

'I didn't think there was any call . . . Miss.'

'Assemble the servants together . . .' she looked at her watch. '. . . In half an hour. I shall come down and talk to them.'

Later as she walked along the stone corridor towards the servants' hall she could hear the buzz of raised voices. It sounded truculent. When she entered the room the belligerence was almost palpable.

'This is a most unhappy occurrence,' she began, once those at the back had been made aware of her arrival. 'I'm sorry it has happened, and for how the innocent among you must feel at having your rooms searched and your possessions disturbed.' She sensed the atmosphere lighten. 'I thank you for your understanding.' One or two had the grace to look shamefaced. 'Something as unfortunate as this always leads to suspicions – usually unfounded – and resentment. But I do hope that will not happen. I'm sure it is all a mistake and we shall be able to laugh at this in the future.' This comment was rewarded with a snort. 'I hope we can resolve it and that it will not be necessary for me to call in the constable. If anyone here is in possession of this trinket I would ask them to own up.' She looked about her questioningly but there was no response – she'd hardly expected one. 'If you are here and you stole it out of desperation, I welcome you to come to me and I shall see what can be done.' Whitaker frowned with disapproval, she saw. No doubt he would have liked the days of transportation to be still with them. 'Are there any questions?'

The group looked about them uneasily, there was much muttering, and a hand was tentatively raised.

'Yes, Dolly.'

'Miss, it's just some of us were wondering why not everyone was searched.'

'I shall be conducting my own search of the rooms of those who weren't.' She saw the furious looks directed at her. 'If that's all?'

'No, Miss, I was wondering . . .' Dolly took a deep breath. 'Is the family to be searched too?' There was a gasp from the assembled company.

'Dolly!' Whitaker and Mrs Gilroy said simultaneously.

'It's a fair question, though I don't think we're likely to steal from ourselves, are we, Dolly?' Although the girl subsided in her seat Hannah felt she was not entirely satisfied with her answer.

'A word.' Hannah beckoned to the senior servants, who followed her out.

'I can't apologise enough for that rude girl, Miss Cresswell.'

'No need, Mrs Fuller, she had every right to raise the issues.'

'But to think that one of the family could be involved. I have never in all my years heard such impertinence.'

'Mr Whitaker, I'm not annoyed. Nor do I want there to be any repercussions on her. I trust that is understood. Now, if I might proceed to your rooms?'

Searching the rooms of senior servants was not pleasant. She had insisted that all four be present as she did so. Whitaker looked close to tears – it was bad enough to witness a grown man so close to breaking down, but even worse that it was the butler, who was normally so dignified. In her room, Mrs Fuller played with her chatelaine until Hannah had to tell her to stop. Mrs Gilroy stood, arms folded over her breasts, with an expression of such fury that Hannah preferred not to look at her. Only Lavender accepted the necessity.

It was embarrassing to find the collection of saucy postcards in the butler's room, and so many empty port bottles – Hannah felt she could never look him in the eye again. She was surprised by the collection of romantic novels in the cook's room, and that her underwear was remarkably flimsy. She avoided looking at the bundle of letters held together with pink ribbon in Mrs Fuller's room, and she would never tell a living soul that the housekeeper kept a photograph of Whitaker under her stockings. How very different they were from how she had imagined them, and how sad.

'I never want to do that again, ever,' she said to Lavender, as her maid dressed her hair ready for luncheon.

'It can't have been nice for you.'

'Will they stay angry with me?'

'I shouldn't think so. They knew it was only fair. Once the dust has settled we'll all be back to normal.'

'Do you think it was stolen or mislaid?'

'I couldn't say, Miss.'

'Dolly's a spirited girl, isn't she?'

'She won't be when Mrs Gilroy's finished with her!'

Her father was waiting for her in the library, and Oliver was lounging in a chair looking at a book on North America.

'What a lovely evening we enjoyed last night,' Mortimer said.

'Wasn't it, Papa?'

'We should have the von Ehrlichs back at the earliest

opportunity. They might be different but they're exactly what this county needs. New blood, new ideas.'

'Some of the fuddy-duddies won't agree with you, Father.'

'Content to eat his food and drink his wine in copious amounts, though, weren't they?'

'The way of the world, Father.'

'And what's this I hear of a thief on the premises, Hannah?'

'I didn't want to bother you. Did James tell you?'

'He did, and he took umbrage at being searched. But what else could Whitaker do? Seems a lot of fuss over such a small thing.'

'But if whoever took it gets away with this it might embolden them to take something more valuable,' Oliver put in.

'That's true. And you, young woman, what's all this gossip I heard last night of you setting up a business on your own?'

'I was going to tell you, Papa, when it was more organised. Do you mind?' Her heart sank that he had been told: she had not yet worked out how to broach the subject with him.

'I'm not sure what I think. It takes some getting used to, my only daughter in commerce.'

'Coral will have the vapours,' Oliver remarked.

'Now, now, Oliver,' Mortimer admonished his son, while smiling broadly. 'And when did this all happen?'

'It was something Lady Prestwick said.'

'Ha! Theo said she was a radical creature.'

'Oh, no, she didn't influence me. She made me realise what I had been thinking – that I wanted to do more with my life than run the house when it isn't mine, paint badly and shop.'

'This is all my fault. If I hadn't stopped you marrying you wouldn't be thinking like this,' her father told her.

'But I'm glad you did. I would have made Simeon a

283

dreadful wife. Laura is much more suitable for him.' At this she looked at Oliver, who had the grace to concentrate on his book. 'And even if I had, I'm sure I'd have thought the same.'

'And what sort of fee are you envisaging, Hannah?'

'Oh, I couldn't charge anyone!' Hannah looked suitably shocked.

'But you should. A labourer is worthy of his hire.'

'Lady Prestwick said that to me. And she also said that people didn't appreciate things nearly as much if they hadn't paid for them.'

'A wise woman. And look how successful she is. What did you decide?'

'I said she should give me a present.'

Oliver laughed. 'You might be in business but you won't make your fortune.'

'Von Ehrlich will expect to be charged for his parterre.'

'He promised he wouldn't say a word to anyone.' Hannah was disappointed in him.

'Never trust the von Ehrlichs of this world.'

'You're such a cynic, Oliver.'

'But, like Lady Prestwick, wise.'

'The only problem I see is that you will soon run out of friends,' Mortimer opined.

'But, Papa, I have another venture. Mr Snape, the architect you found for me, has asked me to be a consultant for some villas he is building in Barlton. I was going to ask you if we could supply the plants from here. We always have more than we need . . .' The words and plans were bubbling out of her. But she stopped when she saw that her father was laughing.

'Good gracious!' was all he could say, and each time he repeated himself he laughed the more.

Oliver laid down his book. 'Did you say we would supply the plants from the gardens here?'

'Yes. We overproduce plants and many are burnt. If I was a success we could open the two large glasshouses at the far end of the kitchen garden and grow more to supply my business – if you see what I mean. After all, our roses are the best in the county – everyone says so. And, of course,' she had a brainwave, 'I would insist on buying them.' She felt pleased with this last comment: it made her sound more serious about the venture, more in control.

'It's an interesting idea, Father.'

'I can see it might be but I could never take money from my own daughter!' he spluttered. 'And I still have to adjust to the idea of my daughter being in *business*.' He was laughing again.

'Father! Please!' Hannah felt quite angry with him.

Her tone calmed him and he frowned. 'This matter requires consideration, Hannah. I'll let you know if you have my approval in good time. Business! My daughter!' He looked as if he was about to start laughing again. 'Come,' he said, at a tap on the door.

A diffident-looking Melanie entered. 'I hope you don't mind me bringing my son with me, Sir Mortimer.'

'Better you have someone with you in the circumstances,' Oliver said helpfully, and Melanie paled visibly. 'You don't look well – do sit down. Father!' Oliver said severely. Mortimer now had a handkerchief laid over his mouth as he tried to control himself.

'Forgive me, Mrs Topsham,' he said. 'I just heard something amusing.'

Hannah looked at him with dismay: he wasn't taking her seriously.

'I asked you here to discuss your future,' Mortimer continued.

Melanie sat rigid, and Hannah noticed that Zephaniah's hands were clenched and the knuckles showed white.

'Yes,' Melanie whispered.

'In the circumstances . . .' Mortimer's voice trailed off as if he was unsure how to proceed. 'You know the

285

Cresswell Arms?' As soon as he had said it he was waving his handkerchief. 'Of course you do.'

'Shall I, Father?' Oliver intervened, aware that Melanie's distress was compounded by his father's odd behaviour. 'We have been thinking for some time that the inn needs to be refurbished and improved, not to just sell beer but food too. In my opinion, and I have talked with others who know more about such matters, the inn is ideally placed for travellers passing on the road to Barlton and Exeter.'

'Yes?' Melanie looked confused.

'We wondered if you would be interested in running it.'

'Me? But I know nothing of the victuallers' trade. I mean – I rarely drink.'

'Even better,' Mortimer said, in control of himself now.

'We would start with just four rooms for hire but we could expand to twenty.'

'Twenty!' she said, in an awed tone. 'But are there many travellers on that road?'

'I've been asking questions and have observed that this summer there have been more family visitors to Cress than usual. If the facilities were available we could become like Torquay, or Paignton.'

'I don't know either place.'

'I assure you, they flourish.'

'Excuse me.' Zephaniah leant forward. 'Before we go further, what would my mother's remuneration be?'

'Her keep and accommodation, of course, and a wage.'

'What would be her security?'

'In what way?' Mortimer seemed puzzled.

'What guarantee would she have that the employment would continue, as you describe?'

'You mean you want a contract?' Mortimer asked.

'That would be acceptable.'

'Zeph!' Melanie whispered urgently.

Mortimer was shaking with laughter. 'Well! You're a good son, Zephaniah. It is commendable that you should look after your mother's affairs. What do you say, Mrs Topsham?'

'I . . .' She got no further before she burst into tears. Speech was beyond her, but she was nodding vigorously in case they thought she was not interested.

An hour later, Stanislas von Ehrlich was closeted with Mortimer. They were alone since Mortimer had asked the others to leave him.

'It was kind of you to come so quickly,' he said.

'Last night I had the impression you wanted me to call as soon as I could. And here I am.' Stanislas gestured, his hand gloved in cream suede, which would have looked more suitable in Bond Street than in the country, as would his patent-leather shoes and his silver-topped cane.

'I need advice,' Mortimer told him.

'*You* need advice from *me*? Then I am flattered.'

'I trust this conversation will remain confidential between us?'

'But of course.'

'I need to make some money as quickly as possible.'

'Yes?' Stanislas looked infuriatingly blank.

Mortimer shifted in his chair, the man was playing games with him. But could he blame him? He himself represented the old order, this man the new. It was human nature, he supposed, to score points. 'Yes.' Two could play at that.

'Am I to presume you wish me to loan you money, Sir Mortimer? I'm not a bank.' He flicked an imaginary speck of dust from his sleeve.

'No, nothing like that. "Neither a borrower nor a lender be."'

'Quite. I'm happy that is not the case since I never lend to anyone. One is so rarely repaid.'

'How unfortunate. Do you know of any ventures I might invest in for a suitable and swift return?'

Stanislas balanced his hands on the top of his silver cane. 'My dear Sir Mortimer, I have one golden rule. I never give such advice to those I regard as friends. And I hope we are friends.'

'We are. But you don't?'

'No. What if the investment was a disaster and you lost your money? You would blame me, I would lose your friendship and I should be sorely unhappy.'

'I see.' What a perplexing individual von Ehrlich was. It was not the answer Mortimer had expected. 'Then that's that, I suppose. Never mind. Worth a try . . .'

'However . . .'

'Yes?'

'Your land marches with mine. If you were interested in selling me those two farms that abut my land, that would be a different matter.'

'Really? I might be.'

'Then we can do business?'

'If I have your assurance that no one else need know.'

'It goes without saying, Sir Mortimer.'

The family were at lunch and all looked up at noises coming from the hall. Whitaker, who was in attendance, steamed across the dining room to investigate.

'Hello, my darling family!'

The door opened with a flourish and there was Penelope Cresswell, arms wide, resplendent in a cream linen suit, her matching picture hat heavy with large pink roses. 'My darling Mortimer, I came as soon as I received your summons.' She kissed him and placed her hand possessively on his shoulder, then looked at Hannah triumphantly.

Chapter Ten
September 1901

Hannah had been avoiding her stepmother. Yesterday's lunch had continued in a mixed atmosphere. Coral and Mortie were overjoyed and fussed over Penelope; Oliver was polite but distant; Hannah had been silent and nervous. Sir Mortimer had looked sheepish.

'Hannah!'

Having returned from her morning bicycle ride to inspect her house, she stopped in her tracks on the upper landing. Slowly she turned. 'Yes – Mother?'

'A word.' Penelope swept into her room, Hannah close behind. Colette, Penelope's maid, was unpacking the numerous trunks that had arrived with her and acknowledged Hannah with a slight bob. She continued to bustle from sitting room to dressing room, her arms full of clothes.

'No doubt you thought you were rid of me. Well, you aren't.'

'I thought no such thing – Mother.' For once she did not blush as she lied.

'Your father has decided to remain here permanently.'

'He told me so.'

'And what do you think of that?'

'It will be better for him to remain in the country. He needs the peace and quiet to recover fully.'

'He looks recovered to me.'

'He still tires easily.'

'I'm not surprised if you keep him out until the early hours.'

'But . . .' She was about to argue that she was not the

only one who had been at the von Ehrlichs and not noticed the time, but she knew she would be wasting her breath. When Penelope decided something there was no changing her mind, and in any case, Colette had returned to scoop up more clothes. She didn't want her to overhear any of this.

'It's a good thing I have returned. He obviously needs someone to look after him properly.'

'I think we did.'

'And I think you didn't. Now, I called for you to inform you that we shall be making changes. I intend to take over the full running of the house. I shall need the household ledgers and inventories of the linen, plate and china.'

'Yes – Mother.' She felt sick. This house had been her life for so long and now it was being wrenched from her.

'Coral has requested that since I am now to be here permanently I should care for the children.'

'Lettice and Young Mortimer hardly need caring for. They are almost adults.' Thank goodness, she thought. They would not allow anyone to cut her out of their lives.

'And what about little Felix – or had you forgotten him?'

'Of course not.' How could anyone think that of her? She loved Felix. This was typical of Coral: she would be happy to deprive, humiliate and hurt her, and her stepmother would gladly take up the baton. But at six Felix was a delightful child, and he amused her, yet she was not as attached to him as she was to the others. She did not find small children engrossing: it was when they reached eight or nine, with their minds formed, that they fascinated her. She saw him every day, and checked his well-being, but he had Nanny Wishart and did not need Hannah, or anyone else, come to that.

'And what is this nonsense about gardening and a *business*?' She said this last word with a marked shudder. 'Colette, have those shoes cleaned.' The maid was on her hands and knees in front of one of the largest cases. 'Well?' Her attention had returned to Hannah.

'It is an idea I've had.' She made her voice as low as possible, hoping the maid had not heard.

'Your father is horrified.'

'I don't think so. He was interested in my plans – amused, even.'

'I beg your pardon?' Penelope looked at Hannah with astonishment. 'Are you disagreeing with my assessment.'

'Yes.'

'Are you ill?'

'On the contrary—'

'Colette, you've dropped a chemise. You're to forget this idiotic idea, Hannah. I will not hear of it. You bring shame on your family.'

Hannah looked at her stepmother. The fear had gone, to be replaced with anger. 'I'll do no such thing. I wish to do something with my life. I don't believe my father would want me to stop.'

'Of course he does. He said—' But Hannah did not wait to hear. She rushed from the room, ran along the corridor and raced down the stairs. She was not sure what she was doing or where she was going, just that she wanted to get out of the house and away from that hateful woman.

'Miss Cresswell, a moment of your time?' Whitaker was gliding across the hall.

'Not now, Whitaker.'

'But it's important, Miss. It's the inventory.'

She skidded to a halt. 'Yes?'

'Several items are missing. There is nothing of any great value, just small items and trinkets, but I was wondering—'

'You had better go and see Lady Cresswell about it. It's none of my business any longer.' She turned abruptly and ran through the corridors to the back of the house. It would never do to cry, not in front of the servants. Then she discovered that she was not crying, that she didn't think she would. Instead she wanted to smash something.

She collected her bicycle from the far stable, mounted it, then headed towards Dunwell Wood and her new house.

'Happy birthday, Laura.'

'You remembered!'

'Would I forget? It's why I couldn't wait until this afternoon. I wanted to give you this.' He handed her a small packet.

'Does that mean we won't meet later?' She looked at him wistfully as she opened the small box he had given her. Inside lay a locket. 'It's adorable, but I can't wear it.'

'Why not? Who would see it under your chemise?'

'I missed you the last few days,' said Laura, as she melted into Oliver's arms.

'I've had to be so careful. I don't want you to be compromised in any way. I would never forgive myself.'

'I fear for you too.'

'But it's you who takes all the risk.'

'And if we were discovered?'

'What could happen to me? I'm a man and we never get the blame. They'd think what a fine fellow I was.' He was smiling, teasing her.

'You might find some people were disappointed in you,' she said quietly.

'Not anyone I know.' He chose not to think of Hannah. 'How unfair it all is, with you so good and sweet . . .'

'How unfair when you're such a wicked man – my darling.' She pushed him playfully.

'For you I would commit every sin known to man if it meant we could meet each other like this,' Oliver told her.

'The days I don't see you are interminably long.'

'I know.' He kissed the tip of her nose. 'Such a pretty nose you have, Mrs Redman.'

She sat up abruptly. 'Don't call me that.'

'I'm sorry, my love. I would never knowingly upset you.'

'I know you would not. It's just that the name reminds me . . .' She brushed back her hair distractedly. 'My darling, I don't want to be married to him. I wish I'd never met him. And thinking in that way makes me feel so guilty. It isn't Simeon's fault. He's been a good husband and doesn't deserve such treatment. When I think of my lovely son, the guilt doubles and I'm afraid of my wickedness. But, Oliver,' she turned to face him, 'it's so hard – when he touches me . . .'

'Don't talk about it.' Oliver thumped the ground beside him. 'At night I can't sleep for thinking of the unspeakable.'

'But what can I do? I think of you – I'm always wishing it was you.' She put up her hand and caressed his face, her face suffused with love for him. 'I know we're sinful – but how can such joy, such bliss, be a sin?' Her words were not matched by her bleak expression.

'It can't be immoral! It would be if we didn't love each other. I tried to explain that to Hannah but—'

Laura broke away from him. 'You told your sister? How could you? This is our secret – you promised!'

'Come back. I didn't tell her – I would have kept it secret to my dying day. She saw us.'

'Just seeing us . . .'

'She saw us kissing.' He laughed. 'I couldn't explain it away – not the way *we* kiss.' He pulled her to him, and kissed her passionately, his hands wandering down her body, relishing her curves, flicking up her skirt, as Laura moaned in his arms.

'Did she understand?' Laura asked, a while later, as they straightened their clothes.

'No.' He rubbed a few blades of grass off her cheek.

'I didn't think she would. She's such a righteous woman.'

'Miaow.' He grinned at her.

'I didn't mean it like that. Perhaps it was the wrong word. She's a *good* woman, was what I meant, not a sinner like me.'

'I told her she couldn't judge us when she had never loved. If she had, she would be sympathetic towards us, not censorious.'

'You can't blame her. Poor Hannah.'

'What makes you say that? She's content.'

'Is she? I don't think so. She longs for love.'

'Does she? I've never noticed. She seems happy enough.'

'You're a man – you don't see as women do. Watch her. Whenever a new man appears she seems to glow with anticipation, as if she hopes he is the one for her. She's a woman searching for love. She's lonely.'

'Come to think of it, a few nights ago we went to the von Ehrlichs and Hannah shone. She was really animated, not at all like her normal self.'

'Is von Ehrlich attractive?'

'His character, yes. Physically, I'm not sure. I never know what women like in men.'

'Maybe he will take to her.'

'He was charming to her, but he is with everyone.' He frowned. 'I don't think he's right for her and I can't see my father approving. There's something too sharp about him. He's a mountebank, I fear.'

'But what if she likes him? It's her life and future, not your father's, not yours. Do you have the right to stop her chance of happiness?'

'It's our duty to her.'

'She might not agree.'

'She would eventually.'

'Would you listen to her if she told you never to see me again?'

'No.'

'Where's the difference?'

'As I said earlier, I'm a man.'

'Then let's hope she is not interested in him. But poor Hannah! First her father objects to Simeon and now, perhaps, this von Ehrlich.'

'She doesn't mind. She's grateful now to Father for stopping her marrying Simeon.' He looked at her and his face flickered with a multitude of expressions. Shame, horror, embarrassment, amusement. 'I shouldn't have said that.'

'And I should be cross with you.' To his relief she laughed.

'I'd be so miserable if you were. You are the answer to my dearest wish. When I first returned I went to the wishing tree over on Childer's Hill and wished for you.'

'You shouldn't have told me. Your wish will be broken.'

'Don't be silly, of course it won't. Not now I have you. Unless, of course, you're going to leave me?'

'My dearest, how could I?' she said, as she slid once more into his arms.

Hannah was pedalling so fast that a cloud of dust followed her along the lanes. She was wobbling alarmingly and the hard tyres of her bicycle ensured that she bounced uncomfortably on the dry, rutted road. As she sped through the gate she braked suddenly and almost went over the handlebars.

'Is there anyone here?' she called, and immediately felt calmer as she entered her house. She was amazed each time she came by the rapid progress. She took out her handkerchief and dabbed her eyes – she didn't want the architect to think she had been crying.

'Miss Cresswell, how fortunate that you're in time to inspect the glass for the dining-room doors. I'd rather you approved it before we put it in.'

'Why? Is it awful?'

'No, not at all. But I think you should see the engraving first. Are you all right, Miss Cresswell? Only . . .' He stopped as if unsure how to continue, with the expression of one who wished he hadn't started.

Hannah touched her face. 'It's the dust from the lane – the grit sets into my eyes. I need goggles really.' She doubted if he believed her.

'What a sensible idea. After all the speed you can travel on your velocipede . . .'

'The floor's finished! How lovely it is.' She gazed down at the light oak parquet she had chosen.

'Just needs polishing now.'

'You know the furniture I liked? How long would it take to have it delivered?'

'A matter of days, once you have chosen the items you want.'

'Then we should order it immediately. When could I move in?'

'But I thought—'

'I've changed my mind. Oh, I love them.' They had arrived in the dining room and the glass for the doors was propped against the wall. Hannah had had a scene of water, reeds and birds engraved on it. 'It's a work of art.'

'Then we should put them in?'

'Most certainly . . . This room is so light. It will be a joy to eat in here.' Light was pouring in through the French windows, which opened on to a terrace. She planned to have tubs of plants there. She was glad she had chosen the blond oak – pitch pine, stained oak, and mahogany had also been put forward, but she had rejected them and she had been right to do so.

'Perhaps we should contemplate the kitchen. I should like to be living here by the end of the month.'

'Yes, Miss Cresswell, whatever you wish.'

Melanie stood in the bar at the Cresswell Arms. Her

heart sank. The place was filthy and run-down – even her cottage was preferable. Still, she told herself, she had no choice. She'd better get on with it. From the bag she had with her she covered her dress with a voluminous apron. In a cupboard she found a broom, a dustpan and brush, and some rags. She opened the door and windows wide, tied a scarf over her head and a piece of rag over the broom's bristles and started to sweep down the cobwebs that festooned the ceiling like ectoplasm.

'It's a mess, mother.' Zephaniah clattered in.

'Nothing some elbow grease and plenty of hot water can't put right.'

'There's six bedrooms up there – the big ones could be divided to make more. There's one huge room, too big perhaps for a bedroom. And in the attics there's another four. Have you seen the kitchen?'

'Not yet. I don't know if I've the strength.' She laughed.

'It's nice to see you laugh. You haven't done much of that in your life, have you?'

'Go on, I wasn't always miserable,' she said. 'If you've found the kitchen maybe you'd get in some wood and light the range. I'd like some hot water and a cup of tea would be nice – I reckon this is going to be thirsty work.'

Half an hour later, the cobwebs dealt with and the floor swept, she went in search of her son and the tea. A black-faced Zephaniah was on all fours in front of the range; it was the filthiest Melanie had ever seen. 'You look as if you've been down a coal mine. Just look at the state of you.'

'I can't get it to light.'

'Here, let me.'

'How did you manage that?' Zephaniah asked, once the fire had taken hold.

'Years of apprenticeship with the copper in the cottage.' She lifted the lid of the kettle and pulled a face. It was caked with fur. 'It will have to do – I'm dry as dust.'

'What about one of these saucepans?'

'Would you fancy anything put in that?' She indicated its interior.

'That Tubs must have been the dirtiest man on the planet.'

'Poor soul. I learnt after the funeral that he had lost his wife and children in a fire. Yet he was always so cheerful. And he had no one. Can you imagine how awful that must be?'

'Horrible.'

One wall of the kitchen was taken up with a pine dresser that needed a good scrub; tall as she was, she would never reach the top shelves. The range covered another. Melanie crossed to the two stone sinks, with a small pump handle over them. She tried it and it worked. 'Well, that's an improvement – no more going to the well.' She filled the kettle, then opened the dresser cupboards and found china, cooking utensils, glasses, jugs. 'Just look at all of this. There'll be no need to buy any equipment.'

They carried the tea-tray into the bar and sat at one of the trestle tables in front of the open window. From here Melanie could see the bustling quay, the anchored ships, the swooping, cackling seabirds and, beyond, the wide expanse of the sea. 'Makes you want to get on one of those ships and sail away, doesn't it?'

'Not particularly. I like it here,' her son answered. Sometimes Melanie felt as though he was the older of them, she the child.

'That breeze is cooling, isn't it? We'll be happy here.'

'You sure you want to take this on, Mother? It's going to be hard work and long hours.'

'That doesn't frighten me. The thought of drunks does, though.' She knew what a drunken man was capable of doing.

'But you just spoke of going away?'

'That was just a dream, I didn't mean it. It's just something you say. Don't you?'

'I can't say I do.'

Melanie smiled at him. He was such a serious young man. 'I think, with a lick of whitewash, a good polish, perhaps a picture or two, some decent chairs, this could look nice.'

'Have you had a chance to discuss what needs to be done with Oliver Cresswell?'

'Not yet. He said he'd be here this morning – he must have been delayed. Perhaps he changed his mind since we're to see his father this afternoon.'

'You're not to be soft with them, Mother. Right from the start you insist on having what you want.'

'I hardly think I shall be in a position to do that.'

'They'll expect you to make a profit so they have to supply you with the wherewithal. And make sure you account for every penny you spend.'

'I'll do that.' She smiled at him, touched by his concern for her. She busied herself pouring the tea so that he could not see how emotional his regard made her feel.

'It's too hot to carry much.' Xenia stood in the doorway, the smallest of Melanie's baskets over her arm. 'I'm exhausted.'

'Come and have a cup of tea.'

'Are you really going to live here?' Xenia looked about her with distaste. 'It's awful, Mama. It's filthy.'

'You should have seen it before I started.' Melanie was laughing again.

'I think you're ill advised to take this on, Mama.'

'Xenia, I have little choice. I have to earn money somehow. But in any case I want to. It will be a challenge.' She was not sure if she was saying that to reassure her children or herself.

'Where was he killed?' The horror of Xenia's words was belied by the casual tone of her voice.

'There.' Melanie pointed to the spot on the floor where

299

Bernard had lain. It had unsettled her to sweep it; she had been certain that a dark stain on the floorboard was his blood.

'I can't say I'm sorry.'

'I wouldn't expect you to be, Xenia.'

'I don't fancy walking over there.'

'I can't say I enjoyed it. Now, wouldn't it be a good idea if you went upstairs and chose a room for yourself while you're here?'

'Me? Stay here? Hardly, Mama.'

'I've no idea where you can go, then.'

'I can stay in the cottage.'

'We have to be out by the end of the week.'

'How can they evict you so soon?'

'They're not evicting us. They need the cottage urgently so I volunteered to go.'

'I wish you'd spoken to me. I'd like to have stayed there.'

'But you'll be returning to Mrs Featherstone's next week.'

'I don't want to go.'

'You never said. I thought you were happy there.'

'It is so tedious, Mama. She's so old and it's tiresome fetching and carrying for her. She smells too.'

'Surely not. I don't believe it.'

'Old people always smell.' Xenia wrinkled her nose.

'But you could have stayed. I'll have struggle enough to keep Timmy and myself. What will you do?'

'I thought to ask Miss Hannah if she needs a companion, or Lettice. They'll help me.'

'I don't think that's a good idea.'

'Why not? You've worked there.'

'That was different.'

'What's different? Why can't I?'

'Because I say so.'

'It's not fair! Why can Zeph stay and I have to be pushed away?'

'Zeph?'

'Oh, hasn't he told you? Then excuse me.' She swished her skirts angrily. 'I'd better leave you to your little *tête-à-tête* then, hadn't I?' She opened the door to the staircase, slammed it behind her and clattered up the stairs, making as much noise as she could.

'Zeph?' Her son was still sitting at the table, looking uncomfortable.

'I should have spoken to you first, mother, but I'd like to stay and help you.'

'That would be wonderful, Zeph. How long for?'

'For good.'

'But you can't do that, Zeph! Your career! I couldn't spoil your chances.'

'I'd rather be here with you – I've weighed up my prospects and I reckon I'll be better off. Mr Battle's nice enough but it'll take me years to get anywhere. I'm kept so busy I have little time for study. Some clerks there are still articled when they retire, and I don't want to be one of them.'

'But it's such an opportunity for you.'

'No, it isn't, Mother. I'm cheap labour, that's all. If we work hard here, though, I think we could make a real success. I've walked round the village – well, it's almost too big to call it that, isn't it? – and it's very pleasant. As Sir Mortimer said, I think there's need for a respectable inn.'

'It would make me so happy but . . .' Her son, she knew, with his serious demeanour, was not the ideal choice of landlord, but she could not bring herself to say so. 'If you're sure.' He should stay with Mr Battle, she thought, she'd persuade him later.

'I'm positive.'

'That makes me want to cry.'

Zephaniah hit his forehead. 'Don't – please don't. Don't cry!' he declared, just like a tragedian. Melanie laughed.

'Excuse me, are you open?' A man was peering in the doorway.

Melanie paused only a second. 'Of course. What can I get you, sir?'

'Hannah, what's the matter? What's happened?' Oliver, riding back from a tryst with Laura, had found his sister slumped on the grassy bank of the drive, a picture of dejection.

'I fell off my bicycle.'

'Have you hurt yourself?'

'I'm just a bit shaken.' She began to get to her feet.

'That machine's dangerous.'

'No, it's not. It's the stupid way I ride it.'

'You look as if you've been crying.'

'I wish people would stop saying I have when I haven't.' She stamped her foot with frustration.

'Something must have happened – you never lose your temper.'

'Why can't I? Everyone else does.' She was brushing down her skirt now.

'Hannah, I don't want to annoy you, but if something's wrong please tell me what it is. Maybe I can help.'

'I doubt that anyone can. I was so happy ... and then ...'

'I think we had better sit down.' He pulled her down beside him. Sergeant pulled contentedly at the grass. 'Is it Mother? Has she said something to you?'

'I wish I could talk to you about it but I can't. But I will say one thing. I'm tired of always having to pretend that all is well when it's far from being so.'

'I'm the one person you can confide in. You know there's no love lost between Mother and myself. You have no need to protect me, and I won't say a word to anyone. I promise.'

'Very well, then. She's trying to control my life again. She says I have no right to pursue my gardening plan—'

'She can't stop you.'

'She says Papa is horrified and will forbid it.'

'I think not. He most certainly doesn't want you to become too commercial – he feels it's not fitting and would prefer you to continue with private commissions – but otherwise I think he's rather proud that you wish to do something.'

'Really?' She ventured to look at him.

'Your eyes are all pink. Are you sure you haven't been crying?'

'No!' she shouted.

'Then why do your eyes look like a ferret's?' he teased.

She chuckled unwillingly. 'Why are brothers always so rude?'

'It's what we're here for – to stop you becoming conceited.'

'Not to make me laugh?'

'That too.' He grinned. 'But you must'nt let Mother hurt you. She's clever – she knows how to upset you.'

'But why would she want to? What have I ever done to her?'

'You remind her that our father loved someone before her. And it would seem to me that your mother was the love of his life. She's jealous of her and punishes you for it.'

'That's what Nanny Wishart says.'

'Wise old bird, Nanny. So, you see, it's nothing to do with you, really. In fact, she probably likes you.'

'If she does she hides it well.' She managed a laugh this time.

'Feeling better?'

'Yes, I am.'

'Good. Shall we go home, then?' He nodded up the drive towards the manor.

'I love that house. Just look at how beautiful it is. To me it's like a living thing. It's as much part of me as my arm. Does that sound silly?'

'I loved it like that once, but I don't allow myself to do so any more.'

'I can't stay, you see. I'm going to ask Papa for permission to move to the new house this month.'

'Because of Mother?'

'Yes. She tells me she's going to stay here permanently. It would be impossible, for her too, if we continued to live under the same roof.' There was a tremor in her voice.

Oliver took her hand and squeezed it. 'It's sad, but probably for the best. You've been mistress of the house for too long—'

'Why did he ask her back? He's been so much happier . . . Oh dear, that's wrong of me. I should be happy they are reconciled. I should be pleased he's not alone any more.'

'If I tell you something, promise you won't repeat it?'

'Of course.'

'He can't afford not to have her here.'

Hannah stopped walking. 'What do you mean?'

'Mother's extravagant, as you know, and supporting her in London is too much for him. He's maintaining three mansions, three sets of servants. And that's without her expenditure on travel, clothes, all the things women find they cannot live without.'

'But why? He's always kept two houses before, I thought your mother's new home was quite modest.'

'I don't want you to repeat this to anyone but he has lost a lot of money recently. The estate is not producing as much revenue as it used to.'

'Oliver, this is dreadful.'

'It came as quite a shock to me too.'

'And I've made things worse with my house. Oh, why did he allow me to be so extravagant? Can't you help him?'

'I offered, but he refused.'

'This is so serious.'

'Less so with Mother returning. The London houses are to be sold – not that she knows.' He laid his finger on his lips. 'Don't look so tragic, Hannah. He's not going to starve or be bankrupted. He's making a few economies, that's all.'

'Poor Papa.'

'Indeed – having to live with Mother again!'

'Oliver!' She pushed him. 'You really are wicked!'

'But you love me.'

'I do. Don't ever leave again, will you? Promise?'

He hugged her in reply. 'Is there anything else?'

Hannah wondered if she should mention the stolen objects, but decided against it. If she was leaving, it no longer had anything to do with her. Let Penelope sort it out.

'Where's Lavender?' Mrs Gilroy asked, as she joined Mrs Fuller and Whitaker.

'Rushed off her feet. Who would have thought so much could change in such a short time,' the housekeeper said, as she handed Mrs Gilroy her cup.

'It's hard to know if you're coming or going. As soon as we think everything's settled it all changes again.'

'It was more peaceful here without Lady C. I can't say I'm happy at her return.'

'Mrs Fuller!'

'I speak as I find, Edward. She upsets all and sundry, she does. And that she's apparently here for keeps fills me with dread.'

'And Mr Greenacre's going. Not that that's any great loss as far as I can make out. Never heard a good word said of him.'

'I hadn't heard there was to be a change in estate manager. Where did you hear that, Mrs Gilroy?' Whitaker asked, looking put out.

'The head gardener told me when he delivered the vegetables today. Sudden it was.'

'Given the push, was he? Can't say I can blame Sir Mortimer for that.'

'Oh, no, Gussie. He gave notice. Apparently his wife made him. Got a position near St Austell, I gather. Not quality like here, of course. But then, beggars can't be choosers.'

'So, is a new manager coming, Eve, since you seem to know it all?'

Mrs Gilroy smiled slightly at the sarcasm. Household servants always thought they should know everything before those who worked in the kitchen. 'Apparently Mr Oliver is taking over everything.'

'Will Mr Mortie like that?'

'I doubt he has much choice, Edward. Everything's changing. It was a difficult meal this evening with Madam and her London ways.'

'There's more to come. Miss Hannah's moving.'

Housekeeper and Cook looked at the butler with astonishment. 'Never!' they chorused.

'I overheard them discussing it at dinner. She's going to the dower house in two weeks. Her father tried to dissuade her but she was adamant. That young woman has changed since his illness, to be sure.'

'She'll be a loss to us. She was always fair, was Miss Hannah. Come in,' Mrs Fuller called to the tap on the door. Lavender appeared.

'What a day! My mistress is beside herself.'

'So it's true?' Mrs Gilroy asked. Whitaker scowled at her.

'I'm afraid so. And I shall miss the little chats we have down here,' Lavender said. 'She'll have a small staff and it'll be quite lonely.'

'We'll visit you, and you can come here whenever you want.'

'We couldn't stay. Lady Cresswell is being horrible to her – after all Miss Hannah's done for this family! It's not right! The old bitch!'

'Really, Lavender, you should not refer to your mistress in such an uncouth manner.'

'She's not my mistress, Mr Whitaker, Miss Cresswell is.'

'But who pays your wages? You should always keep that in mind.'

'From now on Miss Hannah will. She's going to tell her father she can manage her own money. I only hope she's right about that.'

There was a banging on the door.

'Yes, Jock?'

'Sorry to bother you, Mr Whitaker, but you're needed. The bells have been going crazy, sir.'

Wearily he stood up. 'If you'll excuse me, ladies . . .'

'Lovely manners, that man,' said Mrs Gilroy, with a sigh, once he had departed.

'There's something more going on here than meets the eye.' Mrs Fuller ignored her. 'I'm not surprised about Greenacre, or, in a way, about Miss Cresswell, but what about Melanie Topsham and the Cresswell Arms?'

'She's landed on her feet there. Mind you, what does she know about beer and food? Catering for large numbers is hard work. It's the organising – takes years to learn.' Mrs Gilroy looked smug.

'But why? That's what I'd like to know.'

'It's a man's job,' Lavender said, 'running an inn, with all manner of rough people patronising it. And she's never struck me as a happy person. You need someone jolly in a bar.'

'Well, if you ask me . . .' and Mrs Fuller beckoned to the other two to lean forward '. . . I think she knows something about this family and they pay her to keep quiet.'

'I thought you were going to tell us something interesting. That rumour's been going the rounds as far back as anyone can remember. Why, I've even heard she's Sir Mortimer's by-blow.'

'Eve! She doesn't look a bit like any of them.'

'I'm not saying it, others do. But there you are, that's what you get with gossip.' She looked triumphant.

'I've never noticed you didn't like to hear a bit now and then,' Mrs Fuller retorted.

'What sort of thing do you think Mrs Topsham knows, Gussie?' Lavender asked politely.

'There's something fishy. Look how idle her husband was. And there was a lot of bad feeling about them being given that cottage when it's one of the biggest.'

'Is that so, Eve?'

Mrs Fuller fidgeted with her stays. 'And why don't her parents speak to her? Answer me that.'

'They were at the funeral,' Lavender said.

'Don't mean anything. Probably went for show,' was the cook's opinion.

'I reckon she was Sir Mortimer's fancy woman.'

'Gussie!'

'You might look all po-faced, Lavender, but look how Lady C loathes her. Makes you think, doesn't it?'

But none of them had time to think for the door flew open and Whitaker stumbled in.

'Lord above, Edward! You look like you've seen a ghost. What is it?'

'Trouble, that's what it is, Mrs Fuller. Lady Cresswell's sapphire ring has gone missing. In hysterics, she is.'

Melanie could not have chosen a worse time to call on the Cresswells. The house was in turmoil. She wavered on the back step, hearing the raised voices in the corridor beyond.

'Something's happened.' She turned to Zephaniah and Xenia. 'Perhaps we should leave.'

'But you've an arrangement to meet Sir Mortimer.'

'Yes, but if there's a problem . . .'

'Whoever is shouting, it isn't anything to do with us,' Xenia said petulantly. 'I've come all this way and I'm not going back yet. My shoes are hurting.' She was wearing a tight, neat, heeled pair, unsuitable for walking in the countryside. Nothing was ever right for her, Melanie thought. Xenia hated being here – her carping never ceased. Living at the inn was undoubtedly beneath her and Melanie was left in no doubt that her daughter thought she was meant for better things than Fate had given her.

'You didn't have to come. You chose to.' She was on the point of mentioning that she should have worn more sensible shoes for the three-mile walk from the Cresswell Arms, but restrained herself.

'Why shouldn't I see inside the house? Why should I be excluded?'

'No one is excluding you. Oh, it doesn't matter.' She tugged at the bell pull.

'Yes?' The door opened and Dolly Pepper peered out. Her hair was awry and she looked as if she had been crying.

'We have an appointment with Sir Mortimer. These are my children, Dolly.'

Dolly looked at Zephaniah, wiped her nose with the back of her hand, grinned, blushed and gave a minuscule bob. In his turn Zephaniah suddenly found his boots of intense interest. 'If we might come in?' Melanie asked, with a slight smile at the girl's reaction to her handsome son.

'Yes, of course, sorry . . .' Dolly held open the door for them, and they moved in out of the heat of the sun.

'Dolly! Where are you?' a voice yelled.

'Answering the door, Mrs Gilroy,' she called back. 'Like you told me to,' she added, under her breath.

'What's amiss?' Melanie asked.

'It's awful, missus. Everyone shouting at everyone else and everyone accusing everyone. Horrible!' Dolly shuddered. 'I'll find Mr Whitaker for you.'

'It sounds like a madhouse,' said Zephaniah, as

shouting emerged from the kitchen, accompanied by the sound of pots and pans being banged about.

'This is not the best time, Mrs Topsham.' Whitaker had appeared.

'I realise—'

'My mother has an arrangement, sir. It's a long walk from Cress in the heat.' Zephaniah looked the butler squarely in the eye.

'If you insist. There's no doubt you'll have a long wait. If you would follow me . . .' Whitaker led the way, in his stately manner, to the front of the house. 'Sir Mortimer might not be able to see you,' he said.

'At least he will know I came,' Melanie said, with a placid smile.

'Oh, it's lovely!' Xenia exclaimed, as they entered the main hall with its tessellated floor, hammerbeamed roof and the intricately carved Carrara marble fireplace. 'It's just perfect!'

'Mrs Topsham. How nice to see you.' A flustered-looking Hannah had appeared. 'And your children too. Oliver, let me introduce you.' Xenia was rendered speechless as Oliver bowed, and Melanie's heart sank as she saw the effect he was having on her. No! her mind screeched. 'And I think you've met Zephaniah?' Hannah went on.

'Fleetingly. My apologies, Mrs Topsham, for not coming to the inn, but I was delayed here.'

'It was of no matter.'

'In fact—'

'Zeph, I wish you would allow me.' She placed a restraining hand on her son's sleeve.

'How is everything?'

'We've started in earnest on clearing things up. And—'

'My mother works too hard, sir.'

'Zeph!'

'Then we should try to organise more help.'

'I manage.' Melanie flashed an annoyed look at her son. 'The regulars have returned.'

'It's not the regulars we need.'

'But in winter when there are no trippers, Mr Cresswell, we shall need them,' Zephaniah put in.

'You're probably right.'

'I wonder how everyone will mix, though. Some of the fishermen are quite, well, rough.' Melanie had been unsure how to say this: it was the truth, but they had been kind to her.

'Perhaps we should set aside a bar for their exclusive use. A public saloon and, perhaps, a lounge bar and a snug.'

'That would be a good idea, Mr Cresswell. They would be more comfortable with such an arrangement too.'

'The place is filthy.' Xenia had found her voice.

'I don't know why you're complaining. You've had nothing to do with the cleaning,' Zephaniah snapped at her.

'I think we should have a meeting to take some decisions. It is remiss of us that we haven't done so before this,' Oliver told them.

'It's why we're here now, Mr Cresswell. Your father suggested I should report to him at intervals.'

'Mother has spent quite a lot of her own money,' Zephaniah added.

'Zeph, don't exaggerate!' Melanie laughed nervously.

'Then we must reimburse you,' Oliver said.

'That would be very kind. I've all the receipts.' She smiled, relaxing for the first time since she had got here. The subject of money – how much she had spent and if she should ask for it back – had been causing her sleepless nights.

Everyone was startled when raised voices issued forth from the library. Whitaker returned, his face impassive.

'Aren't we becoming quite the little party?' Hannah giggled.

Soon they were joined by Young Mortimer and Lettice, and yet more introductions had to be made. Then Whitaker slid towards the front door as someone banged on it impatiently.

'Hello, everyone, I thought I'd surprise you all!' Esmeralda burst into the hall. 'I bicycled here – it was *so* alarmingly dangerous! It's Miss Beatty's machine but promise me, on pain of death, none of you will *ever* tell her. She'll kill me! Oh, you've visitors! Good morning.' At which point she opened her basket, took out her little dog and placed him on the floor – much to the alarm of Cariad, who at that moment had appeared from the direction of the library. At the sight of Mr Woo she scuttled back in. A tall man was lingering in the doorway. 'And this is Mr Richard Joynston, my father's secretary, whom I forgot about. A thousand apologies from silly me!' Esmeralda flashed a dazzling smile at the unfortunate young man, who blushed deeply.

Melanie's heart went out to him. She thought she had never in her life seen such an exquisite creature as this girl. She wore a boater at a rakish angle and her jet black hair tumbled from beneath it. Her alabaster skin was prettily pink from the exertions of her ride, and although she flounced and prattled there was something charmingly childlike about her. She was someone it would be impossible to dislike. One look at Xenia told Melanie that she was not in agreement. As if sensing this Esmeralda, arm outstretched, rushed towards her. 'I spy a friend!' she said. 'And you are?'

'Xenia Topsham.'

'What a divine name.' So much more interesting than boring old *Esmeralda!*'

'Mrs Topsham is the landlady of the Cresswell Arms. Her son and daughter are helping her,' Hannah said.

'How interesting. I've always thought what fun it must

be to serve in a tavern, meeting all manner of people. You never know who will come through the door, do you?'

She has manners too, thought Melanie, aware that Hannah had been warning Esmeralda that the Topshams were not her social equals. But, given the way they were dressed, she felt it was rather insulting to the girl's intelligence. No doubt she meant well, she thought, then smiled – she often thought that those were the three most depressing words in the English language. At that point there was another burst of shouting from the library.

'Gracious me! Someone's in a fluff!' Esmeralda giggled.

'I suggest we all go into the morning room. Father seems to be engaged at the moment,' Oliver said, and Hannah led the way. Oliver turned to see Melanie and her children still standing in the hall. 'Won't you join us?'

'It's not necessary.'

'Yes, please,' said Xenia, and walked promptly to join him. Melanie, fretting that this was all wrong, followed with Zephaniah in her wake.

In the morning room when everyone was seated, Xenia and Esmeralda were soon chatting to each other. Young Mortimer stood by the window staring at them.

'He's not used to female company of his own age.' Oliver had sat beside Melanie.

'I hope they don't eat him!'

'I can't think of anything nicer.'

Melanie blushed. 'I didn't mean . . .'

'I know you didn't. I was just teasing. Father might be unavailable. Can I help in any way?'

'These are the receipts.' She handed them to Oliver. 'I've made a list of everything I've spent and another of everything we need. I fear both are rather long – but there was so much . . .'

'Mrs Topsham, I don't think we're going to argue about a few shillings.'

'I'm a little confused, Mr Cresswell, at what I should

ask for – what's reasonable. I've never done anything like this before. Business, I mean.'

'Why don't you leave it for me and your son to agree?'

'That would be most kind.'

'He seems quite capable of looking after your interests.'

'Yes,' she said, unsure, then relaxed when she saw Oliver was smiling. 'He has decided to stay and help me – if that's all right with you and your father.'

'Far better for you. And your daughter?'

'She has a position with a Mrs Featherstone at Exeter. She'll be returning soon.' To her horror she found herself hoping it would be *very* soon. 'There was another thing I wished to discuss. While I can cook, I'm finding it difficult with all the other duties . . .'

'You wish to employ someone?'

'Yes. She lives on the estate – Flossie Marshall. She's a wonderful cook, far better than I, and I'm sure it can only help the business – having good food, I mean.' She was afraid she might be asking too much, putting this opportunity in jeopardy, but she wanted to share her good fortune with her friend.

'It sounds most satisfactory to me.'

Xenia rushed over to them. 'Mother, it was Esmeralda's father who brought me here from Exeter in his automobile. Isn't that astonishing?'

'Yes,' Esmeralda chimed in, 'he told me all about your daughter, Mrs Topsham, and what a delight she was. But isn't it sad about Mrs Featherstone?'

'What about Mrs Featherstone?' Xenia asked.

'Why, she's passed away.'

'*Mrs Featherstone?*'

'The very same. Fell down the stairs and broke her neck.'

'When?'

'Last week. Papa had to go to the funeral. He did much business with her, you see.'

'What good news! Now I shan't have to return.' Xenia was smiling broadly.

Melanie was appalled. 'Xenia!' She frowned at her daughter.

'But don't you see, Mrs Topsham? It's wonderful news. Well, it isn't for poor Mrs Featherstone and her family – oh dear, what a dreadful thing to say but of course, she was very old. I mean, you could stay here and be my friend.' Esmeralda looked at Xenia affectionately.

Melanie noticed that Oliver seemed transfixed by her. 'I'm afraid that won't be possible, Miss Ehrlich. My daughter has to earn her living.'

'How beastly for her.' She thought a moment. 'She could come and stay at my house, be my companion.'

'I thought you already had one in Miss Beatty,' Hannah interrupted.

'Yes, but she's old. I'd love to have someone my own age. Please say yes, Mrs Topsham. Please!'

'Esmeralda, I think you should discuss this with your father first.'

'He'll say yes, he always does. Mrs Topsham?'

'I shall have to think about it, Miss Ehrlich. I'm sorry—'

The door swung open. 'Who allowed that foul dog into my hall?' Penelope Cresswell sailed into the room, taking everyone unawares. 'Have you called the police yet, Oliver?'

'Father didn't want them informed.'

'And I do. Get them. Now!' Oliver didn't move, but Penelope didn't notice: she had spotted Melanie. 'And what are you doing here?'

'I was waiting to see your husband, Lady Cresswell. By arrangement.'

'In my morning room?'

'I invited them here – Mother.'

'How extraordinary. And who, pray, are you?' She glared at Esmeralda.

315

'The owner of the foul dog. But he isn't.'

'Don't be rude to *me*, young woman.'

'If you were more polite to me, it wouldn't be necessary.'

The assembled company stood, with bated breath, waiting for the onslaught. Penelope looked the girl up and down, then burst out laughing. 'I like you,' she announced.

'Hannah, where are you? Come quickly!' Mortie stood in the doorway.

'Papa?' Hannah was immediately on her feet.

'No, it's Coral. She's ill – she's fainted! I fear she's dead.'

Mortie led a virtual stampede from the morning room, across the hall and up the wide staircase. Three abreast, they ran along the wide landing and into Coral's bedroom, Penelope bringing up the rear. Coral was sprawled across the fine rug in front of her dressing-table. She was foaming at the mouth and shaking; her shoes beat a rapid tattoo on the floor.

'Open the window!' Hannah ordered. In his haste, Mortie sent a table flying, its bibelots crashing to the floor. He yanked at the window catch.

'She might catch a chill,' Penelope protested, following her son and slamming it shut.

'It's too hot in here for her, she needs fresh air. Now, please, give her space.' Hannah shooed her brothers away. Gently she straightened her sister-in-law as a rattling noise issued from Coral's throat. Hannah looked at Oliver with alarm.

'Is there anything I can do?' Esmeralda had joined them. 'Please let me help. Should I cycle and get the doctor?'

'Would you? Where's Mrs Topsham?'

'She stayed downstairs.'

'Dear Miss von Ehrlich, please find her and ask her to join us.'

'What do you need *her* for?' Penelope asked, as the girl rushed from the room.

'She's . . .' But Hannah did not have an answer. She just knew she wanted the woman here – she was such a calming influence. 'Sal-volatile, that's what we need.' She began to look about the room, wondering where Coral was most likely to keep her smelling-salts.

'Should we get her onto the bed? It's somewhat undignified to have her sprawled on the floor. Oliver, Mortie!' Penelope ordered.

'I don't think you should move her.' Melanie had joined them.

'And what would you know?'

Melanie was on her knees, turning Coral's head to one side, checking she had not swallowed her tongue. We should wait for the doctor. We might do more harm than good if we disturb her. I really think that is best, Lady Cresswell.'

'I agree,' Oliver said. 'Perhaps if we cover her—' But Melanie was already efficiently stripping the bed.

'Where are Lettice and Young Mortimer?'

'I thought it was best they did not accompany me – I wasn't sure what I would find. They are talking with my children.'

'I see you are still taking much upon yourself where this family is concerned, Mrs Topsham.'

'Oh, Mother, not now!' It was an aggrieved Mortie who snapped at her. Since he so rarely did, this took everyone by surprise.

Hannah, still searching for the sal-volatile, was opening drawers in the chest, searching the wardrobe. It was not something she enjoyed since she would hate anyone, especially Coral, to be doing the same in her room. She checked the dressing-table drawers. In one there was a silk sachet for stockings. As she moved it, she felt something hard inside and opened the top. Inside were the family's lost articles, including Penelope's ring. 'No!' The word was out before she could stop herself.

'What's wrong, Hannah?'

'Nothing, Oliver, I caught my finger.' She slammed the drawer. Coral! Surely not. Had she imagined it? Gingerly she opened the small drawer again, but the lumpy-looking sachet was still there. 'I'll fetch my own salts from my room.'

In her room she sat on her bed collecting her thoughts. There had to be a reason for Coral to take the items, and it would be best if Hannah said nothing about them until she could talk to her – *if* she could talk to her. She shook her head with disbelief. It seemed impossible to contemplate that Coral might be dying: she had appeared well over the last few days. Was it something she had eaten? Was it infectious? Should she send the children away? There was no doubt in her mind that Coral was very ill.

With the sal-volatile in her hand she returned to the room to find Dr Shelburn on his knees. 'I could only wish that the families of all my patients were as intelligent as you, Lady Cresswell. So much damage is sometimes done by moving a patient before I have had time to examine them.'

'We do our best, Doctor.' Penelope simpered. Hannah looked at Melanie and smiled sympathetically.

They stood in a semicircle as he listened to her heart. 'She has a high fever. That is why she was having a fit.'

'A fit!' Mortie wailed.

'It is common with a high temperature, Mr Cresswell. Now, gentlemen, if you would assist me, we should get the patient onto the bed . . .'

Coral was laid on her bed. The gurgling noises she was making were louder and even more alarming.

'She didn't say she was ill – she'd a headache. That's all she complained of . . .'

'Poor Mortie. Don't worry, we'll look after her,'

Hannah told him comfortingly. 'Mrs Topsham, a tepid sponge, I think, if you could arrange that for me?'

'Of course.' Melanie sped from the room.

'So fortunate for us all that she was here. Mrs Topsham is an excellent nurse.'

'She proved that with Papa, Doctor.'

Penelope snorted. 'I must go and see what has happened to our delayed luncheon. Call me if there's any change.' With that she bustled out. Mortie was making a strange mewing noise.

'Mr Cresswell, you mustn't blame yourself.'

'What do you think ails her?' Mortie looked at the doctor with anguish written across his face.

He really cares, thought Hannah, and was shocked by how surprised she felt.

'I cannot be certain. She might have the undulating fever or an inflammation of the brain. But first things first. We have to get this temperature down. Mrs Topsham will aid me in this critical matter,' the doctor said, as Melanie returned, barely visible behind a large pile of white towels, closely followed by Molly with large ewers of water.

Luncheon was difficult. For a start they were late, the food was tepid and the staff disgruntled. They had, out of politeness, invited Esmeralda. When Penelope told the Topsham twins to go to the kitchen to eat, Esmeralda begged that they be allowed to stay. 'You see, Lady Cresswell, Lettice and Xenia are my truly best friends – Young Mortie and Zeph too, of course,' she added hurriedly, and bestowed a wondrous smile on the two young men. Esmeralda was evidently someone whom no one could refuse, even Penelope.

Hannah wished that her stepmother, having grudgingly agreed, could have shown better grace afterwards for she did not speak to the Topshams once during the meal, which made everyone else uncomfortable – everyone but Esmeralda, who did not appear to notice. She was engrossed with Oliver, and so, it would appear, was he with her. Hannah was pleased: it could only mean that the unfortunate business with Laura Redman was at an end.

Mortie had bolted his lunch and rushed back to sit with Coral for an hour before taking his mother to Barlton. He hadn't wanted to go but Penelope had insisted and, grudgingly, he had given in. That he should be so concerned had pleased Hannah. He had always given the impression that, while fond of his wife, he was not completely enamoured of her, but now he was showing everyone how wrong that idea was.

Hannah found it hard to talk to Xenia, although she prided herself on getting on with young people. Zephaniah was a different matter: he was interested in all about him, asked intelligent questions and could talk on several subjects with ease. Melanie had succeeded well with him, especially given her circumstances. She was pleased, too, that her father was showing such an interest in the boy – though given his size and age, nineteen next birthday she gathered, 'boy' was a misnomer. He was, with his seriousness, very much a man.

In a lull during the conversation, she had noticed him looking at Penelope strangely. It was not anger, or embarrassment, but rather, she felt, and could hardly believe it, he was feeling a pride in himself that was almost arrogance. There was much that was interesting about this young man.

'Papa, if I might have a word?' she asked, as they dispersed after the meal. The young were going for a walk, and Penelope to rest. Oliver, she presumed, was off for his afternoon ride.

'Of course.'

As she followed him into the library her heart was

pounding so hard she was sure he must hear it. She had been practising what to say to him all day.

'Yes?' He looked up from lighting his cigar, banned by the doctor but he could not resist them.

'I don't want you to be offended, but I want to ask you . . .' She twisted her handkerchief. 'I don't want to continue to be a financial burden to you. I want to meet my own obligations at the dower house.'

'The last thing I would ever call you is a burden. What makes you say this? Who has been talking to you?'

'No one.' She willed herself not to blush at the lie. 'Had I found a husband you would no longer be supporting me, and it seems wrong to me that when I have money you should continue to do so.'

'You're such a moral creature, Hannah, but I would prefer to maintain things as they are.'

'But, Papa—'

'There is nothing more to be said.' He returned to the task of lighting his cigar. 'I shall miss your efficiency.'

'Mrs Fuller knows my ways. You won't notice I've gone.'

'So I can rely on the housekeeper, if not my wife?'

'I didn't mean that, Papa.'

'She lacks your sensitivity.'

'Not really.' That wasn't true either. Look how she was dealing with the staff over the missing objects! But what else was she to say? She had wondered whether to confide in her father about what she had found in Coral's room, but decided not to bother him. He'd enough worries already.

'It's no secret how difficult it is for you here with Penelope. I don't wish you to think I am criticising her – which, of course, I am.' He grinned. 'But I'm sorry it has been such a trial. I understand why you wish to escape before I'm dead.'

'I hate it when you speak like that.'

'It's not as frightening to me as to you, my dear.'

'I shall miss you more than I can say.'

'Don't cry!' he ordered, but smiled at her.

'I won't. I know what you think of weeping women!' She was laughing now.

'After all, you won't be far away.'

'And I can come every day.'

'Of course. And I can visit you – it will be an oasis of calm for me. In fact, I shall look forward to it.'

'I shall miss the smell of your cigars.'

'Then take it up yourself.'

'Me? Smoke? What a novel idea.'

'I was lonely, Hannah.'

'I'm sorry?'

'Inviting my wife back.'

'Papa, there is no need to explain yourself to me.'

'But I must. Admittedly she forced my hand, with the size of the bills she was sending me – but I missed her. It took me by surprise that I did.'

Hannah felt acutely embarrassed that her father was speaking to her in this way. 'Will she stay?'

'Who knows? I doubt it. But I shall remain here. My days of rushing around are over. I'm content. Just one thing bothers me. I would like to see you settled and happy with a good man.'

'Oh, Papa. I doubt there's much chance of that.' She laughed, but more to hide her discomfort than from amusement.

'I don't know what's wrong with men. They don't know what they're missing.'

'I'm glad I never married now. I could never leave Cresswell, and had I been someone's wife I would have had to go to their home and leave mine.'

'Still, it would be a comfort—'

'What do I need a husband for when I have you?'

'But for how long?'

'Oh, Papa, please don't speak like that.'

'I have the impression there is something else you wish to discuss.'

'No, Papa. That's all.' She would not worry him with Coral's hoard. Although he was well now she felt he should be protected from as much anxiety as possible.

That afternoon, with her father resting, the others occupied and Mrs Fuller sitting with Coral, Hannah crept about the house, depositing the various items Coral had stolen, trying to make them appear merely misplaced.

'You look chipper, Edward.'

'And so I should, Mrs Fuller. A most satisfactory morning.'

'It might have been for you, but it most certainly wasn't for me. Three more for luncheon, and me given fifteen minutes' notice!' Mrs Gilroy grumbled.

'Everyone was most complimentary, Mrs Gilroy. It was all greatly appreciated – especially the sole.' The butler took his seat and accepted a cup of coffee. 'I will say this. Miss Esmeralda's father might be a Johnny-come-lately but she's nice manners. And I've other momentous news.'

The two women leant forward in anticipation, but the butler sat mute.

'What?' they chorused.

'I wish to inform the assembled servants. I've arranged that we all meet in half an hour. So, dear ladies, you must be patient for a little longer.' He smiled almost flirtatiously, which made both women twitter.

'Inviting the Topsham twins to lunch struck me as strange.' Mrs Fuller, aware that the butler would not be drawn, changed the subject. 'They'll be thinking they're gentry at this rate. What were they like, Edward?'

'They behaved well. It was Miss Esmeralda who insisted, you know.'

'And was it true, as Jock said, that she had her dog with her in the dining room?'

'On her lap, feeding it titbits.'

'My food – for a dog? Whatever next? Freezes a body's heart, it does.'

'Apparently the creature is a fussy eater but today ate with relish. I trust that is some form of consolation, Mrs Gilroy.'

'Hardly, Edward. I can't believe Sir Mortimer would permit such goings-on. Why, he won't allow Cariad in the dining room.'

'That young minx winds him round her little finger. Men!' Mrs Fuller said, in an aside to the cook.

'Tell us, Edward, is there further news on Mrs Cresswell?' the housekeeper enquired.

'The doctor is flummoxed, that's for sure. A great fever she has, but she's sitting up.'

'Hardly surprising. One as spiteful as she, the poison's coming out of her.'

The butler took out his pocket watch and peered at it.

'If you ladies would care to join us?' He held open the door of Mrs Fuller's sitting room.

The two women rustled along the stone corridor, their high buttoned boots clicking on the stone floor. Ahead they could hear the excited buzz of the junior servants. Evidently someone was watching for them: as they approached, the noise subsided and by the time they entered the servants' hall everyone was quiet. But there was no avoiding the sense of anticipation that pervaded the room.

All eyes were upon them as cook, housekeeper and butler, joined by Lavender and Colette, made their way to the front where four chairs had been set out for the women. The butler stood waiting for the whispering and coughing to subside.

'This has been a most unfortunate and uncomfortable

time for us all. No one has been above suspicion,' he began.

'Took Miss Hannah to search *their* rooms, though, didn't it?' Dolly whispered to Molly.

'Would you care to share that comment with us all, Dolly?'

'I was just saying how hot it was in here,' she lied, blushing to the roots of her hair.

'If you would do me the courtesy of listening,' he said. 'As I was saying . . .' He proceeded to lecture them on trust, honesty, reliability with a good smattering on the subject of loyalty.

'Likes the sound of his own voice,' they both whispered.

Eventually even Whitaker became aware of the fidgeting and shuffling. '. . . So, as I say, much is expected of us in our privileged position. Never let it be forgotten. I make no apology for running a tight ship. But today we are all exonerated. Ladies and gentlemen, I have an announcement.' He paused, as if expecting a roll of drums. 'Lady Cresswell's ring has been found!'

His proclamation was rewarded by a cheer from some, clapping from others and sullen silence from a few. He was smiling broadly.

'You'd think he'd found it himself, wouldn't you?' Mrs Fuller whispered to Mrs Gilroy.

'Where?' an anonymous voice asked from the back.

'Who asked that?' There was silence. 'Under the escritoire in the morning room . . .'

'But . . .'

'Yes, Molly?'

'Nothing, Mr Whitaker.'

'Molly, I would like to hear what you have to say.'

Molly looked trapped. 'What I was going to say . . . It wasn't there this morning.'

'What do you mean?'

'Someone planted it, that's what she means.'

'And what would you know about it, Dolly?'

'It stands to reason! If it isn't there when the house-maids clean the room and afterwards it is, someone put it there.'

'And the matchbox cover? And the card case? And the gold cigar-cutter? Have they been found?'

'All found. Isn't it wonderful?' The butler clasped his hands in the manner of an evangelical preacher.

'Bloody miraculous.' Dolly, standing at the front, made no attempt to lower her voice.

'Language, Dolly!' Mrs Gilroy frowned at her kitchen-maid.

'You must have overlooked the ring this morning, Molly.' Whitaker seemed less sure of himself now.

'I didn't, Mr Whitaker. Tuesdays I always do the skirting-boards in the morning room. You can ask Mrs Fuller.'

'That's right, Mr Whitaker. She does and that means she's on her hands and knees. I'd have thought it unlikely she would miss it.'

'Well, she did on this occasion.'

'I—' Molly was silenced by a glare from the house-keeper.

'The cover and the card case had slipped down behind a cushion in the drawing room. The cigar-cutter must have been overlooked since it was found in Mr Mortie's cufflink box. He must inadvertently have put it in the wrong place.'

'Drunk again!' a man's voice shouted, which made a few laugh, but the majority didn't.

'Which cushions in the drawing room?'

'The blue velvet Knole.'

'Then there's something wrong. I did them cushions meself and there weren't nothing there then,' a second housemaid, protested.

'It has to be said, Mr Whitaker—'

'What, Mrs Fuller?'

'Nothing, Mr Whitaker.' She had evidently thought better of it.

There was a general muttering of discontent. 'I am surprised that all of you are so argumentative.'

'The point is, Mr Whitaker, if Molly and Joan say the things weren't there, then they weren't.' There was a murmur of approval at Dolly's remark. 'So if they weren't, what most of us are thinking is, who put them there?'

'Dolly, don't be silly!'

'I don't think I am, Mrs Fuller.' Dolly bridled. 'It makes things just as bad, Mr Whitaker. You must see that. It can't be only us what's thinking like this. They were planted by the thief. There won't be no change. Everyone's under suspicion still.'

'That is where you're wrong, Dolly. The family is overjoyed to have the items safely returned. We're fortunate that the constable was not involved.'

'Then perhaps it was one of them what nicked them in the first place, got the wind up and put them back.'

'Dolly!' All three senior servants shouted at her in unison.

'That is the worst slander I have ever heard.' The butler sat down with a bump, overcome with shock.

'You should take that remark back, Dolly.'

'But it's what a lot of us are thinking, isn't it?' She turned to face the others – but, without exception, they were either looking at their feet, out of the window or anywhere but at her. 'They're scared, that's why,' she said defiantly.

'Dolly, shut your mouth!' Mrs Gilroy bawled.

'Why should I?'

'Because I say so.'

'But it's not fair.'

'Life often isn't. Now, stop it.'

'I insist that you retract these unpleasant things you said.' The butler was on his feet again.

'Why?'

'Do as you're told, girl,' the cook demanded.

'If you're not careful, Dolly, you'll find yourself in serious trouble.'

'What have I done, Mr Whitaker? Only said what a lot are thinking.'

'They don't seem to be agreeing with you.'

'Dolly, stop it.' Molly, looking anxious, give her a little push.

'No, I won't, Molly. It's not fair. Who do you think would be under the most suspicion if them things was still lost? You and the other maids, that's who. It's always us gets it. It's as if Mr Whitaker only ever thinks the worst of us and the best of them.'

'Dolly, I've warned you. Desist or you will be dismissed.'

'I beg your pardon! Dolly is my kitchenmaid. I say who works for me and who doesn't.' Everyone perked up at the prospect of a row between the butler and the cook.

'I will not tolerate such insubordination. Either she apologises or she goes.'

'Don't argue about me! I'll decide for you – I'm going and that's that.' Dolly stormed out of the room, slamming the door behind her for good measure.

Oliver was lying on the grass, high on Childer's Hill, his arms behind his head as he watched small white puffs of cloud drift in the azure blue sky. It was hot, but not too hot, and the smell of ripe corn was heavy on the air. The buzz of bees, the song of the skylarks high above and the hum of his companions' conversation further down the hill were the only sounds. It was the sort of summer day he had often dreamt of in his self-imposed exile. Now his eyes were heavy and sleep was sliding towards him.

'When you were in America did you ever see any bears, Mr Cresswell?'

He shook himself awake and half sat up. 'Many, Miss

von Ehrlich.' He hadn't realised the others had joined him. 'They're large, fierce creatures.'

Esmeralda squealed. 'I'd be so frightened.'

'I should like to see one close to,' Xenia told him.

'You wouldn't, Miss Topsham.' He lay back again and closed his eyes. He didn't really want to talk, especially not to these young people with whom he would have little in common. His use of her surname pleased Xenia – she hadn't expected such formality from him. It showed respect and she liked that.

'Just as well they're made into our soldier's bearskins. The fewer there are of them the better,' Xenia pronounced.

'Poor bears,' said Lettice.

'I look forward to wearing mine,' Young Mortimer added.

'Shall you be a soldier?'

'Perhaps, Miss Topsham. I think I'd like to.'

'I hope you won't. What if there was another war and you had to go and fight? I'd hate that.' Xenia's eyes welled with tears.

'Then I shan't,' Young Mortimer said shyly, and blushed furiously.

Esmeralda picked a long blade of grass and began to stroke Oliver's cheek with it. Thinking it was a fly, he swatted at it. She stroked him again, putting her gloved finger to her lips to prevent the others saying anything. Oliver brushed his cheek. The third time, he opened his eyes and sat up, but she had discarded the grass and her hands were folded demurely in her lap.

'What was that?' he asked.

'I've no idea.' She looked at him, merriment in her eyes. 'Maybe a fairy kissing you.' She laughed.

'I don't believe in fairies.'

'How very sad for you. I must make you a believer.'

'Was it you? I think it was.'

'Why, Mr Cresswell, are you accusing me of lying? Fie!'

'No – of, pretending.' He was clambering to his feet and Esmeralda, as if reading his mind, was quickly on hers and running across the grass, then round and round the wishing tree, shrieking prettily. Oliver was laughing.

'She's very pretty,' Xenia said, apparently to no one in particular.

'Isn't she? And she has the most wonderful bedroom. I've asked my aunt if I can have one just like it.' Lettice was watching her enviously.

'You don't say anything, Mr Cresswell,' Xenia said.

'She's very lovely,' Young Mortimer replied.

'Do you think so? Honestly? Don't you think she's a little bit . . . how to say? Posed?'

'I think she's very natural,' Lettice answered for him.

'Yes, but an acting sort of natural.'

Lettice frowned. 'Is that possible? You couldn't meet anyone kinder. And please call *me* Lettice. I don't see why we should be formal with each other.'

'I agree,' Young Mortimer added.

'As you wish,' said Xenia, who was enjoying that formality. 'I'm probably wrong about her. After all, I've just met her and you both know her better than I.' The other two did not respond. 'I'm probably being so horrible because I'm jealous.'

'How commendably honest you are, Xenia,' Lettice said.

'I've found it's the best way to be. Then no one can misunderstand, can they?' She paused. 'It's hard to have nothing and to see others with so much.'

'We should have thought. How awful it must be for you. We should make amends, shouldn't we, Young Mortimer?'

'We must. Where's your brother, Xenia?'

'In the library, looking at books.' She rolled her eyes. 'He's so serious.'

'I liked him very much,' Lettice said shyly. 'I like serious people.'

'I can be serious too.'

'I doubt it, Xenia – but, then, I should hate it if you were.'

'Really, Young Mortimer?'

'Oh, yes,' he said, blushing even more furiously.

'Look, they're wishing.' Lettice pointed to her uncle and Esmeralda. 'That oak is our wishing tree.'

'How exciting. Let's wish too.'

'Very well, Xenia, but you mustn't tell what you wished or it won't come true.'

They joined the others. Lettice insisted they hold hands and circle the tree. Oliver had Esmeralda on one side, Xenia on the other.

As they circled the tree three times Oliver wondered what on earth he was doing there with these children. Then he realised he was enjoying himself.

'What did you wish?' Esmeralda asked him, as they began slowly to walk down the hill. He had his hand under her elbow to steady her for it was steep and she had already stumbled twice.

'It's a secret.'

'Tell me, do.'

'No. I want it to come true.'

'Shall I tell you mine?'

'You mustn't if it was important to you.'

Esmeralda stopped walking. 'I wished you would learn to love me.'

He laughed. 'Then it doesn't matter that you told me, for such a wish could not be regarded as important.'

'How beastly you are,' she replied gaily, yanked at his hand and made him run with her the rest of the way.

'Do you want to know my wish?' Xenia asked Young Mortimer.

'You mustn't tell,' he answered.

'But I want to.' She stopped, and Lettice overtook them. 'I wished that you would love me more than Esmeralda.'

'I do,' he said, in all seriousness.

'Good.' Xenia began to walk again, but a judicious trip made sure that Young Mortimer took her hand to steady her.

Laura Redman stood waiting in the wood by the broken gate. She had been there an hour. She had no watch but she guessed the time. She would wait ten minutes more. She wondered where Oliver was. He had never been late before. He had never missed one of their rendezvous before.

Chapter Eleven
September–October 1901

As she sat at Coral's bedside Hannah was riddled with guilt. She had never liked her; after Penelope she feared her most – or, rather, her tongue. She had never voiced her feelings but she had thought them, which was just as bad. Now, as she watched the woman struggle to live, she felt pity for her and was ashamed of her uncharitable thoughts.

'How is she?' Lettice, as quiet as ever, had entered the room unnoticed.

'I think I detect an improvement. A healthier look to her complexion.' Hannah saw no such thing but the child needed comfort.

Lettice bent over her mother, stroked her cheek, then kissed the middle of her forehead, much as a mother kisses a child. 'Perhaps there is a little.' She did not sound convinced. 'A little rosier – perhaps. Poor Mama.' Her face was wan with worry and Hannah was concerned. Lettice was barely sleeping and refused to eat. At this rate she, too, would be ill. 'I don't understand why the doctor does not know what is wrong with her. I don't understand why Papa does not call another who perhaps could tell us what ails her.'

'I'm sure he has his reasons. And Dr Shelburn is a good doctor – remember how well he cared for your grandfather.' Hannah, however, had reached the conclusion that Mortie *had* been told what was wrong with his wife. His silence, she was convinced, was to protect the rest of them from what was presumably bad news. But she thought it would be kinder to let the children know if

Coral was mortally ill. Being prepared for the worst, she was sure, was better in the long run since it gave people time to prepare themselves for the grief to come.

What still shocked her was the suddenness of Coral's illness. One day she was as fit as a fiddle, the next laid low with this appalling fever, which, no matter what they did, would not lessen. It showed how tenuous their hold on life was. She wondered what Coral's beliefs were. She attended church only occasionally and, Hannah had presumed, only out of duty. But she knew that many people who were not regular attenders frequently held beliefs that, at times like this, should not be forgotten. But if she were to mention that to Mortie would it not imply that Coral was not going to get better? She remembered how upset she had been when the vicar was called to her father, and how it had frightened her. But it was none of her business – she should leave well alone. That was what she usually did – and she despised herself for it.

'How long can Mama survive without eating?' Lettice looked at the bowl of soup, which stood untouched on the table.

'The doctor says it is more important that she drinks water. We are not to worry about food, not yet. But I try several times a day – just in case. I could, of course, ask the same question of you, my dear. Nanny Wishart tells me you refuse all food.'

'I can't face anything, Aunt Hannah. Just the thought of it . . .'

'You should try. You won't be a help to your mother if you, too, become ill, will you?' She smiled at her niece, not wanting her to think she was criticising. Anyway, Hannah understood: when her father had been ill she had almost lost the ability to swallow. 'If you have just a bowl of broth, it will help.'

'I will, Aunt.' Lettice fussed about the room, folding

napkins that were adequately folded, arranging ornaments that were already well arranged, looking for dust
that was not there.

Poor child, Hannah thought again. What a good
daughter she was. And when one remembered what a
distant mother Coral was, it showed her in an even better
light . . .

'Thank you, Mrs Fuller. I was just thinking how nice it
would be to have a cup of tea.' They had been joined by
the housekeeper.

'Sometimes I don't know how we'd go on without it.
How is the poor soul?'

'Lettice and I are sure there's an improvement in her
today, aren't we?'

'What do you think, Mrs Fuller?'

'I think you might be right, Miss Lettice. If I might
have a word, Miss Cresswell?'

'Of course.' Hannah left Lettice with her mother and
went into Coral's sitting room. 'Yes, Mrs Fuller?'

'I'm loath to bother you at such a time but I felt you
should know that there's much dissatisfaction among the
servants, Miss Cresswell. Unfortunately there is a suspicion among many of them that the items found last week
were not lost but stolen and then replaced.' The housekeeper said all this quickly, not looking at her.

'What makes them think such a thing?' Hannah hoped
she sounded surprised.

'The maids assure me they had cleaned those rooms
just before the items were found.'

'They might have missed them.'

'Miss Cresswell, I would agree that some of the girls
we've had here recently might have – sloppy, some of
them were – but not Molly. She's one of the best maids
we've had.'

'I see. But what do you expect me to do?'

'Talk to them.'

'I can't see what good that would do, Miss Fuller. I

335

can't explain anything.' She had to look at her shoes rather than at the housekeeper while she said this. 'In any case, it's no longer my business. I've already told Whitaker to talk to Lady Cresswell in future about domestic matters. I shall be leaving here, as you know, as soon as Mrs Cresswell is better.'

'But Lady Cresswell says she doesn't wish to be bothered with the problem.'

'And I cannot.'

'I don't know how long Mr Whitaker and myself can deal with it. Already a kitchenmaid has walked out and I fear there will be others.'

'Surely not. Where would they go?'

'There's a blanket factory newly opened in Barlton. I hear them talk of going there. They can earn more, you see, Miss Cresswell. And the hours are regular.'

'But there's more to life than money, Mrs Fuller.'

'As you say, Miss Cresswell,' the housekeeper answered, in a tight voice and a strange twist to her mouth.

'Who left?'

'Dolly Pepper.'

'No one important, then.' Hannah twisted open the face of the watch she wore on a chain round her neck. 'I'm sorry, what did you say?'

'Nothing, Miss Cresswell.'

'I think you did.'

'It was not important.'

'I'd still like to hear it.'

'I merely said that Mrs Gilroy would not agree.'

'I see.' Hannah frowned. 'That will be all, Mrs Fuller.' She spoke quite sharply.

After the housekeeper had left her Hannah stood for a moment at the window overlooking the park. She had not handled the situation well. She had been insensitive in dealing with Mrs Fuller: of course the cook would be lost without Dolly. But what was she to do? The staff were not stupid. If only she could talk to Coral and find out why she had stolen the objects. What an ugly word 'stolen' was, but the little cache in the dressing-table drawer had not arrived there by magic. She sighed, straightened her hair and returned to the invalid. An excited Lettice was waiting for her.

'Aunt, while you were with Mrs Fuller, I think she opened her eyes.'

'You think? Did you not see?'

'I had my back to her and I felt someone watching me, and when I turned, it was as if she was just closing her eyes. Oh, Aunt Hannah, what if she did? It would mean she really was better.'

'Coral . . . Coral, it's Hannah.' She could not be certain, but had the eyelids flickered? 'Coral . . .' She stood up. 'Lettice, it might be a good idea to call the doctor. What do you think?'

'Oh, yes! I'll go immediately.' Lettice did not need second bidding.

'Shifty, she looked. There's no doubt in my mind, she knows something.'

'Gussie, you're not implying Miss Hannah took the bits and bobs?'

'Of course not, Eve, what do you take me for? She knows something's not right, that's what I mean. Uncomfortable, she was. Wouldn't look me in the eye.'

'If . . . I would like you all to note that I said *if*, I don't wish for any misunderstanding, but *if* a member of the family is the guilty party then perhaps Miss Hannah knows more than she should and is protecting them.' Whitaker was at his most pompous.

'One of the family? What madness would that be? I never thought the day would come when you had a word of criticism for the family.'

'That's because I never had cause before, Mrs Gilroy, but I don't like the servants being put under such pressure. Those objects were not where they should have been. So where were they? Elsewhere. And of course, Mrs Gilroy, it isn't just the juniors who are under this cloud. It's us as well.'

'Surely not! Why would they suspect us?'

'Until this is solved we are all tarred with the same brush.'

'Anyhow, if I might continue?' Mrs Fuller looked archly at Whitaker. 'So . . . if neither of them can deign to be interested in the problem – right uppity, she was – how are we to get to the bottom of it? But if that's how they feel then I don't see why I should bother myself. She even implied it didn't matter that Dolly had left, said as she wasn't important.'

'She said *what*?' Mrs Gilroy exploded. 'How am I supposed to manage with no competent kitchenmaid? Does she think her food comes out of thin air? *Wasn't important*, indeed!'

'Have we had news of Dolly?'

'Not a word. But she's a sensible girl, not like Jose. God alone knows how *she*'ll end up.' Mrs Gilroy glared at Whitaker. It would be a long time before she would forgive him over Jock.

'She'll probably try for employment at the new blanket factory in Barlton, opened by that Mr Ehrlich.'

'Why blankets?'

'Sheep, Mrs Gilroy. Proximity to them and their fleeces. Such as Mr Ehrlich are constantly on the lookout for a business opportunity.'

'I could do with a bit of that sort of expertise.'

'You, Mrs Gilroy? Hardly. You're a professional of some standing.'

'I might have standing, Mr Whitaker, but I'd like some of that there Mr Ehrlich's money.'

Everyone laughed. But suddenly Whitaker was serious. 'I fear the factory will be cause for concern. There's enough unrest among the young here, and the last thing we need is one of ours going to work there, then coming back to tell the rest how wonderful it is. The maids are so easily led.'

'And your footmen aren't wayward?'

'Certainly not!'

'Hm. We shall see,' Mrs Fuller observed.

They were well into a good discussion of how times had changed when they were joined by Lavender. 'And how's the patient?'

'Still not with us.'

'I've been trying to feel sorry for her but I just can't find it in me,' the housekeeper confided.

'Not the easiest of women, to be sure, but you wouldn't wish *her* suffering on your worst enemy, Gussie.'

Mrs Gilroy snorted with amusement. 'Oh, I don't know. I could just see Gussie wishing that on several people we know.'

'Get on with you, Eve. I'm a good Christian woman.' But she was laughing.

'Miss Lettice swears she saw her opening her eyes, so they've sent for the doctor.'

'Have they any idea what ails her?'

'Well . . .' Lavender looked pointedly at Whitaker, who seemed nonplussed, then embarrassed, and got to his feet, muttering about the wine cellar. The three women waited in silence until he was safely out of the room. Lavender continued: 'You know there was blood in the bathroom the day she was taken poorly?'

'Yes, Mr Mortie had a nosebleed. Right to-do, getting it up off them tiles.'

'I don't think it was. I think she had a . . .' Rather than say the word she mouthed, '*Miscarriage*.'

'Poor soul.'

'Then why didn't they say?'

'Because he hasn't told anyone, that's why.'

'But women have miscarriages all the time and they aren't unconscious for days with a high fever.'

'Complications,' said Lavender, sucking her teeth.

'It could be. But at her age she's better off without another baby. Once a woman's in her forties she's better off not having any more, if you ask me,' said Mrs Gilroy, even though no one had asked her.

'And she shouldn't anyhow. Not the most concerned mother, is she? Swanning off and leaving her offspring for others to look after.'

'The aristocracy have a different attitude to parenthood, Lavender. Never been involved, have they? Palm 'em off, that's what they do,' Mrs Fuller said, disapprovingly.

'I always thought Miss Hannah would have made the perfect mother.'

'She's left it a bit late for that, hasn't she?'

'Unlikely she'd find anybody now.'

'Sad,' said Mrs Gilroy, and this time it was her turn to suck her teeth.

With the arrival of the colder weather Oliver's meetings with Laura could no longer take place in the open air. He arranged a suite of rooms at the Cresswell Arms for himself, telling Melanie he wanted some peace and quiet to work away from the main house.

The Cresswell Arms had once been a thriving coaching inn, rather than the run-down establishment it was now. The front of the building faced on to the road across from the harbour wall and the sea. A wide arch led to a galleried and cobbled courtyard, and a smaller one to a lane that skirted the inn at the back where the stables were situated. Oliver had chosen two rooms towards the rear of the gallery, which he had cleared out and had redecorated. They could be accessed from the lane, so he could stable his horse and no one need know he was there. More importantly, Laura could come and go unobserved. When the rooms that opened on to the galleried balcony, which was on three sides of the yard, were ready for letting, it would not be so easy. But work had only started on those furthest from his own.

To establish a routine he often appeared in the bar, with papers in his hands, ordered some wine and retreated to his rooms asking not to be disturbed. After ten days of this he arranged for Laura to visit.

'But it's charming, and if I peer to the right I can see the sea.' She clapped her hands. 'And we're safe here?'

'I've told Melanie I'm not to be bothered, that I'm working.' He grinned at her. 'She won't come anywhere near us. And you weren't seen?'

'No. It's not very busy out there at this time of the afternoon. Are we to have champagne?'

'I thought we should celebrate, don't you?'

'I was so afraid I wouldn't see you, with winter coming. As it is, it's been so long, an agony of waiting.'

'Hasn't it?' He handed her a rummer filled with champagne. 'Forgive the glass. The establishment doesn't run to the correct ones yet.' He raised his and they toasted each other. Laura's eyes brimmed with her love for him. So strong was the emotion showing on her face that he had to look away, as if blinded by its intensity.

Later they lay on the bed, her body curled around his like lichen, her head on his chest. 'What are you thinking?' she asked.

'Nothing.'

'What a disappointing response.' She pretended to sulk.

'What did you want me to be thinking?'

'How wonderful that was. How much you love me. How you can't live without me.'

He kissed her forehead in reply. She uncurled, propped herself on her elbow and looked down at him. 'It's lovely here in this little nest but I miss our river setting.'

'If we went there you'd get pneumonia or rheumatism.'

'Then what use would I be to you?'

'Use? That's an odd word.'

'I don't think so. There's no other way I can serve you but in your bed.'

He kissed her again. 'Don't spoil our time together.'

'I'm so unhappy, Oliver.'

'I know you are.'

'What can we do?'

'I don't see what there is to do but continue as we are. If you didn't have the child it would be different, but you do.'

'I sometimes think I love you more than him.'

He put his finger on her lips. 'You don't mean that so don't say it.'

She was silent for a moment, as if collecting her thoughts. 'I feel you're different with me,' she said eventually.

He sat up. 'I'm not.'

'You're distant. Something has happened.'

'Laura, my dear, you're overwrought, you imagine things,' he said, but felt uncomfortable saying it. He took her into his arms and made love to her to reassure her, but found he was not reassured himself.

They had met several times at his rooms. He did not know what was wrong, why the romance was slipping away from him. He tried to recapture the magic, but failed. Each time they met he knew he was becoming more distant. Sometimes he was late, sometimes he wished he didn't have to go at all – and yet only weeks ago he'd thought he was in love for the rest of his life. He enjoyed the physical aspect of their meetings, the release it gave him, but that was different too. Once, when they had coupled, it was as if they became one; now he always felt his separateness. Why Laura's power over him should have diminished puzzled him: she was still the same sweet person, still willing to risk everything to be with him. He was not being fair to her, he was not behaving as a gentleman should: their affair was coming to an end – but he was too much of a coward to tell her.

On the other hand, his guilt annoyed him. It had been Laura's choice, after all, to become his mistress. It was she who was committing adultery, not him. If there was sin, then hers was the greater. Imperceptibly, so that he was barely aware of it, he began to think of someone else.

He was considering how he could resolve the dilemma as he rode to Longacre Farm, on the edge of the estate, to see to some outbuildings, which were in need of repair.

'Good morning, Fender. Fine October morning,' Oliver said, as he slid from Sergeant in the farm yard.

'It is that, Mr Cresswell. And what can I be doing for you?'

'I came to check those barns. You said the roofs were bothering you.'

'They'm fixed.'

'Really? When?'

'Oh, a good month past.'

'I'd no idea.'

'That Mr Ehrlich was true to his word. Said he'd do them and, bugger me, he did.'

'Ehrlich? What has it to do with him?'

'He owns it. Lock, stock and barrel – and me, of course.' Frank Fender laughed, exposing bad teeth. When he saw that Oliver wasn't amused, he stopped abruptly. 'You'm didn't know, did you? Bugger me, why not?'

'Why indeed, Fender?' He looked about him. The yard was spruce, and he could see how well the barn roof had been mended. 'There's nothing to keep me here, then, is there?'

'You'm welcome to a bite to eat.'

'I'd better be getting back.' He remounted the horse.

'Mr Cresswell, there's just one thing. Perhaps I should mention it, not that it's any of my business, but you'd probably like to know he owns Tithe Barn Farm too.'

'How many acres?'

Frank Fender sucked long and hard at his brown-stained teeth. 'Getting on for five hundred acres.'

Oliver rode away with a collection of emotions swirling in his mind. He was angry. He was disappointed. He was puzzled. Anger held sway.

'You might have told me, Father.' He had not paused to knock at the library door. Neither had he removed his boots, which had left a trail of mud from Fender's yard in his wake – of great interest to Cariad.

'Told you what?'

'Frank Fender has just informed me that you have sold Longacre and Tithe Barn farms to von Ehrlich.' He was stalking about the room. 'I was made to look a fool.'

'They were mine to sell. Or had you forgotten?' There was little spirit in Mortimer's voice.

'I am aware of that. But it alters nothing. Either I am assisting you and you keep me fully informed of your plans, or if you have decided to dispense with my help, you might have had the courtesy to inform me. I am insulted that you have chosen to treat me like a child – a person of no importance. And in those circumstances I shall be on my way.' His voice had grown louder with every word.

'I should have told you.' His father spoke so quietly that Oliver had to ask him to repeat himself. 'I'm sorry.'

Oliver banged his fist on the rent table in the centre of the room. 'I can't believe you have treated me with such disdain.'

'I have apologised. There is little more I can do or say.'

'Why didn't you consult me? Did you think I wouldn't find out?'

There was a long pause. 'I hoped you wouldn't. I had intended to . . . I just kept delaying it.' Mortimer looked suddenly very weary. 'And I was ashamed.' His father seemed defeated, and very old. Oliver hadn't expected the answer he'd received. 'Father . . .'

'I've been a fool.'

'Not in my eyes.'

'I didn't know which way to turn.'

Oliver waited patiently while his father composed his next sentence. 'I had a particularly sticky creditor on my back who needed paying,' Mortimer said eventually.

'Could we not have raised money by mortgaging the farms rather than selling them?'

'I didn't think so.'

'If only you had confided in me, I would have helped you. Better that you sold them to me rather than him – pleasant though he is.'

'I told you, I was ashamed. I didn't want to come cap in hand to my son. And Ehrlich was keen – he'll care for the land. I've done a few calculations – we shall have to cut our cloth—'

'Can I help now?'

'Too late, I fear, but thank you for the offer. You're a good man.'

Oliver realised that despite what he was saying his father looked guilty. 'Father, there's something else?'

'Nothing.' Again the shifty expression.

'Father?' As Oliver spoke it struck him that their roles were changing. He remembered a time in this library when his father had been interrogating him over some misdemeanour and he'd been afraid to look at him.

'Well, there is something. I'm negotiating to sell him Lees Coppice.'

Oliver sat down. 'And how far has this progressed?'

'I haven't signed anything yet.' Another pause. 'The next couple of days,' he mumbled.

'Then we have time. I shall purchase it. I need a property of my own.'

'But I gave my word.'

'Break it. If you would prefer I shall see him for you. I'll explain. He'll understand.'

He waited in a small sitting room off the main hall of Courtney Lacey for Stanislas von Ehrlich to join him. On the ride here he had reached a few conclusions. He was going to have to sit down with his father and find out the full extent of his financial problems – not the vague indications he had given him today. This was unlike the man whom he had thought he knew. His father had always been wealthy so it was difficult to understand why he was in trouble now. As far as Oliver could gather it had been brewing for a long time. Mortimer had once been astute: might there be something wrong with him now? Had his mother had been right after all? Or was he simply slowing with age?

Whatever the reason, the stupidity of investing heavily in a gold mine in America that he hadn't seen, in partnership with men he didn't know, was plain to see, and Oliver could imagine how one bad investment had led his father to think he could recoup by reinvesting in something equally disastrous – as a gambler at the roulette wheel is sure that the next throw of the dice will solve everything.

Had there been no one his father could have confided in? Was he too proud? And yet why hadn't he talked to him during the last year? He knew why, there was always a barrier between them. As soon as he thought he understood his father another hurdle appeared.

It was strange how things often happened to Oliver without him having to make any real decision, and Lees Coppice was a prime example. He looked about him at the ornate cornices, the heavy chandelier of the room where he waited for von Ehrlich. He was sure that everything happened for a reason, so his failure to buy this house meant it would not have been right for him.

346

Lees Coppice, though, might be perfect for him in his bachelor state . . .

'Oliver, what a lovely surprise.' Stanislas von Ehrlich stormed into the room, followed by footmen carrying trays of glasses, decanters and cake. 'Madeira with Madeira, a weakness with me. You will join me?'

'Mr von Ehrlich.' Oliver was quickly on his feet.

'Oh, Stanislas, please.'

The footmen had finished serving them. 'I hear you have opened a blanket factory in Barlton,' Oliver said.

'I have. I was standing here looking out of the window at the pastures full of sheep and I began to wonder . . . Sheep, I thought. How can I use them apart from eating them? Carpets next.'

'You're a man after my own heart.'

'I looked at your inn – happened to be passing. I like what you're doing.'

'The frequency and speed of the trains will revolution-ise our lives in Devon. We were once isolated in the west, but now it is becoming more and more popular.'

'There are opportunities a-plenty—'

The door burst open and Esmeralda flew in, today a vision of cream and primrose yellow satin with matching jewelled boots. 'Papa! You didn't tell me Oliver was here. You're so thoughtless!'

'He came to see me, not you – didn't you?'

'I did, but my visit is made complete by seeing Miss von Ehrlich.'

'Oliver! So formal today?' She smiled at him and flirted with her eyes, and Oliver smiled back – with a rather asinine expression, he knew.

'Then stay, daughter, but keep quiet while we talk.' Oliver was relieved to see that her father looked at her in a similarly besotted fashion.

'Perhaps Oliver wants to talk to *me*.' She pouted.

'Esmeralda!' Stanislas warned benignly. The girl threw herself in a flurry on to one of the sofas and sighed.

'I wanted to talk to you about Lees Coppice, Stanislas.'

'A fine property. I'm pleased with it.'

'There's a problem.'

'And what might that be?' He smiled, but Oliver noticed he had sat up straighter.

'I fear my father has changed his mind. He no longer wishes to sell.'

For what seemed a long time Stanislas said nothing. 'His reason?' he eventually barked.

'He has not been well.'

'He appeared in rude health yesterday, when I was last privileged to see him.'

'Indeed, but he has not been himself for some time.' How true that was, he thought, after what he had learnt today.

'Do you mean that your father is no longer capable of making decisions about his own affairs? I doubt he would be happy to discover his son's opinion of him.'

'I did not mean that.'

'Then what *did* you mean?'

'Stanislas, of course we're sorry if you are disappointed by this change of plan, and we will reimburse you for any expense you might have incurred so far.'

'He gave me his word.' He spoke so quietly that it was hard to hear him, and Oliver found this threatening.

'I know.'

'Is he not a gentleman, then?'

Oliver was on his feet.

'Papa!' Esmeralda exclaimed.

'I beg your pardon, sir. That was not necessary,' Oliver said.

'But I think it was, Mr Cresswell. I am accustomed to dealing with men of principle, who do not go back on their word.'

Oliver knew that von Ehrlich was controlling himself and wondered what would happen if he lost his composure.

348

'It is not a whim. He made an error of judgement. He regrets it and apologises. I resent your implying that he is not a gentleman. Evidently there is no point in discussing this further. The property is no longer for sale. Miss Esmeralda . . .' He bowed to her as he prepared to leave.

Stanislas was breathing heavily, blinking rapidly as if he had something in his eye. 'No one – do you hear me? – *no one* treats me in this manner!' Stanislas was now standing between Oliver and the door, barring his way. He was pale, his fists were clenched. 'How dare you?' he shouted. He began to shake, spittle appearing at the corners of his mouth.

'Sir, this reaction is too extreme. I beg you, sir, take control of yourself.'

'Control myself! *You* tell *me* to control myself? I had plans. I demand you honour your obligation—' The door opened to reveal Agnes Beatty. 'You, out!'

'I beg your pardon, Mr von Ehrlich, I was worried—'

'Mind your own business! Keep your snooping nose out of my affairs! And how dare you not knock?'

'As I have often explained to you, Mr von Ehrlich, one does not knock at a drawing-room door.'

'You!' He dived at Agnes, who stepped neatly out of his way. Stanislas had lost his pallor and was now the colour of old burgundy.

'Take care, sir. Your colour is alarming. You look as if you might be about to have a seizure.'

'Get out!' He was ranting, hitting the palm of one hand with the fist of the other.

He made Oliver think of a child in tantrum. He looked at him with disbelief. 'I can assure you, Mr von Ehrlich, that, in light of this, if we changed our minds you would be the last person to whom we would entrust our property. Now, if you would kindly move . . . I'm sorry, Miss Esmeralda.' He moved towards Stanislas who, for a moment, looked as if he was not going to shift. But Oliver was larger than him and sense prevailed.

Agnes preceded him out of the door and into the hall. 'I apologise for intruding, Mr Cresswell, I heard shouting.'

'Not from me, Miss Beatty, I assure you. Good day.' Oliver found he too was shaking, not with anger but with shock at the scene he had just witnessed.

A groom was holding his horse. 'Oliver, please . . .' He turned to see Esmeralda rushing towards him. 'Please don't leave me!'

'I have to. I could not guarantee to keep my temper with your father.'

'He had no right to speak to you like that. I'm so sorry!' She grabbed his sleeve. 'Please don't go!'

He disentangled his arm from her grasp. 'I'm sorry. I dare not stay, I don't know what I would do. Esmeralda, don't cry. There.' From his pocket he took his handkerchief and wiped away her tears.

'Oliver, you don't understand – I love you!'

Oliver did not know how to deal with her. 'You can't, you don't know me.'

'Love knows no barriers! I don't need to,' she said dramatically.

'Esmeralda, come here this minute!' her father roared from the steps.

'I hate him.'

'No, you don't. Go back to him – he's making himself ill.'

'I love you.'

Oliver bent down and kissed her lips. 'We'll talk later,' he said quietly, leapt into his saddle and saluted an apoplectic Stanislas.

He entered the library.

'Done?' his father asked.

'Yes.'

'He didn't mind?'

'No, of course not,' he lied. 'Here's the cheque for Lees

Coppice, Father. I shall enjoy living there. But I'd appreciate it, in future, if you were entirely honest with me.'

'It's hard to let your son know you've failed.'

'We all make mistakes.'

'Some of us make larger ones than others.' But at least his father was smiling.

As she sat beside Coral, Hannah decided pity was good, not the debased emotion that many regarded it as '*I don't want your pity!*' '*Don't waste your pity on me.*' She'd heard those words said often but never fully understood why it should be so. How could she not have pitied Coral, laid so low by her mysterious illness? Pity was the same as compassion and no one, as far as she knew, rejected that. And the sympathy had replaced the anger Coral had aroused in her.

She looked up as the door opened. 'How is she this evening?' Mortie came to her side.

'She is so much better. She's sleeping peacefully and there's no fever. She was talking to us quite animatedly earlier. Soon she'll be fine.'

'Bit of a fright she's given us, though. Where's the new nurse?'

'She's tired. I told her to go to bed, that I'd sit with Coral tonight.'

'You're always so kind, Hannah. Is the doctor coming?'

'He was here earlier. He's much happier about her.'

'I was scared, Hannah.'

'I'm sure you were.' She took his hand as he sat down.

'I'm not very good at saying what's in here.' He patted the region of his heart. 'But . . . Well, I'm glad.'

'Of course you are.'

'You looked deep in thought when I came in.'

'Did I? I was considering the difference between pity and compassion and I couldn't find any.'

'You always were a bit of a deep thinker, weren't you? Comes of being so clever.'

'Me?' She laughed. 'It's not how I would describe myself.'

'But you are. You grasp things so quickly. You don't have to have them explained to you. You just get on with what's necessary. I don't know what we'd have done without you this past year – first Father and now Coral.'

'I can't say it was my pleasure, since I would prefer that neither of them had been ill. I did what I could.'

'And more. I do understand how difficult it is for you . . . Don't like to say anything bad . . . But, well, there it is, you see.'

'Bless you, Mortie.' A lump formed in her throat.

They both looked up at a tap on the door. To their surprise Simeon's face appeared. 'Is it convenient?' He sidled into the room. 'I was returning from evensong and thought I'd just see how our dear patient is faring.'

'Kind of you, vicar. Much better, I'm happy to report. Come in.' Mortie beckoned.

Had Simeon always walked like a crab, Hannah wondered, as she watched him move sideways towards the bed. 'Simeon, you look tired,' she said.

'Weight of the world, Miss Cresswell, but my shoulders are broad.' Since his were narrower than those of any other man she knew, it was, she thought, an unfortunate thing to say. 'Would you like something to drink? Eat?'

'Always caring for others, aren't you?' He looked at Coral, lying so peacefully. 'Perhaps a prayer of thanks.'

Mortie looked uncertain. 'Don't want to jump the gun, Vicar.'

'That would be most kind.' Hannah said, and slid on to her knees. Mortie followed her, looking uncomfortable.

'*Our dear Lord in Heaven, heavenly Father . . .*' Simeon began. He had a special voice for speaking to God: his normal tone was obsequious, but when he dealt with the Almighty it was stronger, more sonorous, as if he had more confidence in himself. Hannah reprimanded herself for such irreverent thoughts when she should be praying, but something about Simeon made her that way. She opened her eyes and looked at Coral.

She was staring at Simeon with a look of sheer terror, her mouth opening and shutting as if she was trying to say something. Immediately Hannah was on her feet. The men, their eyes still shut, did not see. 'There, there, Coral. It's all right. It's us,' she whispered, trying to comfort her, but Coral's expression did not change.

Simeon's voice droned on. He was reaching what appeared to be the crescendo, so loud now that Hannah expected to hear trumpets at any moment. She realised Simeon's voice had not only woken Coral but was frightening her. As Simeon took a deep breath as if winding himself up for another onslaught on God she leant across the bed and tugged at his sleeve. 'I think our patient is grateful but has had enough for tonight, Simeon.'

Simeon looked at her with glazed eyes. He shook his head, as if to refocus them. It struck her that he seemed to be emerging from a trance.

Coral remained agitated even when the men had left. But at least she was fully awake and Hannah persuaded her to drink. 'Shall I read to you for a little while?' Coral nodded, looking miserable. Hannah picked up her copy of *Kim* and began with the first chapter. She was not sure if Coral was listening but hoped her voice would lull her back to sleep.

'You've been so good to me . . .' Coral's voice, husky with disuse, cut across Hannah's. 'All these days . . .'

'You were aware of us?'

'A lot of the time.' She coughed, clearing her throat. 'I could hear you all, I just couldn't find the energy to respond. I didn't deserve . . .' She was waving her hand as if searching for Hannah's.

'Of course you did. It was my pleasure to care for you.'

'I've always been so horrible to you. I'm sorry.'

'I don't think you have. There's no need to apologise.'

'Hannah, I don't want to die . . .' A large tear, then another, rolled down her cheek. She dabbed them away.

'But you're not going to. You're much better.'

'You lie to me.'

'I promise you I don't. The doctor was here earlier. He said he was pleased with you and he—'

'I've got to tell you . . . tell someone, before it's too late . . .' Coral struggled to sit up.

'Don't tire yourself.' But Coral seemed determined so Hannah propped her up on her pillows. She sat down again, to find Coral searching desperately for her hand, which she grasped so tightly that Hannah winced.

'I'm being punished for my wickedness. I deserve to die!' More tears fell. 'I killed my baby!' she declared. 'God is punishing me.'

Hannah was mystified. What was she talking about? What baby? 'You must have had a bad dream, dear.'

'I have not!' She seemed angry at being contradicted.

Had she had a miscarriage and it had been decided not to tell anyone? 'It could not be helped. It was dreadful.'

'Of course it was. Poor you, poor Mortie.'

'Poor Mortie. He didn't deserve it.'

'It wasn't your fault—'

'But it was. I had to rid myself – it wasn't Mortie's.'

Hannah could hardly believe what she had heard.

'I have to confess to someone. Do you think that because I'm telling you, saying how sorry I am, God will forgive me? I used . . . Oh, my God.' She put her head into her hands. 'I . . . a knitting needle. Oh, Hannah, the pain, the shame . . .'

Hannah could feel herself alternately blushing at the information and then blanching at the horror. Was that what had made Coral so ill? Had she damaged herself? 'I don't think you should be telling me these things.'

'But I can't die without confessing.'

'You're not going to die.'

'I am. Why else was the vicar here?'

'He was giving thanks for your recovery.'

'He was? Why didn't you stop me speaking?'

'I tried. Really, Coral, you've nothing to fear.'

'Why did you let me think I had?'

'But I didn't.'

'That's a matter of opinion.'

Hannah looked at her sister-in-law, who was virtually back to normal. Nothing had changed after all. But this time she wouldn't be intimidated.

'I would prefer you to forget everything I said to you.'

'I've forgotten already. Now, how about some warm milk to help you sleep? You've tired yourself.' She crossed the room and pulled the bell. She ordered milk and asked for Lavender.

'I really am feeling too weary, Lavender,' she said to her maid, when she appeared. 'Would you be so kind as to sit with Mrs Cresswell?'

She could not get out of the room quickly enough. She did not want to be with Coral a moment longer. In her own room she sat on her bed in fury. These were matters she did not want to know. How dare Coral confide in her, of all people? Poor Mortie, poor dead baby. She tried to forget the hateful words, but it was impossible.

Chapter Twelve
October 1901

At the Cresswell Arms two of the rooms on the balcony, overlooking the courtyard, were now ready. Melanie, with a reluctant Xenia, was making the beds and generally checking that all was in place.

'Do you think people will want to come and stay here?' Xenia asked, stuffing a pillow into its case.

'There's no need to shove it like that or the pillowcase will need ironing again.' Melanie brushed the wrinkles out of the coverlet on the large double bed. 'And, yes, I'm confident we shall have guests – I've had several enquiries already. It will look lovely when it's finished. In the spring I plan to plant flowers in tubs. I saw a picture of a house in Austria that looked lovely with tumbling geraniums – it's not dissimilar to this one.'

Xenia laughed. 'You are such an optimist, Mama.'

'It's the only way to survive, Xenia, as you will find.'

'Don't you feel like a drudge? You never stop working.'

'There's much to do. I felt like a drudge at the cottage, but here I'm paid for my labour.' She looked about the room with satisfaction. Last month it had been full of rubbish and filthy. Now she'd whitewashed the walls, scrubbed the floorboards and polished them; she'd cleaned the windows, sewn curtains for them, and buffed the furniture – which she had found abandoned in various rooms – until it shone. If not exactly fit for a king, it was clean and pleasant, better than any bedroom she had ever had.

'It's all right. Not as nice as at Mrs Featherstone's house.'

'Nothing is, is it?' She doubted her daughter heard the irony in her voice.

'Why can't I go to Esmeralda's as she wanted me to?'

'Because I need you here.'

'But I hate it.'

'I can't do it all myself.'

'But you've Zeph to help and Flossie.'

'Zeph is only here at the weekend, as you well know. I'd rather you didn't go, that's all.'

'Why?'

Melanie hugged the sheet to herself. 'I think your time with Mrs Featherstone gave you ideas above your station. The von Ehrlichs are even richer and I fear for you there. When Esmeralda tired of you, as she would in time, you'd be riddled with discontent.'

'But—'

'No, Xenia, I've had my say. You're not going. You've Lettice and Young Mortimer, are they not enough for you?'

'Lettice's mother is ill so she's helping look after her. He's at university.'

'I expect you'll see Lettice soon.' She hoped so. Her daughter was easier to deal with when she had been with her new friend. She did not worry about her with Lettice for the latter was such a sweet, kind girl.

They had just begun to walk along the balcony to the next room when a woman appeared from Oliver's suite. At sight of the Topshams, she froze.

'Good afternoon,' Melanie said, as startled and embarrassed as Laura Redman was. Laura lowered her head and fled along the balcony to the stairs that led to the back entrance arch.

'That was the vicar's wife!' Xenia said. 'What's she doing here?'

Melanie didn't have time to answer before Oliver

appeared. 'How are the six rooms progressing, Mrs Topsham?'

'Two more, sir, so with the others over the bar we've got five now. One more to go.'

'Excellent. And are you happy here, Miss Topsham?'

'It's lovely, thank you, Mr Cresswell.' Xenia bestowed a brilliant smile on him as she bobbed a small curtsy. He was about to turn away, then stopped as if the smile halted him. The two looked at each other intently.

'Is there anything else you require, Mr Cresswell?' Melanie's voice was sharp. She had not liked the look that had passed between the two.

'No, thank you, Mrs Topsham. I was just leaving. Splendid. I'm glad about the rooms.' He ran down the stairs.

'Well!' Xenia was laughing. 'Heavens above, the vicar's wife!'

'She was probably visiting him on business.'

'Then why did she look so guilty?'

'It's none of our business. And I'm shocked at you making reference to things you shouldn't know about.' She collected her basket of cleaning materials. How worldly her daughter was, how shocking. Or was it? she wondered. She herself had been a mother for over two years at Xenia's age.

'He's very handsome.'

'Xenia, I saw how you looked at him. Don't! Our livelihoods depend on that man. I want nothing to interfere with our security.'

'*Your* security, you mean. I can't help it if men like me. I know I have a power over them,' she boasted.

'The only power you have, young woman, is the same that all women have. Don't think you're different. They have one thing in mind, and you know what I'm talking about. But I can assure you, once he's had it, he'll drop you. Fast as anything.'

Xenia looked bored. 'He's too old for me anyway.'

Melanie did not believe her.

They had been at the inn for several months and it was home now. It bore no resemblance to how it had been when they had first moved in. And not only had the building changed: Melanie was aware that she had too. She was happier. She smiled constantly. Although she never stopped working from morning to night she had put on a little weight, which suited her; the strained look had gone from her face, and she looked prettier, healthier, than she had in years. She enjoyed the company, the banter in the public bar, the more serious conversations she had in the lounge. She was not sure which she preferred: she was relaxed with the men in the public bar since she knew them all, and with Bernard's death, and her father's constant presence as he dallied over a pint, the barrier that had been between her and them had tumbled down. She loved the lounge bar she had created, with its comfortable chairs, flowers, heavy velvet curtains and the wrought-iron candlesticks that the blacksmith had made for her. She was shy with the clients here, for they were of the local business community and professionals, she sometimes felt out of her depth with them. But they were always courteous, and some made her feel quite important. Best of all, she was building a lunchtime business, which she hadn't expected. Times were changing and the local businessmen liked to discuss important matters informally over a meal.

Everything was happening so quickly that she was relieved Zephaniah came home at weekends. He continued to work with the solicitor during the week, as Melanie had persuaded him to do. There lay security. While things were going well for her family now, who was to say it would last? Her son balanced the books for her, paid the bills, banked the money, negotiated with the Cresswells and supervised the builders. Without him she did not know how she would have managed. Melanie looked after the guests, which she enjoyed.

There were times, usually when Rob Robertson, his brother and Sol came in, that she remembered Bernard and her guts knotted with anxiety: the day might come when they fell out and the truth would be told. Although her brother was in Scotland, if it ever emerged she knew he was not far enough away.

'Guess who was upstairs, Flossie?' said Xenia, as they entered the kitchen. Two of Flossie's children were at her feet and the youngest was in his crib in a corner.

'Xenia. No!' Melanie remonstrated.

'The *vicar's wife*!'

'So?' Flossie was hauling a large copper pan off the range.

'Visiting *Oliver Cresswell*.'

'So? Would you mind moving? I need to strain this.'

Reluctantly Xenia moved out of her way. Melanie was aware that neither woman liked the other – she couldn't blame Flossie: her daughter was high-handed with her when she chose.

'Hello, who are you?' Melanie had just noticed another young woman sitting in the corner.

'This is Dolly,' Flossie told her. 'She used to work up at the big house as a kitchenmaid but left and she's looking for work. I said as she'd have to speak to you. She's Sol Pepper's niece.'

'What are you looking for?' She had no call for extra staff, but her debt to Sol was enormous so she'd have to find something for the girl to do.

'I don't mind.'

'Have you references?'

'No – I walked out, and Mrs Gilroy told me where I could go when I asked her for a letter of recommendation. I can't say I blame her.' The girl grinned.

Melanie liked her for that: many would have moaned or lied. 'As you know, we've not been in business very long so we can't offer you much. But you'd have room, board and a few shillings.'

'Thank you.'

'Did you try the factory at Barlton? Or wouldn't they take you?'

'They weren't fussy about references. I was there a couple of weeks and hated it. They've got these big machines going thump-thump – I began to think I was turning into one meself. You can't talk to anyone. I thought I'd go mad.'

'When can you start?'

'Now?' She smiled winningly.

They looked round when Zephaniah called: 'You're wanted, mother.' He tailed off when he caught sight of Dolly.

'Who needs me, Zeph?'

'That Miss von Ehrlich. She's in the bar.'

'The bar?' Melanie said, with astonishment, and scurried to see what she wanted. The locals were staring, amazed, at the exotic creature in pink wool and fur wrap who stood among them. Beside her, looking concerned, was Richard Joynston.

'Miss von Ehrlich, how can I help you?'

'I'm searching for Mr Cresswell. I wondered if he was here?'

'Which one? Mr Oliver was here but he's left.'

Esmeralda stamped her foot, as if she was cross with herself rather than anyone else. She opened the small bag she was carrying and withdrew a letter. 'I wonder if, next time he's here, you could give him this.'

'Would you not be better leaving it at the house?'

'No. I can't go there, you see.'

Esmeralda was evidently not about to explain any more so Melanie took the letter and slipped it into her pocket. 'I'll make sure he gets it,' she assured her.

'Thank you, Mrs Topsham, you're very kind.'

The letter bothered Melanie. Did it mean that the girl

had an interest in him? Was he suitable for her? *Was* he involved with Laura Redman? Melanie had tried to persuade herself that the woman had been here on business but she could not forget the panic and embarrassment she'd seen on her face. She had been caught out. If she was right, that young girl was likely to be hurt. And something must have happened between the Cresswells and the von Ehrlichs.

She wished she knew nothing: she never liked to be involved too intimately in other people's lives. And who was she to criticise Laura? No one knew what happened in a marriage other than those who lived it. If she had met someone who could have shown her happiness, might she have betrayed Bernard? She doubted she would have found the courage, but that would have been all that stopped her, she was sure.

Hannah was being driven to Dulcie Prestwick's house. Normally she would have ridden over but she had a cold, and Lavender had made such a fuss about her going out that she had given in and was now sitting in the back of the automobile wrapped in furs and blankets, a hot-water bottle at her feet. She much preferred a carriage to this monster: it was noisy, it rattled, and the smell of petrol made her feel sick so she had to open the windows, whereupon the cold air came rushing in, making her huddle under her covers. She would have preferred not to go out today but there had been a violent storm at the weekend and she was concerned about some of the shrubs she had had planted in October. When a note arrived inviting her to luncheon today she presumed that Dulcie, in her nice way, was summoning her and that something had gone wrong.

Her cold was making her feel wretched. She was one of those fortunate souls who were never ill and when she was it always took her by surprise. She knew she was a dreadful patient and Lavender must have been pleased to see the back of her.

Her misery did not stem simply from the cold. Her father had summoned her yesterday and asked her to reconsider her decision to move into her new home. She did not wish to hurt him by refusing to stay – he was so generous to her and when they had been at home alone with just Oliver it had all been perfect, but it wasn't any more. She could not stay. And, if she was honest, which she always found somewhat uncomfortable, she had become excited at the prospect of her new home, having her own possessions, her own routine, her own little kingdom.

There had been a moment with Coral when she had thought it might be possible. A couple of days after that confession, Hannah had plucked up the courage to discuss the missing items with her. 'I have a problem, Coral,' she had said.

Coral had looked up. 'Yes? Might I be of help?'

'I found certain things in your dressing-table drawer that shouldn't have been there.'

'Oh, my God.' Coral had covered her face with her hands. Her shame, Hannah was sure, was genuine.

'I've managed to get rid of them all. Penelope has her ring back.'

'Hannah, my dear, you are so good to me.'

'There's just one thing.' How best to phrase it? 'Why did you take them?' She had to know: she had read of a woman who had stolen things because she couldn't help herself. And if that was so with Coral, they had to know, they had to watch her, they had to warn people.

'I'm so ashamed!' Coral had burst into tears, and Hannah had had to wait for her to recover herself before proceeding.

'Why?' she persisted.

'I needed money. I'm in debt. I borrowed from a man

and now I owe him more than he lent me. He won't explain why.'

'It's interest, Coral. That's how lenders make their money.' How could she be so stupid? 'Could you not have asked Mortie to help you?'

'Ask Mortie?' She gave a bitter little laugh. 'He would have half killed me if he knew.'

'*Mortie?*' She knew she sounded half-witted.

'He beats me.'

'*Mortie?* I can't believe that!'

'Are you accusing me of lying?' Coral bridled.

'No, of course not, but – he's such a gentle man.'

'Ha. You don't know him. He often beats me black and blue. Says it's his right.' And she was away again, wailing into her handkerchief so that Hannah had to fetch her a clean one. She waited for the crying to cease, still unable to believe such a thing of her brother.

'Why do you owe money?'

'You'll tell Mortie.'

'No, I won't, I promise.'

'Dresses mainly – he keeps me so short. And since your father cut his income, things have been so hard – you can't imagine how difficult it has been. And then I was trying to make things better ... Trying to get some money I could give him to help a little and I played at cards and . . .' She was incapable of continuing, sobbing in the most heartrending way into her handkerchief.

'How much?' she asked eventually.

'You will despise me. Five hundred pounds.'

'I'll pay it for you.'

'Hannah, would you? I mean, I wasn't expecting you to. I'd hate you to think I was begging, but if you could, perhaps I could pay you back.' She sat up straight against the pillows. 'Yes, just a loan from you and I will.'

'It's not necessary.'

'What a dear sister you are. Oh, Hannah, I shall be grateful until my dying day.' And she insisted on kissing her, which since she had that sweet-sour smell of the sickbed about her was not pleasant. 'Do you have to go?'

'To my new house?'

'Don't go. Don't leave me alone with Penelope. I feel safer with you here.'

Life was full of surprises, Hannah had thought. But she wished she didn't know these things. It had started with Oliver and Laura, and now all this. First, the awful reason Coral was ill, then that she had been unfaithful to Mortie, and now that Hannah had promised to deceive him. She felt burdened by the confessions of others.

As she arrived at Dulcie's house she resolved to put it all behind her and enjoy her visit.

'Why on earth did you think I had summoned you to complain? What a sweet child you are. Of course not! It wasn't a summons but an invitation – I wanted to see you. Your company is always such a delight to me.' Dulcie was fussing about her, insisting she sit closest to the fire, pressing warm drinks on her, making her feel warm and cosy. This was what a mother should be like, she thought. 'You don't look well at all. It's my suggestion you should stay here the night. No, it's not even that, I *insist* you stay. It's such a chilly day.'

'But the plants.'

'Oh, bother them, they're fine. Honestly, your man bedded them in so well. Darling Theo checked them for me, I was fussing so. They're like my children at the moment.'

'It would be nice just to relax. Would you tell my father's coachman to return for me tomorrow?'

Hannah had spent her adult life looking after other people and it was a new and pleasant experience for her to be cherished.

'You know, my dear, you have the look of one who is bowed down with worry. I don't mean to pry, but do you wish to confide?'

'It's very kind of you and you're right, but I don't think

you can help me. I have been told things that I would prefer not to know.'

'By knowing them you feel you deceive another?'

'Yes, it's that exactly. I did not seek these confidences – well, only one, and that of them all is the most minor. Now I am as torn with guilt as if I were the miscreant.'

'You must not be. I've found that people frequently confess to their wrongdoings to lessen the burden on themselves with never a thought of how it affects the person they impose upon. Some people can be so self-absorbed.'

'But I don't know what to do about the other person involved.'

'Do nothing.'

'You think so?'

'If it is too awful why make them miserable by telling them something they are in ignorance of, and might never need to know? In any case, they may not believe you and may accuse you of being malicious and thus hurt you – no one ever wants to hear unpleasant matters. They will find out for themselves without you telling them.'

'That makes me feel much better. You're so wise.'

'Not at all, my dear. I've just learnt how to keep myself safe over the years.' And you, young woman, are ill and you are going to bed.'

Oliver was inspecting Lees Coppice. The house was even better than he had remembered it. It had not originally been part of the estate but his grandfather had bought it to acquire the land that went with it. It was a fine Georgian house and he supposed he was fortunate that when the plans had been mooted for Hannah to have a place of her own this one had been tenanted.

Thaddeus Highman had been an old friend of his father's from university days. He was an inventor – not that he had invented anything of significance – who had fallen on hard times; Mortimer had helped out by providing him with this house rent free. A couple of months ago, Thaddeus had announced he was going to Australia to join his brother and Oliver was now the proud owner.

The house was more than adequate for his needs. The rooms, as in most Georgian houses, were high-ceilinged and large. He had a fine hall, a grand drawing room, a capacious dining room, a good library and six bedrooms. He had stabling for half a dozen horses and kennels that would accommodate a pack of hounds, if he was so minded. He'd a trout lake and flight pond, twelve acres of woodland, four of garden and fifty of pasture. It was excellent. And to think he might have ended up with a huge mansion if von Ehrlich had not come to his rescue.

At the thought of the man he frowned. His reaction over this property was out of all proportion to its value. He had certainly shown another side of himself, a most unpleasant one. But Oliver should not have been surprised: he had often found, on his travels, that the most charming of people, when allied with recent wealth, were often the most devious, that they loathed to be thwarted. That their charm was not genuine but merely a tool. And yet, like the rest, he had fallen for Stanislas's charisma.

He continued on the inspection of his new home. He had a notebook with him in which he was listing work to be done, furniture to buy. He'd need paint, paper and curtains. Hannah would help him there.

He should, he supposed, have asked Laura, but the situation between them was difficult. She was aware that his interest was waning and clung to him, which made him step further back from her.

Laura had been in his heart for such a long time that extricating himself was hard. He did not want to hurt her: while he was no longer in love with her, he had a great fondness for her, but that was not enough for either of them, certainly not for him, and it seemed an insult to the love they had once had for each other. She was a sweet woman, and a loving one, and she had taken such risks for him that he felt ashamed of himself and what he had allowed to happen. He hadn't wanted to fall out of love – it had just happened.

The other day at the Cresswell Arms, when Melanie and her daughter had seen her, he had hoped, God help him, that Laura would be so frightened at what they might think she would stop coming. Instead she had been even more clinging, and yesterday when she had come he had been irritated with her, which had heaped guilt on to guilt. The simplest solution, he supposed, was to bolt, as he would have in the past. But he didn't want to – and he most certainly didn't want to leave this house now that it was his.

He ran down the long, curving staircase, in response to a banging on the front door.

'I'm coming,' he called as the banging persisted and he fumbled with the unfamiliar bolts and locks. 'Esmeralda! What are you doing here?'

'I had to come.' She hurtled through the door, an anxious Agnes Beatty behind her. 'It's Papa! He says I am never to see you again. He says I am never to go to Cresswell Manor again. He says that Lettice can't be my friend. But, worst of all, he says I am never to speak to you again!' She threw herself into his arms. Oliver was taken aback and did not know what to do. He looked at Agnes and shrugged his shoulders. Esmeralda nestled into him, which he found pleasant.

'I'm sorry, Mr Cresswell. I couldn't stop her coming here. I had to follow on my bicycle.' It was then he noticed how dishevelled they looked.

'Esmeralda, calm yourself.' She was sobbing so hard it was tearing at his heartstrings.

'Esmeralda, pull yourself together.' Agnes's voice rang out sharp.

'I can't. I love him.'

'Esmeralda!'

The girl stood back from Oliver. 'You can *Esmeralda* me all you like, but it's true.'

'And what would your father say? He'll be furious with both of us.' For a normally calm woman Agnes was agitated.

'I don't care what my father thinks. It's my life, not his.'

'You can't behave in this manner. It's unseemly.'

'I know one thing. If you want something you have to take it. You can't listen to others. We have one life and we have to do what we want, not what others want us to do. I apologise, Oliver, if I speak out of turn, but I am beside myself with misery.'

He brushed a lock of hair off her face. 'Don't apologise, there's no need.' In that moment he knew why he no longer loved Laura.

It was two days before Hannah was well enough to return home. Even then Dulcie begged her to stay, and she was tempted – Dulcie made her feel so important and wanted. 'You're so kind, but I have to go. I've finally decided that I can't leave my father. I'll just have to tolerate my stepmother.'

'Does your father know how miserable she makes you?'

'He does. He says little but observes much.' She found it so easy to talk to Dulcie, whom she knew would never divulge a word of what she said.

'Then I hope you're making the right choice.'

'I nearly lost him earlier this year. How would I feel if I moved and then, God forbid, something dreadful happened to him?'

'But he wouldn't want you to live your life because of him. Still, enough of my snooping. We must discuss our planting plans for the spring. With gardens it's never too soon to start . . .' And they enjoyed a couple of happy hours designing, agreeing, disagreeing, while they waited for Harold, the coachman, to return for Hannah.

As she sat in the back of the vehicle she felt renewed. Perhaps she had needed to get right away from home to be better able to gauge it. She peered out of the window as, having come down from the moor, they joined the road to Barlton. It was a dismal day, raining quite hard now; she hoped her news would lighten it for her father.

The car swerved suddenly and Hannah rocked on the back seat. She turned and looked out of the tiny back window. A woman, bundled up in a cloak, was walking with her head bowed against the rain, barely able to keep hold of her umbrella in the stiff wind, and lugging a heavy-looking bag. Hannah unloosed the speaking tube and blew into it, alerting Harold. 'Stop! That poor woman – we should assist her.'

Harold braked – evidently a little too sharply, for the heavy vehicle swayed alarmingly then lurched to a standstill. He had only recently mastered the technique of driving and was still wary of it. He climbed out and trudged back along the road. Through the lashing rain, Hannah could just make out the two of them in conversation. What a day to be walking! She hoped the woman was a suitable person to invite into the automobile. She must be mad or in distress – she hoped it was not the former. The chauffeur returned and opened the front door of the automobile. Hannah opened hers too.

'Miss Beatty – is it you?' she exclaimed. 'You poor soul! Come in the back with me. I've fur rugs here. Dear me, you'll catch your death.'

'Miss Cresswell, how fortuitous. You are most kind.' And then, to Hannah's astonishment, Agnes Beatty began to cry, not noisily, or obviously, but discreetly. She looked for a handkerchief, couldn't find one, and covered her face with her fur tippet instead. Hannah found her own clean handkerchief, gave it to her, then leant forward and pulled down the walnut cabinet in which the decanters and glasses were neatly stored. 'Here, my dear, a small brandy as a restorative.' She handed Agnes the glass. 'Poor you.' She tucked a fur closer around her. 'As fast as you can, Harold, we must get Miss Beatty into the warm.'

Hannah hated to witness someone else's distress. She never knew who was the more embarrassed, the weeper or herself. It always seemed such an intrusion: if she wept she hated anyone to see her. It was even more difficult when, as now, she did not know the person well enough to touch and comfort them. She sat with her hands folded in her lap and waited patiently.

'What must you think of me? My most heartfelt apologies. Giving way like this is not in my nature, I would like you to understand.'

'But I do. Exhaustion is difficult to deal with,' she said encouragingly.

'You're such a sensitive and kind person, Miss Cresswell. I realised that the first time we met.'

'Thank you.' She smiled, unsure if it was true or if Miss Beatty was just being polite.

'You must be wondering what I was doing out and about in such inclement weather.'

'I wouldn't presume—'

'I think I should explain. Mr von Ehrlich is a man of passion—'

Hannah's gloved hand shot to her mouth.

'No, pray, not to me. Oh dear, I phrased that in the most unfortunate manner. I was trying to find a polite way of saying he has a temper without appearing too disloyal to him.' At least she was smiling now, Hannah saw.

'My fault for jumping to the wrong conclusion. I trust he didn't lose it with you?'

'The whole household. He was angry with Esmeralda and beat her. I intervened so he dismissed me forthwith.'

'No!'

'I wasn't even given time to pack my belongings.'

'The barbarian.'

'Not really. I could understand his distress, even if I find it more than inconvenient.'

The irony was not lost on Hannah. 'He beat that dear child?'

'Yes. Not her face, I'm happy to say.'

'But he should not have hit her anywhere. Is she safe there?'

'Oh, yes. She will cry and he will sulk, and then they will be friends again.'

'Does he do this often?'

'Only when he is totally vexed, as he was today.'

'Might I enquire what made him so?'

'She had an assignation with someone he did not find suitable.'

'Who?'

'I'd rather not say.'

Hannah was glad the light was fading for she blushed to the roots of her hair. 'It was most insensitive of me to ask. So, you have no home?'

'That is correct. And, sadly, no employment. I was walking to the railway terminus to catch a train. I was going to my brother, who lives near Newbury.'

'Not today. I insist you come and stay with us for as long as you like.'

'Really? That is so very kind of you. But I would not wish to impose myself.'

Hannah held up her hand. 'It is no imposition. It would give me enormous pleasure. You need time to recover from this horrible incident, then plan what you wish to do.'

When they returned to Cresswell they were met by Lettice, who threw her arms about her aunt and hugged her. 'I thought you were never coming back.'

'What? And stay away from you? Never! I had a fearful cold and dear Lady Prestwick insisted that I stay with her until I was recovered. I met poor Miss Beatty here walking in the rain – summon Mrs Fuller for me, there's a dear. And I see you have a friend here too, that's nice.'

Xenia Topsham gave her an elegant curtsy – well executed, neither too much nor too little. 'I trust you don't mind me being here, Miss Cresswell.'

'Why should I object? It's nice for Lettice . . .' She laughed. 'I was about to say it was nice for Lettice to have someone to *play with*. Which, of course, would be deeply insulting to two such smart young ladies. You see, Miss Beatty, I find it so difficult to grasp that my niece is becoming a young woman.'

'They grow so quickly, Miss Cresswell. It is one of the sadnesses of life.'

'It's not sad to us, Miss Beatty.' Lettice was smiling.

'I couldn't wait to be an adult,' Xenia added.

'And are you?' Agnes asked, in a kind tone.

'Of course.' The stare that Xenia gave Agnes was bold and, Hannah thought, quite intimidating. 'How's Esmeralda?'

'Miss von Ehrlich is well,' Agnes said pointedly, evidently choosing to put Xenia in her place. The girl really was a trifle forward, thought Hannah.

Having settled Agnes in one of the guest rooms, Hannah returned to her own with the girls in tow. She was aware of them whispering, and out of the corner of her eye noticed Xenia nudging Lettice as if encouraging her.

'Aunt, you'll never guess what Xenia has told me.'

'And what is that?' Hannah asked, as she removed her hat. She put the several hatpins she had worn into the cushion where she kept them, and which made her think they looked like miniature jewelled excaliburs wedged in a pink satin stone.

'She saw someone visiting Uncle Oliver.' Lettice giggled nervously.

'I expect he has lots of visitors. He's a busy man now that he is helping your grandfather.'

'This was a *woman*,' Xenia declared.

'Really?' Hannah had a sense of foreboding from the bold way the girl spoke.

'In his *bedroom*.'

Hannah chose to ignore her. 'Should I wear the pink or the primrose dress tonight, Lettice, which do you think?'

'Oh, the pink – I like that colour with your dark hair.'

'Don't you want to know who it was, Miss Cresswell?'

'Not particularly, Xenia.'

Xenia nudged Lettice again.

'It was the vicar's wife, Aunt.'

'Really? About church matters I expect. And grey slippers or red? Do you think red would go with coral, Lettice?'

'You're not shocked?'

'Why should I be, Xenia? And I really don't know what you're implying, but I must tell you I don't like tittle-tattle or gossip. And I'm surprised at you of all people, Lettice. Now, if you will excuse me, I need to rest before dinner. I suggest Xenia leaves now – it is already dark. And you, Lettice, shall eat in the nursery tonight.'

'But, Aunt, I want Xenia to stay.'

'And I am saying she is to go.'

Lettice said no more.

Rest was out of the question. Was he still seeing the wretched woman? How foolhardy of him, how wicked. And now it was only a matter of time before that wretched girl would have spread the information. She was far from a suitable companion for Lettice.

It had been decided that Agnes Beatty should continue to rest and Mrs Fuller would bring her a tray of broth. Already a plan was forming in Hannah's mind. If Agnes needed employment she would give it to her. Not as a companion, she wouldn't insult her, but as her assistant in the gardening business – once her father had given his permission, which she was sure he eventually would. Hannah loved the creative work, the paperwork that might be involved was another matter. She would be surprised if Agnes could not deal beautifully with such matters. That apart, Hannah had taken to her at their first meeting and would like to have her as her special friend and ally.

She took longer than usual to get ready: she wanted to look nice for this evening when she planned to tell her father that she was not moving to the dower house. And she had resolved to dress up more: in the past she had always felt a bit mousy beside the resplendent Penelope and Coral.

First, there was Oliver to talk to: she hoped to get him on his own – she could not speak to him about such a matter with others present. To her relief he was alone in the drawing room.

'I have been told that Laura Redman was seen coming out of your bedroom at the Cresswell Arms. I am very disappointed,' she said, without preamble.

'Who on earth told you that?'

'I'd rather not say.'

'The Topsham girl? I knew she was trouble when I first set eyes on her.'

'Is it true? I didn't even know you had rooms there.'

'It's an office. There's a lot involved with the running of the inn and I prefer to keep everything to hand.'

'So what was Laura doing there?' she persisted.

'She had come to ask me if I could find work for a young girl she was concerned about,' he said, looking her straight in the eye. 'To be honest, Hannah, *I'm* disappointed in *you*. Why listen to gossip? It does you no credit.'

'I'm sorry, Oliver. I didn't mean . . .' she looked away,

shame-faced. 'But if I were you I'd ask Melanie Topsham to have a word with her daughter. She has a vicious tongue.' She spoke sharply, attempting to lessen her feelings of humiliation. And just in time: at that moment everyone else arrived, except Penelope.

'We were worried about you, Hannah,' Mortimer said.

'I was well cared for by Lady Prestwick, Papa.'

'The hotelier?' Coral said. 'How is her house furnished? Like a hotel?'

'Exquisitely. I'm glad to see you so much better.'

'Coral, sit down this minute.' Mortie pretended to be cross. 'I told her she could only dine with us if she was a good wife and looked after herself properly.' He was fussing over her in a particularly gentle and endearing manner. Would he do so if he knew Coral had said he beat her? Such a lie. And what if he knew the truth about the baby, Hannah thought. This was the first time she had been with both of them in the same room since Coral's confession, and she felt most uncomfortable.

'Where's your mother?'

'Whitaker needed to see her on urgent business, Father. If we're not to die of thirst I'd better pour the drinks. Why couldn't he have sent a footman?' Mortie muttered, as he dispensed the sherry, managing to spill a goodly quantity on to the tray and the carpet.

'So, you're back?' Penelope swept into the room. 'Fuller tells me you have invited a Miss Beatty to stay?'

'I trust that is in order. I met her on the road, soaking wet. I feared she might take a chill.'

'Miss Beatty, out in weather like this? What on earth was she doing?' Oliver asked, with what looked to Hannah like real concern.

'It's a long story.'

'And we've no time for it now. The servants are in revolt.'

'What has happened, Penelope?' Mortimer asked quietly.

'It's those wretched missing objects and my ring.' She waved her right hand, on which flashed the diamond and sapphire band. 'Apparently they have been muttering for weeks among themselves. They don't believe that the things were found. They think one of us put them back and object to being under suspicion. Whitaker says they want a full investigation.'

'What?' Mortimer said, in disbelief.

'The cheek!' added Coral.

'I can see why they'd be upset,' Oliver said.

'I told them I had an inkling who the culprit might be.'

Hannah looked surreptitiously at Coral, who had gone as white as a sheet and was holding on to the arms of her chair so tightly that her knuckles were white.

'And who is that?'

'Why, Mortimer, the one person who remained silent. Your beloved daughter, of course.'

All heads swivelled to Hannah. 'I beg your pardon?' Hannah blushed and rued it: it would be taken as a sign of guilt.

'Honestly, Mother, I've never heard such rubbish. Hannah would be the last person to steal anything.'

'In my opinion it can only be her. The maids are adamant that they had cleaned where the items were all found. I was in Barlton with Mortie that day. Coral was weak in bed. No one is accusing you, Mortimer, and of course you would have been resting. You were out on the estate, Oliver – I checked.'

'You did *what*?' Oliver blustered.

'Which only leaves Hannah.'

'What about the children?'

'How dare you, Oliver?' Coral was on her feet. 'How dare you accuse my little ones?'

'Actually, Oliver, you were with the children, if you remember.'

'Lady Cresswell is right. After all, Hannah is the only one who was here alone that day . . .'

'Coral!' Hannah said, with a mixture of horror, surprise and hurt. She looked at her, but Coral glanced away. 'How could you?'

Now Coral looked straight at her. 'I had no choice,' she said firmly.

Hannah expected to want to cry. But she didn't. She felt a surge of anger. How could the woman be so duplicitous? 'Very well. If that's what you wish to think, then so be it.'

'Hannah, don't!' Oliver was crossing the room to her.

'No, Oliver, stay away. I had been going to tell you, Papa, that, despite the difficulties I find here,' she looked at her stepmother, 'I had decided not to move to the dower house. However, after such accusations I have no choice but to leave. I shall not be dining. I shall be moving tonight.'

'Hannah, you can't! You mustn't!'

'I can and I must, Papa. I have been unwelcome in this house for so many years that I had become accustomed to it. But to have my honesty and integrity attacked in this manner is too much for me. Please visit me.' With that she left the room as fast as she could, determined that Penelope should not see her tears.

Chapter Thirteen
October–November 1901

At all levels, in all departments, the manor of Cresswell was in uproar.

Harold, the coachman, had been called from his fireside. His wife, who had taken to her bed with a heavy cold, had to be roused to find him a change of clothes. The stable lads were bleary-eyed and having to disguise that this was caused by too much beer rather than sleep.

Lavender had been told by Hannah that they were not moving into the dower house so had begun to unpack everything. Now she was repacking while trying to console Hannah, who was in a parlous state.

Whitaker was mortified that he had had to get more wine from the cellar since unusually copious amounts were being consumed in the family dining room. He had always prided himself on judging the exact quantity needed and serving the wine perfectly. The temperature was wrong and he had no time to decant it correctly. He found himself doing the one thing he regarded as desecration – holding a bottle under a hot tap in the butler's pantry, trying to take the cellar chill off it. He felt that all he held dear, all his standards, were being destroyed.

Lavender was flustered as she rushed into the brushing room to collect various items of Hannah's clothing. Then she was searching the laundry for favourite articles. As she rushed along the lower corridor she stumbled and the pile of clothes she was carrying fell to the floor.

'Dear me, Miss Lavender, what's amiss? What now? You've been crying! Jock! Those entrée dishes, quick!

Then return for this wine! Mrs Fuller,' Whitaker called to the housekeeper, who was at the end of the corridor, 'your assistance.'

'Gracious, what have we here?'

'It's dreadful, Gussie,' Lavender sobbed. 'Poor Miss Hannah. She's in a dreadful state. I'm having to pack in such a rush – we're leaving—'

'At this time of night?'

'Have you not heard, Mrs Fuller? Such a cataclysmic argument the family have been having! Poor Miss Hannah,' Whitaker informed her.

'I'd a bad headache – I had to lie down. You can't possibly be leaving, Lavender. Where are you going?'

'To the new dower house.'

'But it will be cold – it's freezing tonight.'

'Miss Hannah says she doesn't care.'

'Who has upset her so?'

'Lady Cresswell.'

'She should be used to that by now.' Mrs Fuller sniffed.

'This was different. She accused her of stealing.'

'Miss Hannah? Has her ladyship gone mad? I've never heard of anything so ridiculous.'

'I fear it's the servants' fault, Mrs Fuller.'

'And how do you come to that conclusion, Edward? Miss Hannah is the most popular member of this family, as far as we're all concerned.' Mrs Fuller looked dismissive.

'Lady Cresswell says that Mr Whitaker told her the servants were discontented and suspicious of how the missing valuables were found, and she said that Miss Hannah had stolen the items, then put them back for fear of being found out.' Lavender related this speedily, as if reciting her catechism.

'It sounds very much to me as if it's *your* fault, Edward. What a thing to say!' Mrs Fuller blustered.

'I spoke the truth. The servants *are* disgruntled. I never said a word about Miss Cresswell.'

'It would seem tactless to tell her anything of how the servants are feeling, Edward. We have always dealt with such matters ourselves. What has it got to do with the family?'

'I would normally agree with you, Mrs Fuller.' Whitaker looked taken aback by this sharp criticism. 'However, I have to say I don't know what is happening here below stairs. Kitchenmaids walking out, disagreements, our position being questioned, insubordination below decks.'

'Are you accusing me?'

'Of course not, Mrs Fuller. Standards are changing. It was never like this in our youth, as I'm sure you'd agree. I, for one, don't like what's happening. For the first time in my professional life I look forward to my retirement. There are days when I feel like bringing it forward.'

'Don't even *speak* of leaving us. What would we do without you?' Mrs Fuller looked shocked. 'Why, when we were young there was a measure of insubordination below stairs – think of the times we had!'

'Not as now.'

'Well, I think we should watch ourselves. No point in us accusing each other and our juniors just because that lot are arguing.' She nodded in the direction of the dining room. 'This business about Miss Hannah, it's all rubbish. It's far more likely to be Penelope Cresswell up to no good than that sweet lady. No wonder she wants to move, but it will break her father's heart.'

'Sir, you're wanted!' Jock called from the top of the stairs.

'If you ladies will excuse me.' Whitaker, looking relieved to escape the housekeeper's sharp tongue, sidled along the corridor.

'What a to-do, Lavender. How could that woman accuse her?'

'The problem is,' Lavender bit her lip with agitation, 'I've got to talk to someone – It's such a burden!'

'Who better than me, Lavender? I like to think we've been friends for a long time.' Mrs Fuller was licking her lips with anticipation.

'You see, I think Miss Hannah *did* replace the things. Not that I know for sure, you understand. But she was behaving strangely that day *and* she didn't say anything when everybody was talking about nothing else – not that I thought it odd at the time.' She looked ill-at-ease for having unburdened herself. 'I'm not saying she stole them,' she added hurriedly.

'If she replaced them, she was doing it for someone else, that's for sure. And what about that poor Miss Beatty? Is she to go too?'

'Heavens! We'd quite forgotten about her. Should we wake her or leave her?'

'I'll see to her. You go and help Miss Hannah.'

Mrs Fuller watched the maid disappear and, when the coast was clear, ran towards the kitchen. 'Eve! It's Miss Hannah! You'll never guess what she's gone and done . . .'

So engrossed was Mrs Gilroy, in the housekeeper's tale that the stock on the hob overboiled and chaos ensued in the kitchens.

'I don't wish to discuss it further,' Penelope said.

'How convenient. You upset my daughter cruelly, then announce you don't wish to talk about it? Well, I do.'

'I felt I had to say something. It was my duty.'

'Why could you not have discussed it with me first?'

'She's not a girl, she's a woman,' Penelope said petulantly.

'She's still my daughter, even if she is an adult. You have demeaned her in front of her family. No doubt the servants are, at this moment, compounding the accusations.'

'That's hardly my fault.'

Whitaker continued impassively to serve them.

'Of course it is. What proof have you?'

'I told you, she was the only one of us here.'

'Coral was here.'

'Sir Mortimer! You can't possibly think it was *me*! I was ill, barely conscious. I knew nothing of this until after my recovery.'

'Then why did Hannah ask you if you were proud of yourself?'

'I have no idea.' But she was blushing furiously and rearranged the remaining cutlery at her place, watched intently by the others.

'Don't you?' Mortimer looked at her sternly. 'I have never had reason to believe that Hannah was a liar, or that she was prone to exaggeration.'

Coral put her hand to her forehead. 'I don't feel well.' She swayed on her chair.

'I expect it's troublesome for you, Coral, but if you could tell us what the problem is, you could retire.'

'Father, I must protest. Poor Coral is weak.'

'We have to get to the bottom of this, Mortie, in fairness to all of us. You were saying, Coral?'

'I'd rather not . . .'

'I think you must in fairness to Hannah,' Oliver interrupted.

'Mortie will be cross with me.'

'Why should I be? When am I ever cross with you?'

'Hannah lent me some money. I had got into a silly tiny debt and she . . . such a kind woman . . . I never asked her for it. She gave it to me.'

'Why did you get into debt?'

Coral burst into tears.

'Father, Coral is still not well. I insist we stop this inquisition!' Mortie had thrown down his napkin and was rushing to her aid as fast as his corpulent frame would allow.

Whitaker could not get out of the dining room fast enough.

'Are you cold, Miss Beatty? Had I known we were coming here tonight, I would have arranged for the boiler and fires to be lit. I can't apologise sufficiently for disturbing you as I have. There I am, trying to help you, then making your situation worse.'

'Not at all. Your kindness has made my situation far better than it was this morning. We both seem to be having quite an adventurous day.' Agnes's smile was one of wry amusement.

'Are you sure you haven't caught a chill?'

'Please, don't worry. It would take more than a little rain to make me ill. I was mentally exhausted with all the drama. There's no doubt that tonight we have become true companions with far too many emotions assailing us.' She got up from the sofa on which she had been sitting and removed her coat, which Hannah thought unwise. 'If you could show me where the kitchen is, I could make us some tea or at least something hot.'

'Lavender can see to that.'

'Perhaps she has enough to do without that, and I am doing nothing.'

'It's this way.' Hannah led the way across the hall and through the swing door into the back area of the house. She felt uncomfortable as they walked along, aware that, in the gentlest way, she had been admonished. Unnecessary, she thought. Lavender wouldn't have minded – she was always so willing.

'What a fine kitchen. So modern.'

'It is, isn't it?' She looked about her at the pale oak cupboards she had had built, the white marble tops on the lower ones. The range was of the most up-to-the-minute design. And she was happy with the pale yellow she'd had the walls painted, and how well they went with the white and blue tiles.

'What a pleasant colour to work in – the kitchen at Courtney Lacey is a dismal green. And such bright lighting too! How fortunate for us the generator was working – it would have been difficult with oil lamps.' Agnes bent and opened the range firebox. 'Unfortunately there is no kindling for the hotplate.' Agnes looked about her.

'It'll be outside.' Hannah did not move. She had never had to search for kindling, but when Agnes did not move either, she said, 'I'll see if Harold can find any.'

She found the coachman in the outhouse where the central-heating boiler stood. 'I'm sorry, Miss Hannah, but this is all a bit beyond me,' he said. 'I'm fearful if I do light it and I haven't got the right valves open or closed there could be an explosion. You need Sol Pepper to look at this, and that's a fact.'

'Could we not get him?'

'I doubt it at this hour.' He refrained from telling her that Sol would be three sheets to the wind by now and would be equally dangerous messing with the boiler.

'Could you try, Harold? But before you do that, could you find us some kindling and logs? We need a fire in the drawing room, and the range lit.'

'Yes, Miss.'

When Harold appeared with a large basket of wood and kindling, Agnes sped to his aid and began to lay the range fire. Hannah watched with admiration. 'How clever of you to know what to do.'

'One never knows when one might need to be self-sufficient, does one?'

'I'm beginning to think I never could be.'

'One quickly learns when necessity dictates.' Agnes was looking into the basket that Lavender had put on the kitchen table. 'Such a treasure, your Lavender, thinking of all this.' She was unpacking tea, coffee, milk, an apple tart, bread, cheese. 'It's like being on a mystery picnic. And, look, a bottle of sherry.' She waved it in the air triumphantly, then returned to the basket in search of further treasures.

'Let's have some sherry. I need a pick-me-up.' Hannah

began opening the cupboard doors looking for glasses. Suddenly she felt a wave of exhaustion and had to sit down quickly as the room rocked in front of her. 'Agnes, what would I have done without you? I've been stupid and too hasty. I let my temper get the better of me. We should have waited until morning. This is all too inconvenient for you.' She was wrestling with the cork in the sherry bottle.

'Let me try.' With a deft twist Agnes had the bottle open. 'From what you've told me you could not have behaved in any other way. You could not possibly have stayed in the same house as your stepmother after her appalling accusations.'

'But I should have waited until morning at least. Nothing's ready here.'

'Nonsense. The house is completed, it's furnished. It has light. All we lack is heat. This is an adventure. And how fortunate you are to have such a lovely home to go to,' she said, as she poured the sherry for them.

Harold tapped on the kitchen door. 'Fire's lit, Miss Hannah. Fortunately it's drawing well. I'll go and see if I can shake Sol up.'

'No, Harold, don't bother, it's too late, but perhaps you would ask him to get here as early as possible in the morning. And thank you for all your help.'

'Yes, Miss. And . . .' Harold paused in the doorway. 'Just to say as, I'm truly sorry, Miss.'

Hannah looked down at the table, knowing that if she caught his eye she risked bursting into tears. What a position to find herself in, accepting sympathy from a servant! 'Good night, and thank you again, Harold.'

She shivered. The lack of heat was irksome but it would not have been right to call Sol out at such an hour – and, she thought with amusement, Agnes would not have approved. Agnes had laid three plates on the table. She'd found the breadboard and knife, had arranged the cheese on a blue and white platter, sliced a large wedge of game pie and unearthed a jar of pickles. 'A veritable feast.'

Hannah smiled at her, but wished she would stop being so cheerful about their situation. She presumed she was trying to help her but it was becoming wearing.

'I've made up the beds, Miss. I've put Miss Beatty in the room next to yours. There's no hot water, so we'll have to boil kettles for washing tonight.'

'Lavender, I've cut you a slice of pie. Do you take milk in your tea?'

Lavender looked at the three place settings and then at her mistress, unsure what to do. 'Should I take yours into the dining-room, Miss Hannah?' She picked up a tray.

'No, it's warmer here. It'll be cosier, the three of us.' She patted the chair beside her. 'Sit down. Agnes, I would like another sherry and this time a very large one. I'm sure Lavender would enjoy one too.'

Instead of going back to his cottage Harold turned down the road which led to Cress-by-the-Sea.

The public bar of the Cresswell Arms was still busy when he pushed open the door. He hadn't been in since before Tubs died and then not often. He was not a drinking man and had only ever popped in for the odd pint. He could never understand other men's devotion to the inn: to him, it was a dirty, uncomfortable place. If he was going to have a drink he'd rather have one in the comfort of his own home. Now, though, he was impressed by the change in the place. It was better lit, with candles in bottles on the tables and oil lamps hanging from the rafters. There was a thick curtain over the door so the log fire no longer billowed smoke into the room when it was opened. The glasses shone too.

'Dolly? What are you doing here?' Behind the bar, Dolly grinned at him. She was a pretty girl but looked even prettier in a blue dress instead of the drab grey she had always worn at the manor.

'I got the hump up at the house. So I walked. I'd had enough.'

'I heard. Caused quite a stir, you did. I might as well have a pint now I'm here. Quite broke our Ferdie's heart, you did. Ta,' he said, as he took the tankard from her.

'Get on with you! I bet he hasn't even noticed I've gone.' She grinned.

'Do you like it here?'

'So far. It's nice meeting people, the hours are better and I don't have to work as hard. You'd never get me going back into service now.'

'Evening, Melanie,' he said, as she appeared behind the bar with a steaming bowl of soup.

'We don't often see you here, Harold.'

'You'll see a lot more of me, the way you've changed it all. Didn't much fancy it before but it looks a pleasure to drink here now.'

'Thank you.'

She went across the room and placed the bowl of soup in front of a stranger sitting by the fire. 'Is there anything else you'll be wanting?' she asked him.

'Perhaps another pint of ale.' He held up his tankard. He looked tired and drained, not helped by the fairness of his skin. Wearily he pushed a hank of blond hair out of his eyes. 'You don't remember me?'

She looked at him, her head to one side. 'I'm sorry, there's something familiar about you . . . but . . .'

'Don't worry.' The young man grinned and his face became almost handsome, she thought. 'I'm used to not being remembered. I'm Richard Joynston. I used to work for Mr von Ehrlich.'

'Of course I remember you now. How silly of me. But I'm so busy, you understand, with different people coming and going.'

'Honestly, Mrs Topsham, I'm not in the least offended. After all, we only met a couple of times.' He should smile all the time, she decided, because when he did he wasn't *almost* handsome, he *was* handsome. 'I was wondering if you have a room.'

'Of course. For how long?'

'I'm not sure yet.' Richard gave a short laugh, more like a snort. 'Mr von Ehrlich dispensed with my services somewhat abruptly, but that's his way.'

'Did I hear right?' Harold interrupted. 'I think the whole world's gone mad tonight. There's that Miss Beatty – rumour has it he threw her out too. There's big upsets at Courtney Lacey and more at Cresswell Manor. Upheaval everywhere.'

'What's happened up at the manor?'

'Poor Miss Hannah's out in the cold. She's moved into that dower house she had built. No heating on a night like this.' Harold shook his head.

'What's happened?'

'Big family row. It's a comfort to know the nobs go in for them too. Lady Cresswell accused Miss Hannah of stealing some stuff and then planting it so as it looked like it had been lost, and her didn't like it and stormed out. Can't say as I blame her.'

'Oh, no.' Dolly stopped drying glasses and looked aghast. 'That's my fault.'

'Can't see as how you can work that one out, Dolly, if you were here.'

'I started all the questioning. I wouldn't accept when they told us, see? I got to arguing with Mr Whitaker and Mrs Fuller. That did for me. But Miss Hannah a thief? Never!'

'That's what everyone's saying. Right old mix-up it is an' all.' He looked about him. 'Have you seen Sol Pepper?'

'He's over there playing dominoes – Uncle Sol!' Dolly shouted. 'You're wanted.'

'Harold! Don't tell me that there deng boiler needs me,' Sol said, as he joined them.

'No, not that one, the one at the new dower house.

389

Needs stoking up. I had a look at it but it was too new-fangled for me. I was afeared of blowing the whole house up.'

'Have I to go now?'

'At first Miss said as I was to come and find you, then her changed her mind and said it was too late and to tell you to come early in the morning.'

'Good God. I almost feel the need of sitting down. Don't tell me the family's getting considerate.' Sol laughed.

'I always thought Miss Hannah was better than the others.'

'So her is, Melanie, sometimes. But there are other times when she's just like the others. Wants everything done there and then.'

'I'd agree with Sol. I don't think she means to be but she just don't think.'

'What's she want the new boiler lit for?' Rob Robertson had joined them. 'She wasn't moving till after Christmas – that was the last thing I heard.'

'There's been a bit of argy-bargy . . .' And Harold recounted all he knew to another audience, none of whom believed that Hannah could be guilty of anything.

It was early the following morning when Oliver arrived at the dower house. He hoped it wasn't too early, but he couldn't wait any longer.

'Such an hour.' Hannah looked at her watch. 'Did you wish to ensure you were my first visitor?'

'Of course. Are you all right?'

'I slept like a log,' she lied.

Oliver looked about him admiringly. 'This is lovely – you've done it well. It's a charming house. I like those tapestries.'

'Aren't they beautiful? It's King Arthur and his knights. They're modern, of course.'

'When things are in such good taste they're timeless, are they not?'

'Thank you. I'm pleased. You must see it all, but we've just started breakfast. Would you care to join us?'

'I should like that. I'm moving too.'

'Really? Not far I trust?' she asked, as they crossed the hall to the breakfast room.

'Lees Coppice.'

'I've always loved that house. Father was wondering what to do with it when Thaddeus left.' She opened the double doors to the dining room with a flourish. 'Agnes, we have company,' she announced.

'Mr Cresswell, how pleasant,' Agnes said, as he entered. Oliver was again struck by what a handsome, dignified woman she was.

'I'm glad you're here. Hannah needs friends to support her at the moment.'

'I feel she can manage very well without me. Your sister is a strong young woman.'

'You're not going?' Hannah said anxiously.

'I should not wish to overstay my welcome. I'd planned to catch the train today.'

'I won't hear of it, Agnes. Please don't go. It would give me such pleasure if you would stay longer – for as long as you like. For ever, if you want.'

Agnes laughed, a delightful chuckle. 'Careful, Hannah, I might just take your invitation seriously. Then you might find yourself burdened and wonder how to be rid of me.'

'You could never be that, Agnes. Miss Beatty saved me last night,' she told Oliver. 'She was so efficient and had us organised in a trice. If you ever find yourself in a jungle, Oliver, Miss Beatty is the person to have by your side.' She laughed.

'I'll bear that in mind. And how wonderful to hear you laughing. I feared you'd be crying.'

'No.' She shook her head defiantly. 'I'm not going to succumb – it's what your mother would expect of me.'

'Bravo!' Agnes clapped.

'Have you told Miss Beatty your circumstances?'

'I have. I decided to have no secrets from my friend. I treasure her counsel. Is everyone talking about me?'

'Mortie said this morning that he had never heard such poppycock in his whole life.'

'Dear Mortie.'

'No one has seen Coral – far too early for her. Last night Mother was threatening to go and Father was threatening to permit it.' He said this with a sardonic smile.

'Not again?'

'I had thought that if she did, you could come back. It would please Father. But, now I've seen this house, I can't imagine you would want to.'

'I couldn't, Oliver. What if she returned as she did last time? No, I've made the break and I shall remain here. In any case, I have so much to do. The bulk of my possessions will arrive today and then Agnes and I shall be busy arranging everything.'

'Have you staff?'

'Mrs Fuller is arranging maids for me. I have Lavender, of course, and also, temporarily, a young girl called Jose working in the kitchen as a cook-general until we can arrange someone more suitable. She was taught by Mrs Gilroy so I'm sure she will be adequate for a short time. I've decided I don't need a butler, but I shall see how we get on.' Hannah continued to chatter about her plans while Oliver longed to get on to the subject he wanted to discuss.

'Did you finally resolve the problem over Lees Coppice, Mr Cresswell?'

Oliver wondered if Agnes had noticed his lack of interest in Hannah's domestic affairs. 'I have. The builders begin next week.'

'You know the house, Agnes?'

'I was there the other day. I didn't have time to see it all but the hall is charming. I am happy Stanislas did not purchase it. I don't think he appreciated it. He prefers houses on . . . , how shall I put it? . . . a much grander scale.' She smiled in that mysterious way she had – it must have broken a hundred hearts, he thought.

'I'm sorry. I don't understand. That is Papa's house,' Hannah said.

Agnes looked at Oliver, one eyebrow slightly raised.

'You'd better be told,' Oliver said. 'I bought it. Von Ehrlich hoped to, and unfortunately we had a falling-out over it. He's now very angry and not speaking to any of us.'

'No! How awful. But I still don't understand why you bought it, and why he was thinking of buying it.'

'He also owns two of our farms.' There seemed little point in not telling her; after all, Agnes might at any time.

'How extraordinary. Is Papa all right, Oliver? I mean . . . Well, after the fuss earlier this year.'

'Nothing like that,' he reassured her.

'I think, Mr Cresswell, that Stanislas is more than a little cross. He intends to ruin you all.'

Hannah let out a squeak of alarm.

'I don't see how,' Oliver told her.

'I fear it is no laughing matter. He can be a dangerous enemy, Mr Cresswell. He is quite ruthless when crossed.'

'But he's so charming,' Hannah wailed.

'Of course, and he can be the kindest of men, unless you disagree with him. Then things can become fraught.'

'Esmeralda?' Oliver asked.

'She is why I am here. After we left you the other day at Lees Coppice, when you so wisely told her she must return home, that it was her duty to be with her father, well, I counselled her to deceive her father.' Hannah gasped. 'Yes, I know, Hannah, it sounds shocking, and so it is. But it is the only way with the man – safer, even. But

393

she ignored me. She told him where she had been, that she had seen you and that . . .' Agnes glanced down at her lap. '. . . and that she loved you and intended to marry you.'

'And?' Oliver leant forward.

'Stanislas hit her. His mother tried to stop him and she was thrown to the floor.'

'No!' Hannah's hand was over her mouth, her eyes wide with horror. 'I can hardly believe it.'

'And then?' Oliver said impatiently.

'Richard Joynston, his secretary, hit him.'

'Oh, the hero!' said Hannah.

'They began to fight. I intervened and I was dismissed as, I presume, was Richard.'

'And?' Why was she taking such an insufferable time to tell them all she knew?

'The following morning before I left his mother came to me. She said he had calmed down and I was to see him. I refused. I had no wish to stay in that house a moment longer.'

'Of course you didn't,' Hannah said sympathetically. 'And Esmeralda?'

'There is talk she is to be sent to France. But I know no more. I tried to see her but I couldn't.'

'How hard did he hit her?'

'He slapped her, really, Mr Cresswell. She screamed a lot but I think it was more from fright than pain.'

Oliver stood up so abruptly that the chair he had been sitting on crashed to the floor behind him. 'This is all my fault.'

'How can it be? It's not your fault if the child thinks she loves you.'

'It was my fault he didn't get the house and that was what started this.'

'It's beyond belief,' Hannah moaned.

'He is prone to childish tantrums, Hannah. The very rich often are, in my experience.'

'I shall go to her,' Oliver said.

Agnes was on her feet now and laid a restraining hand on Oliver's arm. 'If you don't mind me saying so, Mr Cresswell, that would not be a good idea. You might make matters worse.'

'But we can't leave her there alone with him.'

'He is her father, Oliver.' Hannah was frowning, obviously afraid for him.

'I have an idea. I've left much of my property there – you understand the haste with which I left. I could return today to collect it – if you would permit me to store it here, Hannah, until I know where I am going. If I can't see Esmeralda I shall see her grandmother. Then I can ascertain the situation and the best way to deal with it.'

'Agnes, you're a wonder.' Oliver saw his sister looking at her companion with deep admiration.

Mortimer was surprised when Whitaker announced that Stanislas was waiting outside.

'Show him in, Whitaker, then bring in the port, and we need another log on the fire.'

This was most satisfactory, he thought. He'd intended calling on the man and this would save him a trip in this bitter cold. Although Oliver had said von Ehrlich had been reasonable over the house and land, it had crossed his mind that his son might have lied to protect him. Von Ehrlich did not strike him as the sort who would be understanding about a deal falling through. This had bothered Mortimer: no one with any sense wanted to fall out with their neighbours, and everyone had enjoyed the entertainment the von Ehrlichs had provided. He loved this house, he loved country living, but he had always found the social life restricting and Stanislas's arrival had been like a breath of fresh air.

He waited at the door to welcome his guest. 'My dear chap, how pleasant to see you. You've caught me on my own, I'm afraid.'

'It was you I came to see. I trust I'm not disturbing you?'

'No. I was looking at my stamps.' He gestured to the table where his albums were spread out.

'You're a philatelist?'

'I wouldn't give it such a high-falutin' description, but I enjoy it and perhaps one day it will amuse my great-grandchildren to see what stamps we used.'

They took their places at either side of the fire. Jock clattered the fire irons as he tended it and Whitaker returned with the tray of port.

'I'm happy you were so understanding about Lees Coppice, Stanislas. I did not like going back on my word in such a manner.'

'Sir Mortimer, it meant nothing. I was happy to oblige. It was not as if I planned to live there. It was merely an acquisition.'

'No formality, please. I'd be honoured if you called me by my name. You must have quite a large acreage. I heard you'd been purchasing land on the far side of your estate.'

'As you would agree, there's no investment as good as land for the simple reason they're not making any more of it.'

Mortimer slapped his thigh. 'Well put. I must remember that.'

'But I could not possibly accept the money you sent me to cover my expenses.'

'But I insist. It was my son who caused the problem – he was upset that the house was to go. Unbeknown to me, he had set his heart on having it.'

'Does he always get what he wants?'

Mortimer laughed. 'No, not always, but if I can help I like to. As a father yourself, I'm sure you understand.'

'I do. Esmeralda can be demanding. Sometimes, though, they have to be refused to guard them against themselves.'

'Quite,' said Mortimer. 'Thank you for being so charming to him when he called to explain. It couldn't have been easy.'

At this Stanislas smiled – a secret smile, Mortimer thought. 'A busy man like you must be here for a reason. You need more land?' He grinned.

'No, but a few weeks ago you asked me if I was aware of any good investments to be made.'

'I remember.'

'Well, I've heard of something that might interest you.'

'That is most kind of you, but you said you did not like to risk advising friends – and I trust you regard me as that, despite Lees Coppice?'

'That is so. And normally I wouldn't. But this is such a good venture, with no risk as far as I can see. And you have been kind to me and mine, so I decided I could not let slip this opportunity to help you.'

Mortimer leant forward. 'Tell me more, my dear chap.'

'It's in America.'

'America! Um . . .' Mortimer looked doubtful.

'The land of opportunity.'

'Undoubtedly for some. Unfortunately I've had a bad experience there. I'd be wary of ever trying again.'

'Gold, was it?' Stanislas looked sympathetic.

'It was. My own fault, of course. Too trusting.'

'One should never trust anyone where business is concerned, my friend.'

'Oh, I've learnt my lesson. However, what is this venture?'

'I should not have bothered you.'

'Now you've mentioned it, though, I'd like to know, just out of curiosity. Unless, that is, it's a secret and you don't want anyone but investors to know of it.'

'Nothing like that. But if you feel so about America there is no point in telling you.' Stanislas leant back in his chair. Mortimer looked disappointed.

Stanislas said nothing for a while. Then, 'This is a fine

room, and you have a good collection of books. I like the smell of libraries, don't you?'

'Yes . . . ' Mortimer sounded vague. 'I don't want you to be insulted by my reaction.'

'Not at all. I was trying to help you – which was presumptuous of me. That was all. I have investors queuing for suggestions from me.'

'I'm sure you have. Another glass?' He raised his empty one. Stanislas nodded. Mortimer refilled them.

'This is excellent port.'

'Isn't it? Laid down by my grandfather in eighteen fifteen. Waterloo port, they call it.' For a moment they relished it silently. 'What sort of figures are you contemplating?'

'A mere ten thousand but, please, let us not discuss it further.'

'But I'd like to know.'

'Well, if you insist . . . I've purchased . . .'

And as he began Mortimer sat back, absorbing the figures, learning of the crock of gold that would be the reward, registering the lack of risk. He was doing rapid calculations in his head. 'I think you've changed my mind, Stanislas.'

'Are you sure, Mortimer? I've always thought that one's first instincts are the best.'

'I'm ashamed to admit that last time I didn't know the man to whom I entrusted my money. This is different. I know you. You are my friend.'

'Quite,' said Stanislas.

Oliver had wanted to accompany Agnes to Courtney Lacey that afternoon but she had refused. 'It will make things more difficult for all of us.'

'But what if he harms you?'

'He will be calmer now. I implore you to let me go on my own.'

'But he would recognise our carriage, Agnes. That might enrage him again.'

'I can go to Cress and hire a cab.'

'I'll arrange it for you.' Oliver leapt up.

'No, really . . .'

'Let him go, Agnes. Men are better when they're doing things.' Hannah smiled with affection at her brother.

They decided on another cup of tea while they waited for him to return.

'Does he have feelings for Esmeralda?'

'I wouldn't know, Agnes. He doesn't speak of his private life to me.' She would have liked to confide in her the fears she had for him and Laura, but loyalty would never permit it.

'Of course, the girl thinks she is in love with your brother.'

'She told me the same. I presumed it was a childish fancy.'

'Oh, there's nothing childish about it. She means it, and I'm concerned for she is innocent and has no knowledge of men, what they can be like. She knows nothing of lust and sin.'

'You need not fear my brother, Agnes. He is a man of honour.' If only what she had said about him was true – how could a man of good repute be involved with a married woman? Try as she might, Hannah did not believe his denial. 'Would you allow me to accompany you this afternoon?'

'It's kind of you, but if you are with me that, too, might enrage him.'

'Then take care.'

An hour later Oliver arrived back with a carriage and coachman hired from the ostlers in Cress-by-the-Sea. Agnes set off with a letter from Oliver to Esmeralda hidden in the large tapestry bag she had taken with her. She had reservations about the wisdom of his writing to her and had at first intended to 'forget' to give it to her former charge, but he had extracted a promise from her that she would hand it to her. 'If I am fortunate enough to see her,' had been the only assurance she could give him. She was also weighed down with instructions as to what she should say and do. Since neither Oliver nor Hannah knew Stanislas as well as she did, she had listened merely to placate and reassure them. The coachman had been told that she was to be guarded and should he become alarmed he was to go and call the constable. Agnes felt quite sorry for the poor man's bewilderment, and she had seen in him a flicker of fear – evidently news of Stanislas's temper had spread.

As for herself, she was not sure if she felt fear or excitement: the two were so akin, and the butterflies she felt tumbling about in her nether regions were much the same from either emotion, she knew that from the past. She thought it was probably excitement. She was sure Stanislas would be calmer now. His mother was there after all. But, in any case, her life had been so dull for so long that she was enjoying all the drama. And now that sweet Hannah had come to her rescue so many fears had been eradicated.

She would miss Esmeralda, it was true, for she was a dear child. But that was the crux of the matter. She was too young, and what interested Agnes was anathema to Esmeralda. Of course she had enjoyed the travelling that being with the von Ehrlichs had involved, but even that had been steeped in frustration. To go to Florence and not visit the Uffizi, to be in Paris and not enter the Louvre, had been painful for her. To be in Milan and not see an opera had been the greatest disappointment. She knew the shops in every city of consequence in Europe, to be sure – could have written a guide on them – but while she liked nice clothes and to look well turned out, it was not the be-all and end-all of her life.

Teaching Esmeralda how to be a lady had been her task. She felt Stanislas had succeeded there. The girl knew how to behave, she was sure, but intellectually Agnes had to face the fact that she had failed with her. There was nothing but froth in the child's head. Agnes was aware that the girl was intelligent but she'd never been able to interest her in serious pursuits and thought.

Hannah was different altogether. Already the sweep of their conversations had been wide. She felt she had found a kindred spirit and she could not have been happier. It was with a dreamy smile that she looked out of the carriage as it bowled along the Barlton road.

'If you took the carriage round to the back I'm sure the groom there will water the horse and find refreshment for you. I shall have my bags carried down to the courtyard within an hour.'

The excitement was turning to fear, she realised, as she walked round the side of the mansion to a door that she was sure would be open – she did not want to make a fuss by going in at the front where the footman would alert Stanislas. She remonstrated with herself for being foolish. She had every right to collect her possessions.

She crossed the small morning room and gingerly opened the door to the hall. It was empty. She was behaving like a burglar: why didn't she just march in and demand her possessions? She smiled to herself: it was all right to think she might, it was quite another to do it.

If she could pass through the green baize door without being seen, she could sweep past any servants she encountered as if she had every right to be here. Then she could go to her old room by the back stairs. She was ten feet into the hall when she heard a voice on the stairs. Esmeralda. She wavered.

'Miss Beatty! How wonderful – you've come back!' Esmeralda was tripping towards her. She looked pale but was smiling broadly.

'My dear, how are you? Your father?'

'Pouf.' She exhaled. 'He's calmed down. I said I was

sorry, how bad I'd been and I'd never do it again, and he believed me.'

'Esmeralda, take care.'

'Miss Beatty, I was so sad when they told me you were no longer here.' Dulcie Prestwick lumbered down the staircase. 'I hoped we should meet again.'

'Where have you been, Miss Beatty?' Esmeralda enquired.

'Miss Cresswell kindly took me in.'

At this Esmeralda clasped her hands together. 'Then you've seen him? How is he? Did he ask after me?'

Who could resist her when she was so sweet and ingenuous? 'Here.' Agnes delved into her bag. 'I have something for you.' This was the solution, she decided. Dulcie Prestwick had seen her hand over the letter so it was up to her to decide if Stanislas should be told or not. In a roundabout way she was exonerated.

'I've told Lady Prestwick what happened. She says I should be most careful,' Esmeralda went on.

'Lady Prestwick is right.'

'I said I could understand how dizzy she felt,' Dulcie said. 'Love is an all-consuming emotion. And, of course, the gentleman she is honouring is a charming and honourable man, one of the best in my husband's opinion. But I told this dear girl that excitement and novelty are often misdiagnosed as love.'

'I'm glad you're here to advise her so wisely, Lady Prestwick.'

'I counselled time. And, of course, she must never disobey her dear father. That would be very wrong.'

'Of course.' Agnes wished this discourse might reach a speedy end: she felt vulnerable standing in the cavernous hall.

Too late. The library door opened and Stanislas, with Lord Prestwick in tow, appeared.

'Miss Beatty, what a pleasant surprise,' her disbelieving ears heard him say.

'Just to collect my possessions, Mr von Ehrlich. Lord Prestwick.' She dropped him a small curtsy.

'How did you get here?' he asked, ignoring his daughter.

'I hired a carriage.'

'You must stay to tea.'

'I really should like to get back before dark.'

'To where?'

'The Cresswell Arms. I've taken rooms there,' she lied.

'How convenient. Still, we need to have a word together, you and I. If you will excuse us, Dulcie and Theo?' He put his hand under Agnes's elbow and propelled her towards the library. Once the door was closed his demeanour changed. 'You should not have returned here, Miss Beatty.'

'I had left many of my things, Mr von Ehrlich. I feel I have a right—'

'You have no rights in my house, Miss Beatty. I do not wish you ever to set foot here again. I forbid any contact with my daughter. Do I make myself clear? Your property will be sent to the inn. You will not go to your room.'

'As you wish, sir. I should like to point out, since I was not given the opportunity yesterday, that I was trying to protect your daughter, not the reverse.'

'Then you did not do a very good job, did you? I have forgiven my daughter. She had been led astray by the people I entrusted with her care.'

'Really, sir, I must protest—'

'I warn you, Miss Beatty, if you disobey me you will regret it for the rest of your days.'

'I am not used to being threatened, sir. I can assure you that you don't frighten me.'

'You will say nothing of this matter to anyone. If you do, I shall have my revenge and you will be sorely frightened then.'

She took a deep breath. 'There is the matter of my remuneration.'

The look he gave her would have quelled the stoutest soul, she thought, as she made the journey home.

Alone at last in her room, Esmeralda ripped open her letter. She lay back on her swan bed to read it. What a beautiful hand he had!

'*My dear Miss von Ehrlich . . .*' He was so formal, always such a gentleman, she thought. '*I am distressed at the misfortune which has befallen you and Miss Beatty. I feel wretched that because of me you should both be so sorely treated . . .*' He cares about me. She'd been right. '*I shall worry about you and your well-being . . .*' He loves me! She smiled at the painting of cherubs in the canopy above her bed. '*If there is any assistance I can give you to make amends . . .*' He wants me! She hugged herself with joy.

The night was bitterly cold, too cold even for snow. The atmosphere at Cresswell Manor was not happy. Mortimer was barely speaking to Penelope; Mortie was hardly speaking to Coral. The two women were speaking guardedly to each other. Oliver wished his house was ready so that he could move, and Hannah was greatly missed.

This atmosphere had permeated below stairs. Whitaker was missing Lavender more than he liked to admit and wished he had had the courage to tell her he admired her. Still, he consoled himself, it wasn't as if she had gone to Outer Mongolia: she was merely across the park. And even had he spoken, what could they have done? He could not jeopardise his position here by marrying one of the ladies' maids. He knew there were houses where this was permitted but how did one find out how it would be received here? Sir Mortimer might allow it, an amiable soul he was, and Mr Mortie. But Lady Cresswell?

Whitaker puckered his lips as he thought of her likely reaction. It was always women who caused the problems, he told himself. Perhaps it was too risky by half.

'I've reached the point where I wonder if Miss Hannah might be needing a housekeeper. She's only been gone a couple of days and it seems I can do no right.' Mrs Fuller was rubbing her bare foot, sore from her tight boot.

'You wouldn't like a small establishment, Gussie. You'd be lost, wondering what to do with yourself. And it wouldn't carry the same prestige, would it?' Mrs Gilroy was slicing the Victoria sponge Hilda had made for their tea.

'No, but what's the point of prestige when you're spoken to as if you were a tweeny? We had to reorganise all the linen cupboards today. It took Molly and me most of the morning. Then there was trouble because she was late sorting the boudoirs. To cap it all, Lady Cresswell didn't like the way we had done it and it's got to be redone tomorrow. She wanted me to do it today, but I insisted I'd other duties. Another cup of tea would go down a treat, Eve.'

'Edward's not happy. He's been moping all day. It's the atmosphere – they don't understand that it affects us too. And Edward's so sensitive.'

'Why couldn't *she* have stayed away and never come back? But, then, that Mrs Cresswell is little better. There's a new rule: no maids on the upper landing after eleven in the morning – apparently that's what her father the Viscount insists on and, of course, Lady C thought it a wonderful idea.'

'She would. And what if they don't get up until twelve? What then?'

'Precisely, Eve. Still, you're all right down here.'

'Well, I won't put up with any nonsense, that's for sure. I'm good at my job and they know it.'

'You implying I'm not?' Mrs Fuller bridled.

'*No!* Come on, Gussie, the last thing we need is to fall

out.' She tried to placate her. 'But I made a stand, I did. Menus decided in the morning must not be altered. I told her ladyship that if she wanted quality then the menus could not be changed on a whim.'

'How's the new kitchenmaid settling?'

'She'll do – she'll have to. I miss my Dolly, I really do.'

'I hear she's working at the Cresswell Arms.'

'Is she now? She'll be all right there, bright young thing like her.'

'What's going to happen over Christmas? Is Miss Hannah going to come here?'

'I wouldn't, if I were her. It won't be the same. I miss Lavender.'

'Still, we three are here; and we must stick together, mustn't we?'

Whitaker had just joined them. No sooner had he sat down than the front-door bell rang.

'They expecting anyone?'

'Not as I was told.' He began to put on the black jacket he had just removed.

'Can't Jock see to whoever it is?'

'If it's the front door, it'll be someone of quality. I'd better go.'

He reached the hall and opened the door to find on the step the bedraggled figure of Esmeralda, shivering with cold, white with fatigue.

'Miss von Ehrlich?' His normally impassive expression had deserted him.

'Is Oliver here?' she asked, before falling in a faint at his feet.

Whitaker, all decorum lost, crashed into the drawing room where some of the family were assembled, taking tea.

'Whitaker, really!' Penelope looked cross.

'I apologise, Lady Cresswell, but a most unfortunate

occurrence. Miss von Ehrlich is in the hall . . .' He pointed in a vague manner.

'Yes, Whitaker, I know where the hall is. Don't just stand there, show her in.'

'I can't. She's on the floor in a faint.'

Penelope rose swiftly. 'Stupid man. Why leave her there?'

Lettice was already out of the door.

'Shall I come too, Lady Cresswell?' asked Coral.

'Of course you must come.' Penelope bustled out, followed by Coral. Mortie, who had stopped to finish his cake, brought up the rear. They found Esmeralda still unconscious, with Lettice kneeling on the floor beside her, chafing her hand, calling her name.

Attracted by the noise, Mortimer appeared from the library. 'Dear me, what have we here?' He looked down at the girl, damp hair plastered against her skull, her hands blue with cold. 'I suggest we get her to a fire quickly. Lettice, smelling-salts. Whitaker, blankets. Jock, hot-water bottles. Mortie, you carry her.'

Lettice tore up the stairs as Mortie carried Esmeralda into the drawing room and went to lay her on the sofa.

'Not there – she's wet and we've just had that reupholstered.'

'Really, Penelope, does it matter?'

'It does to me. That silk was difficult to find. Put her on the other, Mortie.'

But Mortie had ignored her and was laying her tenderly on the primrose-coloured cushions.

'This is when we need Hannah.' Mortimer looked wistful.

'That's right. Undermine me at every opportunity.' Penelope glowered. 'Do you have to make that infernal racket?'

'Sorry, milady,' said Whitaker, who was stoking the fire. Jock appeared with blankets, closely followed by a flustered-looking Mrs Fuller carrying a stone hot-water bottle wrapped in flannel.

'She's rather lovely even when out for the count, isn't she?'

'Mortie!' His wife objected.

'But it's true!'

'Perhaps we should telephone her father,' Penelope said.

'We don't know why she's here. Let's find that out first. We need to get the doctor.'

Everyone looked with astonishment at Mortie, who normally did what other people told him to do and rarely took the initiative. When Lettice raced back with the small crystal vial of smelling-salts, everyone stepped back to give her room to administer them.

'I still think we should call her home—' Penelope began.

'No!'

'I beg your pardon, young woman.' Penelope glared at her granddaughter.

'I'm sorry, Grandmama, but if she's here it's because she's run away.'

'All the more reason to summon him.'

'We should find Oliver. It's him she's come to see.' Lettice looked agitated.

'How do you know?' Penelope demanded.

'Because she loves him.'

'And how would you know *that*?'

'Because she told me.'

'Then we have to—' Already Penelope was making for the door. Mortie barred her way.

'I don't think that's right, Mother. We should wait for her to tell us herself.'

'Why, Mortie, are you smitten too?' Coral asked, with an unpleasant expression.

'Don't be silly, she's only a year older than our son.' He looked shocked at the suggestion.

'Whitaker, do you know the whereabouts of Mr Oliver?'

'He was practising billiards the last time I saw him, Sir Mortimer.'

'Then fetch him – quickly.'

There was a groan from Esmeralda as Lettice continued to waft the salts beneath her nose. The company, as one, leant forward. She spluttered, her eyes opened, then closed again. 'I'm a nuisance . . .' Her voice was barely audible.

'There! Not at all, my dear. Just rest a moment.'

'Oliver . . .' As she said this, Lettice looked at her grandmother with as much triumph as she dared.

'Esmeralda? What's happened?' Oliver was on his knees beside her.

At the sound of his voice her eyes opened wide and she struggled to sit up. 'Oh, Oliver, I had to come when I received your letter telling me to—'

'My letter?' He looked astonished.

'Oliver, how *could* you?' Penelope remonstrated.

'I didn't—'

'I knew you loved me, I always knew it—'

Oliver stood up, perplexed. 'We must get her out of these clothes and in to bed.' He went to pick her up.

'In the circumstances, Oliver, I don't think that's a good idea. Mortie, take her up to the blue room. Coral, you chaperone.'

'Yes, Lady Cresswell.'

'That will be all, Whitaker, Mrs Fuller.' Penelope waited for them to leave, then swung round to face her son. 'Now what mischief have you caused?'

'None that I'm aware of. I didn't tell her to come – and I never said I loved her, I can assure you of that.' He looked down, remembering the tender moment when she had clung to him so appealingly, but it had not been love, he was fully aware of that. 'She's a child,' he added, for good measure.

'Hardly. At eighteen, she's ripe for the picking. You realise that that young woman is compromised?' Penelope fussed.

'I don't see why. She came here of her own accord. She was not invited.'

'I was right all along. We should call her father and—'

'No!' Oliver almost shouted. 'You can't do that. He's a bully. He's violent. He will hurt her.'

'Stanislas? What rubbish!' Mortimer said.

'No, Father! He's a violent and dangerous man when roused. He does not like to be crossed. If he had an inkling that she likes me he would do all he could to destroy us.'

At this information Mortimer went ashen and sat down awkwardly on the damp sofa.

Chapter Fourteen
November 1901

Hannah and Agnes were sitting contentedly beside the drawing-room fire, reading. Hannah glanced up from her book and watched Agnes without her being aware of it. She had a fine face, with such sensitivity etched upon it, she thought. She was amazed by how quickly they had become close. It was as if Agnes was part of her life rather than a guest, as if she had always known her. Their conversations flowed with such ease. In company Hannah was always wary of silences. She often found herself making inane comments simply to fill the quiet, as if the lack of talk was her fault and her responsibility. Not so with Agnes: their silences were comfortable, natural. In the few days Agnes had been there she had been astounded by how much they had in common. They liked the same composers, writers, poetry. They loved azaleas with a passion, and it was soon apparent that Hannah's interest in gardening was shared. Neither drank to excess but appreciated dry sherry and the odd glass of port. Neither liked chocolate and preferred savoury food to sweet. Both favoured dogs over cats. It was as if they mirrored each other – but only in their minds, for Agnes was a beauty and no one could ever have called Hannah one.

Hannah was curious about her and longed to know more of her background. Apart from her brother in Newbury, a mathematician, Hannah gathered, Agnes did not speak of her parents and Hannah wondered if they had died in tragic circumstances and that to mention them was painful. Something traumatic must have happened, for how could a woman of such style and breeding be a paid retainer?

She knew now that Agnes's role had been to teach Esmeralda Society niceties – another indication that she had fallen on hard times, for how else would she know the labyrinth of etiquette, as she obviously did? But Agnes was not the sort of person she felt she could question. No doubt she would tell her more about herself in her own good time.

When they closed their books, as they did now, it was with reluctance that Hannah said goodnight to her. In her room she suddenly felt lonely in a way she hadn't for a long time.

The next morning her admiration for Agnes grew apace. Her belongings had been delivered from the Cresswell Inn. One lone case stood in the middle of Hannah's hall. Agnes looked distressed and was doing her best to hide it.

'My dear, what is it?'

'Nothing, Hannah. Forgive me, this is the second time you have seen me anguished but I assure you it will be the last. I am not a weak woman . . .' She blew discreetly into her handkerchief.

'I never thought you were. But what is it?'

Agnes pointed at the scuffed leather bag at their feet. 'That was what was in my hand on the day I arrived at the von Ehrlichs'. He has made sure that is all I am left with. My clothes . . .' She waved the handkerchief impotently. 'So silly to be upset about such unimportant things.' She continued to flourish the handkerchief as if it acted as a brake upon her tears. 'But he has confiscated all the little things I purchased with my remuneration.'

'The man is a fiend. How could we all have been taken in by him? It makes me feel quite foolish. He has no right to take what you have bought – that's stealing.'

'The clothes he gave me, or so I thought.' She gave a

bitter little laugh. 'Of course, the jewellery was never mine, that I can understand. But all the little presents that dear child gave me ... gone.' The handkerchief had failed: tears rolled down her cheeks.

'Lavender, if you could take this bag up to Miss Beatty's room and tell Jose breakfast is to be delayed. Come, my dear. Don't fret, we can replace many of the things but, of course, that will not assuage the hurt.' Gently she led Agnes into the morning room. She felt such anger for the man who could do this to her friend.

She had barely settled when she heard a coach arriving in her driveway, then a ridden horse. Lavender entered the room. 'I am not at home, Lavender, and especially not at this unsociable hour.'

'But, it's your brother, Miss Cresswell, and he says it's urgent.'

Now what? she thought. But uppermost was the fear that something had happened to her father. She was momentarily distracted from Agnes's distress.

'Oliver! *Esmeralda!*' Oliver looked cross but Esmeralda was smiling broadly. 'What has happened?'

Before anyone could answer Esmeralda had fluttered across to Agnes and was kneeling at her feet. 'Miss Beatty, why are you crying? Stop, please. You're frightening me!'

'Child, what are you doing here?'

'I ran away. Oliver told me to come. I knew Father would never permit it, but I came anyway.'

Both women looked at Oliver, astonished.

'That was unwise, Mr Cresswell.' Agnes sounded shocked.

'Oh, but it isn't, Miss Beatty. We are to marry.' She was on her feet beside Oliver and firmly holding his hand before anyone could blink.

'So it was you, Oliver.' Hannah looked at Agnes, who glanced away in embarrassment; of course she had known and, sensitive as she was, had refrained from telling her that Esmeralda admired him.

'We would have come last night but Esmeralda was unwell so she slept with Lettice. Cresswell is the first place von Ehrlich will look when he discovers she has gone. I wondered if she might stay here with you, for the time being, Hannah. And it's so fortunate that you are here too, Miss Beatty.'

'So it would seem,' she said coldly.

Oliver chose to ignore her change of attitude towards him. 'Right, I must be on my way. Is that all right, Hannah?'

'Of course she is welcome here, but is this wise?'

Oliver was already leaving the room.

Hannah followed him and Esmeralda trailed behind her. 'Oliver – a moment, Oliver!'

'Esmeralda, if you don't mind, I need to speak to my sister,' he said.

It took time to persuade her to leave them but after a last kiss she went.

'Are you mad?' Hannah asked, as soon as the girl had closed the door to the morning room behind her.

'Where might we not be overheard?'

'In here.' She led the way into her delightful drawing room. 'This is calamitous. Do you understand the problems you've caused? Agnes has lost her position and all her possessions because of you. Evidently the child has lost not only her home but her father – if what I have learnt of von Ehrlich is true.'

'It's not as it seems. It's all a misunderstanding. I never asked her to come. I was fully aware of her father's fury. He and I had had an unholy row over land that he wanted to buy from Father. Esmeralda became involved in her impetuous way. She followed me but I sent her back – ask Miss Beatty, she was there. And why is Miss Beatty so cold with me? What have I done? This is not of my making.'

'Well, of whose making is it, then? You have caused calamity everywhere. Have you no conscience – no shame?'

'I am not proud of what has happened. But Laura is a woman and she made her own choice to be with me.'

Hannah looked at him with horror. 'You and Laura? So you lied to me? I thought you had.'

'I'm sorry. I didn't want you to despise me.'

'You should not have entered into such a liaison. And now Esmeralda! Are you so wicked?'

'For God's sake, listen to me. How many times do I have to explain? Esmeralda misunderstood. The letter I wrote her was to say how sorry I was and to offer my help if she needed it.'

'Well, she has undoubtedly decided she does,' Hannah snapped. 'Did you give her any cause to think her affections might be returned?'

'No. I spent an afternoon with her but I presumed she would take a shine to Young Mortimer, not me. I must be like an old man to her.' He put his head in his hands. 'I find her attractive, of course I do, as any red-blooded man would, but that's all – a passing thought, merely.' This was not strictly true but he was not about to explain to his sister how the girl appeared to have cast a spell on him.

'But marriage?'

'You must see I have no choice. She is compromised. The servants heard it all. I have to make it right for her.'

'But is there no way out? I mean, she's a dear child, but there's the rub – she's a child. Why, Lettice is more mature and she's not fifteen. Esmeralda's empty-headed and thinks only of her appearance. How will you be companions? Where will your shared interests be?'

'She has declared her feelings, she has run away to my home, she has slept under our roof – there is nothing else I can do. She needs my protection. She is an innocent child and my responsibility.'

'I see.' Hannah felt uncomfortable: she had thought immediately of how this would dispose of the undesirable situation with Laura Redman, which was unworthy of her. And hadn't she been relieved by the flirtation she had witnessed between Oliver and Esmeralda, thinking it indicated a death knell in his relationship with Laura? But marriage? That was not what she had hoped for.

Oliver stood up. 'Wish me luck. I'm about to poke the tiger in his lair. I'm going to ask von Ehrlich for his daughter's hand in marriage.'

Stanislas's reaction towards Oliver was as he had expected: unwelcoming. As Oliver stood in the hall, the abuse that deluged upon him was as destabilising as any torrent of water. He felt anger at the injustice of the attack and it was all he could do not to shout back at the man or, worse, hit him. His temper was not helped by the ominous presence of two large manservants loitering in the shadows. But then he rationalised their attendance – no doubt Stanislas had expected him to become violent, and that Oliver had come with no intention of being so gave him the moral high ground. He was then able to watch, initially with amusement and then with pity, von Ehrlich stamping about his hall, bellowing, ranting, hitting inanimate objects. To have such a temper, he concluded, was a monumental disadvantage.

'Have you nothing to say?' Stanislas bellowed at him.

'There seems no point. You're not in a mood to listen to me.' He spoke quite calmly – too calmly, for his voice reignited the man's rage. He continued to let the abuse tumble about him. In truth the whole situation seemed unreal: he had been catapulted into this situation, which was not of his making, and there seemed little he could do but let Fate take him where she wished. He appeared to have no control of his own destiny.

'Stan!' a female voice shouted from above. 'Stop this noise. You're making a fool of yourself and in front of the hired help too.' Stanislas's mother was descending the stairs and, to Oliver's astonishment, he did as she ordered. 'Let the man speak, and in private.' She held open the library door and they trooped into the beautiful room.

'You need not stay, Mother.'

'I think I should – stop you making more of a fool of yourself.' She sat down in a rustle of silk. Oliver noticed that her worn hands were at odds with her expensive clothes. 'Now, what have you to say, young man?'

'I have come here to apologise and to ask Mr von Ehrlich for the honour of his daughter's hand in marriage.'

Stanislas's mouth had been open as if he was about to speak. He slammed it shut and stood in silence. Then he broke it: 'Never!'

'What do you mean, never? He's a nice enough young man.'

'He stole her. First Lees Coppice, then my daughter. And I'm to forgive him? Allow her to marry a thief?'

'I am no such thing. She came to me of her own free will. I did not encourage her. I realise that such an action has compromised her reputation and I am willing to make amends in the only possible manner.'

'I don't believe you. If you've laid a finger on her . . .' Stanislas moved ominously towards him.

'Stan!' his mother screeched.

'I swear to you I have not touched her.'

'I think you should believe him, Stan. You know Esmeralda – she does what she wants and gets what she wants. And if anyone's to blame it's you for spoiling her the way you have. You've made her how she is.'

Stanislas sighed with exasperation and sat down.

'Mr von Ehrlich, I am sorry this has happened. I'm sure I'm not at all the man you had envisaged for her.'

'You would be correct in that assumption. A *second* son!'

'I fear I cannot alter my position in my family, sir, but we are an honourable clan and I have means. She will be well cared for.'

'Not as well as I can look after her.'

'I will do my best.'

'But it won't be enough for Esmeralda – you'll see. She'll beggar you in a couple of years.'

'And how would you know? Are you privy to my wealth?'

'I know my daughter.'

'I trust we can come to some understanding. If you cannot agree, I am sad for Esmeralda. If you will not give your permission I should tell you I am prepared to elope with her. Then her wedding day will be a sorry occasion, not the happy one she dreams of.'

Stanislas looked morose. 'Do you love her? Do you *want* to marry her?'

'I am fond of her – who could not be?' *Fond?* More than fond, Oliver realised. 'She is an adorable young woman. But I would not have proposed had this situation not arisen.' That was true. She was not the sort of woman he would normally be attracted to, and certainly not as his wife.

'Why? What's wrong with our little girl?' It was the turn of von Ehrlich's mother to take umbrage.

'I'm being honest, Mrs von Ehrlich.'

'I respect it.'

Stanislas sat morose and silent. Oliver did not know what more to say. Suddenly Stanislas looked up. 'I have a solution. You will become engaged, a notice will be posted, the banns read. Then Esmeralda will call off the wedding.'

'The damage to her reputation will not be repaired.'

'But it will. We shall ante-date the betrothal. She was merely visiting her future in-laws.'

'The servants heard.'

'They can be bought. It's the only thing I will agree to, Mr Cresswell.'

'And what if Esmeralda won't do as you wish?'

'She will. She'll have tired of you in a week. You're not what I wanted for my daughter.' He stood up, as if dismissing him. 'I have not, as yet, finished with you and your family, Mr Cresswell.' He strode from the room, leaving Oliver perplexed. He was sure that the problem was far from resolved: would Esmeralda agree to any of this?

Hannah could not relax. It had been foolhardy of Oliver to rush off in such a manner. Esmeralda, it would appear, was not in the least concerned.

'But you said your father was cross. That he had attacked you.'

'Yes, but that was when he was angry. He'll be calmer now. He'll respect Oliver for daring to go to see him.'

'He'll never agree.'

'I think he will, provided Oliver doesn't lose his temper.'

That was not what Hannah had wished to hear. She had nothing against Esmeralda, she was a sweet girl who made her laugh, but instinctively she knew that a marriage between these two could not work.

'It might,' Agnes counselled her, when Esmeralda had gone with Lavender to have her hair washed.

'Might what?' Hannah looked up from her book.

'Be a happy marriage.'

Hannah was astonished. It was as if Agnes could read her mind.

'Esmeralda is highly intelligent, you know. She keeps it well hidden, as I advised her to do.'

'Wise, indeed.' Hannah knew only too well how disadvantageous it was for any woman to show she had a brain.

'But, of course, she can use that cleverness with her

419

husband to make him think he has the quiescent creature he wishes, while getting whatever she wants. She will appear to be whatever he requires in a wife. Esmeralda is expert in that – she has learnt, of necessity, with her father.' This was said with a wry smile. 'Only, of course, if he doesn't beat her – that is what breaks a woman's spirit.'

'Oliver would do no such thing.'

'I'm more than pleased to hear it.' Agnes returned to the book she was reading.

'I've never looked at our sex, or marriage, in the way you describe.'

'Have you not? I've always thought we women were far superior in every way.'

'Really?' Hannah liked this theory and turned it about in her mind. Of course she was cleverer than Mortie, she'd always known that, but it didn't mean much since most people were. She could not regard herself as superior in any way to her father and younger brother. To her they were perfect, apart from their taste in women – Penelope and Laura.

'From my experience, men are so easily led by their emotions – especially where women are concerned – and can make such foolhardy mistakes. We are far more capable of using our heads and not allowing our hearts to rule.'

'Really?' How extraordinary – there it was again: Agnes was reading her mind. 'But is Esmeralda? It would not appear so.'

'Undoubtedly. She will not wish to upset her father too far – frighten him, yes, but all will be resolved.'

'Because she loves him so much. That's nice.'

'One reason.' Agnes looked at her intently but said no more.

Getting to know Agnes was proving an illuminating experience for Hannah. Their talks roamed wide. Agnes, like Dulcie Prestwick, was radical in her thinking. Like her, she did not believe in primogeniture, and the more Hannah thought about that the more unfair it seemed – especially when one remembered that it was Mortie, sweet but dim, who would have everything. And despite the laws that had been made in regard to women's property, she had had to agree that she knew no woman who controlled her own money: it was always looked after by the men in the family. She was a case in point – not that she had admitted as much, for to discuss her finances with anyone was too vulgar to contemplate, but it didn't stop her thinking about it. Certainly she had her own money, left to her by her mother, but she had no idea how much there was or where it was invested. She simply had a bank account into which money was placed and which she was now intending to spend.

'I have my own bank account,' she had said, as a bit of a defence for the men.

'But you can only have it with your father's or husband's permission.'

'True.'

'And why should women of good family not have a profession other than that of governess or companion? What is wrong with honest travail?' Agnes had queried.

That, of course, had struck a little too close for comfort: her father had said no more about whether he was going to allow her to carry on with her garden business. From that it was a short step to asking herself why she, a mature woman, needed his permission. Such thoughts were quite liberating and made her feel dizzy with excitement. But when Agnes confided she had friends who were wondering why they, too, should not have the right to vote in elections, provided, like men they fulfilled the necessary property qualifications, well, that was too much. How would she know how to vote when she knew nothing of politics and the world?

'Then learn,' was Agnes's short answer, which had made her think that perhaps she should. That was why this morning, after Oliver had left, she had been engrossed in *The Times* and read more than her customary intake of the obituaries, betrothals, births and the social diary – but she had found it tedious: if that was what men wanted, then let them get on with it.

Esmeralda, hair wet and flying about her shoulders, came squealing down the stairs. 'He's back!' she called to the two older women, who were taking tea in the drawing room.

'I fear that the way she flings herself about, she will be classed as one of my failures,' Agnes said, with a smile.

'But she's so joyous with her spontaneity, isn't she?'

The young couple joined them, entwined about each other. Oliver, Hannah thought, looked remarkably happy. Perhaps she was being unnecessarily pessimistic. And she thought she detected a smidgen of envy in herself – she must watch that.

'So, all went well?'

'Eventually,' Oliver said, with a grin, as he sat down and took the cup of tea Hannah had poured for him. 'It was a touch hot to begin with.' The grin grew wider.

'So he agreed!' Esmeralda was jumping up and down like a jack-in-the-box, clapping her hands with excitement, then running around the room. 'I'm happy, happy!' She was crying.

Hannah could not help but be glad for her, and managed to stop her cavorting for long enough to kiss her. 'I'm so happy for you,' she said, and it was true. What a sourpuss she had been! How could one possibly disagree in the face of such joy? 'Oliver, my fulsome congratulations.' She kissed him too. 'And, Oliver, the cellar! We must have champagne.'

'I'll come with you in case you get lost,' Esmeralda said, laughing.

Luring him away for a kiss, Hannah thought.

'You didn't congratulate them, Agnes?'

'I'm not sure if it's in order,' she said enigmatically, but did not elaborate.

Hannah accompanied the young couple as chaperone when Oliver took Esmeralda home to her father. It was a strange experience for her, when she had heard such bad things about the man, his temper, his violence. She watched the smiling father welcome home his errant daughter, who was already bubbling with plans and deciding whether to wear white or a pastel. Stanislas thanked her charmingly for taking care of Esmeralda for him. More champagne was served and she began to feel quite tipsy.

'Nothing is as it seems, Hannah,' Oliver said, in the carriage on the way home. 'Stanislas is not our friend and you'd be wise to remember it. You've nothing to fear any longer, sister. I shan't be marrying the wrong woman.'

'I don't understand.'

'I have agreed with her father . . .'

As he explained the arrangement they had made Hannah's smile slipped from her face. 'That is deceitful.'

'But for the best reasons.'

'How can that be? You'll break her heart.'

'Hannah, I won't. She will think she made the decision. She thinks she loves me, but how can she? We barely know each other.'

'People do fall in love like being struck by lightning – a *coup de foudre*.'

'Yes, and as quickly fall out. This is the kindest way.'

'I think it's despicable.' And she moved away from him in the carriage and refused to let him hold her hand.

Oliver climbed into the saddle and trotted out of the manor stableyard. It was cold, bitterly so, inside and outside, he thought ruefully. The house was not the same without Hannah – it wasn't running as efficiently as it had when she had been in charge. His mother was not interested in its smooth functioning and Coral, he presumed, did not like to interfere. It was making his father testy. Only Mortie sailed through it all, unaffected by the problems swirling around them.

He would be glad to move out now. Nothing would ever be the same again so it would be best to make a break and start anew in his own establishment. He was excited about the venture, and it was time to go.

He was on his way to the Cresswell Arms. He had been surprised this morning to receive a note from Laura, delivered by a boy, requesting they meet that afternoon. He was concerned, since she would never normally take such a risk. He had not seen Hannah this morning and he was glad. She was so angry that she was barely speaking to him and he preferred to avoid her.

Women, he had decided, were exasperating. One moment Hannah had been advising him it would be a disaster if he wed Esmeralda, then she was overjoyed when he said he would, and furious when he confided he was not going to. 'I suggest you make up your mind as to what you want me to do,' had been his final comment to her last night when they had returned to her house.

The news of his 'engagement' had met with mixed reactions. Mortie had nearly knocked him over with his good-natured thump of congratulations. Coral was horrified, as he had expected she would be, at his apparent choice of wife, facing the prospect of having a sister-in-law in trade. He was not sure what his mother thought: she neither congratulated nor castigated him. As for his father, he had been vague, as if his mind was elsewhere.

Once Sergeant had been settled in one of the stables at the back of the inn he made his way through the building to the bar. 'Mrs Topsham.' He handed her the leather pouch that contained the money they owed her.

'Thank you, Mr Cresswell. Would you be wanting something to eat or drink?'

'No, thank you. I've got some letters to write and then I'll be on my way. Good morning, Miss Xenia.'

'Mr Cresswell.' She gave a smile that belied her youth. 'Visiting again?'

'Far from visiting, Miss Xenia, working.' He did not like the knowing look she gave him. She was dangerous, he thought, as he made his way up the steps that led from the yard to the balcony above.

When he pushed open the door it was to find Laura already there. She was sitting upright on a wooden chair in the middle of the room. There was an aura of stillness about her. Certainly she did not rush towards him as she normally did. Instead she remained with her hands folded in her lap.

'You're early. I had hoped to be here before you.'

'I think you owe me an explanation.' She looked at him steadfastly.

He tilted his head with a quizzical smile. 'Esmeralda?'

'Yes.'

'How did you hear?'

'Everyone is talking about your *good fortune*.' She emphasised the words. Her mouth twisted, making her face look bitter. 'Congratulations.'

'It isn't as it seems.'

'You are engaged?'

'Well, yes . . .'

'I wish you had told me yourself.'

'I haven't seen you. Everything has happened so quickly.'

'Evidently.' Again that frosty, twisted look.

'Laura, don't be bitter . . . You see . . .'

'What else am I to be? I feel used, and deeply disappointed in you. I had expected better.'

Should he tell her the truth? He didn't want to, and yet he owed her an explanation. He had not thought through what he would and wouldn't tell her. How could it be fair to Esmeralda if he told her the truth? But, then, if he didn't she would remain disillusioned and she deserved better than that.

'I'm not going to marry her. It's a ruse . . . It wouldn't be fair to Esmeralda if we went ahead.'

'Does she not want to marry you?'

'Yes.'

'Then if you don't her father will sue you for breach of promise.'

'He doesn't wish me to marry her.'

'I have a certain amount of sympathy with him.'

'Laura! Esmeralda is a child. She did something silly in relation to me and this way we can extricate her with her honour intact.'

'So she doesn't know of this stratagem?'

'No, and she must not – no one must know. I trust you will keep this to yourself?'

'I would not wish the girl to be further humiliated.'

'But she won't be.'

'Did you really think I would congratulate you on behaving in such a devious way? The plan and you are despicable.'

'Laura!' She and Hannah thought the same, yet he was convinced he was acting in the best way to protect Esmeralda.

'For such a situation to arise, this girl must have had some indication that you were interested in her. You were using her while bedding me.'

'It was not so.'

'And you expect me to believe you?'

'Yes, I do.'

'Then I'm sorry but I can't. When I think that I risked everything for you!'

'I know you did, and I'm grateful.'

'You've changed.'

'So you frequently tell me.' He was irritated now and wished she would stop this: it was not helping anyone, including herself.

'You had already tired of me.'

He could not look at her.

'It's true. For the past few weeks you have come here simply because you could not think of a way of extricating yourself from our relationship.'

He stared out of the window, noting the men in the yard rolling barrels noisily across the cobblestones towards the inn.

'It would be more courteous if you would look at me and answer. You are not normally so ill-mannered.' He did not answer her. 'You have become withdrawn and cold.'

He looked at her as she had demanded. 'I wish you'd stop, Laura. You're damaging all that was good.'

'I? I am doing the damage?' Her voice was shrill. 'The damage had been done, and by you. You are a hypocrite, Oliver. Like all of your sex, you take what you want with no thought of the consequences. You are immoral, Oliver.'

She looked as if she hated him. Where had the love gone, the magic? How had it been replaced with this? He looked about him at the little room that had once been their sanctuary, their secret. Now it seemed small, shabby, drab, despite the new whitewash; it was in need of more furniture, silk and chintz. Had he deceived himself over his feelings for Laura just as he had imagined this room to be different from how it really was? Had he thought himself in love to cover his loneliness?

He took a deep breath. 'Very well, yes. I don't think I've changed, but our relationship has. I don't know why – I didn't want it to happen. It simply did. It was as if it had nothing to do with me. I wish you to believe me.'

'As I am to presume you did not pursue Esmeralda? God help her, is all I can say, involved with such a duplicitous man as you.'

Oliver stood up. He collected his crop from the side table where he had put it. 'There is no point in continuing this conversation. It would appear you have made up your mind and have no intention of listening to me.' He moved towards the door, held it open and gestured to it.

'I wish to stay here a while. On my own.'

'So be it.'

'You are squalid!' she shouted after him.

Slowly he turned to face her. 'No one asked you to be involved with me, you came because you wanted to. Stay as long as you wish . . .'

Outside, on the balcony, he stood a moment, breathing deeply. He was alerted to a great wail from the room behind him, like that of an animal in pain. He turned back.

'Don't leave me,' he heard her wail. 'I can't live without you!' She was sobbing and he heard her drumming her fists on the door. He wavered, then put on his hat and was gone.

The weekends were always the busiest time, not that Melanie was complaining. 'You're a wonder, Flossie. Nothing seems to fuss you.' She watched in admiration as Flossie, a perpetual whirl of movement, rushed about the kitchen. While she herself had stood at the table ironing methodically, Flossie had dealt with the butcher's boy while checking a roast, making soup, feeding a cat, wiping her child's nose and chopping herbs. 'How *do* you manage to do so many things at the same time?' Melanie was laughing.

'If it makes you laugh I'd stand on my head in the yard. It's wonderful to hear.'

'You know, Flossie, I think this is the happiest I've ever been, yet I'm doing what I've always done and more of it – more cleaning, more laundry . . . admittedly less cooking, thanks to you. I never stop working. I'm getting up earlier and going to bed later. I should be a crabby old so-and-so yet I wake up smiling.'

'Because you're getting paid for what you do, you're appreciated, and no bully is beating you up. Simple.'

'I sometimes feel guilty that I am so happy and Bernard's dead. Remember when he died? It didn't bother me at all. Now I feel ... not exactly sad, but regret, I suppose.'

'If he could have been happy too, not bitter, if he had appreciated you, he might still be alive and you might not have hated him. It's nice you feel this way – it would have been horrible for you if you had carried hatred with you for the rest of your life. Someone else is happy.' She nodded towards the corridor where they could hear someone singing.

'Is that Xenia?' Melanie was surprised.

'She received a letter.'

'Who from?'

'Very mysterious she was about it. She wouldn't say.'

'Maybe she has an admirer. That would be nice. Perhaps it would cheer her up too.'

'I hope so, for all our sakes,' said Flossie, with feeling ...

Melanie changed the iron for a hotter one from the range. Flossie was right. Xenia in a temper, or simply in a bad mood, affected all of them. She was the one thing that marred life here. She and her brother were so different. Zeph was always calm: if he had a problem he approached it logically; he did not fly off the handle as his sister did. Her security here was because of him and the relevant questions he had asked Sir Mortimer. He cared about her and told her constantly how he loved her. Xenia lost her temper too easily, sulked, ranted and constantly complained. It was as if she thought the world was against her. She was often heard to say, 'It's not fair.' Obviously nothing was – for her. It made Melanie sad that her daughter should be like this. She wanted to love her, be her friend, but there was a barrier between them. She'd heard other women say they preferred their sons and had always thought that unfair. Now she understood how it happened.

'Mum, I've done my books. Can I go and see Sammy?' It was Timmy.

'Of course, just for an hour.'

Another son to be proud of. He had settled well at his new school, worked hard and was never any trouble. He was even sweet-tempered when she had to wake him in the mornings to catch the train to Barlton. Daughters! she thought again, as she finished ironing the pillowcases.

'Dolly!' she called. 'I'm ready.' She ran up the stairs carrying the clean linen. She was lucky, too, with her helpers. She couldn't fault Dolly, and was sure she would never regret employing her. She was a hard worker, and always sunny. She had a suspicion, not that she had said anything, that Zeph liked her too. She had mixed feelings about that. While she could not think of a nicer girl for her son, and pretty too, they were both far too young to settle down, Zeph was approaching his nineteenth birthday and Dolly, she guessed, was only fifteen. She knew better than most that a girl should not marry too early. If she was right about them she hoped they would wait. But, then, at Dolly's age had she? No! She sighed as she pushed open the door to the bedroom they were about to get ready for new guests.

'Is the pudding to your liking, Mr Joynston?' She paused at his table.

'Excellent. As every meal has been.'

'Might I?' She gestured to the seat opposite him. 'There's just one thing, and I'm not sure how to say this . . .'

'You're concerned about my bill?'

'Well, yes. It's so difficult . . .'

'It shouldn't be. You've every right to ask. I'll be honest, it's been worrying me too.' He grinned ingenuously. Melanie's heart sank. She had been trying to pluck up courage for days to ask him and had feared this. She could not afford for people to avoid paying their dues.

What upset her most was that he was such a nice young man and she enjoyed his company: since he had been there they had sat up late talking once or twice.

'Don't, please, look too aghast. Mr von Ehrlich owes me money – it's just a matter of asking him for it. And tomorrow I have an interview with Sir Mortimer for a position at the manor. If I'm successful, all my problems will be over. So, Mrs Topsham, if you could find it in your kind heart to be patient with me . . .'

'Of course, Mr Joynston. You've set my mind at rest. And good luck for tomorrow.'

'I wish you would call me Richard.'

'Very well, then, Richard, and I'm Melanie.' As she spoke she felt quite skittish. The door opened. 'Zeph!' She rushed across to welcome her son, who stood wet and shivering in the doorway. 'Come in the warm. Flossie's made some soup.'

Zeph watched Dolly as she moved about the room helping Flossie with serving food, so Melanie found it difficult to talk to him.

'I've been thinking, Mother.' Finally he looked intently at her but only, she realised, because Dolly had left the kitchen. 'I like it here. I've been wondering if I should give up the work at Barlton and come here permanently.'

'We've already discussed this, Zeph. I thought we'd agreed. You know how proud I am of you and the future you could have if you continued working for Mr Battle. One day you might be a solicitor. Imagine! My son a professional.' She smiled at him.

'The work here is too much for you.'

'I have all the help I need. Really, I'm very content.'

'I still think it's my duty.'

'Sure it's not Dolly?' She grinned. 'A dear and pretty soul,' she added hurriedly, not wanting him to think she disapproved for that would only make him more determined to be with her.

'Of course not. She's too young, and I've no time to

think of such matters.' He spoke crossly but Melanie was sure he had flushed. 'I'm shocked you should think so, Mother.'

She was right, she concluded. 'Dear Zeph, don't be cross with me. I think only of what's best for you – but, in any case, it's early days here. Could we afford to have you here? You shouldn't work for nothing, as you told me.'

'I must get on with the books. Are they in our little snug, Mother?'

'All laid out for you ready to check with the receipts.'

The door of the bar opened and the curtain swung back. 'Why, Young Mr Mortimer. This is a pleasant surprise. Back from university, are you? For Christmas?'

'I came to see . . . Zeph,' he said, blushing to the roots of his hair.

'He's in here.' She showed him the way. Poor boy, to be so shy, she thought. 'Here he is. Now, if you'd excuse me . . .'

Eventually, with her customers served and Dolly back from her shopping, Melanie joined Zeph in the small sitting room she had created for them behind the bar. It was a private place where they could be on their own – when business allowed – but she could keep on eye on things though a small window in the corner that opened on to the public bar.

'Where's Young Mortimer?'

'I think he left.'

'Aren't you sure?'

'He said he'd things to do.'

'But you should have escorted him out, someone important like him.'

'He's old enough to open a door for himself.' He sounded irritated and his face was flushed. 'I see Mr Joynston hasn't paid yet.'

'No, but I've had a word with him. He's explained his situation.'

'And you believed him?'

'I'd no reason not to.'

'I should speak to him.'

'I'd rather you didn't, Zeph. He's had a misfortune but I'm assured he's resolving it.'

'Then I hope you're right. You should be wary of people, Mother.'

'I know. But this time I think you're wrong. Listen, can you hear Xenia? She's been singing like that all day.'

'Has she? Must be the letter I heard she received this morning.'

'Has she an admirer?'

'I don't know.' But he didn't look at her so she presumed he did.

'I think she has.' Melanie tried to sound light-hearted, but she felt sad that Xenia hadn't seen fit to tell her there was someone she liked.

As she returned to the bar she heard a sudden pounding of feet along the back corridor behind her. She turned to see Laura Redman rushing towards her, her face distorted, smeared with tears.

'Mrs Redman! I'd no idea you were here!' The woman did not reply but instead shoved her to one side, so roughly that Melanie almost fell.

'Here, don't push!' Richard shouted, as she cannoned into him too . . .

Heeding no one, Laura ran across the room, leaving stools flying, jostling people. She yanked at the heavy curtain, which fell from its pole, then wrestled with the door. It flew open and she burst out into the dark street.

'Mrs Redman!' Zeph was the first into action and he ran out after her, then Melanie, Richard and some of the customers. Melanie looked left and right up and down the street.

'No!' she heard her son shout, and looked towards the harbour. Silhouetted against the one light on the whole street Laura teetered on the harbour wall.

'No!' came a chorus of shouts.

For a second Laura glanced back at them as Zeph sprinted towards her. She paused, then jumped.

'Zeph, don't!' Melanie screamed, but he had reached the wall, was clambering upon it. He peered into the murky water. Then, without a backward glance, he plunged in after her. Melanie heard herself scream. People stampeded to the wall.

'There, Zeph!'

'To the right, Zeph!'

'Get out, you silly bugger, you'll die of the cold!'

The shouting echoed along the quay, men running up and down, pointing, gesticulating, one instruction cancelling another.

Melanie could not look any more. She stood beside the inn rocking back and forth, mewing in fear. She was not even aware of Richard's comforting arm about her, his soothing tones, the light kiss on her forehead.

It seemed a lifetime before she heard heavy footsteps on the cobbles. Then she saw her son being carried along by four burly men.

'Sol!'

'Don't you fret, Melanie. He's all right. 'Tis the cold what's gone and got him.'

Melanie felt she was about to faint with relief.

'Come on, Melanie, he needs warming.' She heard Flossie speak as if from far away. She followed them into the bar. Someone had thrown more wood on the fire, and they had laid Zeph in exactly the spot where Bernard had died. She wanted him moved.

'Zeph.' She knelt down beside him, but he could not speak because his teeth were chattering. His lips were blue. She took his hand and began chafing it to warm it. 'You're all right, son.'

'What about the vicar's wife?' Flossie asked.

'That there water's too cold for a soul to survive more than a few minutes. She's a goner, to be sure.'

Chapter Fifteen
December 1901

The shock of Laura Redman's death reverberated within the community. Suicide was shocking enough, but for Simeon, a man of the cloth, it led to a different sort of shame and dire consequences. Would he be regarded as unsuitable to continue in his present position? There was his son to consider too: he would be tainted by his mother's sin for the rest of his life. It was Sol who suggested that, in deference to Simeon's feelings and standing and for the sake of the child, all those who had witnessed the tragedy should agree on an explanation: Laura had climbed the sea wall in pursuit of a small dog, then slipped on the icy surface and fallen into the sea. It had been an accident, they declared to the constable. With the constant telling of the tale, many quickly came to believe their lies as the truth.

Melanie, walking to the church for the funeral, was worried about the deception. She had agreed to it, but whether the secret could be kept, with at least eight witnesses, was a different matter, and she was not sure what repercussions might follow if the truth got out. And pretending that Laura did not kill herself did not alter the awful truth that she had. No amount of falsehoods would remove from her mind the distraught expression on the woman's face as she had pushed past her in the corridor. Someone had done or said something that had made Laura want to kill herself. Should not that person be brought to account? But who was Melanie to question the morality of the events? Was she not hiding behind lies about her own husband's death? She wished she could make a joke of it all, as Sol and the other men did. 'We'm getting expert at hiding what's what, bain't we?' Rob had remarked, and the others had laughed but she couldn't.

She heard footsteps behind her. 'Mind if I join you? I hate funerals.'

'Can't say I know anyone who enjoys them.'

'You'd be surprised.' Flossie laughed. A few of the others trudging along the lane, heads bent against the icy rain, turned to frown at her. 'Oops, I shouldn't laugh but I can't help it – I always gets the giggles in church.'

'Then I shan't sit with you or you'll set me off. Is your mum looking after the children?'

'She is. She should be here rather than me, she likes a good funeral, but her's chapel, thinks old Simeon's a papist.'

'Poor man.'

'And her poor son. She's a selfish bitch, in my opinion.'

'She couldn't help it. Accidents happen.'

'Don't give me any of that rubbish, Melanie. You knows, as I knows, it weren't no accident.'

'Perhaps she couldn't help herself. Perhaps she was driven to despair.'

'And forgot her own child? I'd never put myself before my little ones.'

'No, I don't think you would.' They trudged on. But, come to think of it, how often had she wished to end it all after a beating from Bernard? But because of her children she'd never have harmed herself. 'Took courage, though.'

'Not if she was mad.'

'If she was mad then she wasn't selfish. You can't have it both ways.'

'That's true.' Flossie grinned.

'In any case, it was an accident.'

'Tragic.' She grinned again. They walked a little further in silence. 'Do you think Oliver Cresswell had something to do with it?'

Melanie swung round to face her friend. 'What makes

you ask that?' In the circumstances, the friendship between Laura and Oliver was not something she wished to dwell on.

'Your Xenia, she said he were involved with her.'

'My daughter has more imagination than sense.'

'She must have had a reason.'

'Xenia does not need reasons. She talks without thinking.'

'You don't like her very much, do you?'

Melanie stopped dead in her tracks. 'Flossie, sometimes your idea of being honest borders on plain rudeness. Of course I like my daughter.' She put her head down and walked faster, furious with Flossie for saying what she herself had thought.

'Mrs Topsham, a word.'

She paused in the church porch, stepping back to let others pass. 'Mr Cresswell, this is a sad day.'

'It is.' He looked dreadful, she thought, pallid and weary, dark rings under eyes that contained a sadness she was sure was not in her imagination. 'I was wondering, were you there? Did you see what happened to Laura?'

'Unfortunately I did.' She noticed his use of the woman's Christian name.

'Did it happen as everyone says?'

Before she could stop the familiarity, she put out her hand and touched his arm. 'It was an accident, Mr Cresswell, as everyone says.' She could not bring herself to look at him as she lied, but what was the point of distressing him further? Whatever had happened was their business, none of hers.

'Thank you, Mrs Topsham. I heard your son tried to save her.'

'He did.'

'You must be proud of him.'

'I am. I wasn't at the time.' She smiled.

'He should be rewarded.'

'He would expect no such thing,' she said and moved

437

into the church. Why did the Cresswells always think money could absolve them of guilt?

'Is the vicar conducting the service himself?' Agnes writing letters, looked up from her task.

'I believe the Bishop of Exeter will officiate.' Hannah marked her place in her book and looked at her watch. The service would be well under way by now. Such sadness, she thought.

'Do you think it was an accident?'

'Laura would hardly be laid to rest in consecrated ground if it wasn't, would she?' She was aware she spoke too sharply, but it was a subject she would rather not discuss or dwell on.

'It seems such an odd time of the evening for the vicar's wife to be visiting such an area.'

'I don't think so. There are many unfortunates down by the harbour. No doubt she was attending them – she was a good woman.'

'I heard she ran out of the Cresswell Arms.'

'A respectable establishment run by a woman of the highest integrity. Now, if you wouldn't mind, Agnes, it distresses me to talk about her.'

'Of course, you must have known her well.'

'Not intimately, but we were acquaintances. I would put it no higher than that.'

'How unthinking and insensitive of me. Forgive me.'

Hannah smiled at her new friend. 'I understand. No doubt we are no different from everyone else on the estate. They must be talking of nothing else.' And those who weren't gossiping were surely thinking about it, as she was, she thought. She was bothered – more than that, if she was honest. Although she knew that Oliver had been nowhere near Laura when the tragedy occurred – he had been visiting Hannah – she could not forget how distracted he had been that afternoon, not concentrating on anything she said to him. When she had asked him what was the matter, he'd apologised and mentioned problems with von Ehrlich and his new house.

What a muddle Oliver had made of everything – the last thing she would have expected of him. Until now, as far as she knew, he had lived a blameless life.

At least since last night she had felt better about Esmeralda. She had had a long talk with Agnes who, much to her surprise, had said that perhaps it was for the best. She admitted that, like Hannah, she found herself swinging between wanting them to marry and not wanting them to, of approving and disapproving. 'It's just as well no one ever proposed to me. I'd have vacillated for so long my poor swain would not have known if he was coming or going,' Agnes had joked.

Hannah had known only too well what she meant, and that was when she had confessed to her about Simeon and her narrow escape. It was nice to have such a friend to talk to.

'Do you hope still to marry, Hannah?' Agnes now said, as if she had been reading her thoughts about their conversation last night.

'For a long time I did. But just recently I've thought I don't. I'm content with my life.'

'It is a liberation when one reaches such a plateau, isn't it?'

'*Liberation?* What an interesting word to use and, yes, apt. Now I am in my own establishment I have only myself to think of. For so long I have had to defer to my father and brothers, let alone my stepmother. Yes, you're right. I am enjoying my *liberation* . . .' She smiled at Agnes, who bowed in acknowledgement. 'It would be irksome now to consider the demands of a husband.'

'Bravo!' Agnes clapped. 'Welcome to the sisterhood. Men are such selfish creatures, are they not?'

'I had never thought about it, but now you mention it . . .'

'And unreasonable.'

'And noisy.'

'And impolite!'

'And smelly.' At that Hannah doubled up with laughter, then heard scratching at the drawing-room door. 'Cariad?' She sped to open it and found her father and his little dog outside.

'I rang the bell,' Mortimer said.

'Lavender must not have heard. Your coat – come in. You shouldn't be out on a day like this. It's bitter,' she chided, as she fussed about him.

'I'm wrapped up warm. I've been to that poor woman's funeral. It pulled me low, reminded me of my own mortality. Why, Miss Beatty,' he said, as he entered the room, and bowed to her.

She returned an elegant curtsy. 'Sir Mortimer.'

'Tea, Papa?'

'I'd prefer a whisky.'

'Papa, should you?'

'I most certainly should. Purely medicinal on a day like this.'

Hannah pulled the bell to summon Lavender.

'How was the funeral, Sir Mortimer?'

'Dignified and unutterably sad.' He coughed, as if to put a full stop to the conversation. 'So, you've settled in? Isn't this a fine house, Miss Beatty?'

'The very best, Sir Mortimer.'

'And what was the cause of all the mirth I heard when I was in the hall?'

'We were agreeing how difficult men could be and how lucky we were not to have any here – except you, of course, dear Papa.'

'Just as well since I've come a-begging. I was wondering if you had a cranny in which this old man and his dog could spend Christmas?'

'Of course! You, of all people, need not ask. But the others?' She looked worried: she had already decided she would not spend the festival with her family. She was not yet ready to be in the same room as her stepmother.

'Oliver is going away. He's just told me – very abrupt about it.'

'Did he say where to?'

'No. He seems to have taken Laura Redman's death badly. Odd, if you ask me.'

'They were friends many years ago,' Hannah explained, 'before she was married,' she added. Poor Oliver, she thought. He must be suffering. 'And the others?'

'Coral and Mortie are going to her parents – her father is not well. Another one going skywards before long.'

'Papa!'

'The children will accompany them.' He waited while Hannah dealt with Lavender. 'Penelope has announced she wants to join them. I don't want to go anywhere, so I'm an orphan, alone in the snow.'

'There isn't any snow!'

'No, but there might be and it makes me sound more pathetic.'

'I hope we won't be too quiet for you?'

'Peace is what I am looking forward to.'

'And to have Cariad here too! How wonderful.' She patted the little dog, who leapt up to lick her enthusiastically.

The one advantage of a funeral, Melanie learnt, was that the sale of cider and beer tripled. People wanted to forget where they had been, needed to drown their own fears of death. The disadvantage was that she had to work even harder.

Dolly was ill – something she had eaten, she claimed. Although Melanie suspected it might be the amount of cider she had drunk the night before, she did not want to make too much fuss since Dolly was the best worker she could wish for.

Dolly's claim about the food had upset Flossie so much that she had stormed off in a huff; it was the first time Melanie could remember seeing her in a temper. Zephaniah had returned to Barlton immediately after the funeral, and of Xenia there was no sign – not that that surprised Melanie: the girl had an annoying habit of disappearing when she was most needed.

'If you could just bear with me,' she called to a group who were banging their tankards on the bar in frustration. 'It's not as if you're likely to die of thirst, is it?' They laughed good-naturedly. You have to keep them amused, she told herself, as she flew into the kitchen to stir the pot of soup that Flossie had made before she swept off. She needed to wash some glasses too – she was running out. She hauled the kettle off the range, and poured hot water into a bowl, gave some glasses a quick swirl, then an even quicker wipe with the tea-towel and hurried back to the bar. To her horror, it looked even more crowded than when she had left it.

'Richard, what are you doing?'

'You need help. Here, let me . . .' She had been manhandling a new barrel towards the trestle table. 'That's too heavy for you.'

'Thank you.' She watched admiringly as, with ease, he lifted it on to the table, removed the bung, inserted the tap, then turned it over ready for use. He was far stronger then his slim frame implied. 'You look as if you've been doing that all your life.'

'My father had a coaching inn. I learnt from him.'

'Really?' She was unable to hide her surprise. Given his position with von Ehrlich, she had presumed he came from a more genteel background.

'I vowed never to go into the same trade as him.' He laughed.

'And why would that be?' she asked, as she filled tankards.

'Too much hard work – my father never had a moment

to himself. But I discovered when I was working for von Ehrlich that although I never got my hands dirty I had to work longer hours even than my father with far more abuse hurled at me.' He grinned as he spoke, as if the experience hadn't troubled him. Melanie admired the lack of bitterness she observed in him: he was one of those souls who, no matter what bad fortune befell them, always managed to stay cheerful. Just like Flossie.

She served beer, informed the customers she'd only got soup and bread to sell them, ignored their protests and returned to stand by Richard.

'I've a confession, Melanie . . .' He looked worried, which she hadn't expected.

'Mr von Ehrlich didn't pay you what he owes you?'

'You guessed correctly. In fact, he was even more irate with me than usual. He's taking his anger out on me.'

'Why should that be?'

'I suppose I've let him down. He always thought I wanted his daughter.' Melanie found herself surprisingly disappointed. 'But I didn't. Oh, she's a sweet girl, but I didn't admire her in the way he imagined,' Melanie was even more surprised by the relief she now felt, 'and she's taken a fancy to another who, presumably, is even more unsuitable than me. But none of this solves my obligation to you. I never guessed he'd let me down.'

'And Sir Mortimer?'

'I didn't suit.' He shrugged.

'Ah, well. It can't be helped. So, what do we do?' She knew she couldn't throw him out. When Zeph was away who else was there to talk to? Flossie went home in the evening, and as much as she liked Dolly they had little in common, with such a wide discrepancy in their ages. And if she sent him packing what would it solve? She'd lose not only his money but his companionship. 'You could always work off what you owe us.'

'What would Zeph say? It would be a marvellous opportunity for me.'

'He won't mind and, in any case, I'm in desperate need of help.'

Richard was soon back behind the bar, and the two of them worked well together through the rest of the evening.

About ten o'clock Melanie was in the kitchen clearing piles of crockery while Richard looked after the bar. On hearing a noise from the region of the back door, she went to investigate. Xenia, boots in hand, cheeks flushed, was tiptoeing along the passage to the stairs.

'You weren't quiet enough. Where have you been?' Melanie asked.

'Gracious, Mama, you made me jump!'

'I thought you were in your room.'

'I couldn't sleep. I needed some fresh air.'

'In this weather? Have you lost your senses?'

'Good night.' She continued towards the staircase.

'Not so fast. You come in here, young woman.' Melanie pointed sternly towards the kitchen. 'Now, tell me, where have you been?'

'I told you. Is there any soup left?'

'Who were you with?'

'Mama, I don't know what you mean.' Xenia opened her eyes wide in astonishment.

'I think you do. And I want to know.'

'I went for a walk. Why must you always think ill of me?'

'I don't like being lied to and I don't want you risking your reputation, or worse, on some worthless churl.' Melanie did not like the sly, rather smug smile that flitted across her daughter's face either.

'Mama, I promise I simply went out for some fresh air, and you're right, the weather is awful. I was creeping along because I didn't want to wake you. Do, please, believe me.' She smiled at her mother disarmingly.

Once again Melanie was reminded of how beautiful

her daughter was. 'You're so lovely, I live in fear that something bad might happen to you.'

'Mama, don't. I'm wise beyond my years.' She kissed her mother's cheek, which was such a rare gesture that it took Melanie by surprise.

'Everyone always thinks they know everything when they're young, when in fact they know little.'

Xenia laughed. 'If I am pretty it's because I've such a good-looking mother. Thank you.' She kissed Melanie again, then waved airily and ran up the stairs.

'That's a happy smile,' said Richard, as she returned to the bar.

'My daughter kissed me and paid me a compliment.'

'As she should. She's lucky to have such a mother.'

'Heavens above, my head will be turned by all these compliments.' She felt quite flustered as she folded the tea-towels behind the bar. 'It looks as if you've done most of my chores for me.' The room was tidy, the glasses washed, the fire banked up. She was tired, yet did not want to go to bed just yet.

'Perhaps we might share a nightcap. I'll pay, when I can,' he added hurriedly.

She laughed. 'After all you've done this evening? What would you like?'

'A glass of red wine?'

'I know little about wine, so you must choose. Here, take the lantern and the key to the cellar. Mr Cresswell has purchased some bottles.'

As she waited, she added a couple more logs to the fire then sat down beside it. She stretched, enjoying the heat of the flames, feeling tired but knowing it was worthwhile, that the business was succeeding and that, barring accidents, she was secure.

'He's laid down some good ones,' Richard said, as he returned with a bottle. 'I wouldn't have thought the clients you have here would be interested in a fine cellar.'

'He hopes we shall attract others who might, in due time. You like wine?'

'Only the best.' He pulled the cork and poured a small amount, which he tasted, then more into a glass for her. 'Excellent,' he said. The way he did that made her feel cared for. 'Why did Flossie leave so early?' he asked.

'She had a falling-out with Dolly. I hope they're friends again in the morning. I can't cook as she does.'

'You're a courageous woman. You deserve success.' He put out his hand and touched hers so lightly that she wasn't even sure he had. She must have been mistaken, she thought, when he picked up the bottle again – he must have brushed against her.

'Not too much or I'll get tiddly!'

'When you work as hard as you do, it's good to relax in this way. Decent wine never harmed anyone.'

'I don't mind the hard work when I can see the results improving every day. And the clients are kind to me. When I make mistakes they're so patient.'

'*You* make mistakes? I don't believe it.'

'I do. I never could add up . . .' She laughed, thinking he was teasing her, but stopped abruptly. He was looking at her with such intensity that she felt flustered, embarrassed and excited all at once.

'Melanie . . .' His voice was low and husky.

'But I learn each day – I would never have thought there was so much to know.'

'Melanie . . .'

'I'm proud of this inn. We shall make it the best in Devon. I'm determined.'

'I'm falling in love with you.'

She stood up, feeling awkward. 'Of course, without Flossie it would be hard. I could never—'

'Did you hear what I said?'

'Really, Richard, please . . .'

'I can't help myself. The first time I saw you . . .' He had stood up, too, so she sat down. 'The weeks I've been

446

here I've watched and admired you. Your grace, your sensitivity.' Abruptly he knelt at her feet. 'You're so beautiful. You're all I've ever dreamt of . . .'

She looked down at him, at his dear face, then put out her hand and stroked his fine blond hair. 'Richard . . .'

Oliver had risen early. Since Laura's death he had been unable to sleep. Last night he had walked for several hours trying to clear his head of confusion and guilt. By the broken gate he had stopped, thinking of her, of the love they had felt for each other, which had changed to such destructive pain. He had brought with him a small wreath of holly, which he laid by the gate in remembrance. In the spring he would have a bush of rosemary planted.

He had taken a walk to tire himself, but it had been pointless. Sleep had been impossible for, on top of everything else, he was beside himself with anger. Returning late and working in the library, he had come across his father's bank statement – the red ink in one of the columns had jumped off the page. In the past it would never have occurred to him to breach his father's privacy, but with his new role in his father's life he had read it. He had immediately gone in search of him.

'Father, what's this?' He waved the paper at his father, whom he had found still in the dining room, an almost finished decanter of port in front of him.

Mortimer was making patterns with walnut shells on the white damask tablecloth. The servants had been dismissed. He glanced up at his son. 'Did I ask you to look at my private papers?'

'No, but . . .' He had blustered in but now felt reduced to a young boy again. 'Look at this.' Oliver laid the documents on the table and stabbed at the red-ink entries, hoping to recapture his former confidence.

'You have a problem with the bank's calculations?'

'No, but I thought we agreed—'

'What I do with my money is my business.'

'I know, but—'

'So I would appreciate it if you kept to the affairs of the estate and did not intrude into mine.'

'Father, I'm sorry, but I'm concerned. You have signed over a considerable sum to von Ehrlich. He will cheat you out of it.'

'He might. On the other hand he might not.'

'The former, I fear. You didn't see or hear him threaten to ruin us.'

'If I lose this money it is hardly going to ruin us, is it?'

'No . . . But it will hurt. Unnecessarily so. If only you had listened to me.'

'I like the man.'

'He's a mountebank.'

'But amusing and generous with it.'

Exasperated, Oliver had turned away. 'I shall be leaving tomorrow – earlier than I had intended. Obviously I'm wasting my time here.'

'Oh dear, I've hurt your pride.'

'No, you haven't. I just don't like being used when it's convenient to you and cast aside when it isn't.'

'Then I apologise and will consult you in future.'

The way he smiled as he spoke made Oliver wonder if he meant what he had said. 'I trust you will have a pleasant Christmas,' he said.

'As I hope you do. I'm going to stay with your sister.'

'Hannah will enjoy having you all to herself.'

'Hardly. Young Mortimer has decided to join us, and the Beatty woman will be there. Since you're so expert on the Courtney Lacey household, what do you think of Miss Beatty?'

'She's pleasant, and I'm happy that Hannah has someone with her. Don't you like her?'

'There's something strange about her and I cannot put my finger on it . . . Ah, well, no doubt I'm being over-protective. It's time to let go.' He was rearranging the nutshells. He looked up at his son with a sad expression. 'Oliver, I'm touched you're so concerned for me but, really, it amuses me to play this little game with Stanislas. Don't worry.'

But he did. He was certain that his father was being cheated even if he could not, as yet, fathom how.

'Whitaker, could you ask one of the footmen to pack for me? I'm going away for a few weeks.'

'Somewhere pleasant, I trust, Mr Oliver?'

'Brussels, Whitaker.'

'I hear it is a most excellent city for a visit, sir.'

'And could you arrange for Ferdie to saddle Sergeant?'

He had ridden hard, wanting to dissipate his anger, knowing it would be of no use to him in his dealings with von Ehrlich. Anger in business always put one at an immediate disadvantage. Now he was riding up the drive of Courtney Lacey, working out how best to approach the problem.

'Oliver! What a wonderful surprise!' Esmeralda had arrived in her usual squealing hurry. Seconds later, her father appeared, alerted by his daughter's high-pitched welcome. The two men observed the charade of civility.

'Esmeralda, my dear, I've come to say goodbye and to bring you this.' He produced a small packet from his pocket.

'Where are you going? You're leaving me?' She took the little parcel.

'I have to go away for a short time.'

'But I wanted you to spend Christmas with us!' She pouted.

'Next year. This year I can't.'

'And might one ask where you are going?'

'Geneva, Mr von Ehrlich. Business.'

'We poor men – our pleasure is always spoilt by business.'

449

'I shan't let you go. I insist you stay. With me!' Esmeralda stamped her foot.

'Dear heart, I wish I could.'

'May I open it now?'

He grabbed it back. 'No, you must not. It's to be opened at the right time. I shall give it to your father for safe-keeping. Might I have a word, sir? In private?'

'I want to come.'

'Esmeralda, go and find your grandmother. Tell her Mr Cresswell is here.' Stanislas ushered Oliver into his library. 'So?' he asked abruptly.

'Do we have to continue in this way?'

'You want us to be friends again? You have changed your mind about the land?'

'No, sir.'

'Then I did not make myself clear enough to you. I am never crossed by anyone.'

'Is that why you persuaded my father into this latest investment?'

'It was an opportunity I thought he might enjoy.'

'But on the other hand you threaten us. The two do not go hand in hand.'

'He was pleased.'

'And how long before he finds he has lost it? I gather he has made two payments to you. There won't be a third.'

'Surely that is your father's decision, not yours. Or does your arrogance involve him too?'

'This is pointless.' Oliver stood up to go.

'I was sorry to hear of the death of your mistress.' Stanislas remained seated.

'I don't know what you mean.'

'Suicide is always such a bitter business for those left behind. No doubt that is why you're scuttling out of the country – to escape. But, of course, you can never escape your guilt, or did you not know that?'

Oliver had to admire the man's ability to read his

mind. A slow, insufferably smug smile spread across von Ehrlich's face, as if he felt he had won this particular battle. But it was this smile that altered everything.

'Are you still determined to involve my father in our feud?'

'It was his land, his broken promise. Are you stupid as well as deceitful—?'

Oliver stepped forward but then, aware of what he might do, stepped back, bowed and said, 'Good day, to you, sir.'

Esmeralda was waiting for him in the hall. He crossed to her, put his arm about her and kissed her, hoping her father had followed him and would see. He looked over his shoulder, but Stanislas was not there. 'Did you mean you wanted to spend Christmas with me?'

'Oh, I do, I do!' She began to jump up and down.

'Shush. Don't let your father hear.' He leant forward and whispered in her ear.

'You mean it?' She clasped her hands together, her eyes sparkling with excitement.

'Don't tell a soul.' He kissed her full on the lips. God in heaven, what was he thinking of?

It had to have been the wine . . . She was not used to drinking . . . It had gone straight to her head . . . She felt sick . . . Melanie lay on her bed, looking at the ceiling. How stupid she was!

But in blaming the wine was she not lying to herself? The truth was . . . She shuddered. She didn't want to think of that . . . But if she didn't . . . She had no one to blame but herself. She had wanted this to happen even if she hadn't planned it. She had most certainly taken too much wine, to make it easier for herself. She had wanted him to hold her . . . to rid her of loneliness, that was all. No, it wasn't. She closed her eyes as if to eradicate the truth. She had not been aware of how much she had desired him until he had touched her. Then she had known and, from that moment, she had ached for love. That was what had happened.

How strange it all was, she of all people to feel longing. With Bernard, their coupling had been a duty to endure. There had never been any desire on her part, nor any pleasure in it. What mischief had entered her brain last night and made her so forward and lustful? The wine, she said to herself, and this time she believed it.

She turned her head gingerly and looked at Richard lying beside her, soundly asleep. She had not known that lovemaking could be the gentle sensuous thing it had been last night. There had been none of the brutality she was used to. She had felt new emotions and sensations. Her body had reacted in an enjoyable way – it still felt different this morning. Her head might be in turmoil but her body felt as relaxed as if she lay on a bed of swansdown.

Joy – she had known joy last night. She had been shown a fleeting glimpse of what life could be like. *Laura Redman*. Suddenly, from nowhere, with no apparent relevance, she thought of her. Had she felt like this? Had she found the wickedness of her actions too much to bear? Had shame made her take her own life?

Slowly she slid from the bed. She looked down at him. He looked too peaceful to wake. But what if Xenia saw him? She picked up her wrap. She was worrying unnecessarily: Xenia rarely came in here and, in any case, she did not wake early. Looking at him again made her body stir. She wanted him inside her again, wanted to feel the weight of him, his thrusting . . . She bent and put on her slippers. No. She moved quickly across the room to the door. She needed time.

She ran down the stairs into the bar to open the windows and air the room of the stale tobacco smoke and beer fumes. How would she be when he came down? How could she face him, embarrassed and full of shame?

She tried not to look at the place on the floor in front

452

of the fire where Richard had first taken her, and was soon busily collecting the few glasses they had missed last night. But however she tried to distract herself, her eyes were continually drawn to the spot on the wooden boards. She put her hands over her face. They must have lain on the very place where Bernard had died. Oh, the wickedness!

'Sorry about yesterday.' Flossie was already at work in the kitchen. 'It isn't like me to lose my temper.'

'We all have moments like that.' Melanie carried the tray of glasses to the sink. 'Dolly didn't mean to offend you, you know.' She kept her head down, afraid that what she had experienced would be writ large on her face, afraid for even Flossie to know.

'She told me when I got here. We made it up. She's still being sick ... If you ask me ...' Flossie arched an eyebrow.

'You don't mean?' Melanie put her hand to her neck, a gesture she often made when distressed. *Zeph*! her mind shrieked at her. Surely not.

'And what have you been up to?' Another raised eyebrow from Flossie as she nodded at Melanie's neck. 'Well I never! Who's the lucky fellow?'

'I don't know what you mean.'

'I suppose a vampire gave you that love-bite.' Flossie was laughing.

'Don't, Flossie. I'm so ashamed.'

'Don't be silly! What's wrong in having a man when the fancy takes you? You're a woman on your own. Have a cup of tea.' She was already pouring it.

'I didn't know I wanted one – well, perhaps I did.' She laughed nervously. 'But it just happened. I had some wine ...'

'Ha! I thought it'd need something like that to release the strings on your knickers.' And Flossie was laughing again.

'But what will he think of me? I'm not a loose woman, but that's how he must see me now.'

'Richard, was it?'

'Yes.'

'He's a nice chap. I can't see him taking advantage.'

'But he's so young.'

'So?'

'Well, it's wrong.'

'I'd be surprised if he thinks that.' And she was grinning from ear to ear.

'Flossie, don't, please. I am so ashamed.'

'Oh, love, you're just being human.' Flossie took her hand.

'But what if he tells someone? What if the children find out? What if I lose my reputation?'

'Why should they know? Honestly, Melanie, you're being too hard on yourself. What's wrong with a bit of a tumble? Who are you hurting? No one. It's time you began to enjoy life. All you do is work and worry. For one night you were yourself.'

Melanie remembered her groans of pleasure and had to look away, knowing she was blushing. Had that been the real her, that woman who had wanted more and more enjoyment for her body? 'Still I must get on. Sitting here gossiping won't pay the bills.' She stood up, then realised that to get dressed she would have to go back into her bedroom and see him. She couldn't.

She hurried along the corridor to the laundry room. When she was in a panic, as she was now, her memory seemed to desert her: she'd no idea what clothes of hers were in there.

In the piles of washing she found a skirt that wasn't too dirty. Then, from the clean clothes, she selected a blouse that needed ironing. From the wooden drying rail she pulled down a cotton jacket. It was not warm enough for today's weather, but it would have to do – at least it would cover the creased blouse. At the back of the room

454

she slipped round the side of a large cupboard and changed out of her nightclothes. She splashed some water over her face. There was a small mirror over the sink. She caught sight of herself and stopped trying to rearrange her hair. She looked different. She peered more closely. She did not look as if she had been awake half the night, she did not look guilty. She could not put her finger on what was different, but there was something. She twisted her head to one side. She could see the bite now, turning blue – how shameful. She dived back into the laundry basket, found a red kerchief of Zephaniah's and tied it round the mark. Her hair defeated her: it was too long and tangled. She would have to brave Flossie's teasing again to borrow a comb.

'Hello.' She knew it was him without turning. She had known it was him the minute he had entered the little snug where she was sorting out the bills for Zephaniah to deal with at the weekend.

'Hello,' she answered, continuing with her work. At least, that was what it might have looked like to a casual observer, but she didn't know what she was doing.

He leant over, removed the paper from her hand and turned it round. 'You're reading it upside-down. It's easier the right way up.' His voice bubbled with amusement.

'Have you had breakfast?' she asked, still unable to look at him.

'Not yet. Flossie's cooking me something.'

'You've seen her. How was she?'

'Very considerate. I gather she knows.'

'She won't say anything.'

'I see. So I'm to be a secret?'

'It's better that way.'

'It'll be difficult to keep up.'

'No, it won't, because you won't be here.' There was silence. Still she did not turn; still she could not bring herself to look at him. She was aware that he was taking a seat in the old armchair, whose springs stuck up. She should have warned him about them, but somehow it didn't seem appropriate.

'I see.'

'I wish you'd stop saying that.'

'It's difficult to know what else to say in the circumstances. I'm sorry you want me to go.'

'As I said, it'll be easier.'

'Who for? Certainly not me.'

She risked a glance. He looked pale and his skin was almost waxen. Worst of all, he looked sad. 'I'm sorry,' she said.

'I'm hurt, Melanie.'

'I'm sorry,' she repeated.

'I could say that I wish you'd stop saying that.' She detected the smallest hint of mirth in his voice, but she couldn't be sure. 'I meant what I said to you last night.'

'Please don't.' It had been wonderful when he told her he loved her. She'd only been told that once before, a long time ago, a time best forgotten. She felt tears prick her eyes.

'I love you, Melanie. I didn't mean to but I do. It happened.'

'Please stop!'

'Why should I? If I'm to leave you I should be allowed to say what is in my heart.'

'Except I don't wish to hear it.' She bowed her head, collecting herself. She looked at him. 'I will forgo your bill. It's been pleasant knowing you, but I would prefer it if you were gone within the hour.'

'Melanie, you can't do this to me. To us. What have I done?'

'Nothing. It's me. I should never have permitted such intimacy. It was wrong.'

'Why, for God's sake?'

'It was the wine.'

'Oh, no! That's the one thing it wasn't. You wanted me, Melanie. You were hungry for me too. We wanted and needed each other.'

'You're too young.'

'What has age to do with love?'

'A lot. I must be ten years older.'

'Eight.'

'How do you know my age?'

'I asked.' He was grinning again. Then it *was* all words, she thought, for if he was being honest how could he smile? How could he find anything amusing in this?

'There are my children.'

'They like me. I made sure they did before I dared to say a word to you.'

'As a guest. Not as their mother's lover.'

'Then marry me, and I wouldn't be.'

His words took her breath away. 'How dare you?'

'But I mean it.'

'How can you? You hardly know me. You use it as a ruse.'

'I don't. Dear Melanie—'

'Please go. I don't want my daughter to have any inkling of this, and if she sees us now, she would.'

'I can't—'

'Richard, I would be happier if we parted as friends. Please go. If you stay and continue to argue with me we shall become bitter with each other. I have nothing further to say to you.' She turned her back on him and, with every fibre of her body, willed him to leave the room and her life.

When she heard the door shut she broke down. It had been a magical experience and she felt bereft.

Chapter Sixteen
December–January 1901–1902

'This Christmas is going to be an odd kettle of fish and no mistake,' Mrs Fuller said, as she swept into the kitchen.

'And why in particular, Gussie?' Mrs Gilroy looked up from the haunch of venison she was larding with pork fat.

'They're closing up the house. Not one member of the family is staying.'

'You don't mean we've all got to pack our bags and go to London? I hate London, especially at this time of year, all fog and smelling with the sulphurs of hell.'

'We're to go our own ways. I'm to tell the others.'

'What do they mean?'

'Go home. Her ladyship has just informed me that those who have to travel will have their fares paid for them.'

'That's nice.' Mrs Gilroy looked thoughtful and added a few more juniper berries to the wine in the china bowl. 'Did I tell you my old mother lives in Paris – or was it Biarritz?'

'I never knew that.'

'Come off it, Gussie! I was joking. My mother's been in her grave these twenty years. But how are they to know where we come from? I've always had a fancy to visit Scotland. Still, I doubt they mean that far.'

'Jock's getting his ticket. He's the furthest of anyone. And it would be dishonest to lie. Where will you make tracks to?'

'I quite fancy Torquay. Or perhaps Ilfracombe. Who knows?'

'And you've people in both places?'

'The Gilroys are universal,' she announced airily. 'Where are the family going?'

'Sir Mortimer and Young Mortimer are going to Miss Hannah's, the rest are off to the stuck-up Mrs Cresswell's family home.'

'Why's the boy staying?'

'Something to do with his studying.'

'A girl, more like.'

'Eve, you're such a suspicious creature.'

'At his age a maid'll be the cause, not his books – I'd put a sovereign on it. Who's going to look after the house?'

'I told her ladyship I would, as a favour.'

'I trust she was suitably grateful. Why did you offer?'

'Someone had to.'

'Don't see why. They could pay for a caretaker to come in.'

'But it had to be a body they knew was honest.' She had sat down and was looking intently at Mrs Gilroy's receipt book. 'You could make a good soup if you boiled this.' She held it up: some of its pages were stained with food from meals prepared long ago.

'I keep promising myself to make a new one, not that I ever seem to get the time.' Mrs Gilroy placed a tea-towel over her marinating meat, carried it to the larder and put it on the slate shelf. When she returned it was to see Mrs Fuller in an uncharacteristic slump. 'What's the matter, Gussie?'

'Nothing. Just a little tired.' She sat up straight.

'What is it? It's me you're talking to.'

The housekeeper looked everywhere but at the cook. 'Oh, what's the point? I volunteered because I've nowhere to go. There, I've said it, and I don't want you feeling sorry for me and that's flat.'

459

Mrs Gilroy sat down beside her and put out her hand. 'Well, that makes two of us. I've no family neither.'

'But you just said . . .'

'I didn't want you to know, that's all. My silly old pride.'

The rest of the staff were jubilant at the unexpected holiday.

'The chatter and excitement of them young ones quite wore me out,' Mrs Gilroy said, over coffee in the housekeeper's room.

'I gather you're staying here with Mrs Fuller, Mrs Gilroy.'

'I am, that. A rare old time we shall be having. I trust you'll be leaving the wine-cellar keys with us just to make sure we do, Mr Whitaker.'

'I shall ensure you have an adequate supply of good cheer, Mrs Gilroy.'

'Sad, though, isn't it, at our age? No one to go to, no one who cares. Miserable old maids!' She laughed.

'Gussie, don't let it upset you.' Mrs Gilroy was not taken in by the housekeeper's laughter.

'But don't you sometimes worry about the future, Eve? I know I do. Don't you sometimes wonder where we'll be, what we'll be doing in ten, fifteen years' time? And who will there be to care for us when we're old and infirm?' Mrs Fuller felt for her handkerchief.

'Get on with you, Gussie. No point in worrying about something that hasn't happened yet. You might fall under an omnibus tomorrow.'

'Unlikely, Mrs Gilroy, there are no omnibuses at Cresswell.' Mr Whitaker beamed, evidently pleased with his little joke.

'Sometimes I can't sleep for worrying about the future.' Mrs Fuller was screwing her handkerchief into a ball.

'Forgive my levity. I'd no idea.' Whitaker looked upset by his insensitivity. 'But there's no need to concern yourself. When has this family not looked after those who have given them faithful service? I've no reason to believe we shall not be housed with a pension.'

'Sir Mortimer might do that, but what about when Mr Mortie inherits? What then? His wife's never struck me as a woman with a tender heart.' She began to cry.

'Come on, Gussie. This won't do. Think what fun we three musketeers will be having here all alone with no one to wait on.'

'Three, Mrs Gilroy?'

'Hilda has no home to go to either.'

Whitaker was silent for a minute. 'I doubt if you'll agree, but would you like a fourth musketeer to join you? A man to look after you all?' He smiled.

'You, Edward? We'd be honoured, wouldn't we, Gussie?'

'Not as honoured as I.' Whitaker bowed to them. He was smiling even wider. He had a brother he could visit but at the mention of Hilda he had changed his mind. When Lavender had been about, he had not noticed her but lately he had been struck by what an attractive young woman she was.

As evening fell, Oliver said goodbye to his family and climbed into the hired carriage he had ordered earlier in Cress-by-the-Sea. He did not want to use the family vehicle and have Harold know where he had gone and with whom. First he went to Hannah's. 'If anything should happen and you need to contact me, open this – it will tell you where I am.' He handed her an envelope with her name scrawled on the front.

'Wouldn't it be simpler just to tell me?' She smiled at the dramatic way in which he had spoken.

'I prefer it this way. Have a happy Christmas.'

'I can't believe I shall have Father all to myself, with Young Mortimer as a bonus.'

'He's staying behind?'

'He needs to study. Why do you laugh?'

'Nothing.' He was still grinning.

'It's most annoying when people say that.'

'I expect it is.' He kissed her forehead as he wondered which young woman his nephew was interested in. 'And, Miss Beatty, you're still here?'

'Evidently, Mr Cresswell. Hannah is most kind.'

He left after a few more minutes of pleasantry, anxious to be gone. The longer he stayed, the more convinced he was that his sister would know he was up to no good – as she would put it.

Hannah knew him too well, he thought, as he climbed into the carriage and told the coachman to drive on quickly. He was not proud of what he was doing. He knew only too well that he had acted in the heat of the moment, that his anger with Stanislas for cheating his father – he had no proof yet but he was sure it was so – had overcome consideration for Esmeralda. He should never have asked her to meet him but it was too late now. The girl would be giddy with excitement because she had what she wanted. He couldn't let her down now.

He told the coachman which way to go. They passed through a lower gate of the Courtney Lacey estate where there was no gatehouse and no one to hear them. Having once considered buying this property, he knew it well. The carriage breached a slight rise and he saw the house, a blaze of lights, in the distance. He ordered the coachman to stop and then, on foot, he walked rapidly towards the maze. It was cold and he hoped she had been able to wrap up warmly. As he approached he saw a ghost-like figure huddled against the hedge.

'Esmeralda?' he whispered.

'Oh, Mr Cresswell, sir.' A young girl spoke through chattering teeth.

'Who are you?'

'I'm Miss Esmeralda's maid, sir.' She gave him a little bob. 'Her's gone into the maze.'

'What on earth for?'

'She said she felt safer there.'

'And what's that?' He pointed at the trunk, bags and hat boxes beside her.

'Her packing, sir.'

'So much? Wait here, and put a coat on or you'll catch your death.'

'I haven't got one, sir.'

He removed his own cape and gave it to her, then strode into the maze.

Unable to call her name it took time to find her in the dark. She was sitting on a bench by a frozen fountain in the centre, well wrapped up in a fur coat. 'There you are.'

'Oliver!' She rushed towards him, threw herself into his arms and hugged him. 'I thought you weren't coming.'

'It's taken me an age to find you. Had you stayed where I told you to we'd be on our way by now. We must get going.' He had memorised the route through the high hedges and turned confidently to the right.

'Are you cross with me?'

'A bit, yes.'

'Please don't be.'

'Why did you bring your maid?' Next was a turn to the left, then left again.

'Dearest Oliver, you can't expect me to travel without Bridget!' The very idea made her stop dead in her tracks.

'We could have got someone else.' He cursed mildly: he had taken a wrong turning. They turned to retrace their steps.

'You don't understand how important she is to me.'

'How important? The poor woman was freezing. I think we go right here, then left.'

'Was she? I'm so thoughtless.'

'And so much luggage! Yes, I was right. Next it's left and then left again . . .'

463

When they arrived at the entrance the maid was in tears.

'Bridget, what's the matter?' Esmeralda asked.

'I thought I'd never see you again,' the girl sobbed.

'There, there . . .' Esmeralda began to comfort her.

'Would it be possible for us to move on?'

'Dearest Oliver, don't be so grumpy.' She stood on tiptoe to kiss him.

'We can't take all this baggage.'

'But I have to have my clothes.'

'How did you get so much here?'

'One of the footmen helped me.'

'Oh, Esmeralda!' He had to smile. What was the point in being cross with her? 'This was supposed to be a secret.'

It took twenty minutes to get back to the carriage and another twenty for the coachman and Oliver to return for the cases. He'd never have dreamt that eloping could be so complicated.

'We've missed our train.' He looked at his watch as the coach began the trip to Barlton, the two of them huddled under fur rugs, the maid wrapped up beside the coachman.

'I'm sorry. Are you still cross with me?'

'Crosser.' He grinned. She really was exasperating but how could he be angry with her?

'What shall we do?' She snuggled close to him.

'I hope there's a later one.'

'And then where do we go?'

'Tomorrow we catch a boat for Calais, then travel on to Paris.'

'How perfect! But I thought we were going to Geneva.'

'That's what I wanted your father to think. Everyone else thinks we're going to Brussels since I have friends there.'

'Darling Oliver, you're so clever.'

He kissed the top of her head. Suddenly she sat up,

moved apart from him and looked at him seriously. 'There is something I must ask you.'

'Yes?'

'Mrs Redman. My father says you were indiscreet with her.'

'I was.'

'He says she killed herself for love of you.'

'It is my fear that she did.'

'How could that be?'

'Because I told her my feelings for her had died. It made her sad.'

'Poor woman. But she could not have loved you very much, or why should she hurt you so by killing herself in such a cruel way, leaving you with torment and guilt? And her child motherless! It was selfish of her.'

'I believe her despair took control of her mind. She was a good woman and I treated her badly.'

'Thank you for being so honest with me. My father said you would deny it all.'

'Your father does not know me.'

The clatter of the horses' hoofs made more noise now as they reached the road to Barlton and they clip-clopped on the tarmacadam.

'Oliver, you need not do this.'

'Do what, Esmeralda?'

'Run away with me. I understand why you're doing it.'

'Really? Well, I don't.' He wondered what she was going to say next.

'You're angry with my father, and this is a way of punishing him.'

'What a strange thing to say!'

'I don't think it is. It's the truth. I'm not cross or hurt. But I love you, Oliver. I never thought it was possible to love someone as much as I do you. But I only want you to continue with this adventure if it is what *you* want – if you wish me to be your wife. Because, you see, I want only what is good for you. I love you enough that if you don't want me I will let you go. I want only your happiness.'

'Esmeralda, of course I do.' But it was hard to look at her and a lump was forming in his throat.

'You see, Oliver, I'm not stupid – you probably think I am, and most people do. But if you were eloping with me for all the wrong reasons and did not love me, would I be happy or would the rest of my life be miserable? It would be a great risk.'

'I do love you.'

'I don't think you do, well, not as I love you. But I have so much to give you that it might be enough for the two of us. Would that save us?'

'I know one thing and I will be honest. I didn't know it until now, but I do wish to marry you – I want to spend the rest of my life with you. I love you.' And he knew he was speaking the truth even if it came as an amazing shock to him.

Dolly was in tears. 'Mrs Topsham, I'm so ashamed.'

'Please, Dolly.' While Melanie felt sorry for the girl she was also irritated by her. 'Crying isn't going to make things better, now, is it?'

'I don't know what got into me. I'm usually a good girl.'

'Perhaps you had fallen in love.'

'Yes, that's it.' At least this notion stopped the weeping, if only for the moment.

'And might I ask who with?' Melanie's heart was thumping with anxiety.

'I can't tell you.' She burst into sobs again.

'Very well, if you feel you can't confide in me . . .'

'I would if I could.'

'You can, of course, continue working here.'

'Did you say I *can*?'

'I did.' Melanie smiled at her reaction.

'Oh, Mrs Topsham, I didn't expect you to. Thank you – how can I thank you enough?'

'By stopping crying. That would make a good start.'

'I'm sorry. If I were still up at the big house I'd have been out on my ear.'

'When the baby arrives it might be more difficult. We can't have it crying and upsetting the customers.'

'No, of course not, but I'd make sure it didn't bother anyone, honest I would.'

'On the other hand no one is going to throw you out into the cold world. We shall arrange something, I'm sure. Meanwhile, will you continue to help Flossie?'

Alone, she sat for some time looking out of the small window in the wall of the snug and into the bar, but she did not see the people there: her mind was far away. If only she had been treated in the same way when she was young, everything might have been different. She could still remember the fear she had felt when she found she was with child. Her insides, it seemed, had turned to water. She had wished she could faint and slip into darkness so that the fear would go away. She remembered the horror of telling her mother, the screaming, the accusations, the abuse ... But it had been partly her mother's fault: she had been sent from home an innocent. 'Don't let no man into your knickers,' was the only advice her mother had given her with which to face the world. She had known nothing of men until it was too late. She sighed. Now, too young, Zephaniah was to be a father – at least, she was fairly certain he was. She'd had such dreams for him, but recently she had wondered if they were simply *her* dreams. If only she could keep the information from her mother. She could just imagine her, arms akimbo, sucking in her mean mouth. 'Blood will out!' she would say.

And Melanie would be a grandmother. Well, there was a novel idea. She hoped she didn't look like one – she wasn't ready for that yet. It was just as well she'd sent

Richard packing: if anything showed how wrong the discrepancy in their ages was, it was this.

She was alerted by shouting in the bar, then a heated response from Dolly, but could not catch the words. She took off her apron and went through.

'Mr von Ehrlich, what can I do for you?' She did not like the way the man was looming over the bar, his arm raised as if he was about to hit Dolly. In his other hand, he held Young Mortie by the collar of his coat. The boy looked terrified.

'Let him go!' Xenia was screaming at von Ehrlich.

'Xenia, leave this to me.' Melanie turned to face him. 'What is the matter?' She spoke as calmly as she could, wishing there was a man on the premises to protect her. She could not rely on those in the bar to help her, for von Ehrlich was rich and powerful, and they would be frightened of him. Worse, behind him stood two large men, whose faces told of a hundred fights and whose fists were clenched as if in readiness.

'This scut won't tell me if that bastard Cresswell's here.'

'Which Mr Cresswell would that be?'

'Less of your cheek.'

'I'm not being cheeky. There are three Mr Cresswells and you are holding one of them. Is it Mr Mortie or Mr Oliver you require?' She had amazed herself with the calm, controlled way in which she had spoken. It was a good thing he couldn't see the turmoil of fear inside her.

'Oliver.'

'Then, he is not.'

'How do I know you're not lying?'

'Why should I?'

'To protect him, that's why. I know you're in cahoots with them.'

'I can assure you he is not here, nor has he been all day.'

'He has rooms here?'

'He does. But as far as I am aware he is not in them.'

'So you don't know?'

'Would you like to check for yourself?'

'I would.'

'Then please follow me . . .'

A relieved Young Mortimer was let go. The two tough-looking men stepped forward. 'I shall not escort you if those two gentlemen accompany us, Mr von Ehrlich.'

To her relief he barked an order for them to wait outside. She led the way, always conscious of him behind her. She had no idea if Oliver was there or not since he so often came in through the back arch. She just prayed he wasn't – this man was in a fury. Offering up a prayer, she tapped on the door, and then, lifting the bunch of keys she always carried, she opened it. 'Please, see for yourself.'

Stanislas insisted on peering into the cupboards, even looking under the bed – at which she experienced an almost uncontrollable urge to kick him.

'Thank you, Mrs Topsham. I am obliged.'

She did not answer him but led the way back to the bar. With no ceremony she pulled back the heavy curtain and opened the door wide for him to pass through.

When she turned back she was rewarded by a round of applause from her regulars.

'Cor, what a bully!' Dolly said.

'Are you all right, Young Mr Mortimer?'

'Yes, thank you. Bit shocked, it was all so sudden. I can't think what my uncle has done to make him behave in that way.'

'I think you should stay here for a while. I don't think it's safe for you to walk back alone. What do you think, Rob?'

'We'll all walk back together, sir, if you'd like?'

'I'm not frightened,' the youth protested.

'Of course you're not.'

'There's safety in numbers, Young Mr Mortimer. I'd

feel much happier if you'd accompany us. The more the merrier, and we could do with youth on our side.'

'It would be my pleasure, Sol.'

'Thirsty work, a walk like that . . .'

'Yes, of course. Drinks all round, Mrs Topsham.' The boy grinned: he would be safe, and his pride intact.

Much later, when everyone had gone to bed, Melanie asked Zephaniah, who had arrived on the evening train, to join her in the snug. 'There's no point in beating about the bush, Zeph. I know Dolly's with child and I suspect you're the father.'

'I am.'

'I'm disappointed in you.' But she was pleased he had not tried to lie to her.

'I expect you are.'

'You're not going to apologise?'

'I don't think I have anything to say sorry for. I love Dolly, she loves me. Perhaps we should have waited but we didn't, and I shall marry her.'

'I presumed you would.'

'We're both grateful that you've been so kind to her. Dolly was frightened to tell you, but I said you'd understand, and you did.'

'I see her fears.' She'd found the 'we' disturbing: in the past it had meant herself and him; now she must adjust to it meaning him and another woman. It was hard, and made more so by the suddenness. Dolly had usurped Melanie's importance in his life. Such silly thoughts, she decided. They'd get her nowhere. 'It will not be easy for her even if you do marry – think of the gossip. Will you stay?'

'I hoped you would allow us to. I told you some weeks ago I was not happy at the office in Barlton.'

'How will we all manage? Business is improving but not sufficiently. I don't know what Mr Cresswell would have to say.'

'I don't need to work here. I can get employment hereabouts.'

'Doing what?' She hoped she didn't sound too dismissive.

'I shall approach Mr von Ehrlich. I was talking to Richard Joynston the other day and I could do what he used to. And since you can't afford to pay a wage then Dolly could work for our accommodation.'

'You have everything planned.'

'There's Dolly and the baby to think of.'

'Of course.' She had always known what a responsible person he was, but this was still a surprise. 'I'd rather you found someone else to work for, though. He's not a nice man, Zeph.'

'I'm not interested in that. I need his money, that's all.'

'You've changed.' Her voice was tinged with sadness.

'Where's Richard? I need to talk to him.'

'He's gone.'

'Why? I'm surprised. And let down too. I got the impression that . . .' He trailed off.

'What?'

'I thought he was in love with you, that you would be married.'

She looked away. She didn't want him to see her sadness.

After he had gone to bed she sat alone for a long time. Her little boy had gone: he was truly a man now. She was proud of him, but her work with him was almost done.

Hannah welcomed Simeon Redman into her drawing room. She had been dreading his visit to discuss, as usual, the distribution of Christmas presents. It was the first time she had seen him since his wife's death. She paused outside the door, took a deep breath and went in, her arms outstretched in greeting. 'Dear Simeon, I've been thinking so much about you.'

'Hannah.' He took her hands, and held them tightly.

'If you would let go of me I can arrange some refreshment for you.' She laughed nervously.

'I'm so sorry. It's just that it's good to see an old friend after the trying time I've recently endured.'

'Of course. I do understand. I had thought to visit you but I did not want to intrude on your grief.' Which was half true, she thought. In fact she had been avoiding him. As Agnes had pointed out, there was no reason why Hannah should find him any more congenial just because his wife had died – every day she blessed her impulse in inviting her friend to stay with her. 'How is your dear son?'

'He is well, a courageous child, but he needs a mother.'

'It must be difficult for you.'

'Life must go on.' He dropped her hands and rubbed his together.

'Quite. Now, as you know, Cresswell Manor will be closed over Christmas so everyone will have to come here. It will be a bit of a squash as my hall is a fraction of the size of the one at home – I must stop saying that. This is my home now.'

'And charming it is too.'

'We shall have two parties – one for the estate children, one for the workers and pensioners. What do you think?'

'An inspired solution.'

She smiled at Simeon's choice of phrase. 'Of course, Laura always did the list for me – she was so meticulous in keeping track of who had new babies, who had died. I shall miss her terribly. So here is the one I have made and I wonder if you would check it for me.' She crossed to the table on which she had placed it. She was about to turn when she felt arms about her, hot breath on the back of her neck. 'Simeon! Really! What are you about?' She pulled his hands from her waist and whirled round to face him.

'Forgive me, but you said you had been thinking of me . . . and I had been thinking of you too. Now, at last, I am free, and you and I were always destined for each other.'

'Simeon, I don't know what to say!'

'I am inflamed with passion for you!' He lunged at her.

Hannah stepped back sharply and, knocked a small table, which toppled over. A crystal ornament crashed to the floor and broke into a hundred pieces. 'Simeon!'

'Hannah, I love you!' Once more he advanced towards her.

'But your wife died less than a month ago.'

'We never loved each other, not as you and I—'

'I must insist you stop this. I do not love you.'

'But you do. You must.'

'There's no reason why you should think so.'

'But you have permitted me to think so. You are always so charming to me, you are always looking at me in a conspiratorial way. I have known for so long and it has been an agony for me.'

'Were it not for Laura and the sad way she died I would be laughing at you. But this is not amusing. You are making yourself a fool.' But she could not finish for he had leapt upon her and was showering her face with wet kisses. 'Help!' she cried. 'Someone, help me!'

She heard the door open.

'Vicar, desist this minute! How dare you?' Sir Mortimer stood in the doorway, with Agnes peering over his shoulder. 'Hannah, are you hurt? Has he violated you?'

'I'm not hurt, I'm angry. How dare you abuse me in that manner, Simeon?'

'You encouraged me.'

'How dare you lie? And you a man of the cloth!'

'I suggest you leave this minute, Redman, and never return.' Sir Mortimer held the door wide open.

Agnes stood back to let the vicar pass, then rushed to Hannah's side. 'How abominable! Are you all right?'

'He kissed me!' She shivered. 'I have to wash my face – wash him away,' she said, and raced out of the room.

The rest of the Christmas holiday passed joyfully.

The following morning Mortimer had caught the train to Exeter to see the bishop, to complain of Simeon's behaviour. Hannah had tried to stop him since she felt that he should not be judged too harshly, given the circumstances of Laura's death. Distasteful as his presumption had been, she could still feel pity for him. But Mortimer would have none of it and, since the living was in his gift, arranged with the bishop for a replacement vicar to be sent forthwith.

It was a mammoth task to find and wrap presents for everyone on the estate. Mrs Gilroy helped Jose to make the sausage rolls and mince pies that accompanied the mulled wine Whitaker concocted in Hannah's new kitchen. The fire in the hall was banked up and roaring; the tree was decorated by Hannah and Agnes. Cariad wore a scarlet bow that looked well against her white coat.

As she did every Christmas, Hannah cried when the carol singers arrived, and as usual her father teased her. The children's party was the best and Young Mortimer performed conjuring tricks, a talent Hannah had not known he possessed. For the first time, Sir Mortimer agreed to dress up as Father Christmas to give out the presents.

It was a timeless moment, thought Hannah. Every year of her life they had had these ceremonies, which would continue for ever more. She had feared it it would be different this year, in her house instead of the manor and with only a small part of her family present. But as she went to bed on Christmas night she thought it had been the best ever, and certainly, despite Simeon, the happiest.

For once Melanie had been able to buy presents for her children, admittedly only small ones. She had a pair of kid gloves for Xenia, a wool scarf for Zephaniah, a kite for Timmy and for Dolly, since she would soon be her daughter-in-law, a box of lace-trimmed handkerchiefs. She was overwhelmed when they gave her a seed-pearl brooch – 'To the best mother in the world,' the card with it had said. She had shed tears of happiness over it. 'You shouldn't have,' she said, dabbing at her eyes.

'Oh, yes, we should,' the four had chorused, and they all collapsed laughing.

Compared with last year's rabbit the meal they had was a banquet. Last year she had endured a beating; this year she was surrounded with love. Everything had happened at such a speed that she was sometimes afraid it was all a dream and would disappear in a trice.

Her disappointment over Zephaniah and Dolly had dissipated rapidly when she saw how happy they were together. They loved each other, it was plain to see. And she had liked Dolly before so it would have been illogical to like her less now she was carrying Melanie's grand-child. The one thing that still concerned her was the thought of Zephaniah approaching von Ehrlich, a bully of a man if ever she'd seen one. But he would not budge. She supposed she should be proud of his independent nature.

Even Xenia was happier. There had been days when Melanie had despaired of the girl ever being content, but she had settled. Yet there had been no sign of a young man. Although she had grown to hate Bernard, she had always been conscious that he was Timmy's father, and he might grieve for him, but she could see no sign of this. In fact, and she hoped this was not wishful thinking on her part, she thought he was happier than he had been before.

Business over the holiday period had increased, which she had not expected. Flossie's cooking was so appreci-ated by the locals that she had decided to ask Oliver when he returned from his holiday if she should open a dining room. Not only could they offer lunch – a few of the business community had become regulars – the overnight guests could breakfast there.

'I'd no idea we could build up such business,' she said to Flossie, in the kitchen. With Christmas over they were getting back into their old routine.

'It's all them commercial travellers. There's plenty about.'

'I'd never given much thought as to how things got into the shops before. Someone's always selling something.'

The back door slammed. Melanie looked up as Flossie stood on tiptoe to peer out of the window.

'Your Xenia's gone out again. Busy little soul, isn't her?'

'She's made friends with a girl called Veronica, whose father owns the hardware shop on the other side of the harbour. It's nice for her, and it makes her easier to live with.' She laughed.

'Is that what she told you?' It was Flossie's turn to laugh.

'Why? Do you think she was fibbing?'

'More likely to be that Young Mortimer. Haven't you noticed he spends a lot of time here? Aiming high, isn't she?' she said, in her usual forthright way.

'He comes to see Zeph. They're friends.'

'Humph!'

Melanie had to leave the room. Flossie couldn't be right ... but Young Mortimer did pop in frequently – he'd even arrived on Christmas Day with presents, but they had been from Hannah. What to do and what to say? Recently Melanie had come to the unpleasant conclusion that she was a bit frightened of Xenia's moods, the sulks, the door-slamming and screaming. That was why her daughter's new happiness had come as such a relief. Like it or not, she must talk to her.

'Xenia, have you an admirer?' she asked that evening, when she found herself alone with her daughter.

'No. More's the pity.' Her daughter was helping her to

fold the piles of newly laundered linen – something she would not have deigned to do a mere two weeks ago. 'Why?'

'I just wondered.'

'Who would I be interested in here?'

'There are the fishermen.'

'They smell of fish.'

'I thought young Henry Robinson was giving you the eye the other day.'

Xenia stopped working. 'Henry? He's stupid.'

'Young Mortimer Cresswell seems to spend a lot of time here.'

'He's too young – and stupid.'

'He's clever enough to be at university.'

'He might know books but he doesn't know what to say to a girl. All hands and feet and ums and ahs.'

'I'm glad to hear it.'

'Why shouldn't he like me?'

'Because it never works, the likes of us and the likes of them. They show interest in our sort, say sweet nothings to get what they want, and when they've had their fill they disappear back where they came from.'

'You sound so angry.'

'It does anger me. You hear of it all the time.'

'Well, it won't happen to me, I can assure you. No one would take advantage of me, and that includes Young Mortimer. If he ever dared to try – which he wouldn't.'

When Melanie went to bed that night she hoped her daughter spoke the truth.

If there was one celebration Hannah did not enjoy it was New Year. 'Either the past year has been so wonderful one is sad to see it pass or, as this one, it has been so horrible that one is afraid of the next year in case it brings worse,' she had explained to Agnes, when she had suggested that they should have a little celebration. 'Silly, isn't it?'

'I've heard other people say that. But I can't help thinking how sad it is for you. I regard the festival as a new beginning, an excitement, something to look forward to. But that might be because of my Scottish blood.'

'You are Scottish? I did not know.'

'I was born in England but my mother was a Scot. I regard myself as English.'

'How exotic. Where was your mother from?'

'Edinburgh, I believe.'

How strange not to know for sure, thought Hannah. Had her mother never said? Had they never discussed it? There must be a thousand other things she did not know about Agnes. But, then, how little Agnes knew about her, even though they were so comfortable together.

It might be Hannah's house but she was not to get her wish: On New Year's Eve, her father appeared with a bottle of champagne. 'We have to welcome the new year while saying goodbye to the old. It would be discourteous not to. In any case I promised Young Mortimer we should have some champagne.'

In the end, and despite her reservations, Hannah enjoyed herself. Jose had surpassed herself with the five-course meal she served, and Hannah had decided not to look for a cook but to confirm the girl's position and increase her wages. This news had made Jose collapse in grateful tears.

Her father was in fine form, amusing them with stories of his youth, and Hannah found herself learning more about his past too. Did one ever really know people when one thought one did, she wondered. But, then, she had secrets too: she'd never told anyone what she knew about Coral, or of her own longing for love.

'About my garden plan, Papa, have you made a decision?' Since her father was mellow with champagne she had found the courage to ask the all-important question. She was unaware that she was holding her breath.

'This is a new century, the second year of it about to dawn. I must move with the times. You do as you wish, my dear – and you can start with the sunken garden to the side of the manor. I fancy a new scheme there – perhaps with a fountain. Yes, that would be amusing.'

She kissed and hugged him until he pleaded with her to stop or she would crush him to death. To confirm his decision he produced another bottle of champagne although Hannah said she thought they had had enough.

In consequence Young Mortimer was quickly fuddled in the head but so funny when he tried to string a sentence together that Hannah hadn't the heart to remonstrate with him – or to stop her father when mischievously he kept filling his grandson's glass. As Agnes pointed out in a whisper to her, it was better that he learnt to drink at home safely, than experimenting at college.

By the time they retired at long past one and into the New Year, Hannah was tired but happy and could not imagine why she had been so frightened. After all, it was merely a date on the calendar.

It was still pitch dark when Hannah sat bolt upright, immediately awake. What had woken her? She listened and heard nothing, then settled back on her pillows. She must have been dreaming. Then she heard scratching and whimpering. It stopped, then started again. Cariad. Had she been locked out? Silly dog.

She switched on the small light beside her bed – no fumbling with matches and candles in this house – slipped on her dressing-gown and felt for her slippers under the bed. On the landing she paused to listen again. Then she ran, fear clutching her.

She pushed open the door without knocking. Cariad jumped up at her, then, whimpering, rushed across the room, jumped on to the bed and began to lick Mortimer's face.

'Papa.' She could hear his breathing, loud and laboured. She'd heard that once before. 'Papa!' she cried. She left him, ran to Agnes's door and pounded on it, shouting to her to get the doctor. Then she was back at his side. His face was twisted in a grimace of intense pain. 'Dear darling Papa, I'm here. You're not alone. The doctor is coming. Please . . . dear Papa . . . please.' She jumped on to his bed and held him in her arms. She whispered her love for him, and willed him to live.

Then Cariad sat up, put her nose into the air and howled, a primaeval sound. Mortimer had breathed his last.

Chapter Seventeen
January–February 1902

It was inevitable, with his family, that Mortimer's funeral would not pass without problems. On many occasions Hannah had seen the shiny black hearse with its rococo silver decorations, the Barlton undertaker's pride and joy. The four black horses were matched, their harnesses as ornate as the carriage, black plumes dancing on their heads. She hated it. To her it was ostentatious, unseemly, shouting of wealth.

Instead she had chosen a simple farm cart to carry her father to his grave – the one they had used for Bernard Topsham. It stood outside the front door of Cresswell Manor. It had been lovingly decorated by the gardeners with greenery and the many hellebores that were in flower. Fresh, sweet-smelling straw had been laid in the well. What had finally persuaded her that this was the best choice was the discovery, on going through her father's albums, that this was how his own father had been laid to rest.

'He can't be transported in that! It's too undignified,' Penelope fumed, when she saw it waiting for Mortimer's lead-lined oak coffin. The two mighty shire horses, their brasses gleaming and tied with black ribbons, were pawing the gravel with their great hoofs. 'And not those great clod-hopping beasts.'

'It is what he would have wanted,' Hannah said.

'And how would you know?'

'Because I knew him,' Hannah replied, with uncharacteristic sharpness.

'It has to be changed.' Penelope scowled. Widow's

weeds did not suit her complexion, and she looked old suddenly. Some might think it was from grief but Hannah knew it was the colour of her dress.

'I tend to agree,' added Coral, whose looks were not improved either by the sombre clothes.

'It's too late now to change. Had you wanted to arrange Papa's funeral, you should have been here to do so,' Hannah snapped at her stepmother. Her nerves were taut and her mounting irritation was stretched almost to breaking point.

'Do you have to be so insolent—'

'Ladies, please.' Mortie, smart in mourning apparel, stepped forward. 'This is neither the time nor the place. I like the cart and the Clydesdales. Father would have too.'

'Do we have to have the carthorses? Change them at least.'

'The coffin is too heavy for the hunters or carriage horses. Hannah has done well for us all.' He clapped his top hat on to his head. He did not see his wife looking at him with surprised admiration.

There was a flurry of horses' hoofs as a carriage careered up the drive. Before it had ground to a halt, Oliver leapt out. He went straight to his sister and scooped her into his arms. 'Dear Hannah, I'm so sorry . . .' His voice was muffled against her shoulder, but she knew he was weeping.

'I'm so glad you got here in time.'

'As am I.'

Esmeralda descended, looking ethereally beautiful in black, her eyes tinged pink from weeping. Hannah kissed her new sister-in-law. 'Welcome back, sister,' she said simply. There was much to find out and much she did not approve of, but it would have to wait: this was not the time for recriminations.

'So you condescended to come?' Penelope said to her son, ignoring her new daughter-in-law.

'There was a mix-up with Hannah's telegram. We came as quickly as we could.'

'And you got here, Oliver, for which I'm grateful.' Mortie hugged his brother.

'Is my papa here?' Esmeralda asked, more in hope than expectation.

'Hardly. What on earth did you expect, young woman?' As always Penelope was quick to speak when she saw the chance of delivering a reprimand.

'I hoped he would be,' she said.

'He would make a fuss over your behaviour, and rightly so, but that is something we can do without today, I can assure you.'

Fortunately for Esmeralda, Penelope was interrupted by the sound of heaving and grunting in the hall. Whitaker held open the front door as eight of the largest and burliest estate workers struggled across the hall and down the front steps with the coffin. Hannah put her handkerchief to her mouth to stop herself crying out. Sad though she was, incredulity was her strongest emotion. She could not believe her beloved father was in that oak box, or that she would never see him again.

She remembered the last moment she had seen him, just before Rob Robertson had screwed down the coffin lid. She had refused a shroud and he was dressed in his favourite velvet smoking jacket, a crisp white cravat at his neck, on his feet the slippers she had embroidered with his crest and which he had loved. She had asked that his linen be sprayed with his sandalwood cologne. He had looked as if he was sleeping and at any moment would wake up to demand a cigar and some brandy. It had been necessary for her to fuss over these preparations. For Hannah, who had cared for him in life, it was important that she should do the same in death. It had felt right, too, to slip a letter into his pocket declaring her love for him, and a small enamel box with a cutting of Cariad's fur.

A crowd of folk, simply dressed, their heads bowed, stood to one side of the sweep in front of the house. There were those who had served Mortimer's father, others who had served him, and their families. There were many children who, in their turn, would serve future generations. Many were in tears. The coffin was slid on to the planking, the cart sagged, the mighty muscles of the horses took the strain. Before anyone could stop her Cariad had jumped up beside it.

'Get that dog away. It's unseemly.'

'Father would be proud of her devotion, Mother.'

A group of men stepped forward. No word was said, no permission sought, but the horses were released from the traces.

'What on earth are they doing? They can't do that,' Penelope said, as the men took up their positions. 'It's too heavy – they'll drop him. Mortie, stop them!'

'They intend to take Father to his last resting-place, Mother. Have no fear, they will take care of him.' Mortie, blinking away tears, took up his position behind the cart, with Young Mortimer and Felix beside him.

Hannah stepped forward with Oliver.

'Hannah, you're not considering attending the funeral?' Penelope objected.

'Yes, I am – Mother. He's my father and I wish to be with him until the last.'

'I'll come too – hold your hand.' Esmeralda joined her.

'Me too.' A sobbing Lettice stepped forward. They walked at a snail's pace behind the cart, watched by a disapproving Penelope and Coral, in step to the mournful sound of the keeper bell as it tolled the years of Mortimer's life.

Melanie stood at the back of the crowd around the mausoleum that had been opened to receive Mortimer's body. It was a glorious crisp day of bright sunshine, the sort of day on which it was good to be alive. She could

484

see her mother and father. At the start of the service her father had kissed her; her mother had ignored her. Nothing had changed. Zephaniah was with her, but she had no idea where Xenia was or if she had come. She hoped she had: her absence would be noted.

Since Sir Mortimer's death she had been unable to sleep. Zephaniah had reassured her that her position at the Cresswell Arms was safe, that he had seen to it, and Sir Mortimer had promised. But she did not believe it. She was sure that there were ways for the rich to wriggle out of obligations that did not suit them. Not that she had said so to her son: she didn't wish him to think she mistrusted his competence; neither did she want him to worry as she did.

She had felt safe with the old man alive, but now . . . Mortie looked as if he was having difficulty in controlling his emotions. Oliver was weeping as if he did not care who saw. She liked that. As everyone else, she had been shocked to learn he had eloped with von Ehrlich's daughter. There would be trouble from that source, to be sure. But the young girl with him was deeply in love, Melanie could see. At least Oliver was a gentleman.

There had been quite a buzz of whispering when the three Cresswell women had arrived. Women of quality did not normally attend a funeral. But they had been at Bernard's funeral too – Melanie had been proud of that. To be in this graveyard again had made her think of him. If only memories were like school slates and could be wiped clean.

The large iron doors of the Cresswell mausoleum slammed shut. The crowd began to disperse. Melanie looked about her for Xenia so that they could all walk back together. And then she saw her. She was laughing. Melanie frowned. Had she no shame? She worked her way towards her daughter. Then, to her horror, she saw Xenia lean forward and kiss the young man she had been talking to. Melanie pushed through the crowd. 'Home,' she ordered, on reaching Xenia's side.

'Mrs Topsham.' It was Young Mortimer, blushing, looking as if he wished the ground would open up beneath him.

'I don't think either of you are behaving in a decent manner. We're leaving, Xenia.'

'I want to stay.'

'She would be welcome at the house, I'm sure.'

'I doubt it, Young Mr Mortimer, at a time like this. If you will excuse us, I wish to take my daughter home.'

'Of course, Mrs Topsham, I'm sorry.'

'I hate you! You spoil all my fun.' Xenia turned to follow him, but Melanie grasped her arm. 'Let me go! You're hurting me.'

'I'll hurt you some more—' She stopped. That was the sort of thing her husband had said to her. 'We have to go home now.'

'You heard him – I can go to the house. I don't want to be with you! I want to be with him!'

'You're coming with me.'

'Jealous, are you?'

'Not in the least.' She was virtually frogmarching Xenia through the gravestones, praying that she would not make a scene.

'Mrs Topsham, a word, if I may?'

'Mother, this is Mr Battle, whom I used to work for.' Zephaniah had stepped forward.

'Mrs Topsham.' The man had doffed his top hat. 'I am instructed to invite you to the house.'

'Me?' She looked about her with surprise, as if someone else might explain why she should be so honoured. Or was it an honour? Were they about to tell her she must vacate the inn? 'Zeph, take your sister home and don't let her out of your sight. Hold her arm tight. I have to talk to her.' She was aware that Mr Battle was amused.

'Can't she see herself home?'

'No.'

'Do you want me to come too, Mr Battle?' Zephaniah asked.

'It's just your mother who is needed. I trust you understand, Zephaniah.' Mr Battle moved off.

'Don't let them bully you, Mother.'

'Silly! No one's going to. Not me!' She laughed, but it was a thin sound. 'And I mean it, Zeph – lock her up if necessary.'

Whitaker and the footmen moved about the library smoothly, offering drinks from silver trays. Chairs had been arranged and, from the back row, Melanie could see the family at the front. Hannah's shoulders were shaking and Oliver's arm was round her. The servants sat behind them, including Melanie's father. Mr Battle positioned himself at the wide, leather-topped desk, a large whisky beside him. He looked as if he was in need of it.

He coughed, and the chattering ceased. 'As I finish reading each series of names, will those who have heard their own please leave.' Another cough, and he began. It was then that Melanie discovered she had been invited to the reading of the will. Had she been afraid for nothing?

'To the following members of staff, I leave the sum of ten pounds for each year of service with me . . .' At this there was a swell of satisfied whispering. There followed a long list of names, maids, footmen, coachmen, gardeners. She smiled when she heard Flossie's husband's name – they needed that money. Woodmen, keepers, on and on it went. From time to time Mr Battle would look over his spectacles and a group would leave. Some looked disappointed – she wondered if that was because they had expected more. Or perhaps they had wanted to hear more.

Her father, Nanny Wishart, Whitaker, Mrs Fuller, Mrs Gilroy, James the valet received sums varying from twenty pounds for each year of service to a hundred. They left, and Melanie saw that she was the only non-family person left.

'At least that's out of the way, now do get on, Mr Battle,' Penelope demanded as he took a swallow of his drink.

'I have not finished with the retainers yet, Lady Cresswell.' His nerves made him cough.

Slowly Penelope turned in her seat and looked behind her.

'What's *she* doing here?'

'To Mrs Melanie Topsham, landlady of the Cresswell Arms, of Cress-by-the-Sea, I bequeath the freehold of the aforementioned property, the contents therein—'

'*What?*' The word exploded from Penelope like gun-fire.

'. . . and the sum of five hundred pounds to be set aside for the purchase of an annuity for her benefit . . . In the event of her death a similar sum shall be set aside for the benefit of her children . . .'

Melanie sat transfixed, holding her breath. She had to be dreaming. She felt such sorrow, such gratitude . . .

'We shall contest this stupidity!' she heard Penelope screech, and the spell was broken. Melanie stood up and fled from the room.

'I said he was senile. What on earth possessed him to leave such a valuable property to *her*?' Penelope was puce with anger.

'Mr Battle, there must be ways that we can object. It will make my husband the laughing-stock of the community.' Coral was pink with indignation.

'I can assure you it was very much what Sir Mortimer wanted to do.'

'We would cause far more scandal by objecting. He must have had his reasons – and I, for one, do not mind,' Oliver said.

'What has it to do with you? There's nothing here for you to inherit,' his mother hold him waspishly. Oliver shrugged and smiled. Lettice looked tearful and Young Mortimer confused as the argument swirled around them.

'Sir Mortimer was Oliver's father. Of course he has a right to an opinion,' Esmeralda said, indignant.

'You have been in this family for a mere five minutes and none of this is your business.'

'I'd rather you did not speak to my wife in such a manner, Mother.'

'Damn me!' Mortie rumbled, and lumbered to his feet. 'This is appalling. If Father wanted Melanie Topsham to have the inn, then she has it. I don't wish to hear another word on the subject.' He sat down again. All those around him looked astonished.

There was a loud cough from Mr Battle. 'If I might proceed?' Everyone settled down. To everyone's astonishment he had left his stamp collection to Stanislas von Ehrlich because he had shown an interest in it.

'How very sweet of him. Papa will be so pleased.' Esmeralda dabbed at her eyes with a wisp of lace, her handkerchief.

Mr Battle continued: 'To my daughter, Hannah Rose, I bequeath . . .' Her father had left her the dower house, thirty acres of the land around it, and a thousand pounds a year. Hannah began to cry again.

'That's ridiculous! What does she need all that for? She has her own money. It's Mortie's. How dare he squander my son's inheritance—'

'Mother, if you're going to object to everything we shall never finish. Let Mr Battle continue, for heaven's sake,' Oliver said.

The look she gave her son would have destroyed a weaker man.

'Thank you, Mr Cresswell.'

Penelope was silent when they reached the portion of

the will that affected her. She had been left no property but a large annuity. Sir Mortimer had requested that Mortie house his mother for the rest of her life. At this Coral looked remarkably put out, and Penelope as if she had been cheated.

The rest of the will was presented to a chorus of 'Rubbish!', 'Impossible!' and 'How dare he?' Some of the objections were Coral's but the majority were Penelope's. Sir Mortimer, it transpired, had set up a trust, and she almost exploded into smithereens to learn that the trustees were Oliver and Hannah. Fearing for her health, the proceedings had to be halted for a while as brandy was fetched for her.

But this was nothing to the storm that followed. Mr Battle, voice shaking with nerves, read the rest, which told them all that the trust included the majority of the land at Cresswell which was to be managed by Oliver, and would expire when Young Mortimer inherited

'This is monstrous. Mortie, say something! You're being defrauded! Stand up for yourself. Stand up even!' Penelope was on her feet screaming at her eldest son.

'I can't bear this.' Hannah put her head into her hands. Esmeralda was immediately at her side.

'Battle, you're a fool!' Unable to persuade Mortie to react, Penelope turned on the lawyer. 'This will is negated. The estate is entailed – it was not my husband's to dispose of as he wished. It has by law to pass to the firstborn son. What are you going to do about it?' She plopped back on to her chair, looking remarkably pleased with herself.

'I'm afraid you are misinformed, Lady Cresswell.'

'I am no such thing.' She was back on her feet. Like all bullies, she felt more in control standing up.

'You are correct in your assumption that there is an entail, but it is on this house, the pleasure grounds, the parkland and two thousand acres. This was the extent of the estate when it was put in place. All the other land was acquired by Sir Mortimer in his lifetime, and his father in his. Sir Mortimer was quite at liberty to do this, and as he says in his will it is to protect the land for Young Mortimer.'

'Even from the grave he insults you, Mortie. You must go to law.'

Finally Mortie was on his feet. 'Mother, I don't wish to offend but will you please be quiet.'

'Well!' Penelope collapsed back on to her chair, her skirts billowing around her. Her face had gone through every variation of red to settle on magenta.

'I shall do no such thing as to go to law. It would be a foolish waste of money. I think Father has been very sensible. Oliver will manage the land far better than I. He was wrong to think I would damage Young Mortimer's inheritance, I'd never have done that, but it's wiser this way.'

Hannah stood up and hugged her brother. 'Oh, Mortie!' Oliver shook his hand.

'It that all?' Penelope asked Mr Battle in her imperious tone.

'It is, apart from this list of his personal possessions and his wishes as to their disposal among the family – of which I have had several copies made.'

'You will be hearing from my lawyer forthwith. There has been professional misconduct here. Coral, Mortie, we've guests awaiting us in the drawing room. Hurry. Come.' She swept out, but neither followed her.

Mr Battle slumped back into the carved chair with a look of sheer relief that his adversary had departed.

'We're sorry, Battle.' Oliver offered his sympathies. 'Another whisky?' But Mortie was already filling the lawyer's tumbler.

'Thank you, Mr Cresswell, Sir Mortie. Unfortunately I'm rather too familiar with this sort of reaction, but I fulfilled your father's wishes to the letter. If your mother

491

wishes to consult lawyers, of course she is at liberty to do so but I would advise against it.'

'She won't. I won't allow it.' The new, forceful Mortie had spoken.

'I can see Father's plan but what bothers me is the lack of income the estate is generating. I've done some quick calculations,' Oliver held up a piece of paper, 'and his bequests to the staff can be met.'

'I don't need the money he left me,' Hannah put in.

'I'm sure that can be managed. No, it's the amount we will need if we are to put the estate to rights. It has been sadly neglected. Unfortunately, just before his death, he made a disastrous investment on a friend's advice. I fear we shall lose the lot.'

'That was my papa, wasn't it?' Esmeralda asked.

'Darling, it doesn't matter who it was.'

'It matters to me. I shall ask for it back.'

'Esmeralda, I didn't say it was him and even if it was I forbid you to do any such thing.'

'The bequest to the Topsham woman was strange. You don't think they were once lovers?' Coral mused.

'Oh, how romantic.' Esmeralda clapped her hands.

'Don't say such things, Coral. He liked the woman, that was all,' Mortie snapped at his wife.

Downstairs everyone was content, and working out how much they would get.

'Now, everyone, this won't do.' Mrs Fuller clapped her hands. 'Plenty of time for that later. Get upstairs – we've guests to see to.' She shooed them away, and followed to keep a check that all was well.

It was several hours before she could return to the warmth of the kitchen. 'Drunk, most of them. Call themselves landed gentry?' She sniffed disapprovingly. 'I lost count of the number of times I saw Edward dashing off for more wine. And they couldn't stop eating!'

'So they liked my efforts?'

'Liked them? They devoured everything.'

Mrs Gilroy glowed with pride. 'Good job the poor-house wasn't depending on the leftovers – take care with that china!' She shouted as several maids appeared with laden trays. 'Leave it to soak. You can run off and work out how rich you are. Little minxes.'

'Nanny Wishart will be as rich as Croesus. She must have been working for the family a good hundred years!' Mrs Fuller joked.

'Well, forty years, if not longer.'

'Makes you think about the wisdom of giving up a good position, doesn't it?'

'What do you mean, Eve?'

'You yourself was saying only the other day that you didn't know if you wanted to stay with the new regime.'

'We're shaking down nicely. You have to make sure they understand what they can and can't do, what you expect of them.'

'Which is exactly what *I* said to *you*.'

'Edward will be in for a pretty penny too. Quite a catch he's turning into.' Mrs Fuller chuckled.

'Always was, in my eyes,' the cook countered, with a simper.

'You've been busy, Hilda.' Mrs Fuller looked longingly at the plates of miniature meringues and chocolate éclairs Hilda was putting on the table. 'Mind if I just slip my boots off in your kitchen, Eve? All that standing around, my feet are killing me.'

'Be my guest but make sure you can get them back on again. I thought they wouldn't leave us anything.' Mrs Gilroy opened the oven and took out a tray of cheese straws, sausage rolls and vol-au-vents. 'You're just in time, Edward. You must have smelt them.'

'You're a magician, Mrs Gilroy.' He sank wearily on to one of the kitchen chairs.

'Don't make yourself too comfortable, Edward. We've

493

got to toast the old boy and his generosity to us all. What do you suggest?' Mrs Fuller asked.

'Champagne, of course. Everyone agreed?' He returned a minute later with a bottle and four crystal glasses. 'I thought some of those guests would never go. But all went well. I'm sure Sir Mortimer would have been pleased at the turnout. Most satisfactory.' Skilfully he withdrew the cork from the bottle, allowing only the faintest pop. He handed each woman a glass.

'Sir Mortimer,' he intoned as he raised his.

'Sir Mortimer,' the three echoed.

'God bless his cotton socks,' Mrs Gilroy added.

'He certainly did everyone proud,' the housekeeper agreed.

'A good man.'

'And them upstairs. Any mishaps that you might just have overheard, Edward?' Mrs Gilroy looked at him slyly.

'Lady Cresswell is none too pleased . . .' He had positioned himself outside the library door to stop everyone else doing so, and was in command of the whole story.

'Wise of him, if you ask me. That Mortie's too dim to look after this place.'

'In the circumstances he behaved with remarkable dignity. I begin to wonder if we're in for a few surprises where he's concerned. Mind you, it was nothing to the surprise when the solicitor announced Sir Mortimer had left the Cresswell Arms to Melanie Topsham.'

'Never!' Mrs Gilroy exclaimed.

'You're teasing us,' Mrs Fuller accused him.

'It's the truth. Caused quite an upset.'

'I imagine. Makes you think, doesn't it? There's more to that than meets the eye.'

'Still waters – never trust the quiet ones. I always said she was a minx.' Mrs Fuller's face expressed disapproval.

'I never heard you say that,' the cook objected.

'Well, I did!'

'Ladies, ladies.' Whitaker was beaming at them. 'I have another toast for you. More exciting news.'

Gussie and Eve leant forward. 'What?'

'With the passing of the old order, I took it upon myself to speak to the new captain of our ship, Sir Mortie – it will take us a while to get used to saying that. Well, he was understanding, despite the unusual nature of my request – which is unconventional in the extreme.'

'What?' The cook and the housekeeper mirrored each other's exasperation.

'Sir Mortie bestowed upon me the honour of permitting Hilda and myself to marry, and remain here in our positions.' He beamed as he topped up their glasses.

There was a stunned silence. Mrs Fuller and Mrs Gilroy stared at him, at Hilda and then at each other, as myriad emotions flitted across their faces.

'No!' Mrs Fuller said, with a wail. She stood up and rushed from the room.

'Congratulations,' Mrs Gilroy managed then followed in hot pursuit.

Whitaker looked at Hilda, astonished.

'Dear Edward. They are two disappointed women. They both loved you and, I think, always hoped.'

In one swig Whitaker downed his champagne, then picked up Mrs Fuller's and drank that too. 'Well I never!'

Melanie walked so fast she was virtually running. It was impossible for her to take in what she had just been told. She must have imagined it. Things like that didn't happen, not in real life.

The bar was full of estate workers still drinking their dead master's health. The noise was intense, the air foul with tobacco fumes. She pushed her way through to a harassed Dolly, who was attempting to serve them, helped by Flossie. 'Where's Zeph?' she asked.

'Arguing with Xenia,' Dolly answered.

495

Melanie could hear them before she opened the door to the snug. 'You will stay until she returns,' she heard Zephaniah shout.

'I'm here,' she said.

'Mum, are you all right? You look as if you've seen a ghost. What is it?'

'Zeph, could you get me some sherry? I've had a bit of a shock.' She was taking off her coat and hat. There was no need to order Xenia to stay: curiosity kept her anchored to the easy chair. But she was glaring at her mother.

'There's no need for you to look at me like that, young woman.'

'Do you know what annoys me most? The way you call me that.'

'And do you know what annoys *me* most? Your insolence.'

Zephaniah returned. 'Dolly said this would be better for you.'

'What is it?' She looked at the dark red liquid with suspicion.

'It's port and brandy mixed. Dolly says it's good for shock.'

'Then it's exactly what I need.' She sipped the drink gingerly, expecting to dislike it, but instead found it pleasantly warming.

'So, what's happened?' Zeph looked worried.

'It's all right. It's not bad news.' She reached up and stroked his face. 'Sir Mortimer has left me this place and an annuity that will go to you two when I die.'

'He did what?'

'How much?' asked Xenia.

'I can't remember the amounts. All the way back here I was going over and over it in my head, not believing it. But the man read it out for all to hear, so it wasn't a dream.'

'Mother, this is the most wonderful news! You need never worry again!'

'Except if the business is working or not.' She shivered, scared of her new responsibility.

'You sure he left you it, not just a right to the tenancy?'

'Freehold. That's what he left me.' She took another sip of the wine.

'Why?' Xenia was asking the question that everyone would be asking soon.

'He felt he owed me a debt.' She looked down at the glass. 'I presume.' She added.

'We heard how generous he'd been to his servants,' Zephaniah told her.

'Yes, but not like this.' Xenia was staring at her.

'You don't seem very pleased for me, Xenia.'

'Why should I be? You humiliated me in front of everyone.'

'It was necessary to prevent you making a fool of yourself.'

'I wasn't at risk of that, but you were. And I'm not so sure it *is* good news. This estate goes to Young Mortimer's father and then to him, so why should you have any of it? It's his. He told me.'

'Presumably it wasn't. Don't spoil Mother's pleasure, Xenia.'

'She's only too happy to spoil mine. While I was waiting for you to get back I did some thinking. I am eighteen years old, a woman, and I shall decide my own destiny. I'm going to see Mortimer – he won't have to be called Young Mortimer any more, which he hated. I shall see him whenever I want and you can't stop us. So there.'

'I told you, you are not to. I won't allow it.' Both women were standing now, facing each other across the hearthrug. Zephaniah looked anxiously from one to the other.

'I'll do as I wish. You can't stand in my way.' She moved towards the door.

Melanie barred her way. 'Where are you going?'

'To see Mortimer. To tell him what sort of mother I have.'

'He will use you, Xenia. I warned you – his type regards girls like you as mere playthings. He'll dally with you, tire of you and marry someone else.'

'No, he won't. He wants to marry me. He asked me already. And if you forbid it we shall elope to Scotland. See if you can stop us.'

Melanie's face was ashen. She held up her hand as if that alone could stop her headstrong daughter. 'Xenia, I beg you, listen to me. Don't disobey me.'

'Out of my way, Mother. There's nothing you can do.'

'There is. But please don't make me.' Melanie was shaking now from head to toe. 'Please.' Tears rolled down her cheeks.

'Mother?' Zephaniah stepped towards her, but she was backing away from them now until she leant against the door.

'If you wouldn't mind, I wish to pass.' Xenia spoke coldly.

'You can't.'

'I can do as I want.'

'You must to listen to me.' She shut her eyes and took a deep breath. 'He's your brother.'

Chapter Eighteen
January–February 1902

Hannah was exhausted. It had been a dreadful day. Burying her father had been almost more than she could bear. The sound of the mausoleum doors slamming still reverberated in her ears, and the distasteful scene Penelope had made would haunt her for a long time. Then she had had to face Oliver, who seemed oblivious to the distress and trouble he had caused, and she still did not know how best to deal with him. Coral's dreadful secret bothered her constantly. What upset her was the way it did not appear to trouble Coral, who carried on as if nothing had happened, and – Hannah didn't think it was her imagination – was treating Hannah with marked disdain, as if she were the sinner.

'Agnes, if you knew something truly dreadful about a wife, would you tell the husband? You see, a friend of mine has just such a problem and she doesn't know what to do.'

Agnes absorbed this information. 'If she was likely to be harming someone else, her children say, yes, I would be duty-bound. If it was something that, if kept secret, harmed no one, I don't think I would.'

'Not even if you thought she might do it again?'

'No. If it is adultery you refer to, it is better to let him find out for himself, which in time is invariably what happens.'

'But this is my friend's brother, surely that makes a difference?'

'All the more reason to say nothing. She would risk

losing her brother's affection, which would be much more serious than if it were a friend.' Agnes smiled.

'This friend has another problem. She has been accused of doing something the wife did. If she argues her innocence she can only prove it by naming her sister-in-law. What should she do?'

'Dear me, your friend leads a complicated life. Is she hurt in any way by these accusations – other than her pride?'

'I don't think so. Of course, her feelings are very hurt.'

'Then again I would advocate saying nothing. Such matters usually blow over and rapidly become forgotten. Hurt feelings will heal.' Again the smile. For an uncomfortable moment she wondered if Agnes knew what she was talking about, then dismissed the idea.

'The reading of my father's will was terrible. Such arguments! I couldn't believe it was happening – and on the day of his interment too.'

'My poor, dear Hannah, how sad for you. From my experience will readings are never happy occasions. Some people think they have not been left enough, and disagree with what others have been given. It is their misfortune to carry such bitterness, not yours. My own father, such a spiteful man, continued his vendettas from beyond the grave – he cut off my brother and me without a penny. Left everything to a woman he barely knew.'

'Oh, the shame of it!'

'What shame?' asked Oliver, striding into the room.

'Wills, Oliver. What beastly things they are.'

He laughed. 'I thought today was grand theatre.'

'Is Esmeralda with you?'

'No, the poor lamb's very tired. She was deeply upset today. Now she's arranging her dressing room, which is restoring her spirits faster than anything else would. We had a successful time shopping in Paris before your telegram arrived.'

'Thank goodness you gave me that letter. I can't bear to think you might not have been here.'

'If only I hadn't gone when I did.'

'Oliver, I must talk to you.'

'I thought you might want to.' He grinned, like a small boy caught scrumping apples.

'If you would both excuse me.' Agnes got gracefully to her feet and left them.

'Agnes is such a sensitive woman,' Hannah said.

'She probably didn't want to witness you berating me.' He was still grinning.

She looked stern. 'Why, Oliver? Why did you run away with that child? Tell me that.'

'For all the wrong reasons, Hannah. I am shamed by what impelled me. I wanted revenge on her father, pure and simple. He had threatened to ruin us, risked Father's money when he knew Father could ill afford it. She is his most prized and loved possession so I took her.'

Hannah's hand flew to her mouth. 'Oliver, how could you?'

'There is nothing you can say that I don't think of myself. But she is a remarkable young woman. I can hardly dare to believe it but she is now my wife. I've fallen in love, Hannah. I adore her. She is my sun and moon, and it happened so quickly.'

'Oliver!' She felt tears. 'Oh dear, all I ever seem to do at the moment is cry. But at least these are happy tears. This is the truth? I don't want her hurt.'

'I swear to you on our father's grave that I love her, pure and simple. And the miracle is, she loves me in return. I might have lived thirty-three years and she eighteen, but she's wiser than I am.'

'Agnes said she was clever. But what about her father?'

'We have to see him tomorrow and beg his forgiveness. I just pray that, for her sake, he will forgive me.'

'I doubt it.'

'I fear you may be right.'

'But tell me the good things. How did you marry? Where? When?'

'On Christmas Eve in Paris.'

'Not in a Roman Catholic church?'

'You look so shocked and I thought you were a non-believer. Yes, but Esmeralda is a Catholic. We found a priest who took pity on our predicament after we'd given him a wedge of francs!' He laughed.

'You're happy, so I'm pleased for you.'

Cariad scratched at the door.

'You're keeping her?' Oliver said, as he opened the door for the dog.

'Yes. Didn't she behave wonderfully today? Penelope wanted her but she ran back here this evening. I've decided not to tell your mother. Much simpler all round.'

Xenia was hurrying along the Barlton road. Her face was streaked with tears. Anger was mounting in her heart with bitterness. She felt as if her life was over. All her dreams had been shattered by three words: '*He's your brother.*'

She was on her way to Courtney Lacey. Not knowing what to do or where to go, she had remembered that happy day back in the summer – how long ago it had been! Then Esmeralda had asked her to go to Courtney Lacey as her companion and her mother had stopped her. Now she couldn't.

She stepped to the side of the road at the sound of a motor vehicle approaching from behind. She lowered her head, not wanting anyone to see her like this. The car stopped. A man got out. 'It's a cold day. Would you care to join me? No need to look so alarmed. Von Ehrlich, at your service. Remember? The friend of Mrs Feather-stone.' He bowed.

'How wonderful.' She climbed into the back of the car. 'I was coming to your house. I want to see Esmeralda.'

'She's not there.'

'Then perhaps I should get out and go back to Cress.' She looked downcast.

'You may continue with me, if you prefer.' He pulled up a rug and offered to put it over her knees. 'She has eloped.'

'No! And, you love her so.'

'You didn't know?'

'I'd heard rumours, but this awful place heaves with them so I didn't believe it.' she lied. 'I thought she was far more sensible than that. And Oliver Cresswell is so old!'

He patted her knee. 'A girl after my own heart.'

The minute they arrived at Courtney Lacey, Xenia was sent to Esmeralda's room to bathe if she wished and to choose whatever she wanted to change into. The luxury of the room, the bathroom that adjoined it, the contents of the drawers and cupboards did more to mend her broken heart than anything else could have done. This was the sort of life she could get used to, she thought.

Two hours later, in a pastel blue silk dress, with a white cashmere shawl about her shoulders and her hair up in a knot, she descended the wide staircase.

'What a vision of loveliness,' Stanislas said, upon seeing her.

'Why thank you, kind sir.'

'Champagne before dinner?'

'Please.' She sat up straight in the chair, just as Mrs Featherstone had taught her, and looked about the magnificent room. Every surface gleamed, crystal sparkled, tables were packed with bibelots, the walls covered with paintings. She felt as if she had come home.

'My mother will be joining us in a little while.'

'How nice,' she said, and hoped she had covered her disappointment.

'Now, tell me, what was a young maiden doing alone on the road at evening dusk with tragedy in her eyes?'

'My mother told me something that destroyed my life.'

'I sincerely hope not.'

'Coming here has cheered me enormously.' And then, wondering if she should have said that, she added, 'For the time being.'

'Is there something I can do?'

'I fear not. But I would like to discuss it with someone more mature and wiser than me. You see, I thought I loved a young man, and today my mother told me I couldn't for the simple reason . . .' She looked away from him, brushed her face with her hand. 'Oh, this is so difficult for me . . . so . . . mortifying and embarrassing.'

'Don't proceed if you'd rather not.'

'No. You have been so kind to me. He is my brother. There, I've told you.'

Stanislas looked at her for a moment without speaking. 'That must have been a dreadful shock.'

'It was. I mean, it is.'

'Isn't your mother the tenant of the Cresswell Arms?'

'She is. Only she's no longer the tenant, she owns it. Sir Mortimer left it to her in his will.'

'Did he now? So your brother is . . . ?

'Young Mortimer Cresswell.'

'I see. So you are Miss Xenia Cresswell.'

'No, my name is Topsham.'

'Should it not be Cresswell?'

Xenia laughed. 'Good gracious me, I suppose it should.'

'Then you must change it.'

'How do you do that?'

'My dear, leave it with me. It will be my pleasure to make the arrangements for you. Ha! Here's my mother. Come, dearest, let me introduce you. Mother, this is Miss Xenia Cresswell . . .'

Zephaniah was angry. Melanie had only seen him like this once before, and that was at the time of Bernard's funeral when he'd met his grandmother. This fury, though, was worse because it was directed at her. She sat at the table in the snug, which she had once regarded as her sanctuary and felt certain she would never again see it in that light. She played with the tiny loops of the moquette cover – ruby red it was; she'd been so proud when she had purchased it. She did not defend herself, but allowed the tirade to crash about her, as if she was in the midst of a storm. She could not defend herself for she had no defence; he had a right to this passionate outburst of hurt. She sat willing him to stop, to understand. Bernard had schooled her well for she could absorb the anger. She waited.

Eventually the demented pacing of the room, the banging on furniture, the slamming of books ceased. He sat down, put his head in his hands, and wept. She sat opposite him, longing to comfort him, but refrained, knowing that she was the last person he would want to touch him now.

Dolly crept in. She looked as if she was about to go to him, but Melanie mouthed, 'Let him be'.

'I'll make us some tea,' Dolly mouthed back.

Melanie watched her fingers playing with the fabric. Wouldn't it be nice to be an ant and get lost in the fabric jungle? Hadn't she wished herself an ant once before, or felt like one? Nothing had changed since then. If anything, the burdens she carried had become heavier.

Dolly brought the tea. The rattling of the cups distracted Zephaniah. He turned his face so that she could not see his tears, and wiped it with the back of a hand, just as he had as a small boy. How awful it was to sit here and know that she, his mother, who all his life had tried to protect him, had caused the unmanly weeping of which he was ashamed, but which, no doubt was the best thing for him to do.

The tea poured, Dolly left them again. When they were alone he lifted his head and looked at her. 'Why?' was all he said.

'Why did it happen? Why did I have you? Why did I

not tell you? Why did I deceive you? Which question do you want me to answer?' She knew she sounded cool and distant, but she was having difficulty in controlling her own misery at the lies and deceits of the past nineteen years.

'Why did you not tell us?'

'What good would it have done?'

'It would not have come as the shock it is. Xenia would not have been humiliated. I would never have had to accept their charity.'

'Paying for your education was never charity. Sir Mortimer regarded it as a moral obligation.'

'Guilt money.'

'Perhaps, but better to have felt guilt than nothing.'

'But he was not my father.'

'No, that is true, but your real father was always childlike.'

'Irresponsible, you mean.'

'Perhaps I do. He's a pleasant man but he lacks imagination. His father has always taken the decisions for him. He is not, however a bad man.'

'You should have told us.'

'I hoped it would never be necessary. And I would never have had to if Xenia and Young Mortimer had not met and liked each other so. Don't you realise how sad I feel for her, that she is deprived of a friendship because of me? But, then, that's not strictly true, for if they had not been related who is to say that Young Mortie would not do to her what his father did to me?'

'Why did we ever come back here? How could you be so stupid as to think you could keep the secret?'

'We came because I was at my wits' end. We were in danger of starving. Bernard and I were reduced to our last pennies and I had you three to think of. I had to risk it.'

'Did he know?'

'Yes. It was why I stayed with him through all the

506

beatings. He had been good to us. He knew why my parents had thrown me out of their house. He married me knowing I was carrying another man's child. He paid for us to move away. He gave up a good job to do so. And he was never cruel to you.'

At this Zephaniah laughed. 'Hating us. Never caring about us. Making us endure the way he treated you – you think that showed he cared?'

She bowed her head, weariness engulfing her.

'And how could you let us think he was our father? That evil man. I was terrified I might grow up to be like him. I hated myself for his blood flowing in my veins.'

'I didn't know.' She was fighting back tears.

'But to return . . .'

'I thought it was safe. Apart from Bernard and I, only three others knew my secret.'

'Who?'

'Mortie, his father and grandmother – but she has been long dead. They promised they would never tell another soul and I had no reason to disbelieve them. I thought Lady Cresswell knew, since she was horrible to me, but when he was ill last year, Sir Mortimer assured me he hadn't told her. It transpired she is like that with nearly everyone.' She allowed herself a small smile.

'Your parents?'

'I refused to tell them who the father was, and my mother believed I didn't know. I let her think it.'

'How old were you when he seduced you?'

'I wouldn't say he seduced me. We loved each other, he promised to marry me . . .' She smiled again, at the memory of the naïve child she had been, their dreams and plans. 'I was fifteen and he was twenty.'

'And you don't think you were seduced. Really, Mother!'

'He didn't seem to be a twenty-year-old. He was like me – a child.'

'So you weren't good enough?'

'I didn't know it at the time but, yes, that's so. I realise it now.'

'Well, I don't. You're as good as any woman. I want to kill him.' He slammed one hand into the palm of the other.

'Dear Zeph. My champion.' And her heart lifted at the notion that he was, perhaps, going to forgive her. 'It was wrong of me to let you think Bernard was your father.'

'The best thing about the discovery is finding out that he wasn't.'

Another sign, she thought, that he might be forgiving her.

'What did you think, seeing them again?' he asked.

'The difference between the way they live and the way we were, even though you were Sir Mortimer's grandchildren, was difficult to accept. But you must remember that he and his mother paid for your and Xenia's education. That was a blessing.'

'But money isn't love and acknowledgement, is it? I liked him too, when I was working with Mr Battle. He was kind to me. Now I see why.'

'It must have been hard for him. And in the end . . .' She looked about her. 'He gave us this inn and money for life. I have no hard feelings for Sir Mortimer – or Mortie.'

'I don't know if I can stay here now, Mother.'

'I thought you might say that.' She could not hide her misery. 'But I do understand. It would be difficult for you.'

'I might become bitter and I don't want that.'

'What will you do? Where will you go?'

'There's Mr von Ehrlich.'

'I meant it when I said I didn't want you to go to him. He's a hard man. I talked to Richard about him – he's vicious with an evil temper and Richard says some of the things he does in business are perhaps not legal. I don't know that you would be safe with him and if, God forbid, he ever found out who you were he would make your life doubly difficult – I gather he hates the Cresswells.'

'Mr Battle would have me back, he said.'

'I could help you with money – I'm in a position to now.'

'I couldn't take it.'

'But I insist. That's my grandchild Dolly's carrying, and it's money from your grandfather – look at it in that way.'

'I'm sorry I lost my temper just now.'

'My darling Zeph, what other way was there for you to behave?' Now she could kiss him. 'I love you, my son. I'm sorry.'

'Don't be. There's no need. After all, if you hadn't been with my father I wouldn't be here and I'd rather be alive.'

'Where do you think Xenia's gone? To Lettice? I hope not. She'll end up telling her and that would never do.'

'She's probably trying to find Esmeralda.'

'Oh, no! She's not there – she eloped. No doubt he'll send her back. Oh, dear God, what a night!' And at last she was laughing.

Esmeralda had insisted on accompanying Oliver to see her father the following morning.

'I'd rather go on my own,' he said.

'And I'd rather go with you. If I'm there he'll behave better. At the end of the day he loves me.' She laughed. 'But you must wait for me. I have to look my best.'

It took time for Esmeralda to look her best and they were two hours later arriving at Courtney Lacey than he had intended. As soon as the carriage stopped, Esmeralda was racing up the stone steps and bursting into the hall before the footman could open the door. 'Papa!' she called. 'Papa! I'm back, Papa!'

Stanislas stood on the great staircase with a thunderous look on his face. 'What are you doing here?' he demanded, as he descended the stairs.

'I've come to say I'm sorry. Oliver is sorry too. Aren't you, my darling?'

'Esmeralda insisted on accompanying me, sir. Really, I wished to see you alone.'

'You deserve whipping, if not shooting.'

'I agree with you, sir. What I did was unforgivable, and I beg to apologise.'

For a second Stanislas said nothing, as if caught off-guard. 'Your apology is not accepted.'

'Papa!'

'I wish you both to leave my house.'

'But, Papa, I love you.'

'If you loved me you would not have done what you did, putting me through the agony of the last weeks. You are selfish, spoilt and thoughtless. All I have ever given you is my love and attention, and you repay me in this manner.'

'Sir, it was my fault. I acted in anger. My motives were of the worst.'

'Your honesty is commendable, but it makes not a jot of difference to my opinion or my intentions. Get out.'

'But, Papa, I'm married. Look.' Esmeralda removed her glove to show him the rings on her finger.

'I am aware of it. Had you not been he would have been a dead man.'

'Papa, you frighten me.' Esmeralda became tearful.

'Good. That was my intention.'

'Esmeralda, we should go.' Oliver put an arm protectively about her.

'I can't leave my father. I just can't!'

'I think you must. I shall return, sir, at a later date.'

'Then you will be wasting your time. I shall instruct my servants that neither of you are to be given entry. Now, good day to you.'

Esmeralda's sharp intake of breath sounded loud in the cavernous hall. Oliver took her hand, just as a young woman appeared and came down the stairs, dressed becomingly in lilac satin.

'Xenia! What are you doing here?' Esmeralda exclaimed.

'You know Miss Cresswell?' Stanislas smiled.

'Your father has been kind to me. My mother will no longer want me to live with her,' Xenia explained.

'It must be catching,' Oliver said, under his breath.

'Did I hear you're returning? If so, will you carry this note to her at the inn? I would be so obliged.' She held it out and Esmeralda took it.

Stanislas turned on his heel and stamped out of the hall.

'Come.' Still holding her hand Oliver led Esmeralda out to the carriage.

Once inside, the enormity of what had happened precipitated a paroxysm of weeping. Esmeralda cried, screamed and beat at the sides of the carriage. Oliver was worried that she was going to do herself a mischief. All his soothing words were to no avail. In the end he held her, stroked her hair and murmured his love for her. They were nearly home when, as swiftly as the storm of emotion had began, it ended. She sat up. 'Have you a handkerchief? Mine is . . .' She held out the scrap of damp lace to show him. He burrowed in his topcoat and handed her his clean one. 'That was my dress Xenia was wearing,' she said indignantly, which made him smile.

'That's better, my darling. I'm so sorry I've caused you such pain.'

'He can't love me very much if he wouldn't even listen to me.' She pouted.

'I'll double my love for you to make amends. And I'll always be there for you, you know that, don't you?'

'Yes, I do. I'm so glad we did what we did. If you hadn't been so cross with him I doubt you'd ever have asked me. Then I would really have been sad for the rest of my life!'

'Sweetheart.' They journeyed along, holding each other close, Oliver marvelling again that he hadn't known he loved her. Once again he thought how much wiser she was than he.

'And why did he call her *Miss Cresswell*?'

'I've no idea.' But suddenly everything was making sense.

Melanie held the note in a shaking hand.

> *Mother, I am to be employed as a companion to Mr von Ehrlich's mother. He has been most kind to me, and fortunately, for me, understands my predicament.*
>
> *I do not wish you to come in search of me, or to contact me. I do not want any of my possessions sent to me, since I want no memory of my life with you. Mr von Ehrlich has generously given me all I need.*
>
> *I will never forgive you for the shame you have brought upon me, and I hope never to speak to you again.*
>
> *Xenia.*

All those years with Bernard had been for nothing. Her parting from Richard had been for nothing. In twenty-four hours her children had left her. She would see Zephaniah again, but Xenia ... A wave of misery threatened to engulf her. But what was she thinking of? She still had Timmy, and he loved her. As he grew older he might change, but for now she had him. There was only one solution to this: she would work all the hours of the day and she would succeed.

There were days when the longing for her father was almost too much to bear. Then Hannah threw herself into her work, trying to blot out her yearning for him.

She still could not believe that he would not return, still felt that at any moment she would hear him call her name in the hall. It seemed impossible to her that the void he had left would ever be filled.

There were times when she would have given all she owned, her soul even, for just five minutes with him, enough time to tell him what he had meant to her, how much she loved him. She watched her brothers and, though they were sad, it was not grief like hers. She was consumed by it: she could not eat or sleep. Why were they not like her in their suffering? It was Agnes, wise Agnes, who pointed out that they had others to love: Oliver had his Esmeralda, and Mortie his children, if not his wife. Hannah had her friendship with Agnes, and Cariad. She became obsessive about the little dog, afraid something might happen to her, and that then her link with her father would be broken.

There were nights when she cried. She never fought it, just let the tears flow. No longer was she concerned that she was the weeping woman he so loathed. She always hoped it would make her feel better, but it never did.

One particular night when she had been crying she heard the bedroom door opening and Agnes crossing the room. 'Would you like me to sleep with you tonight?'

She could not answer but rolled over to give her room. It was comforting to feel Agnes beside her, her arms about her, her hand stroking her hair, soothing her. Her weeping gradually subsided and finally Hannah slept.

It was pitch dark when she woke to the most wonderful feeling, as if her blood had been turned to honey, a glorious sensation she had never known before. 'I love you,' she heard Agnes whisper, before she slid down Hannah's body and she felt a mouth at her breast . . .

In the morning she lay for some time looking at the woman sleeping beside her. How beautiful she was; how sweet she tasted. Had what they had done in the night been wrong? How could it have been when it was so joyful, such pleasure? She had not known that a woman could make her feel such delight, that another woman could awaken her body as this one had. If it was a sin, she would have to be sinful.

She put out her hand. 'Agnes,' she whispered, 'I'm here.'

The bar had emptied and Melanie was counting the evening's takings. A knock at the door made her heart lurch. She was alone in the inn. The knocking was repeated. Her pulse racing, she moved towards the door and pulled back the curtain. 'Who's there?'

'It's me.'

Hurriedly she pulled back the bolts, fumbled with the large iron key. 'Richard!' she said, her joy evident in her voice.

'I couldn't stay away. I'm sorry.'

'Don't be. I've missed you so.' And she fell into his arms.

All Orion/Phoenix titles are available at your local bookshop or from the following address:

Mail Order Department
Littlehampton Book Services
FREEPOST BR535
Worthing, West Sussex, BN13 3BR
telephone 01903 828503, *facsimile* 01903 828802
e-mail MailOrders@lbsltd.co.uk
(Please ensure that you include full postal address details)

Payment can be made either by credit/debit card (Visa, Mastercard, Access and Switch accepted) or by sending a £ Sterling cheque or postal order made payable to *Littlehampton Book Services*.
DO NOT SEND CASH OR CURRENCY

Please add the following to cover postage and packing

UK and BFPO:
£1.50 for the first book, and 50p for each additional book to a maximum of £3.50

Overseas and Eire:
£2.50 for the first book plus £1.00 for the second book and 50p for each additional book ordered

---

BLOCK CAPITALS PLEASE

name of cardholder ....
....
address of cardholder ....
....
....
postcode ....

delivery address
(if different from cardholder)
....
....
....
postcode ....

☐ I enclose my remittance for £ ....

☐ please debit my Mastercard/Visa/Access/Switch (delete as appropriate)

card number ☐☐☐☐☐☐☐☐☐☐☐☐☐☐☐☐

expiry date ☐☐☐☐   Switch issue no. ☐☐

signature ....

prices and availability are subject to change without notice